image comics presents

THE WALKING DEAD
™

ROBERT KIRKMAN
CREATOR, WRITER

CHARLIE ADLARD
PENCILER, INKER

CLIFF RATHBURN
GRAY TONES

RUS WOOTON
LETTERER

CHARLIE ADLARD & CLIFF RATHBURN
COVER

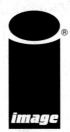

IMAGE COMICS, INC.
Robert Kirkman - chief operating officer
Erik Larsen - chief financial officer
Todd McFarlane - president
Marc Silvestri - chief executive officer
Jim Valentino - vice-president

Eric Stephenson - publisher
Joe Keatinge - sales & licensing coordinator
Betsy Gomez - pr & marketing coordinator
Branwyn Bigglestone - accounts manager
Sarah deLaine - administrative assistant
Tyler Shainline - production manager
Drew Gill - art director
Jonathan Chan - production artist
Monica Howard - production artist
Vincent Kukua - production artist

www.imagecomics.com

THE WALKING DEAD, VOL. 8: MADE TO SUFFER. Second Printing. Published by Image Comics, Inc. Office of publication: 2134 Allston Way, 2nd Floor, Berkeley, California 94704.

PRINTED IN CHINA

ISBN: 978-1-58240-883-5

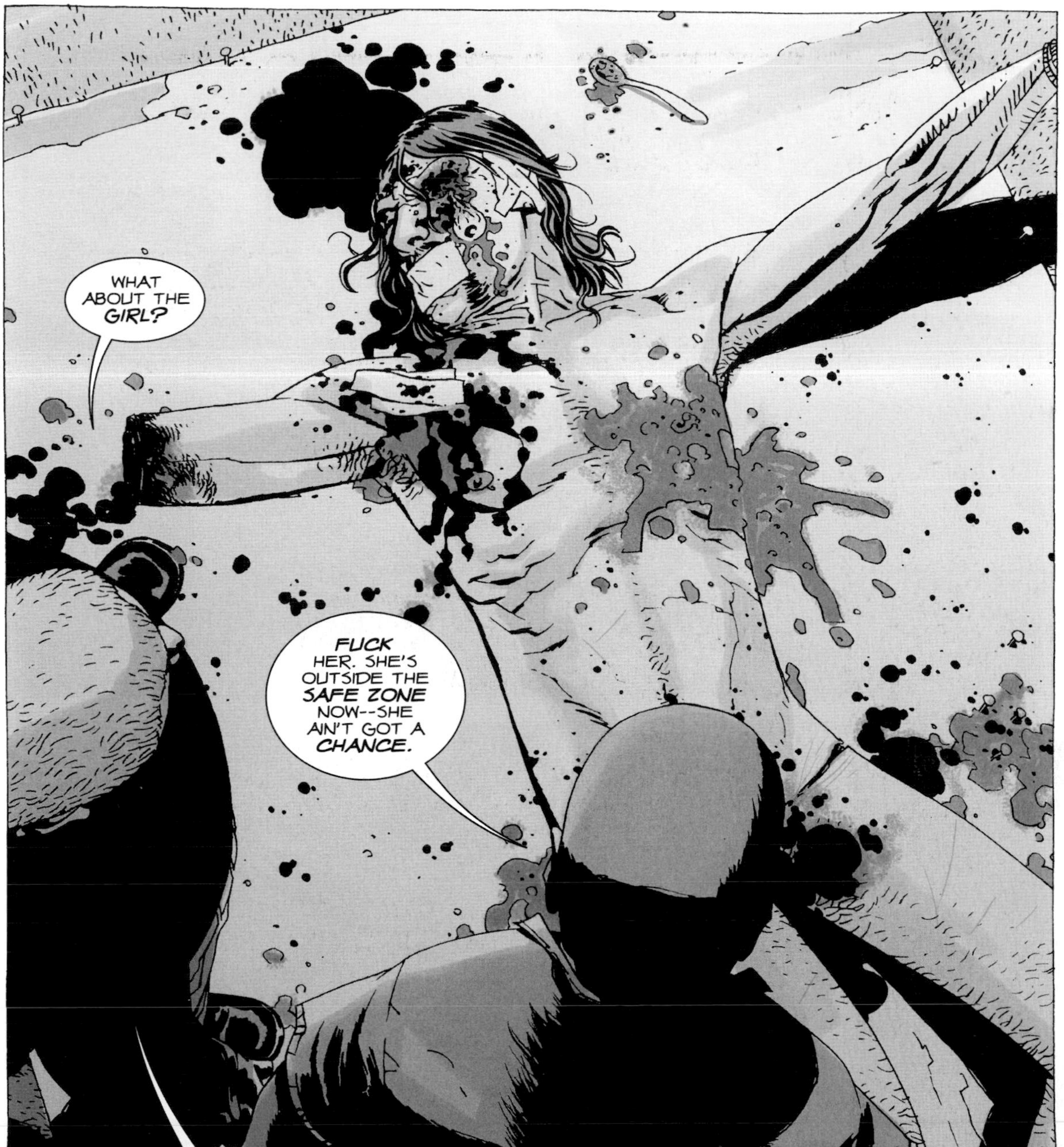
WHAT ABOUT THE GIRL?
FUCK HER. SHE'S OUTSIDE THE SAFE ZONE NOW--SHE AIN'T GOT A CHANCE.
WHAT ABOUT HIM?

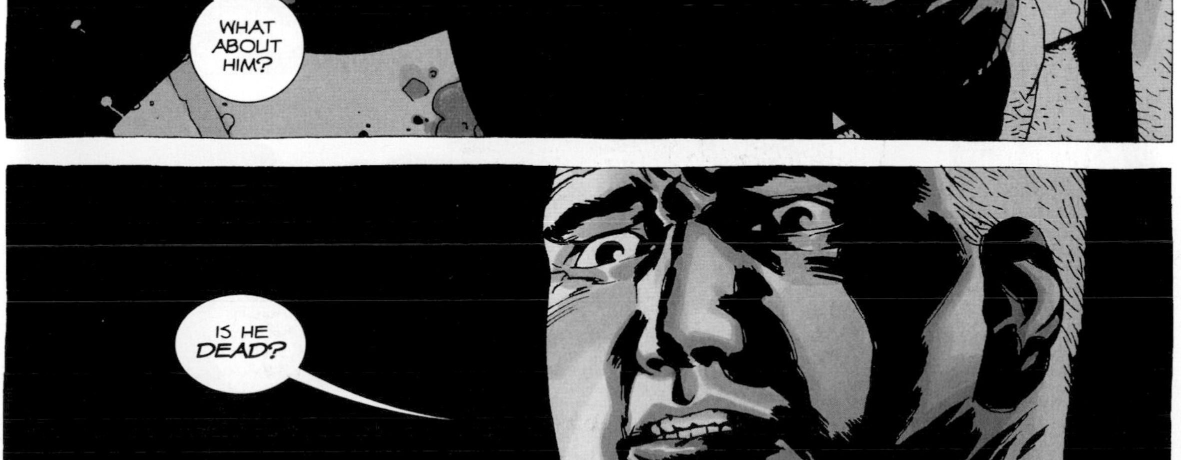
IS HE DEAD?

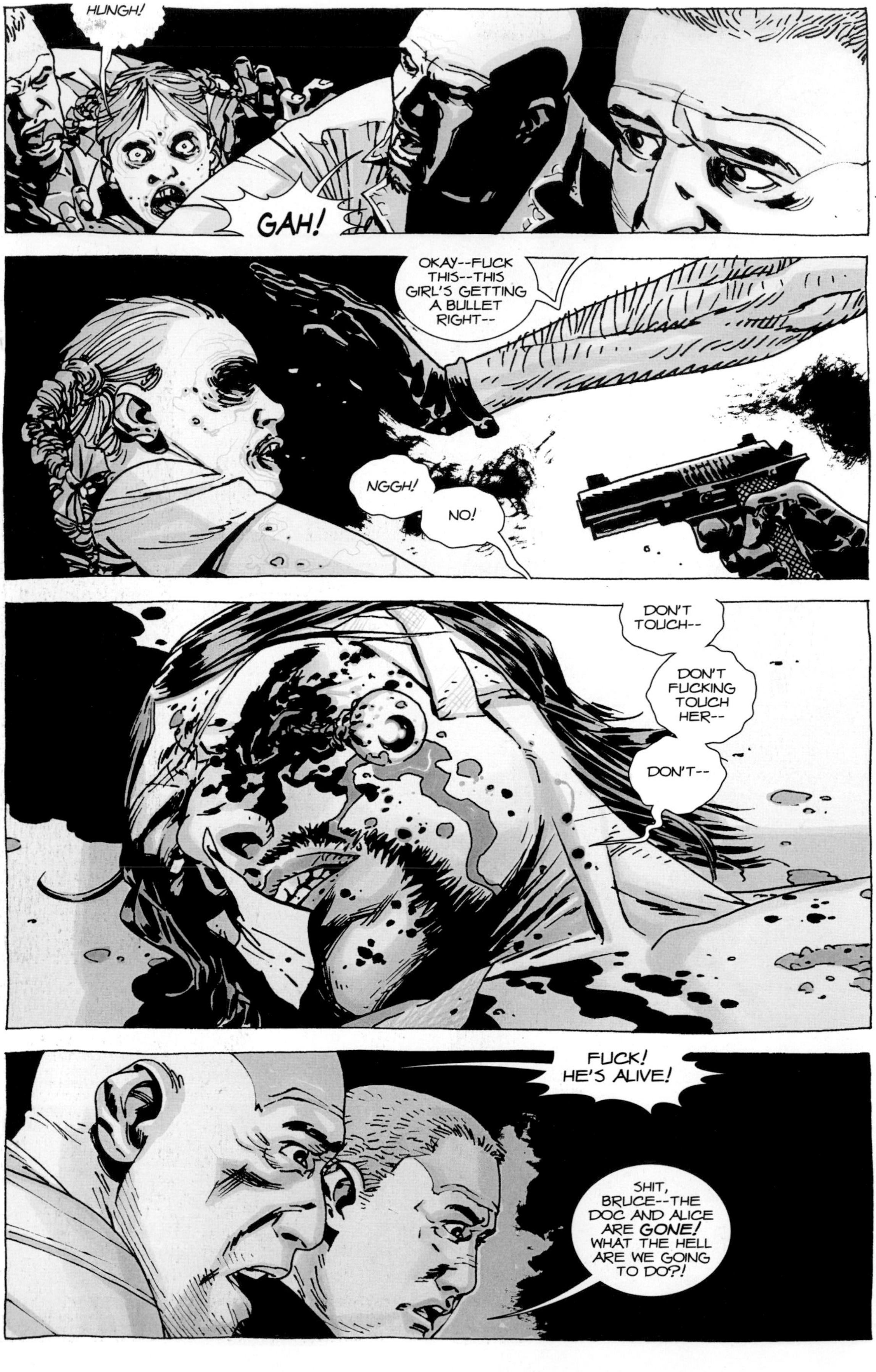
HUNGH!
GAH!
OKAY--FUCK THIS--THIS GIRL'S GETTING A BULLET RIGHT--
NGGH!
NO!
DON'T TOUCH--
DON'T FUCKING TOUCH HER--
DON'T--
FUCK! HE'S ALIVE!
SHIT, BRUCE--THE DOC AND ALICE ARE GONE! WHAT THE HELL ARE WE GOING TO DO?!

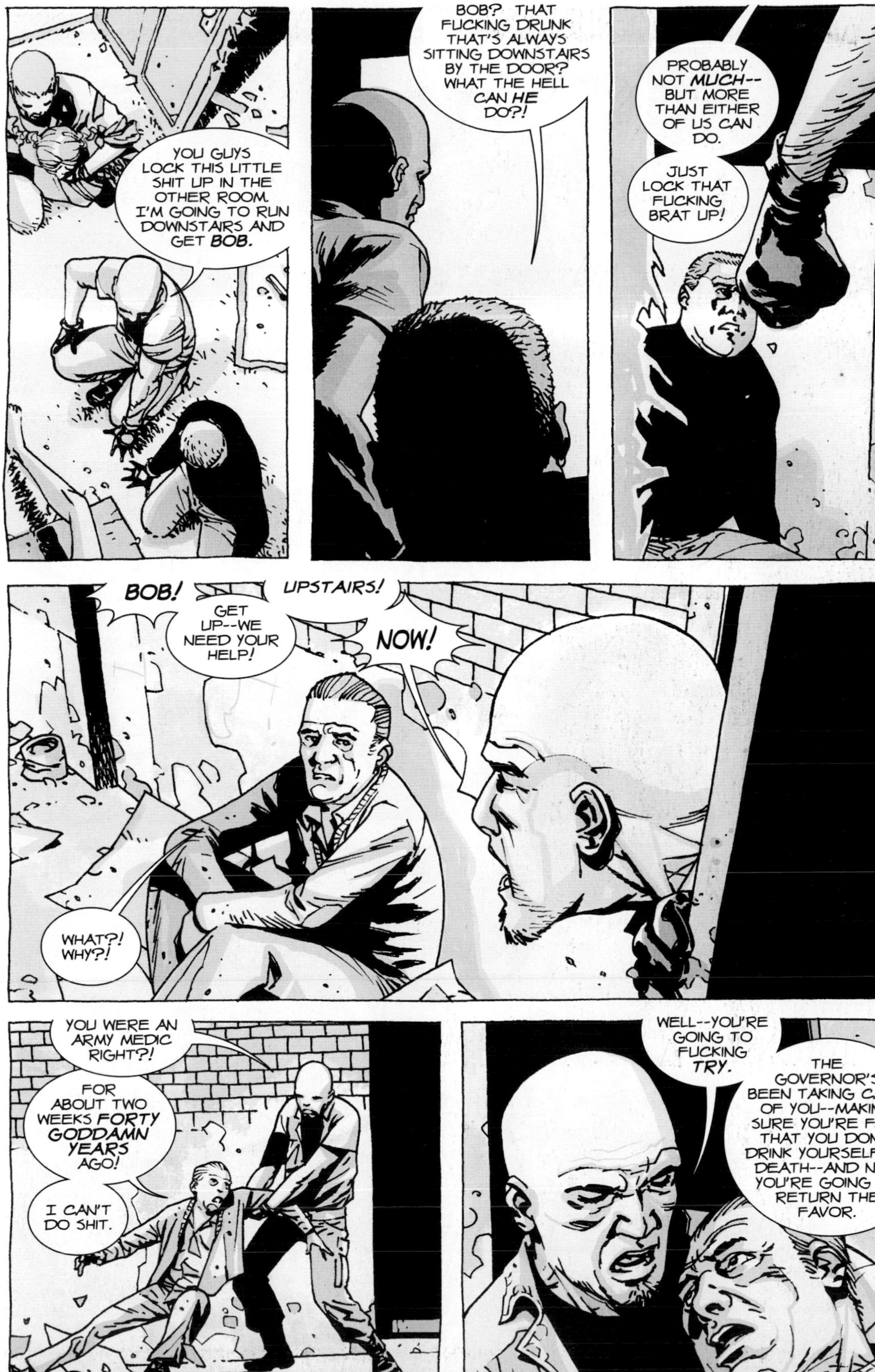
YOU GUYS LOCK THIS LITTLE SHIT UP IN THE OTHER ROOM. I'M GOING TO RUN DOWNSTAIRS AND GET BOB.
BOB? THAT FUCKING DRUNK THAT'S ALWAYS SITTING DOWNSTAIRS BY THE DOOR? WHAT THE HELL CAN HE DO?!
PROBABLY NOT MUCH-- BUT MORE THAN EITHER OF US CAN DO.
JUST LOCK THAT FUCKING BRAT UP!
BOB!
GET UP--WE NEED YOUR HELP!
UPSTAIRS!
NOW!
WHAT?! WHY?!
YOU WERE AN ARMY MEDIC RIGHT?!
FOR ABOUT TWO WEEKS FORTY GODDAMN YEARS AGO!
I CAN'T DO SHIT.
WELL--YOU'RE GOING TO FUCKING TRY.
THE GOVERNOR'S BEEN TAKING CARE OF YOU--MAKING SURE YOU'RE FED, THAT YOU DON'T DRINK YOURSELF TO DEATH--AND NOW YOU'RE GOING TO RETURN THE FAVOR.

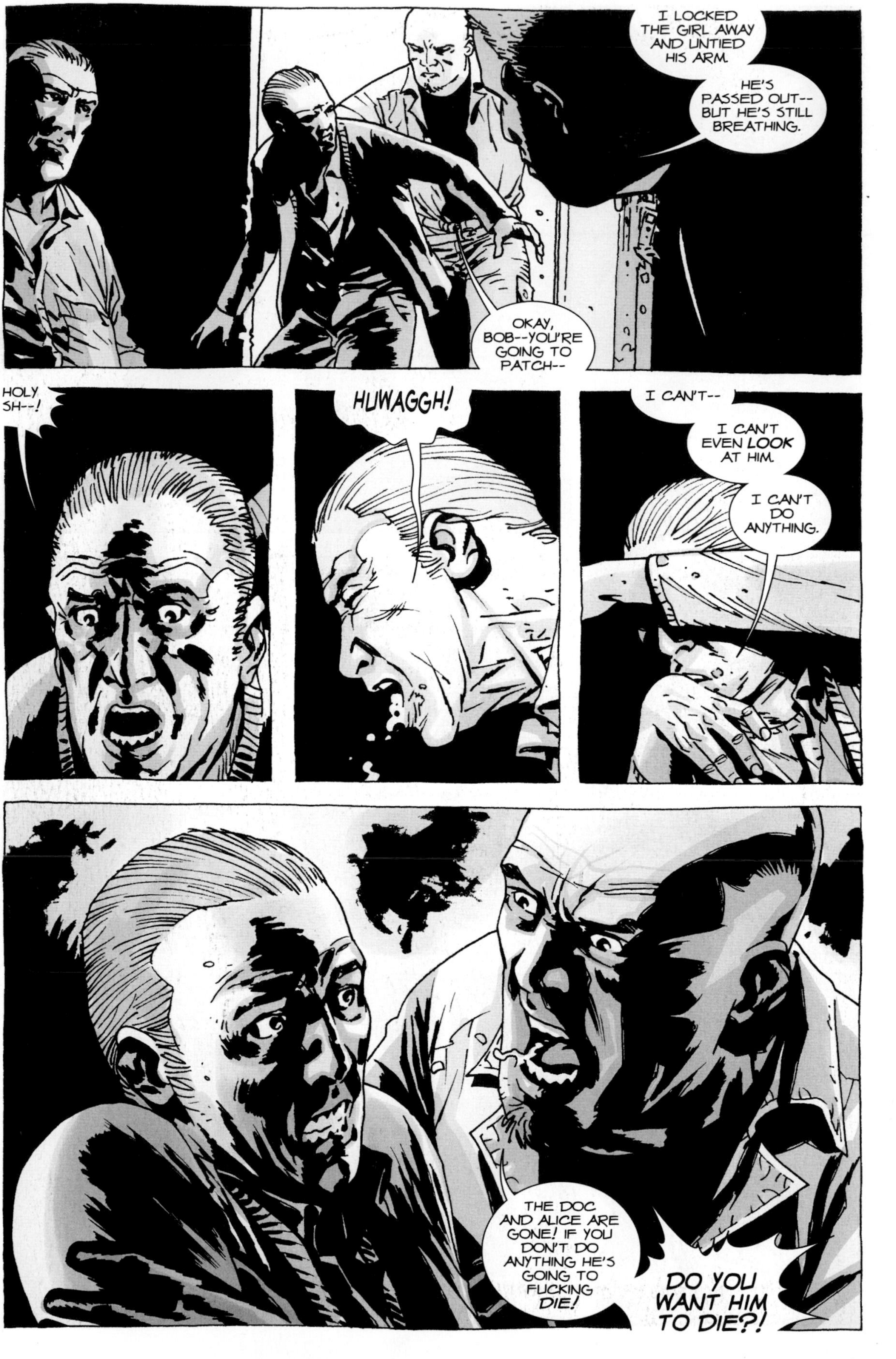
I LOCKED THE GIRL AWAY AND UNTIED HIS ARM.
HE'S PASSED OUT-- BUT HE'S STILL BREATHING.
OKAY, BOB--YOU'RE GOING TO PATCH--
HOLY SH--!
HUWAGGH!
I CAN'T--
I CAN'T EVEN LOOK AT HIM.
I CAN'T DO ANYTHING.
THE DOC AND ALICE ARE GONE! IF YOU DON'T DO ANYTHING HE'S GOING TO FUCKING DIE!
DO YOU WANT HIM TO DIE?!

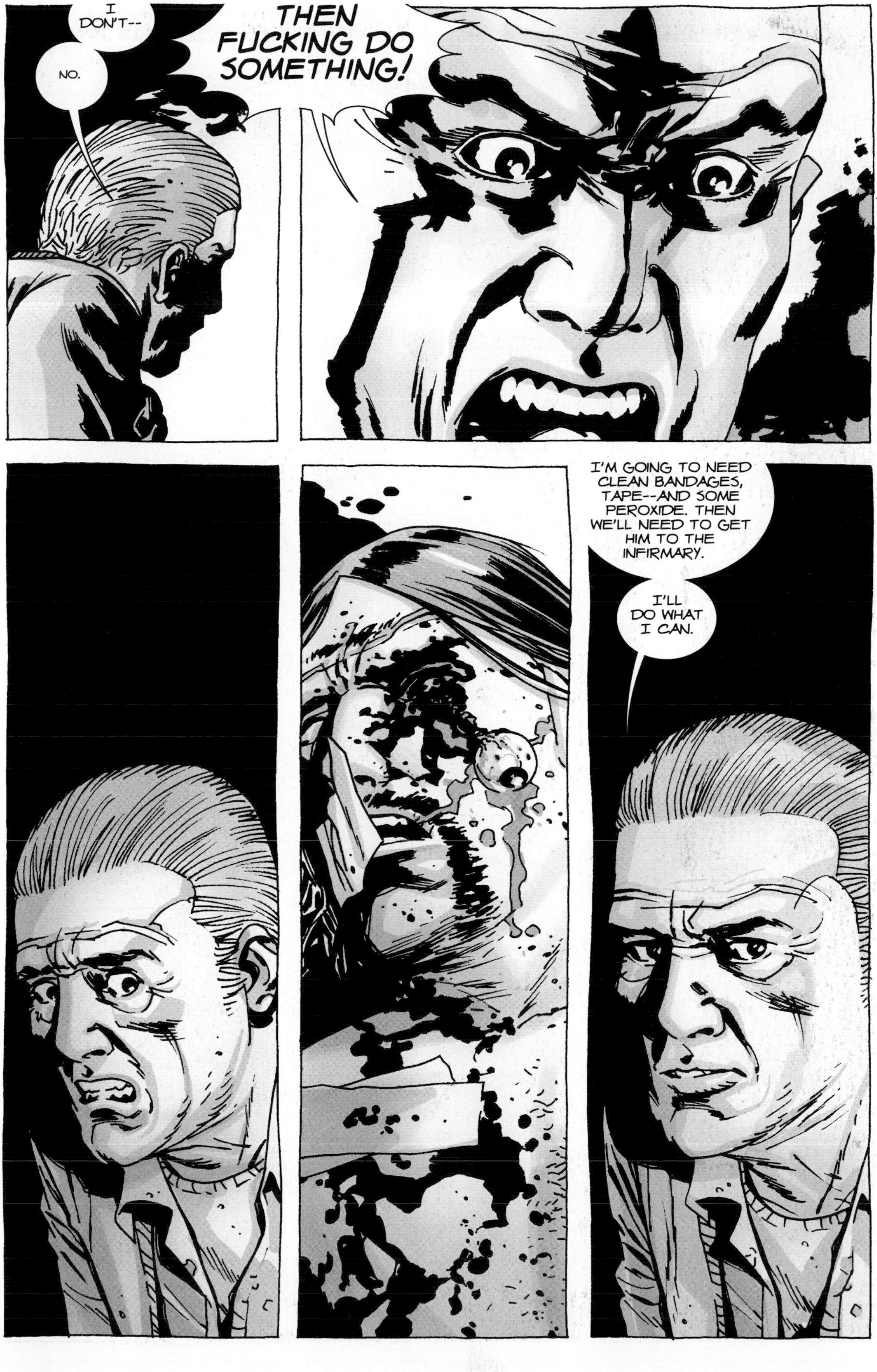
I DON'T--
NO.
THEN FUCKING DO SOMETHING!
I'M GOING TO NEED CLEAN BANDAGES, TAPE--AND SOME PEROXIDE. THEN WE'LL NEED TO GET HIM TO THE INFIRMARY.
I'LL DO WHAT I CAN.

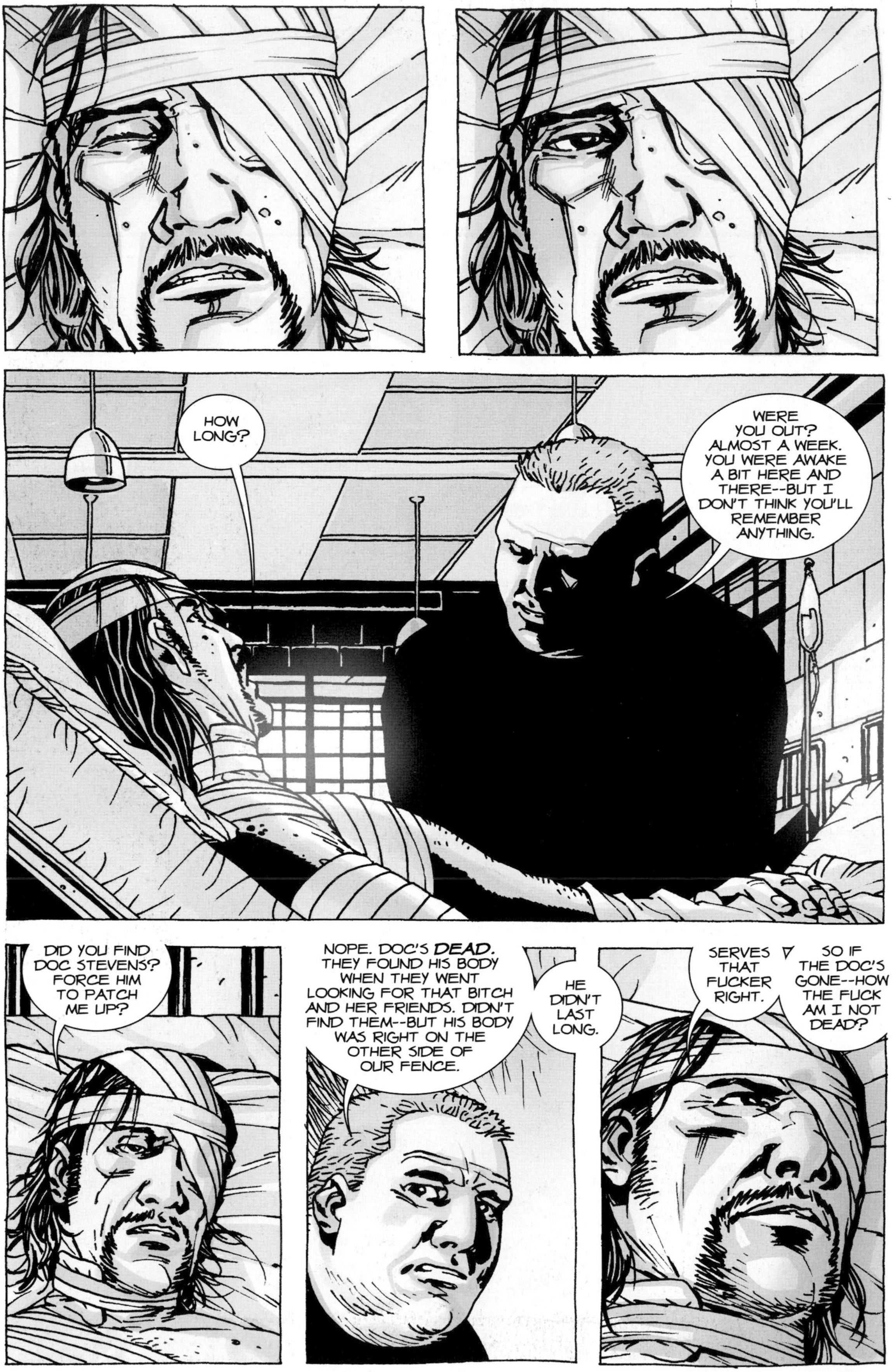
HOW LONG?
WERE YOU OUT? ALMOST A WEEK. YOU WERE AWAKE A BIT HERE AND THERE--BUT I DON'T THINK YOU'LL REMEMBER ANYTHING.
DID YOU FIND DOC STEVENS? FORCE HIM TO PATCH ME UP?
NOPE. DOC'S DEAD. THEY FOUND HIS BODY WHEN THEY WENT LOOKING FOR THAT BITCH AND HER FRIENDS. DIDN'T FIND THEM--BUT HIS BODY WAS RIGHT ON THE OTHER SIDE OF OUR FENCE.
HE DIDN'T LAST LONG.
SERVES THAT FUCKER RIGHT.
SO IF THE DOC'S GONE--HOW THE FUCK AM I NOT DEAD?

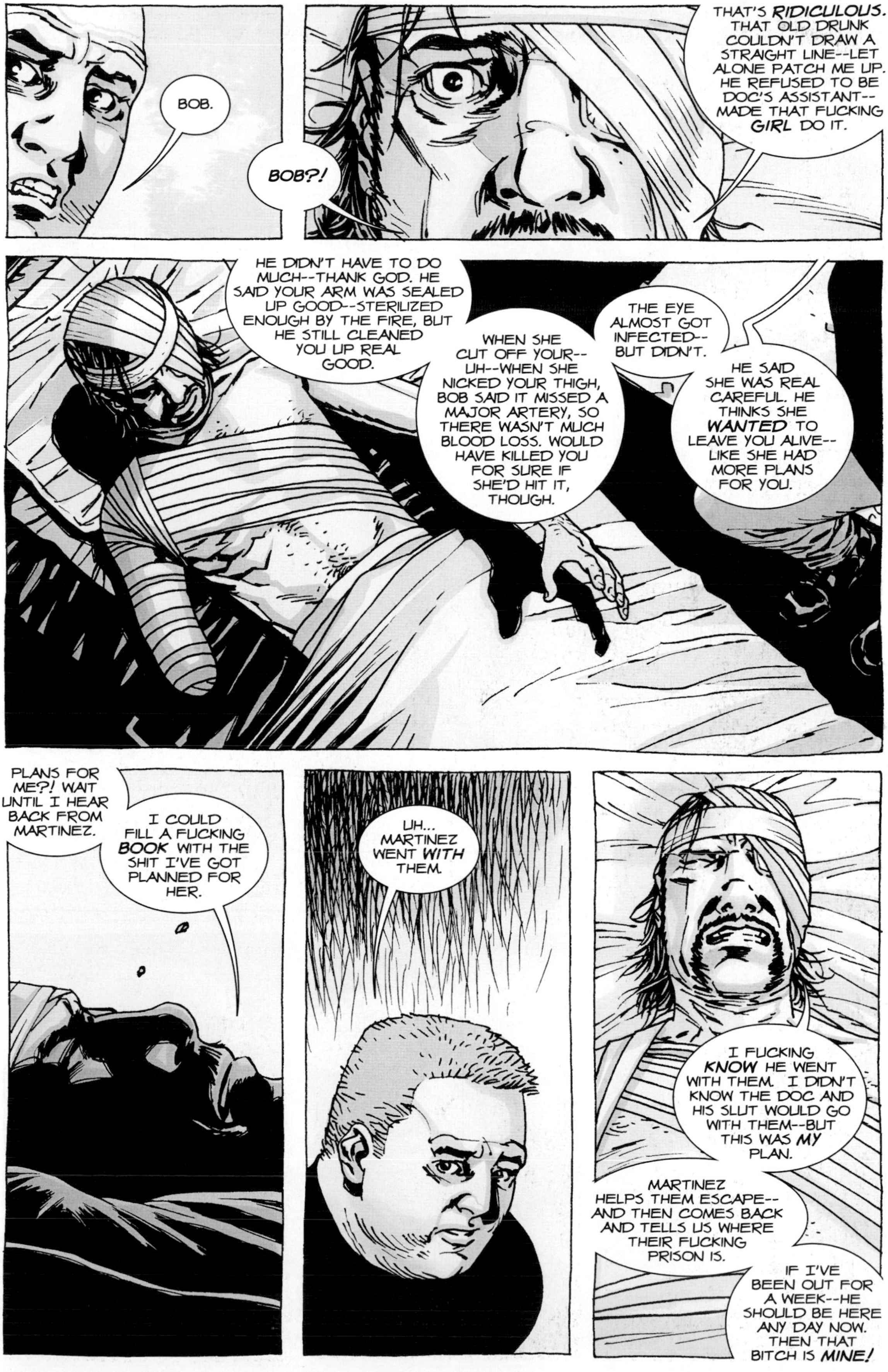
BOB.
BOB?!
THAT'S RIDICULOUS. THAT OLD DRUNK COULDN'T DRAW A STRAIGHT LINE--LET ALONE PATCH ME UP. HE REFUSED TO BE DOC'S ASSISTANT--MADE THAT FUCKING GIRL DO IT.
HE DIDN'T HAVE TO DO MUCH--THANK GOD. HE SAID YOUR ARM WAS SEALED UP GOOD--STERILIZED ENOUGH BY THE FIRE, BUT HE STILL CLEANED YOU UP REAL GOOD.
WHEN SHE CUT OFF YOUR--UH--WHEN SHE NICKED YOUR THIGH, BOB SAID IT MISSED A MAJOR ARTERY, SO THERE WASN'T MUCH BLOOD LOSS. WOULD HAVE KILLED YOU FOR SURE IF SHE'D HIT IT, THOUGH.
THE EYE ALMOST GOT INFECTED--BUT DIDN'T.
HE SAID SHE WAS REAL CAREFUL. HE THINKS SHE WANTED TO LEAVE YOU ALIVE--LIKE SHE HAD MORE PLANS FOR YOU.
PLANS FOR ME?! WAIT UNTIL I HEAR BACK FROM MARTINEZ.
I COULD FILL A FUCKING BOOK WITH THE SHIT I'VE GOT PLANNED FOR HER.
UH... MARTINEZ WENT WITH THEM.
I FUCKING KNOW HE WENT WITH THEM. I DIDN'T KNOW THE DOC AND HIS SLUT WOULD GO WITH THEM--BUT THIS WAS MY PLAN.
MARTINEZ HELPS THEM ESCAPE--AND THEN COMES BACK AND TELLS US WHERE THEIR FUCKING PRISON IS.
IF I'VE BEEN OUT FOR A WEEK--HE SHOULD BE HERE ANY DAY NOW. THEN THAT BITCH IS MINE!

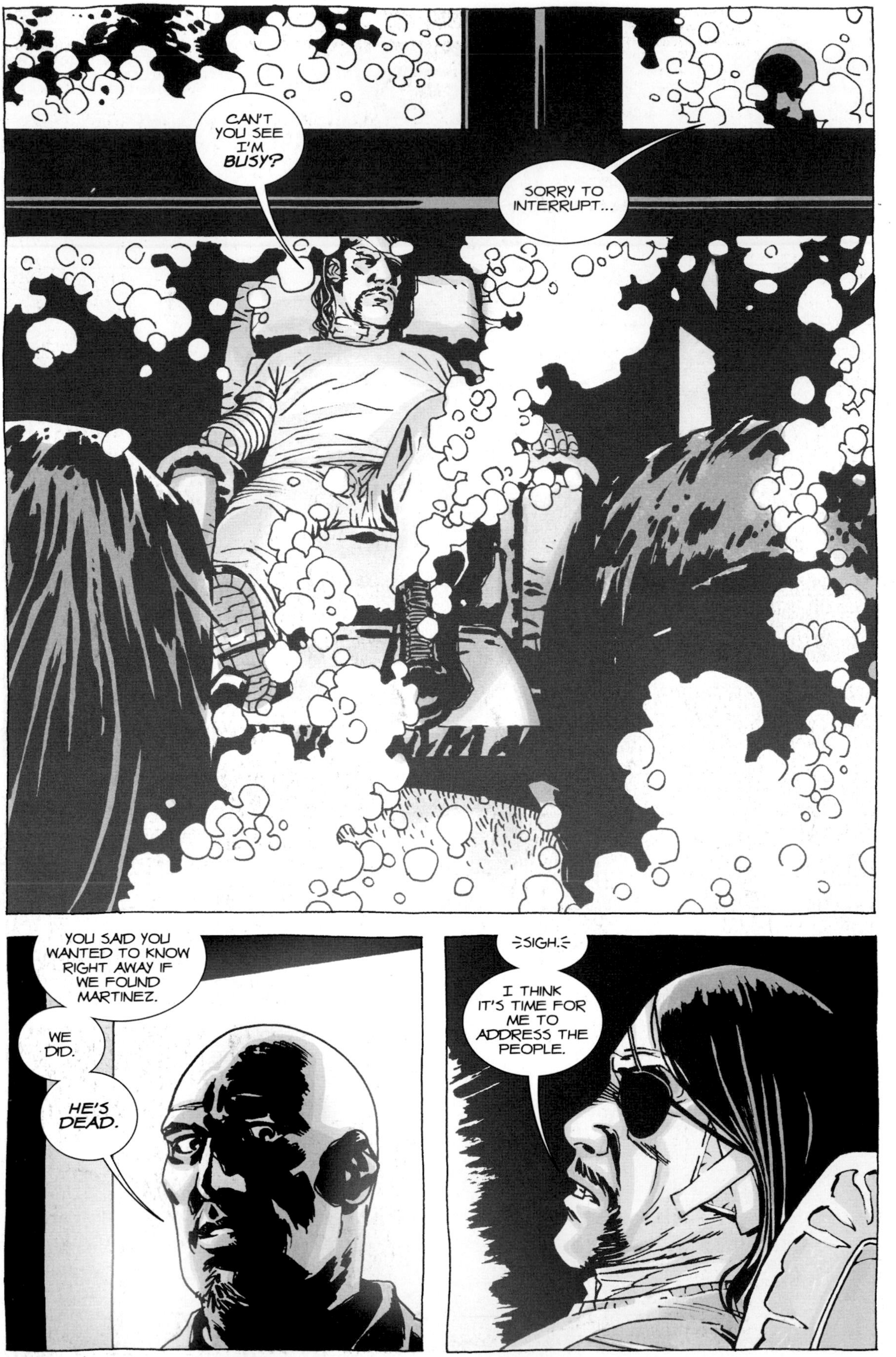
CAN'T YOU SEE I'M BUSY?
SORRY TO INTERRUPT...
YOU SAID YOU WANTED TO KNOW RIGHT AWAY IF WE FOUND MARTINEZ.
WE DID.
HE'S DEAD.
=SIGH.=
I THINK IT'S TIME FOR ME TO ADDRESS THE PEOPLE.

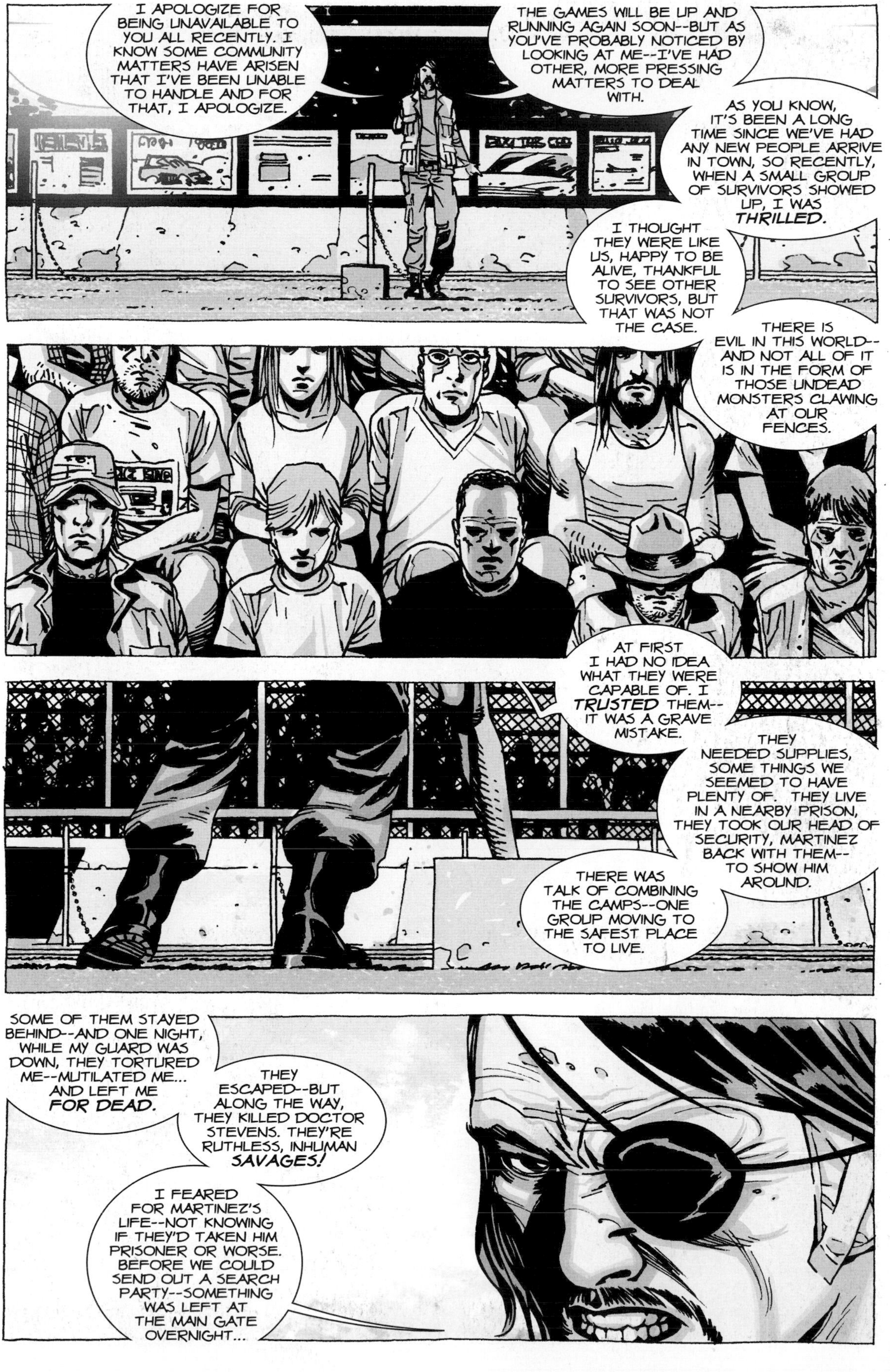
I APOLOGIZE FOR BEING UNAVAILABLE TO YOU ALL RECENTLY. I KNOW SOME COMMUNITY MATTERS HAVE ARISEN THAT I'VE BEEN UNABLE TO HANDLE AND FOR THAT, I APOLOGIZE.
THE GAMES WILL BE UP AND RUNNING AGAIN SOON--BUT AS YOU'VE PROBABLY NOTICED BY LOOKING AT ME--I'VE HAD OTHER, MORE PRESSING MATTERS TO DEAL WITH.
AS YOU KNOW, IT'S BEEN A LONG TIME SINCE WE'VE HAD ANY NEW PEOPLE ARRIVE IN TOWN, SO RECENTLY, WHEN A SMALL GROUP OF SURVIVORS SHOWED UP, I WAS *THRILLED.*
I THOUGHT THEY WERE LIKE US, HAPPY TO BE ALIVE, THANKFUL TO SEE OTHER SURVIVORS, BUT THAT WAS NOT THE CASE.
THERE IS EVIL IN THIS WORLD--AND NOT ALL OF IT IS IN THE FORM OF THOSE UNDEAD MONSTERS CLAWING AT OUR FENCES.
AT FIRST I HAD NO IDEA WHAT THEY WERE CAPABLE OF. I *TRUSTED* THEM--IT WAS A GRAVE MISTAKE.
THEY NEEDED SUPPLIES, SOME THINGS WE SEEMED TO HAVE PLENTY OF. THEY LIVE IN A NEARBY PRISON, THEY TOOK OUR HEAD OF SECURITY, MARTINEZ BACK WITH THEM--TO SHOW HIM AROUND.
THERE WAS TALK OF COMBINING THE CAMPS--ONE GROUP MOVING TO THE SAFEST PLACE TO LIVE.
SOME OF THEM STAYED BEHIND--AND ONE NIGHT, WHILE MY GUARD WAS DOWN, THEY TORTURED ME--MUTILATED ME... AND LEFT ME *FOR DEAD.*
THEY ESCAPED--BUT ALONG THE WAY, THEY KILLED DOCTOR STEVENS. THEY'RE RUTHLESS, INHUMAN *SAVAGES!*
I FEARED FOR MARTINEZ'S LIFE--NOT KNOWING IF THEY'D TAKEN HIM PRISONER OR WORSE. BEFORE WE COULD SEND OUT A SEARCH PARTY--SOMETHING WAS LEFT AT THE MAIN GATE OVERNIGHT...

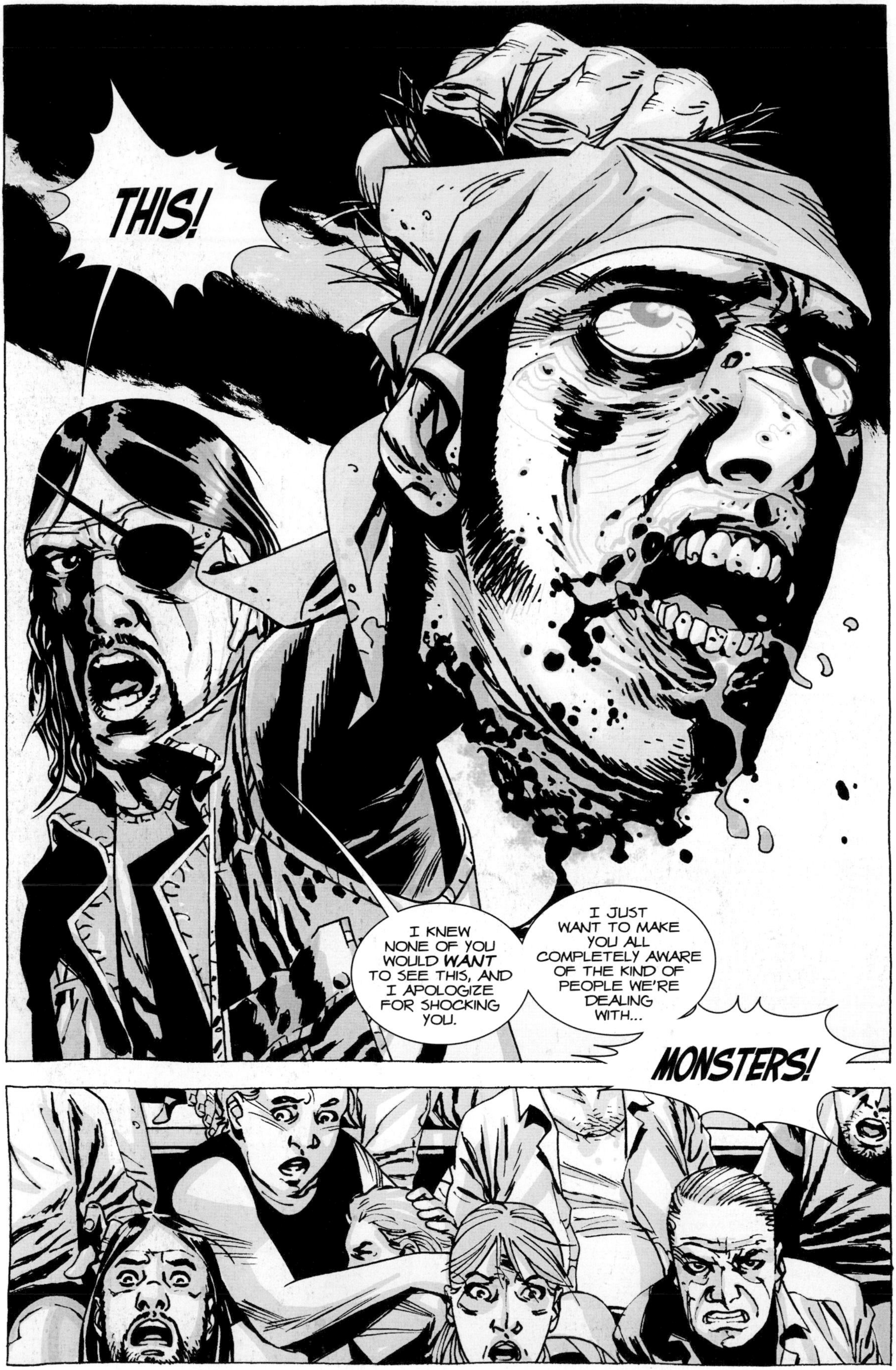
THIS!
I KNEW NONE OF YOU WOULD WANT TO SEE THIS, AND I APOLOGIZE FOR SHOCKING YOU.
I JUST WANT TO MAKE YOU ALL COMPLETELY AWARE OF THE KIND OF PEOPLE WE'RE DEALING WITH...
MONSTERS!

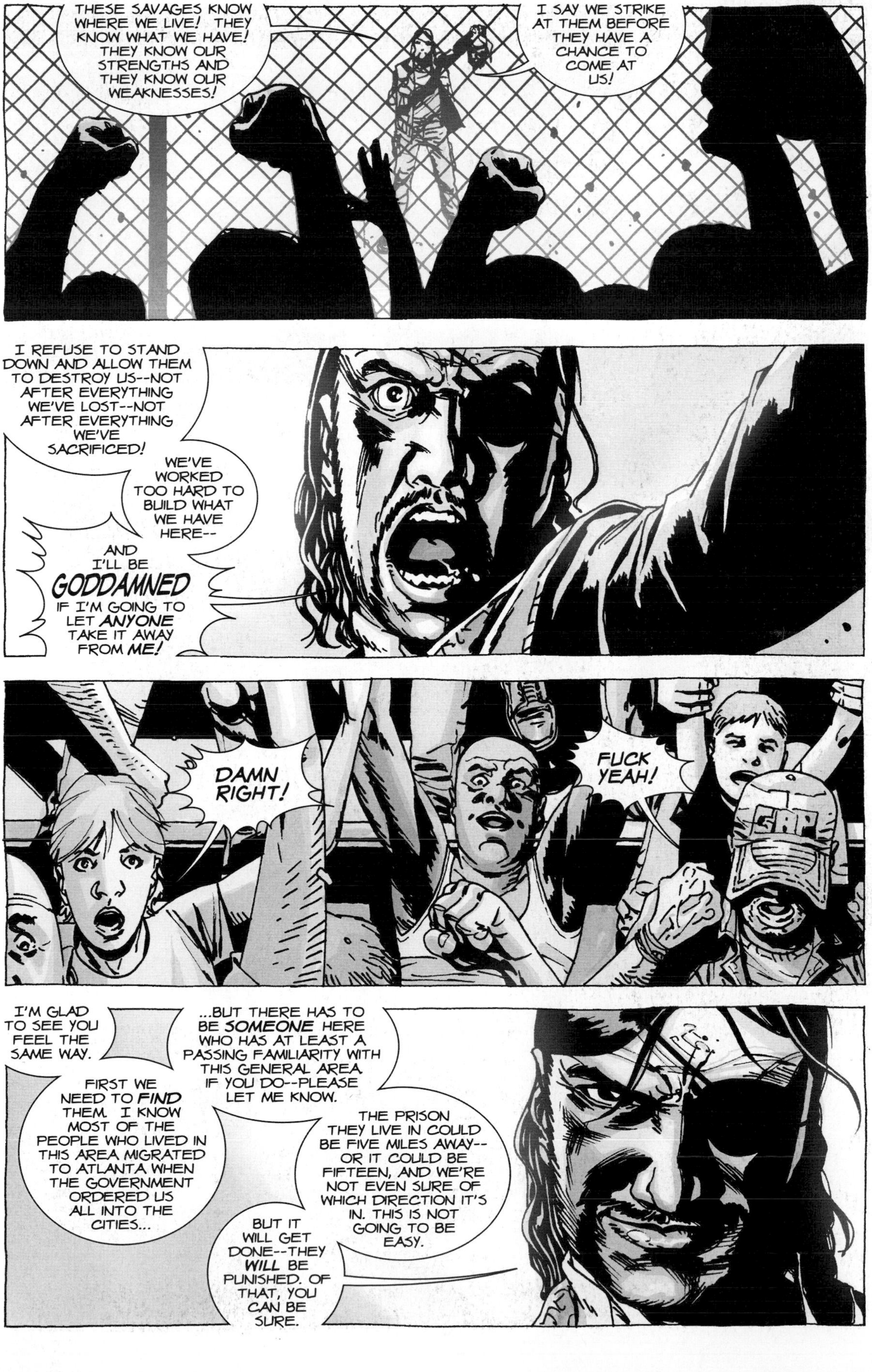
THESE SAVAGES KNOW WHERE WE LIVE! THEY KNOW WHAT WE HAVE! THEY KNOW OUR STRENGTHS AND THEY KNOW OUR WEAKNESSES!
I SAY WE STRIKE AT THEM BEFORE THEY HAVE A CHANCE TO COME AT US!
I REFUSE TO STAND DOWN AND ALLOW THEM TO DESTROY US--NOT AFTER EVERYTHING WE'VE LOST--NOT AFTER EVERYTHING WE'VE SACRIFICED!
WE'VE WORKED TOO HARD TO BUILD WHAT WE HAVE HERE--
AND I'LL BE GODDAMNED IF I'M GOING TO LET ANYONE TAKE IT AWAY FROM ME!
DAMN RIGHT!
FUCK YEAH!
I'M GLAD TO SEE YOU FEEL THE SAME WAY.
FIRST WE NEED TO FIND THEM. I KNOW MOST OF THE PEOPLE WHO LIVED IN THIS AREA MIGRATED TO ATLANTA WHEN THE GOVERNMENT ORDERED US ALL INTO THE CITIES...
...BUT THERE HAS TO BE SOMEONE HERE WHO HAS AT LEAST A PASSING FAMILIARITY WITH THIS GENERAL AREA. IF YOU DO--PLEASE LET ME KNOW.
THE PRISON THEY LIVE IN COULD BE FIVE MILES AWAY--OR IT COULD BE FIFTEEN, AND WE'RE NOT EVEN SURE OF WHICH DIRECTION IT'S IN. THIS IS NOT GOING TO BE EASY.
BUT IT WILL GET DONE--THEY WILL BE PUNISHED. OF THAT, YOU CAN BE SURE.

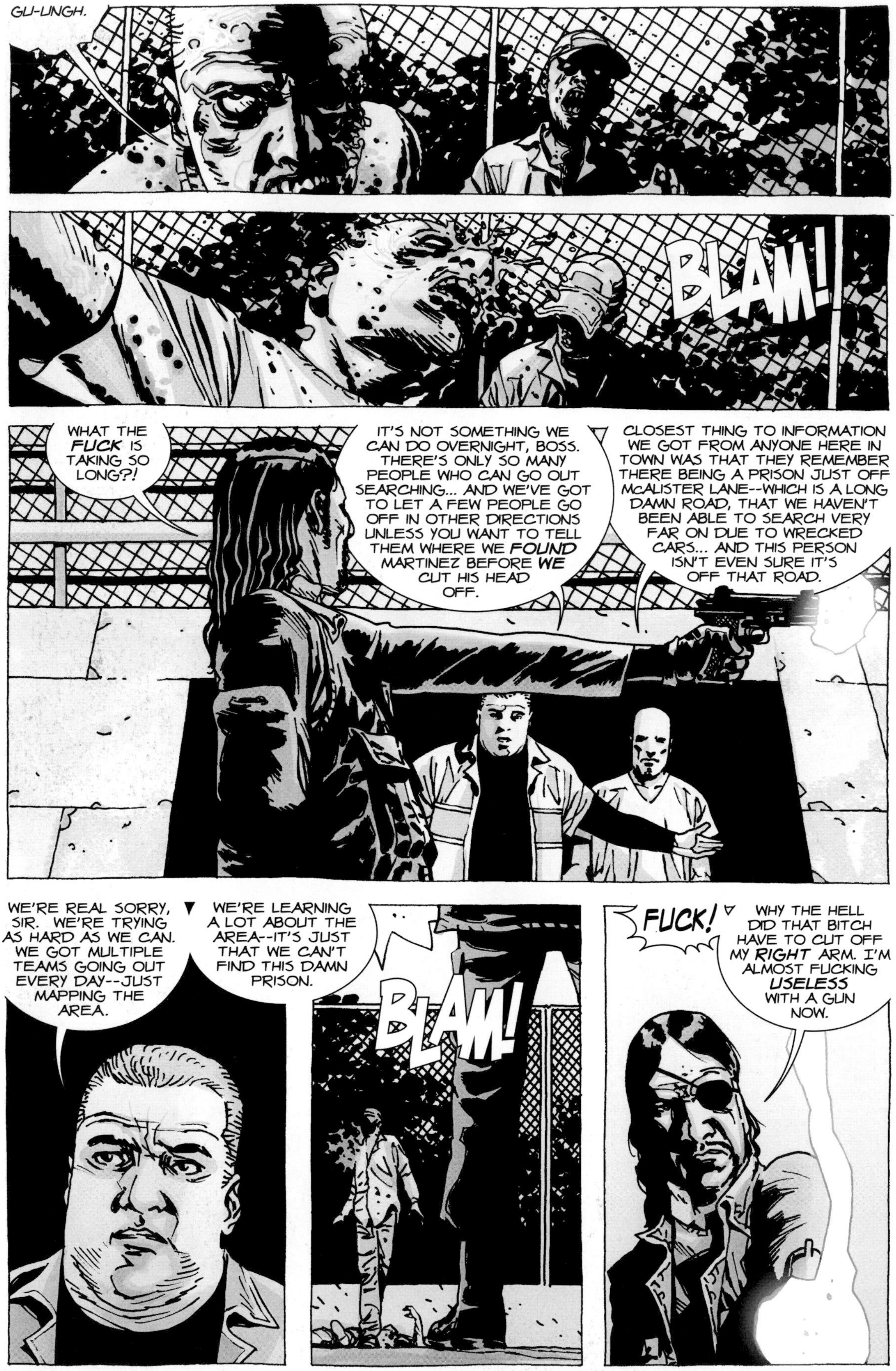
GU-UNGH.
BLAM!
WHAT THE FUCK IS TAKING SO LONG?!
IT'S NOT SOMETHING WE CAN DO OVERNIGHT, BOSS. THERE'S ONLY SO MANY PEOPLE WHO CAN GO OUT SEARCHING... AND WE'VE GOT TO LET A FEW PEOPLE GO OFF IN OTHER DIRECTIONS UNLESS YOU WANT TO TELL THEM WHERE WE FOUND MARTINEZ BEFORE WE CUT HIS HEAD OFF.
CLOSEST THING TO INFORMATION WE GOT FROM ANYONE HERE IN TOWN WAS THAT THEY REMEMBER THERE BEING A PRISON JUST OFF McALISTER LANE--WHICH IS A LONG DAMN ROAD, THAT WE HAVEN'T BEEN ABLE TO SEARCH VERY FAR ON DUE TO WRECKED CARS... AND THIS PERSON ISN'T EVEN SURE IT'S OFF THAT ROAD.
WE'RE REAL SORRY, SIR. WE'RE TRYING AS HARD AS WE CAN. WE GOT MULTIPLE TEAMS GOING OUT EVERY DAY--JUST MAPPING THE AREA.
WE'RE LEARNING A LOT ABOUT THE AREA--IT'S JUST THAT WE CAN'T FIND THIS DAMN PRISON.
BLAM!
FUCK!
WHY THE HELL DID THAT BITCH HAVE TO CUT OFF MY RIGHT ARM. I'M ALMOST FUCKING USELESS WITH A GUN NOW.

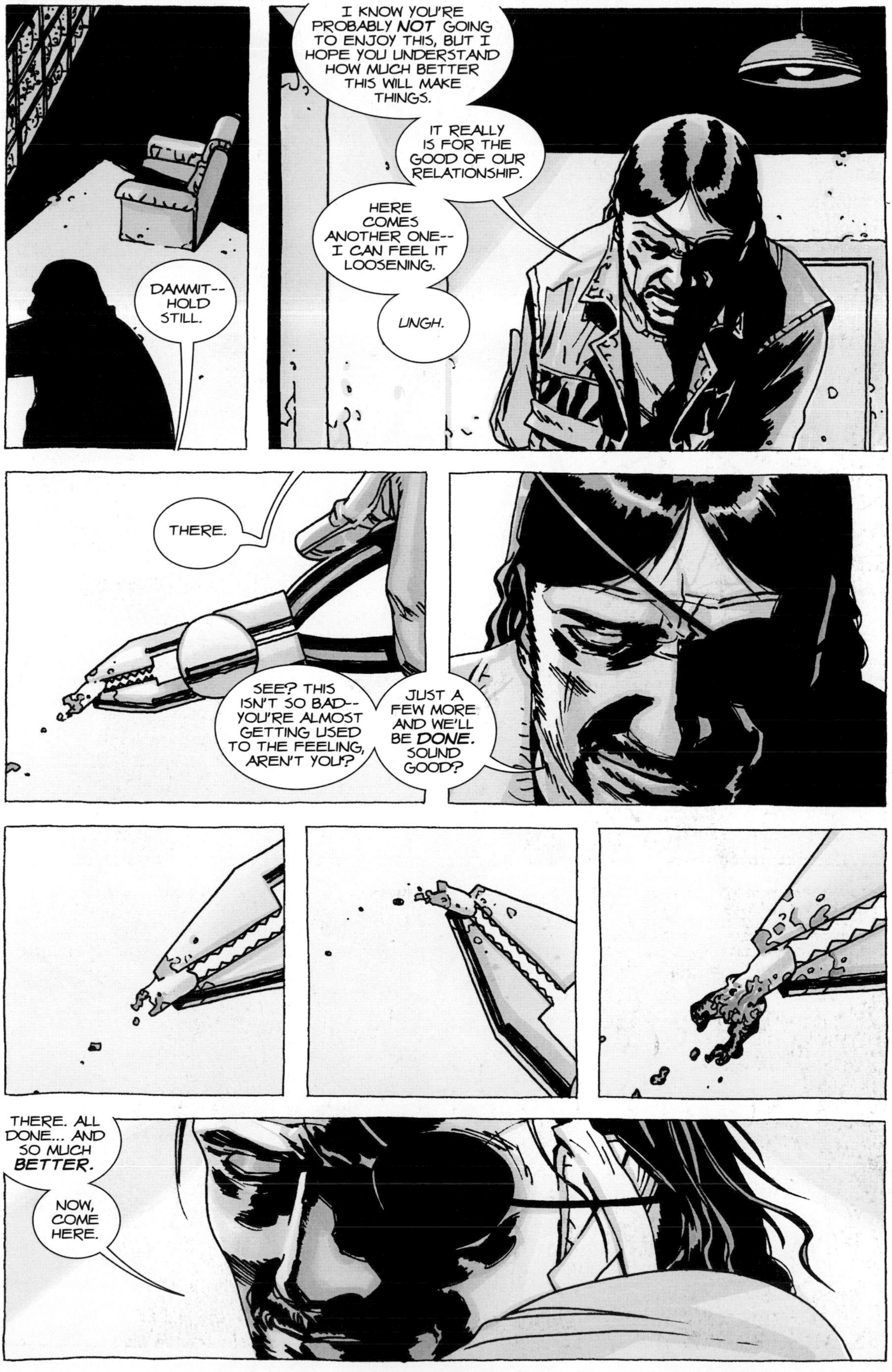
I KNOW YOU'RE PROBABLY NOT GOING TO ENJOY THIS, BUT I HOPE YOU UNDERSTAND HOW MUCH BETTER THIS WILL MAKE THINGS.
IT REALLY IS FOR THE GOOD OF OUR RELATIONSHIP.
HERE COMES ANOTHER ONE-- I CAN FEEL IT LOOSENING.
UNGH.
DAMMIT-- HOLD STILL.
THERE.
SEE? THIS ISN'T SO BAD-- YOU'RE ALMOST GETTING USED TO THE FEELING, AREN'T YOU?
JUST A FEW MORE AND WE'LL BE DONE. SOUND GOOD?
THERE. ALL DONE... AND SO MUCH BETTER.
NOW, COME HERE.

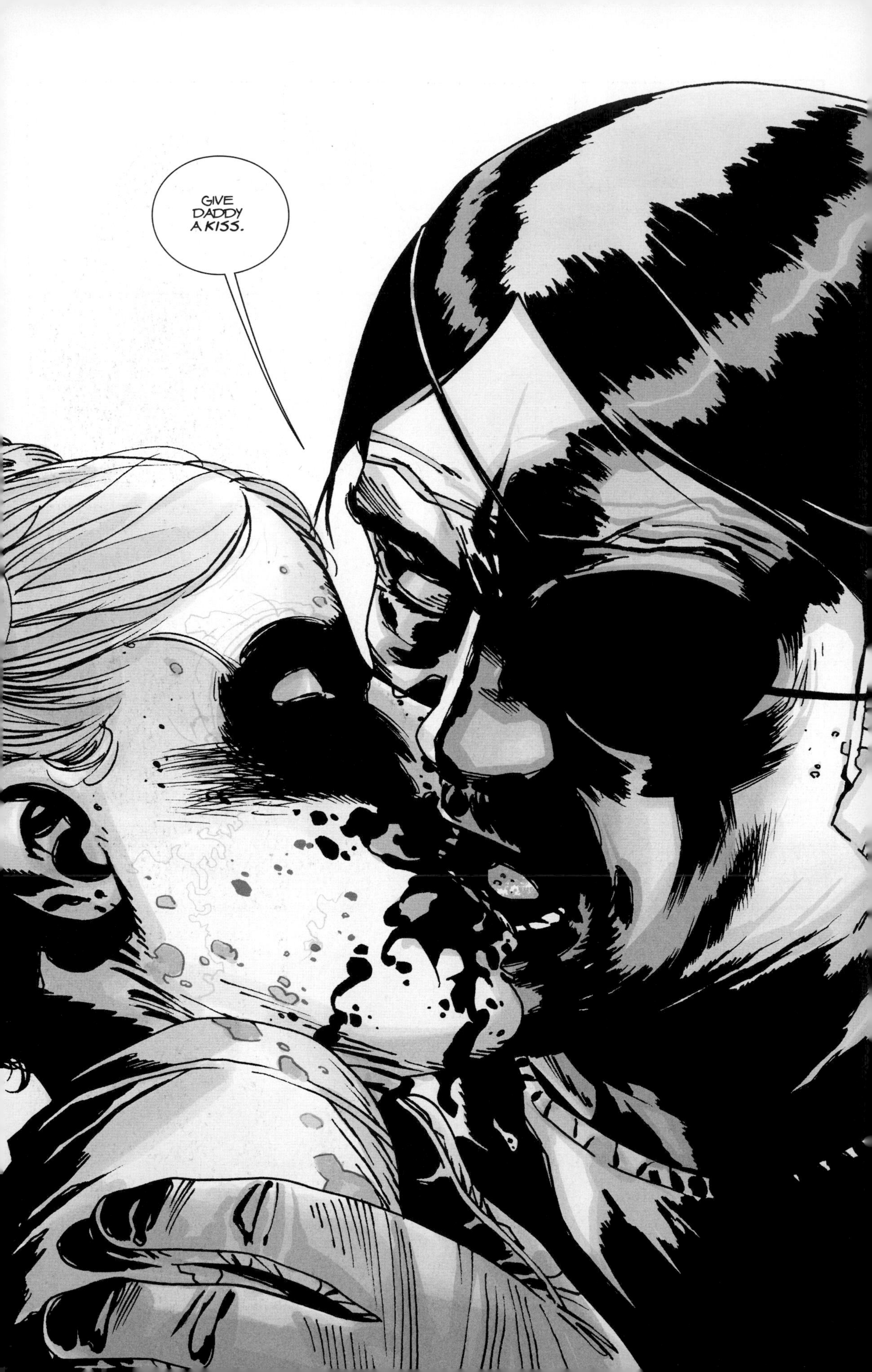
GIVE DADDY A KISS.

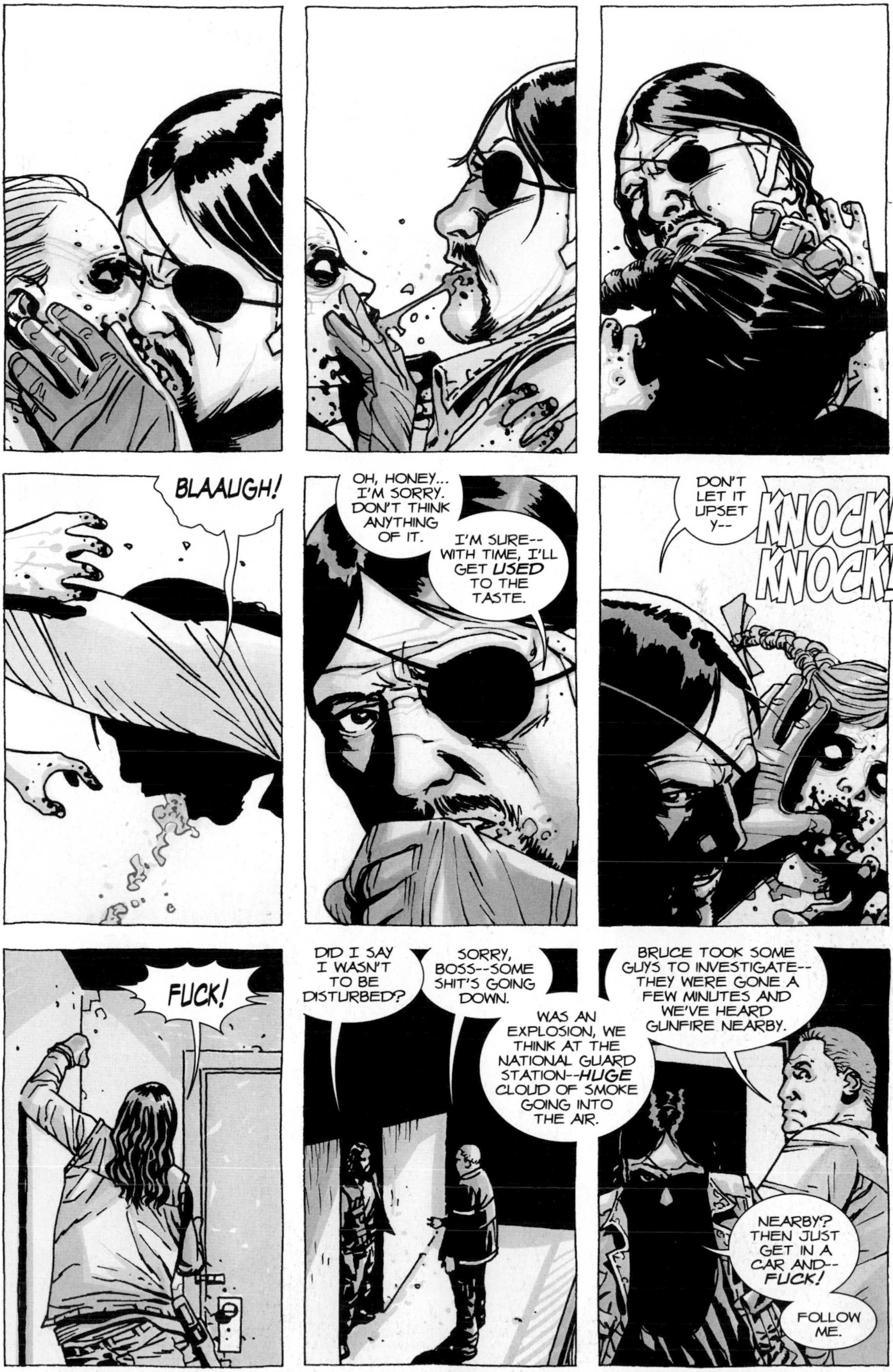
BLAAUGH!
OH, HONEY... I'M SORRY. DON'T THINK ANYTHING OF IT.
I'M SURE-- WITH TIME, I'LL GET USED TO THE TASTE.
DON'T LET IT UPSET Y--
KNOCK! KNOCK!
FUCK!
DID I SAY I WASN'T TO BE DISTURBED?
SORRY, BOSS--SOME SHIT'S GOING DOWN.
WAS AN EXPLOSION, WE THINK AT THE NATIONAL GUARD STATION--HUGE CLOUD OF SMOKE GOING INTO THE AIR.
BRUCE TOOK SOME GUYS TO INVESTIGATE-- THEY WERE GONE A FEW MINUTES AND WE'VE HEARD GUNFIRE NEARBY.
NEARBY? THEN JUST GET IN A CAR AND-- FUCK!
FOLLOW ME.

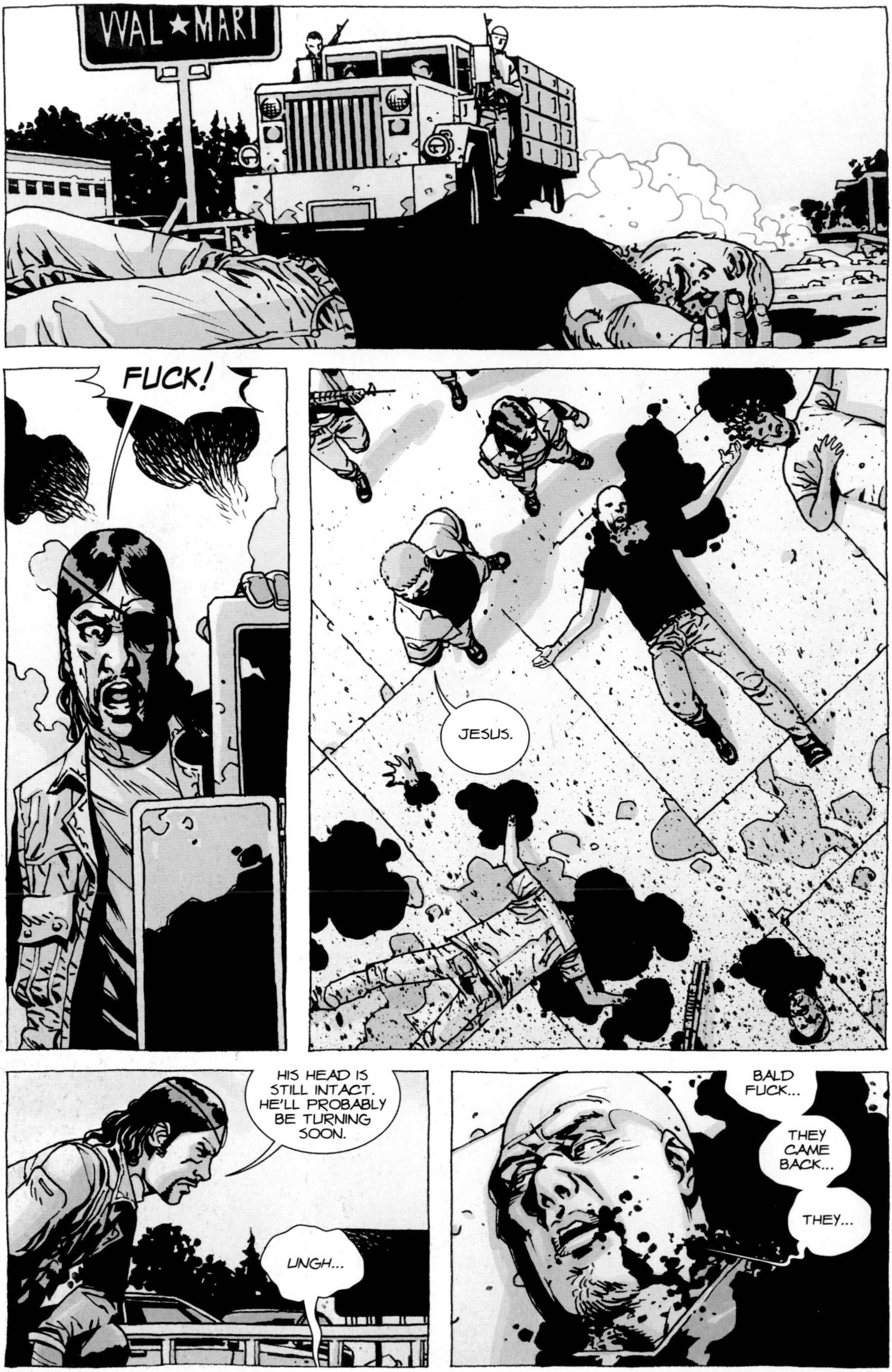
WAL★MART
FUCK!
JESUS.
HIS HEAD IS STILL INTACT. HE'LL PROBABLY BE TURNING SOON.
UNGH...
BALD FUCK...
THEY CAME BACK...
THEY...

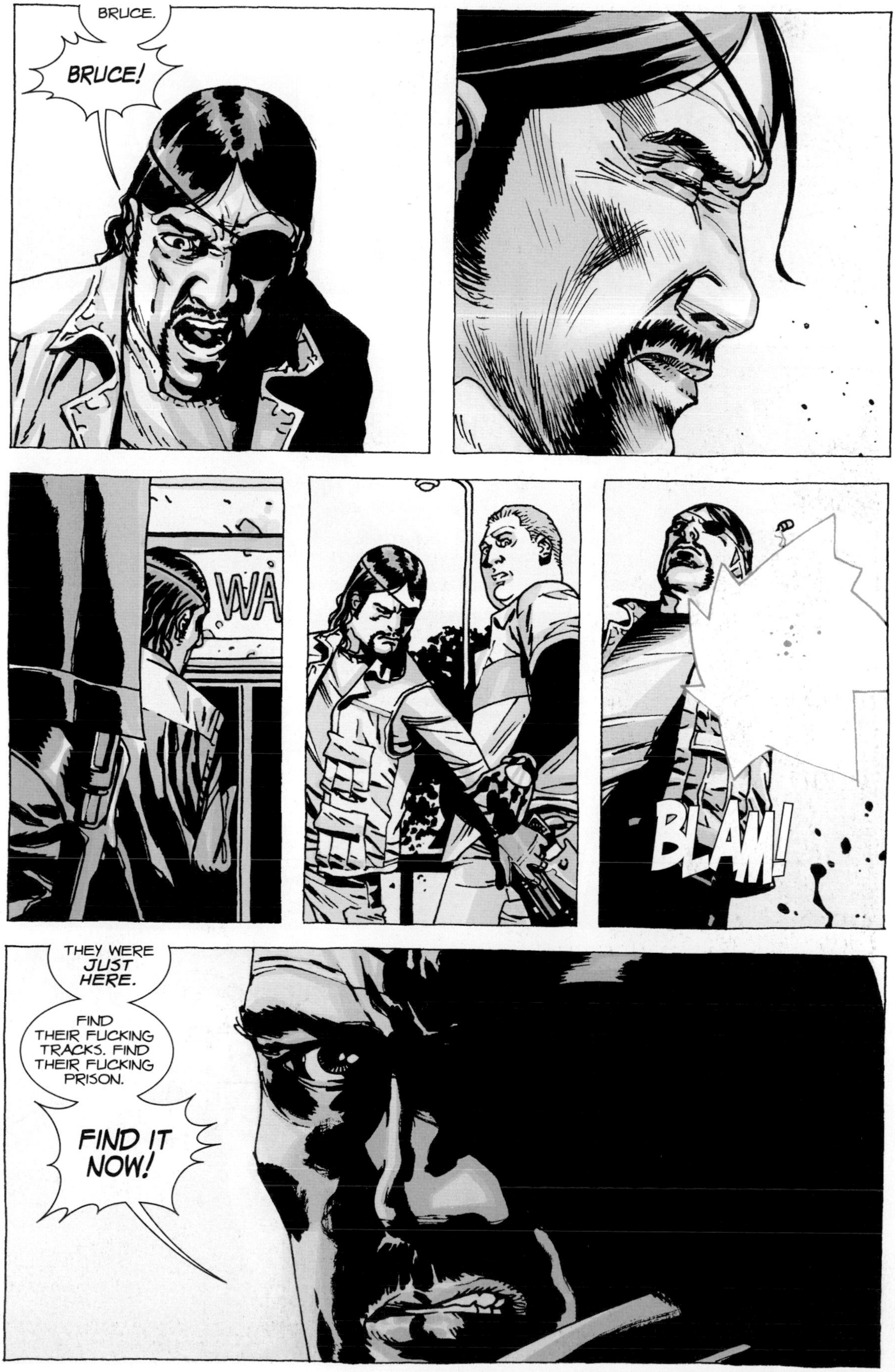
BRUCE.
BRUCE!
WA
BLAM!
THEY WERE JUST HERE.
FIND THEIR FUCKING TRACKS. FIND THEIR FUCKING PRISON.
FIND IT NOW!

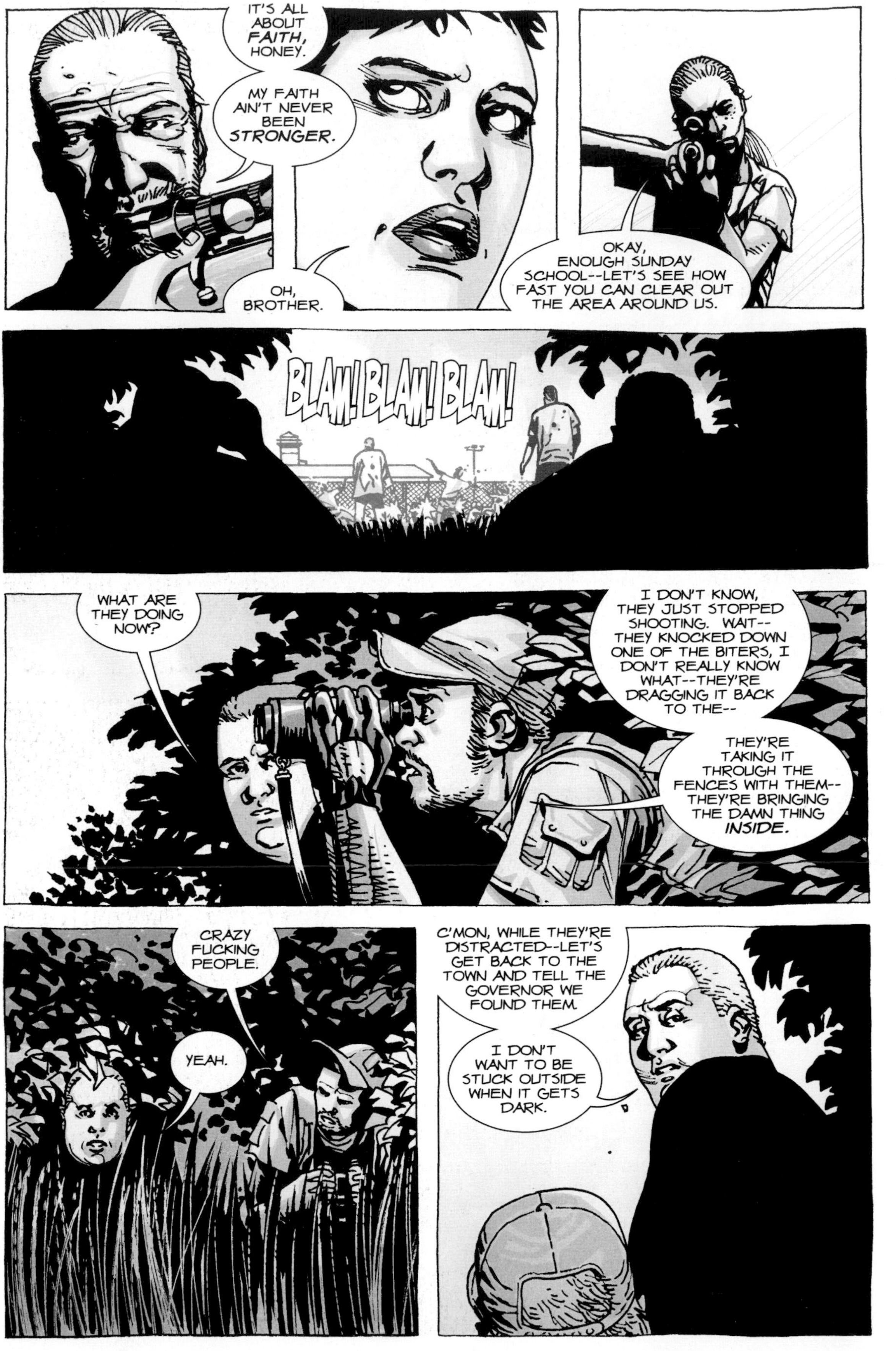
IT'S ALL ABOUT FAITH, HONEY.
MY FAITH AIN'T NEVER BEEN STRONGER.
OH, BROTHER.
OKAY, ENOUGH SUNDAY SCHOOL--LET'S SEE HOW FAST YOU CAN CLEAR OUT THE AREA AROUND US.
BLAM! BLAM! BLAM!
WHAT ARE THEY DOING NOW?
I DON'T KNOW, THEY JUST STOPPED SHOOTING. WAIT-- THEY KNOCKED DOWN ONE OF THE BITERS, I DON'T REALLY KNOW WHAT--THEY'RE DRAGGING IT BACK TO THE--
THEY'RE TAKING IT THROUGH THE FENCES WITH THEM-- THEY'RE BRINGING THE DAMN THING INSIDE.
CRAZY FUCKING PEOPLE.
YEAH.
C'MON, WHILE THEY'RE DISTRACTED--LET'S GET BACK TO THE TOWN AND TELL THE GOVERNOR WE FOUND THEM.
I DON'T WANT TO BE STUCK OUTSIDE WHEN IT GETS DARK.

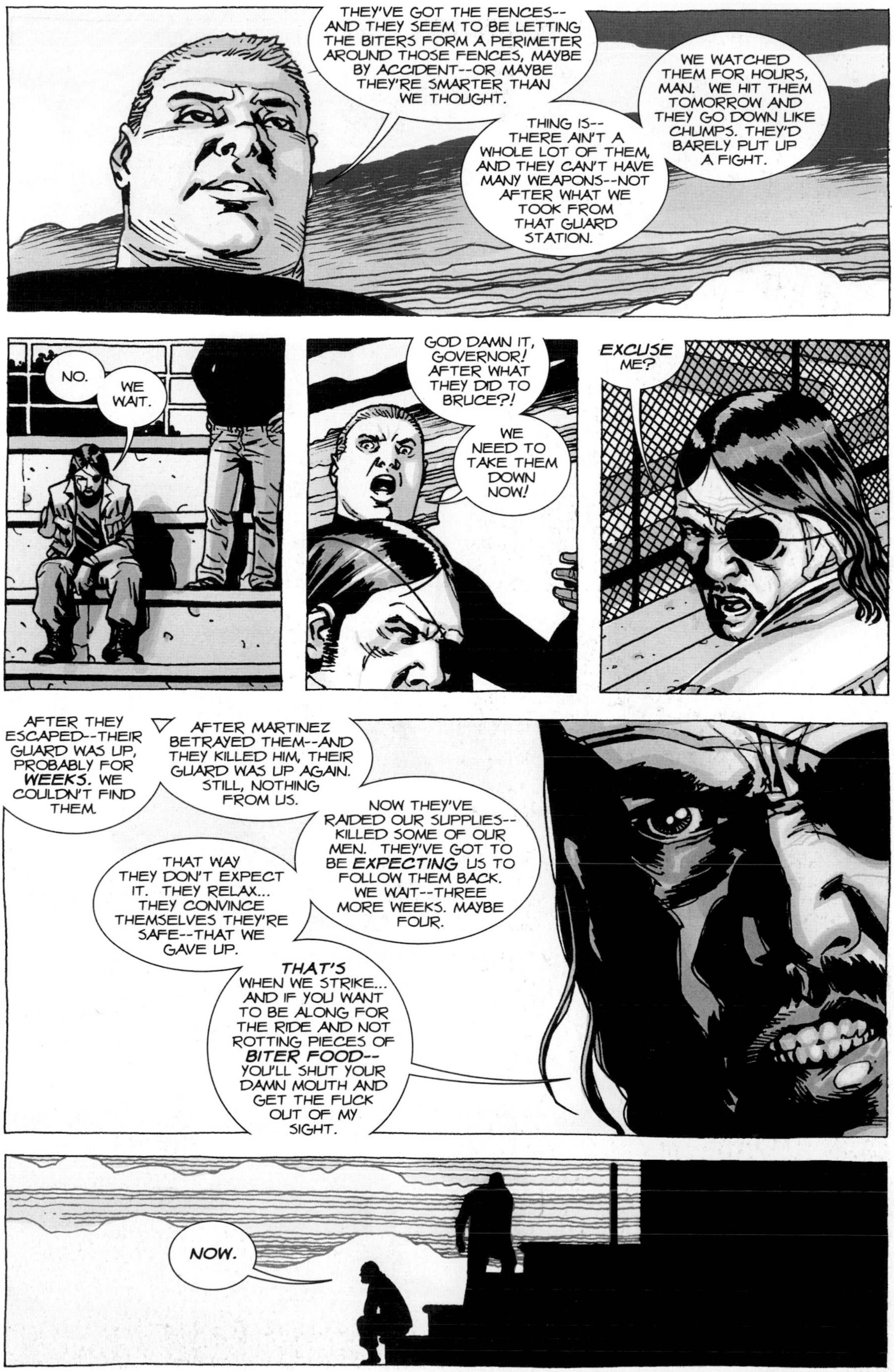
THEY'VE GOT THE FENCES--AND THEY SEEM TO BE LETTING THE BITERS FORM A PERIMETER AROUND THOSE FENCES, MAYBE BY ACCIDENT--OR MAYBE THEY'RE SMARTER THAN WE THOUGHT.
THING IS--THERE AIN'T A WHOLE LOT OF THEM, AND THEY CAN'T HAVE MANY WEAPONS--NOT AFTER WHAT WE TOOK FROM THAT GUARD STATION.
WE WATCHED THEM FOR HOURS, MAN. WE HIT THEM TOMORROW AND THEY GO DOWN LIKE CHUMPS. THEY'D BARELY PUT UP A FIGHT.
NO.
WE WAIT.
GOD DAMN IT, GOVERNOR! AFTER WHAT THEY DID TO BRUCE?!
WE NEED TO TAKE THEM DOWN NOW!
EXCUSE ME?
AFTER THEY ESCAPED--THEIR GUARD WAS UP, PROBABLY FOR WEEKS. WE COULDN'T FIND THEM.
AFTER MARTINEZ BETRAYED THEM--AND THEY KILLED HIM, THEIR GUARD WAS UP AGAIN. STILL, NOTHING FROM US.
NOW THEY'VE RAIDED OUR SUPPLIES--KILLED SOME OF OUR MEN. THEY'VE GOT TO BE EXPECTING US TO FOLLOW THEM BACK. WE WAIT--THREE MORE WEEKS. MAYBE FOUR.
THAT WAY THEY DON'T EXPECT IT. THEY RELAX... THEY CONVINCE THEMSELVES THEY'RE SAFE--THAT WE GAVE UP.
THAT'S WHEN WE STRIKE... AND IF YOU WANT TO BE ALONG FOR THE RIDE AND NOT ROTTING PIECES OF BITER FOOD--YOU'LL SHUT YOUR DAMN MOUTH AND GET THE FUCK OUT OF MY SIGHT.
NOW.

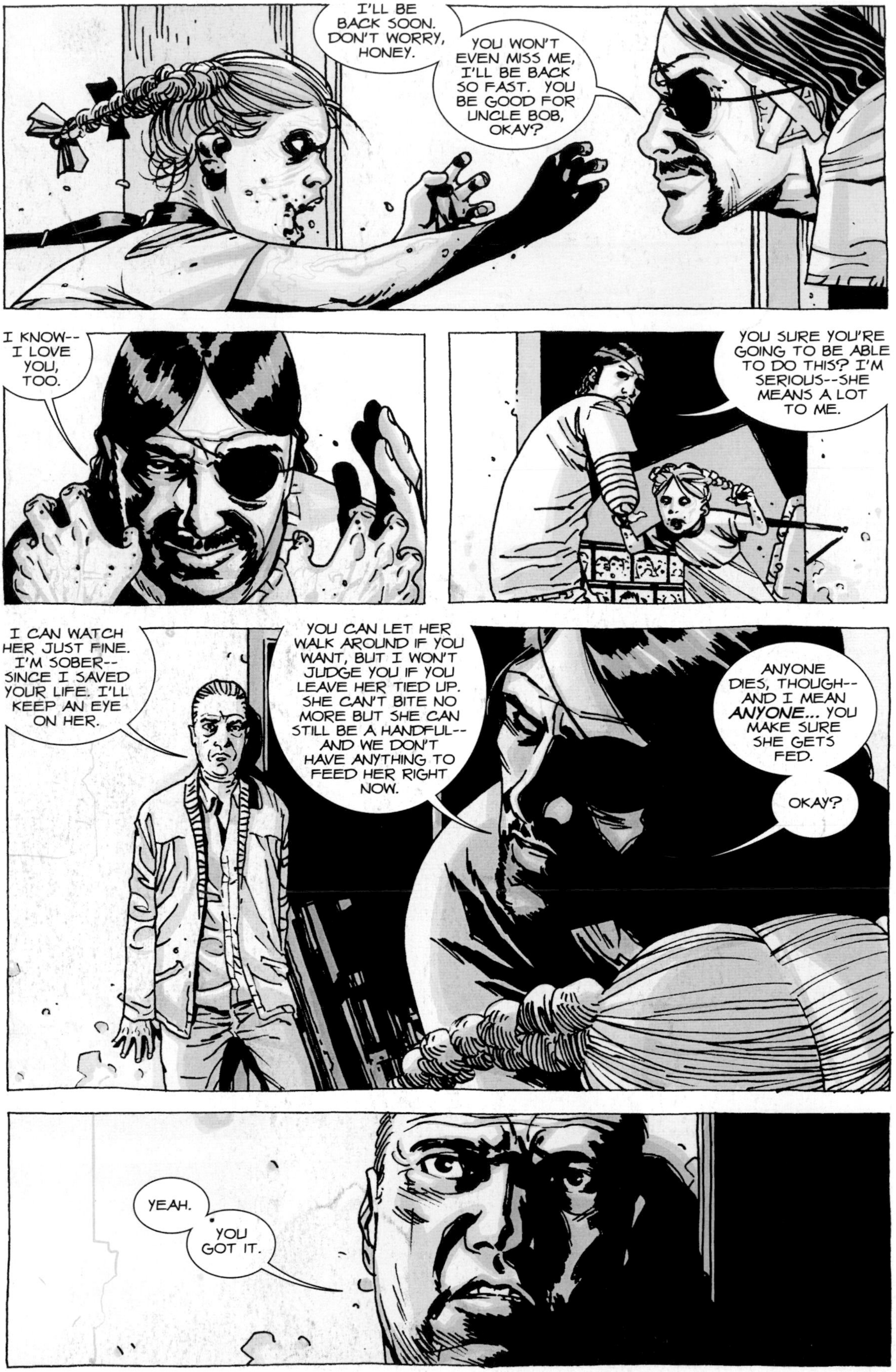
I'LL BE BACK SOON. DON'T WORRY, HONEY.
YOU WON'T EVEN MISS ME, I'LL BE BACK SO FAST. YOU BE GOOD FOR UNCLE BOB, OKAY?
I KNOW-- I LOVE YOU, TOO.
YOU SURE YOU'RE GOING TO BE ABLE TO DO THIS? I'M SERIOUS--SHE MEANS A LOT TO ME.
I CAN WATCH HER JUST FINE. I'M SOBER-- SINCE I SAVED YOUR LIFE. I'LL KEEP AN EYE ON HER.
YOU CAN LET HER WALK AROUND IF YOU WANT, BUT I WON'T JUDGE YOU IF YOU LEAVE HER TIED UP. SHE CAN'T BITE NO MORE BUT SHE CAN STILL BE A HANDFUL-- --AND WE DON'T HAVE ANYTHING TO FEED HER RIGHT NOW.
ANYONE DIES, THOUGH-- AND I MEAN *ANYONE*... YOU MAKE SURE SHE GETS FED.
OKAY?
YEAH.
YOU GOT IT.

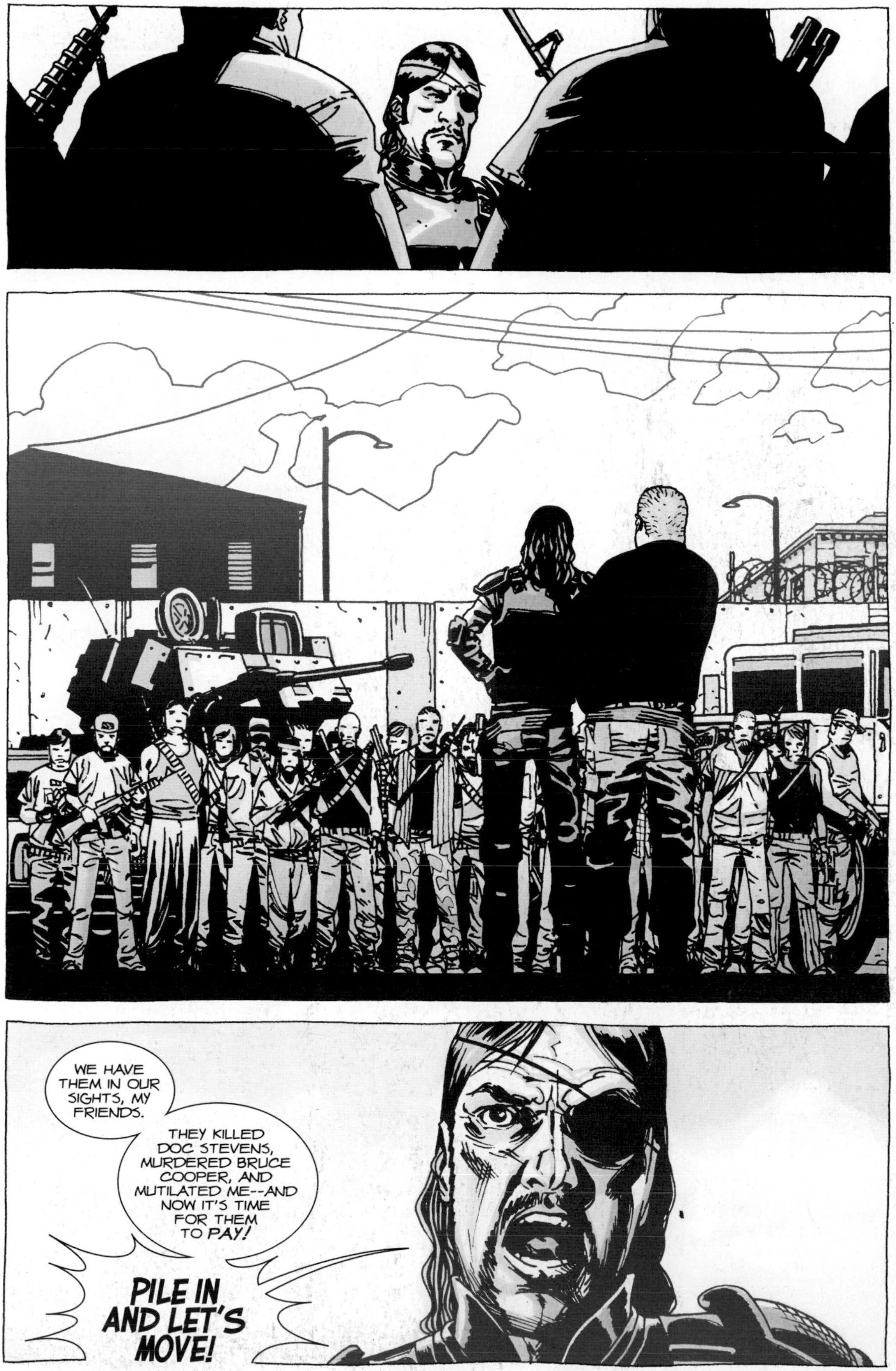
WE HAVE THEM IN OUR SIGHTS, MY FRIENDS.
THEY KILLED DOC STEVENS, MURDERED BRUCE COOPER, AND MUTILATED ME--AND NOW IT'S TIME FOR THEM TO PAY!
PILE IN AND LET'S MOVE!

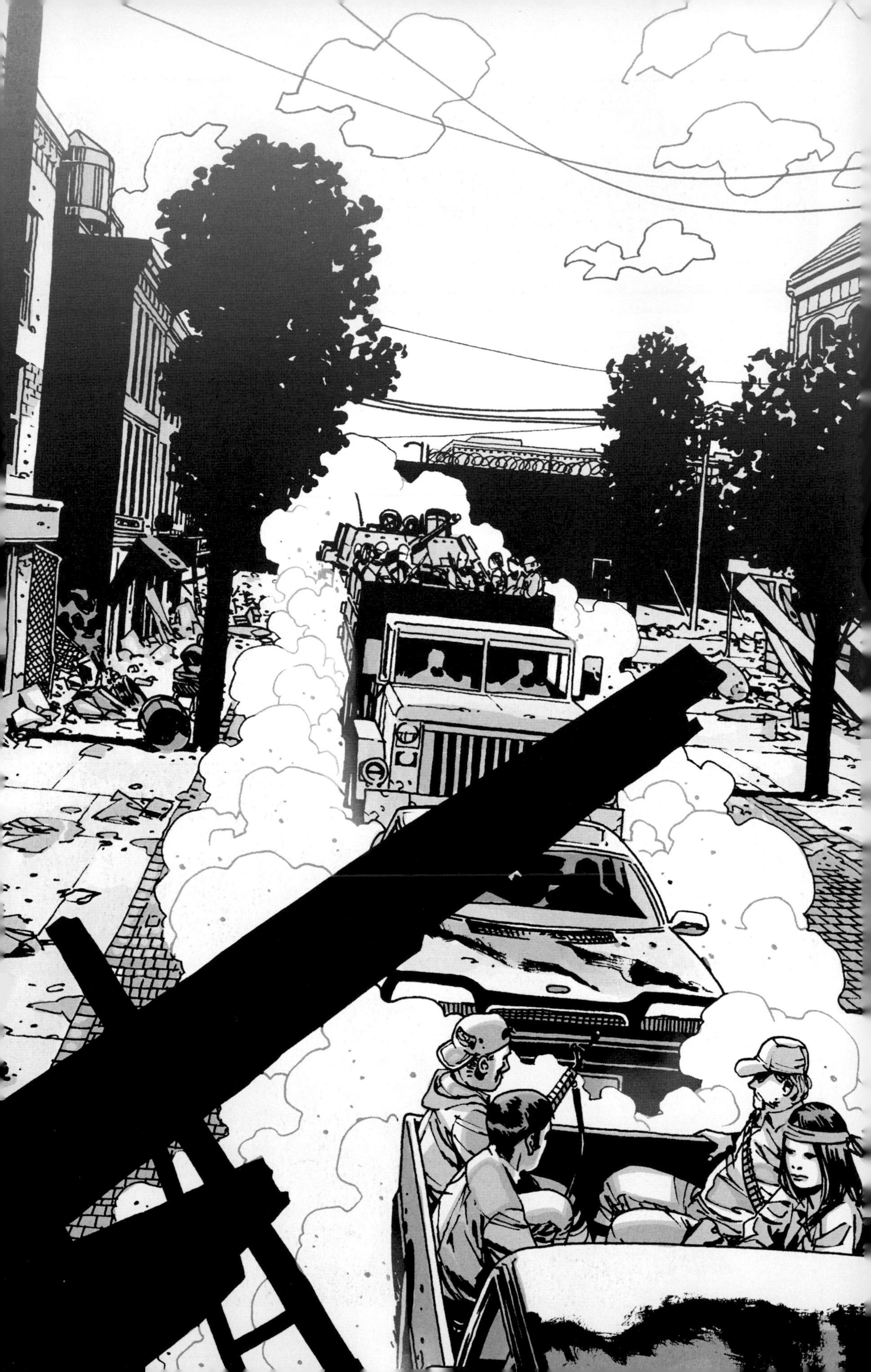

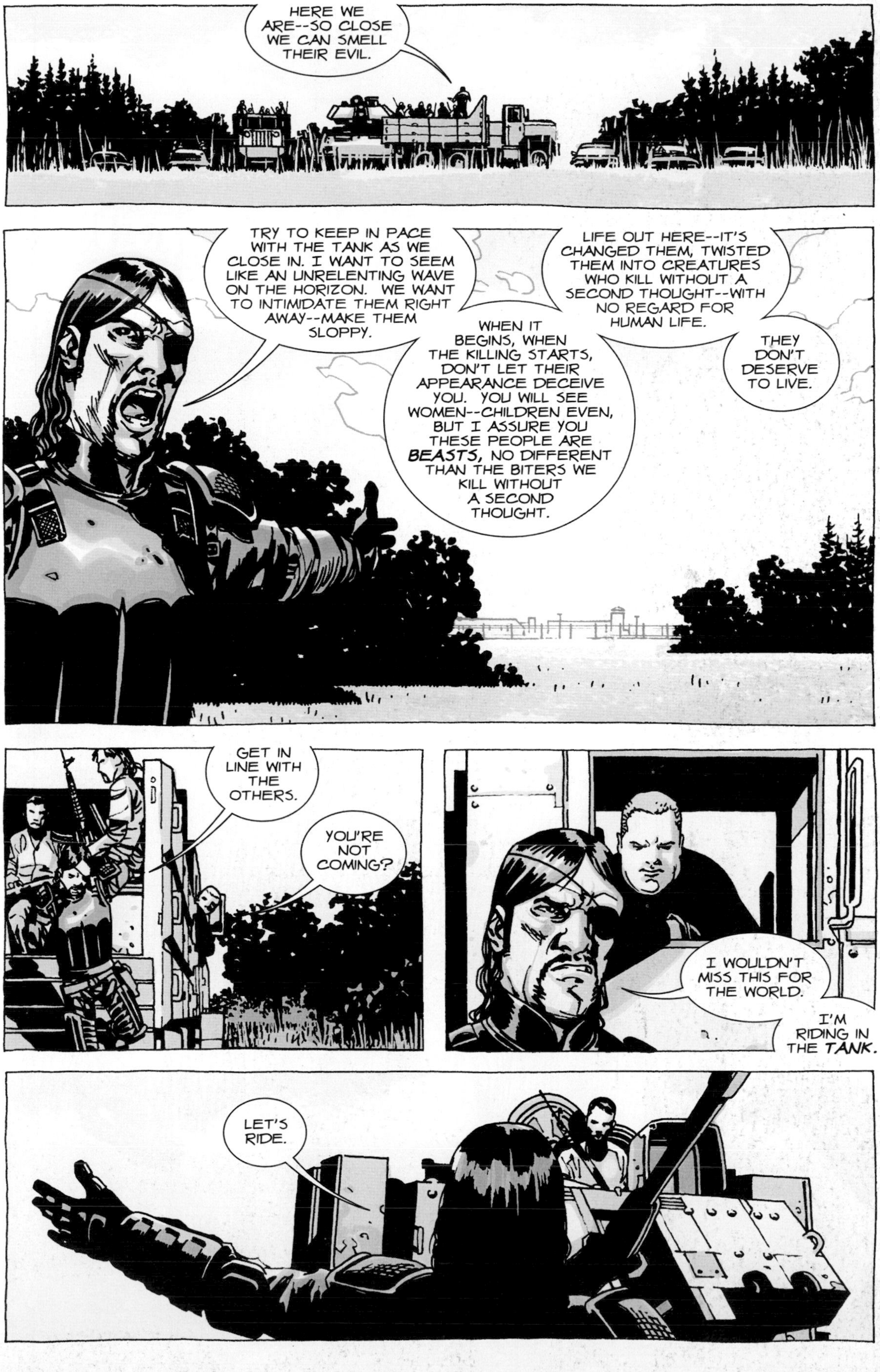
HERE WE ARE--SO CLOSE WE CAN SMELL THEIR EVIL.
TRY TO KEEP IN PACE WITH THE TANK AS WE CLOSE IN. I WANT TO SEEM LIKE AN UNRELENTING WAVE ON THE HORIZON. WE WANT TO INTIMIDATE THEM RIGHT AWAY--MAKE THEM SLOPPY.
WHEN IT BEGINS, WHEN THE KILLING STARTS, DON'T LET THEIR APPEARANCE DECEIVE YOU. YOU WILL SEE WOMEN--CHILDREN EVEN, BUT I ASSURE YOU THESE PEOPLE ARE *BEASTS*, NO DIFFERENT THAN THE BITERS WE KILL WITHOUT A SECOND THOUGHT.
LIFE OUT HERE--IT'S CHANGED THEM, TWISTED THEM INTO CREATURES WHO KILL WITHOUT A SECOND THOUGHT--WITH NO REGARD FOR HUMAN LIFE.
THEY DON'T DESERVE TO LIVE.
GET IN LINE WITH THE OTHERS.
YOU'RE NOT COMING?
I WOULDN'T MISS THIS FOR THE WORLD.
I'M RIDING IN THE *TANK*.
LET'S RIDE.

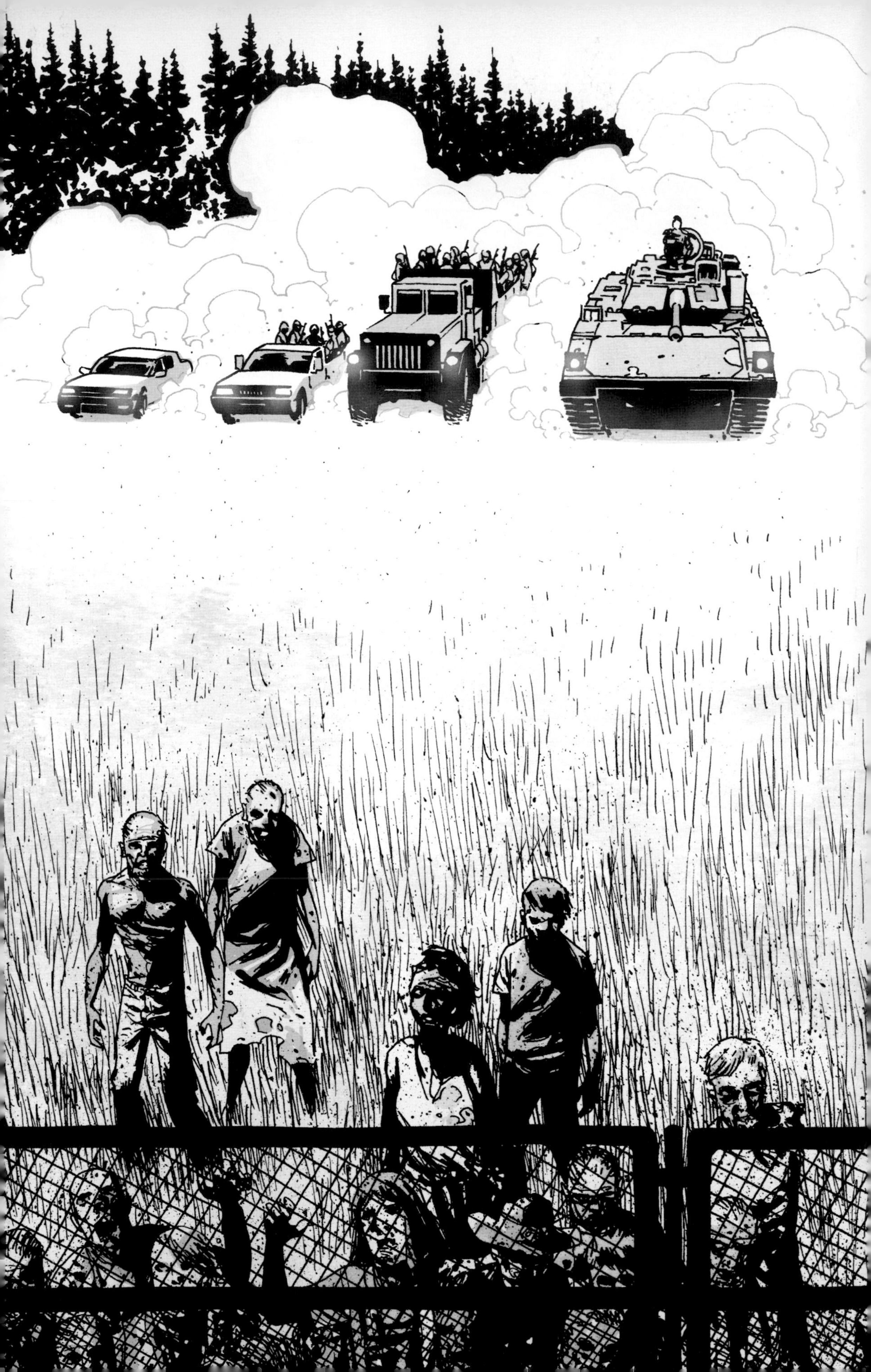

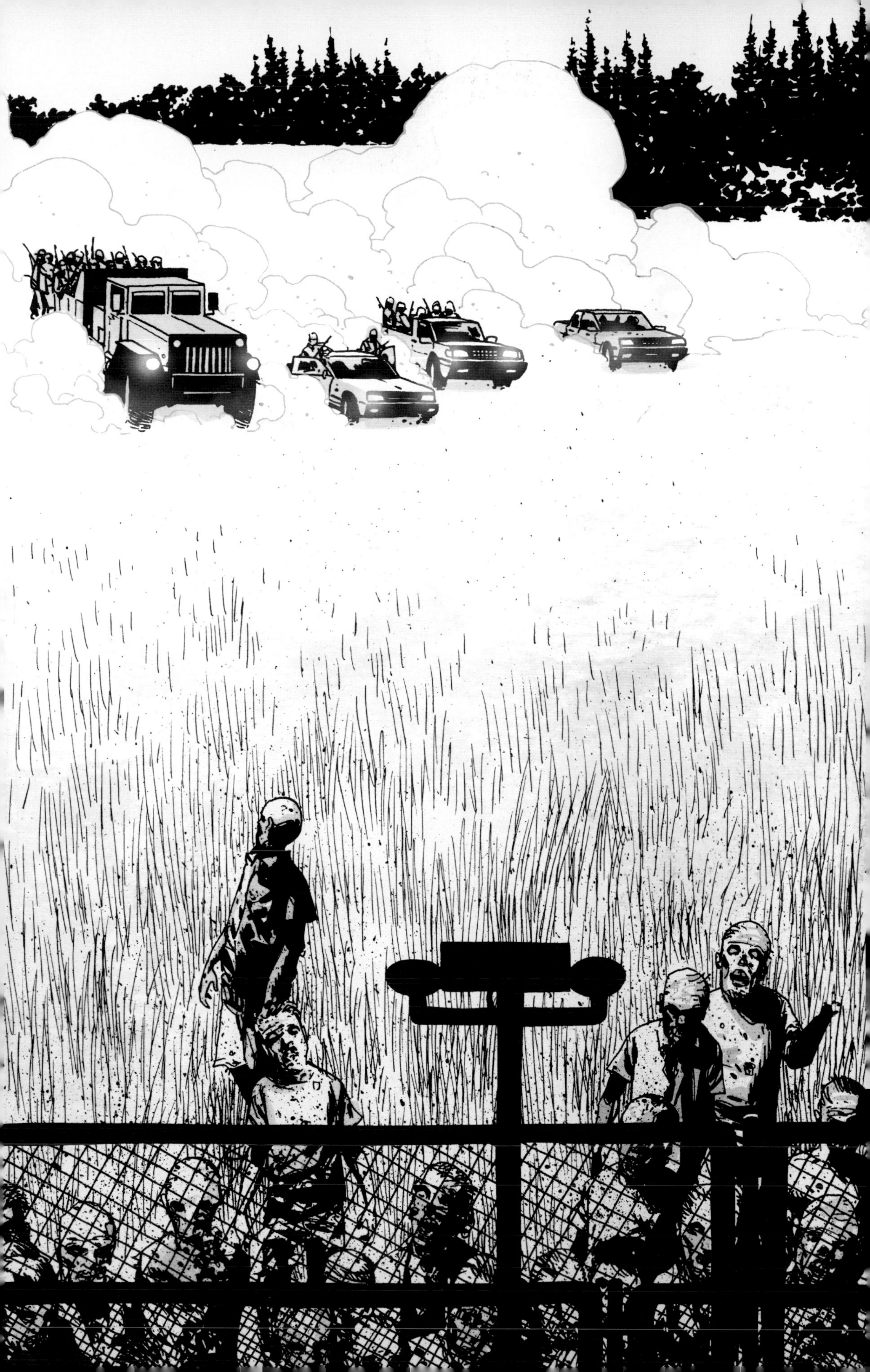

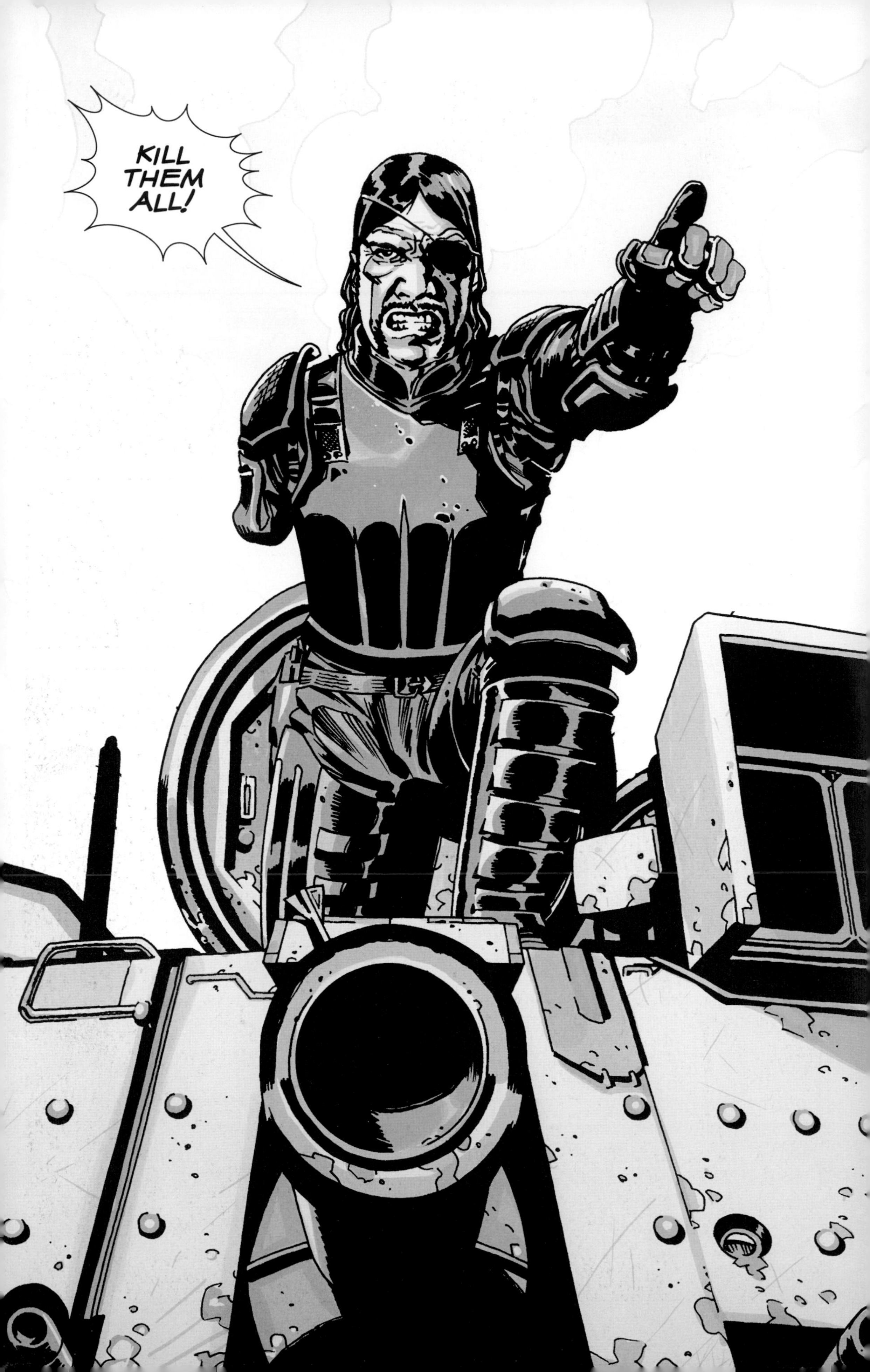
KILL THEM ALL!

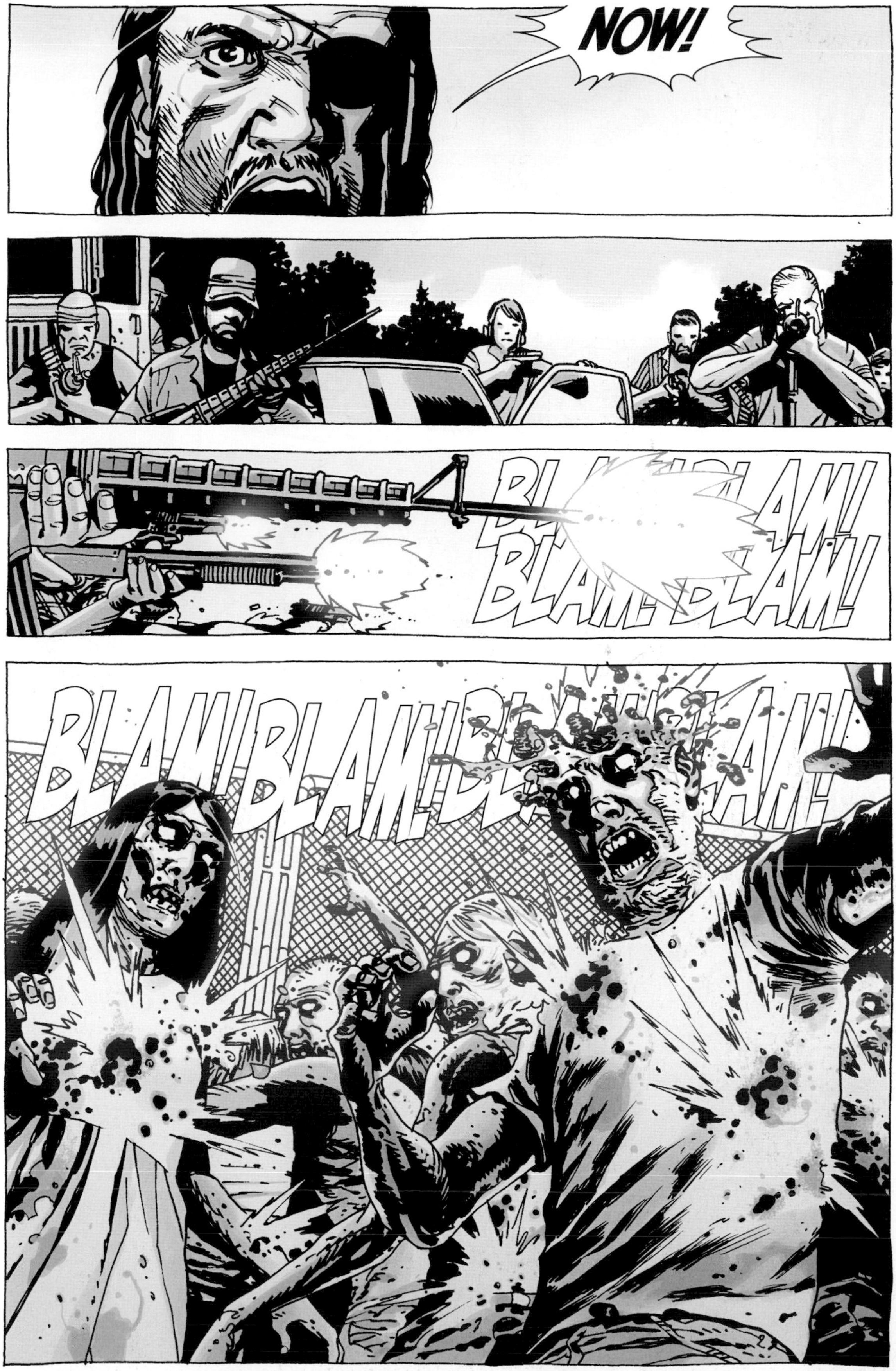
NOW!
BLAM! BLAM!
BLAM! BLAM!

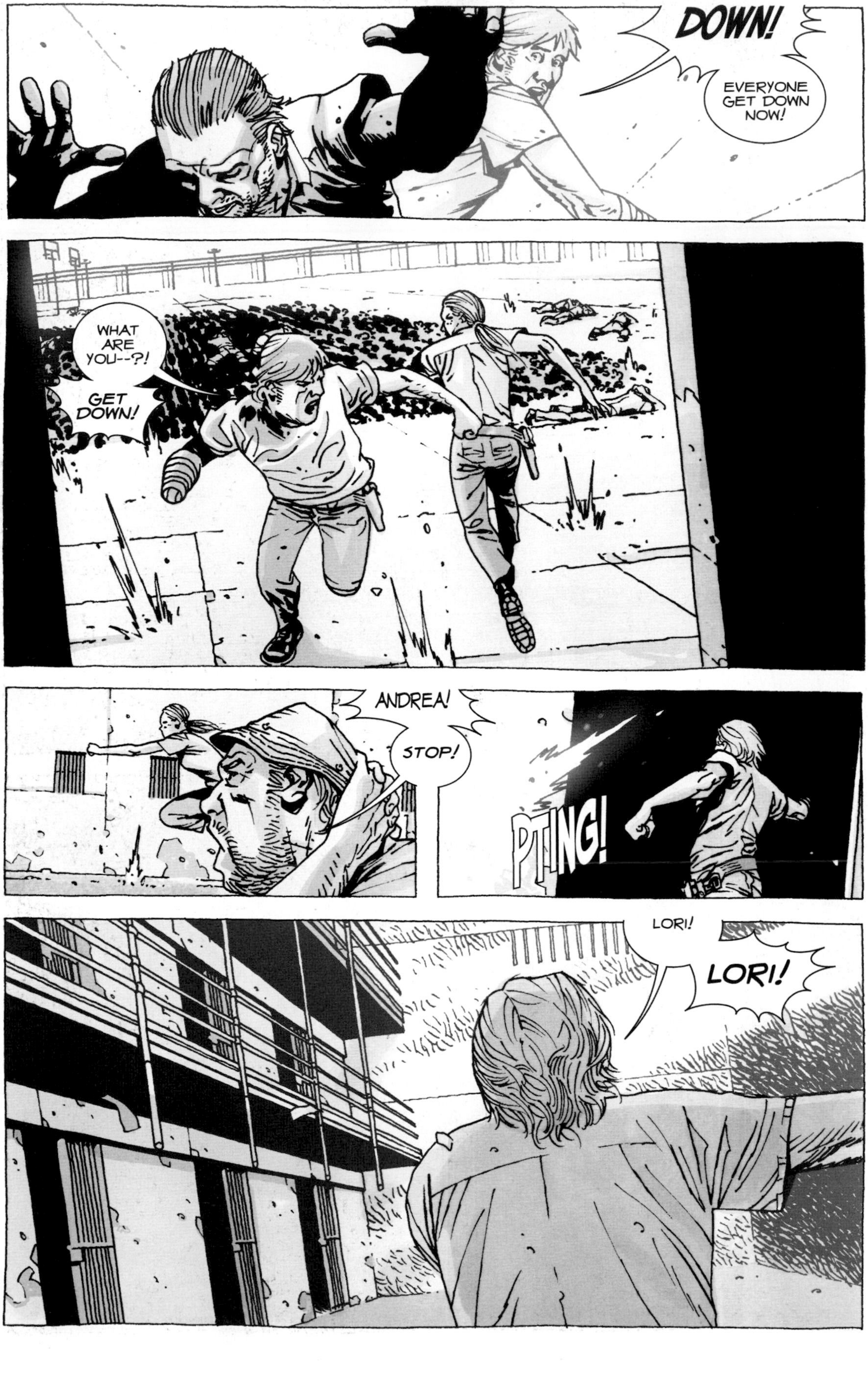
DOWN!
EVERYONE GET DOWN NOW!
WHAT ARE YOU--?!
GET DOWN!
ANDREA!
STOP!
PTING!
LORI!
LORI!

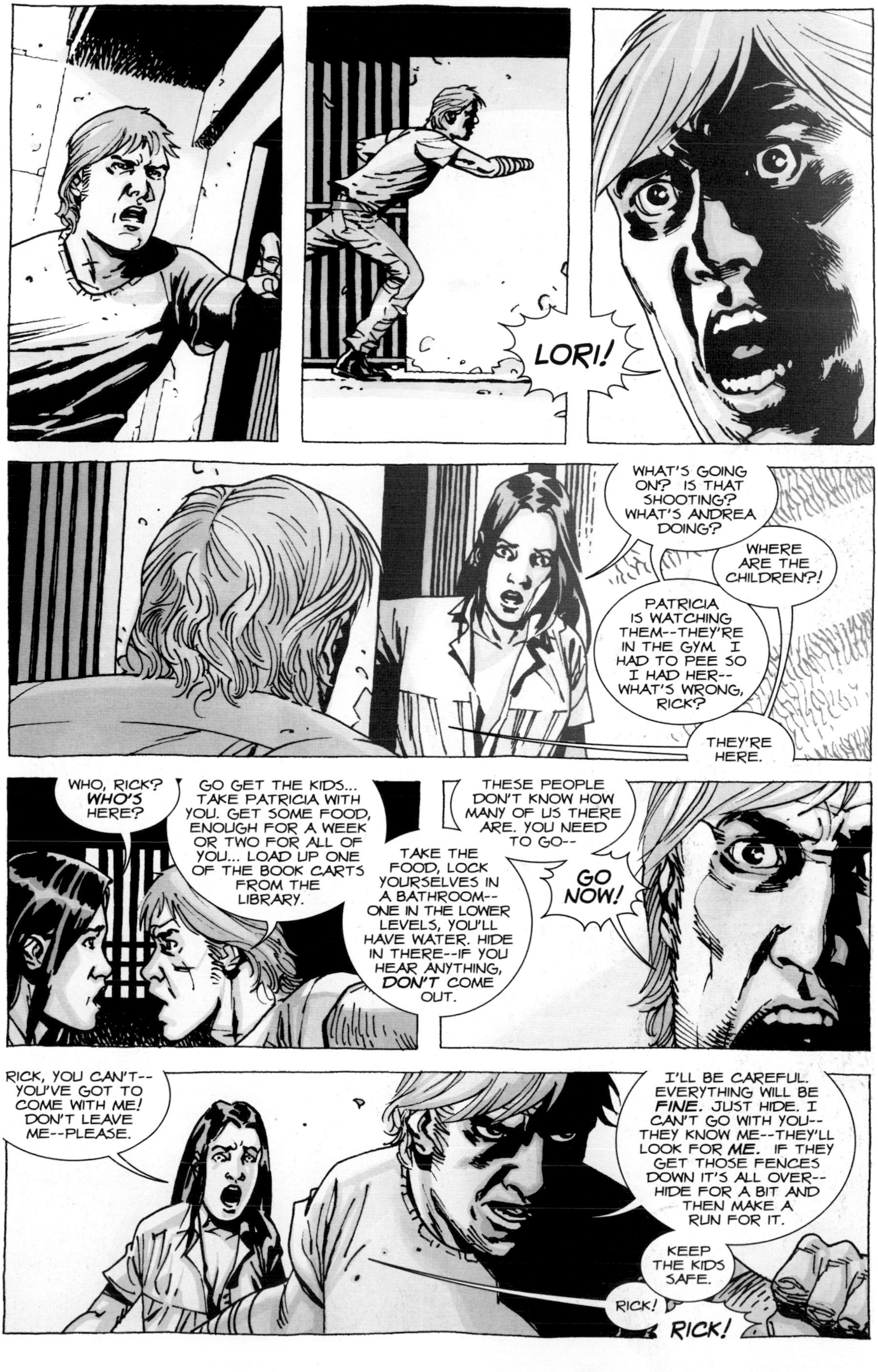
LORI!
WHAT'S GOING ON? IS THAT SHOOTING? WHAT'S ANDREA DOING?
WHERE ARE THE CHILDREN?!
PATRICIA IS WATCHING THEM--THEY'RE IN THE GYM. I HAD TO PEE SO I HAD HER-- WHAT'S WRONG, RICK?
THEY'RE HERE.
WHO, RICK? WHO'S HERE?
GO GET THE KIDS... TAKE PATRICIA WITH YOU. GET SOME FOOD, ENOUGH FOR A WEEK OR TWO FOR ALL OF YOU... LOAD UP ONE OF THE BOOK CARTS FROM THE LIBRARY.
TAKE THE FOOD, LOCK YOURSELVES IN A BATHROOM-- ONE IN THE LOWER LEVELS, YOU'LL HAVE WATER. HIDE IN THERE--IF YOU HEAR ANYTHING, DON'T COME OUT.
THESE PEOPLE DON'T KNOW HOW MANY OF US THERE ARE. YOU NEED TO GO--
GO NOW!
RICK, YOU CAN'T-- YOU'VE GOT TO COME WITH ME! DON'T LEAVE ME--PLEASE.
I'LL BE CAREFUL. EVERYTHING WILL BE FINE. JUST HIDE. I CAN'T GO WITH YOU-- THEY KNOW ME--THEY'LL LOOK FOR ME. IF THEY GET THOSE FENCES DOWN IT'S ALL OVER-- HIDE FOR A BIT AND THEN MAKE A RUN FOR IT.
KEEP THE KIDS SAFE.
RICK!
RICK!

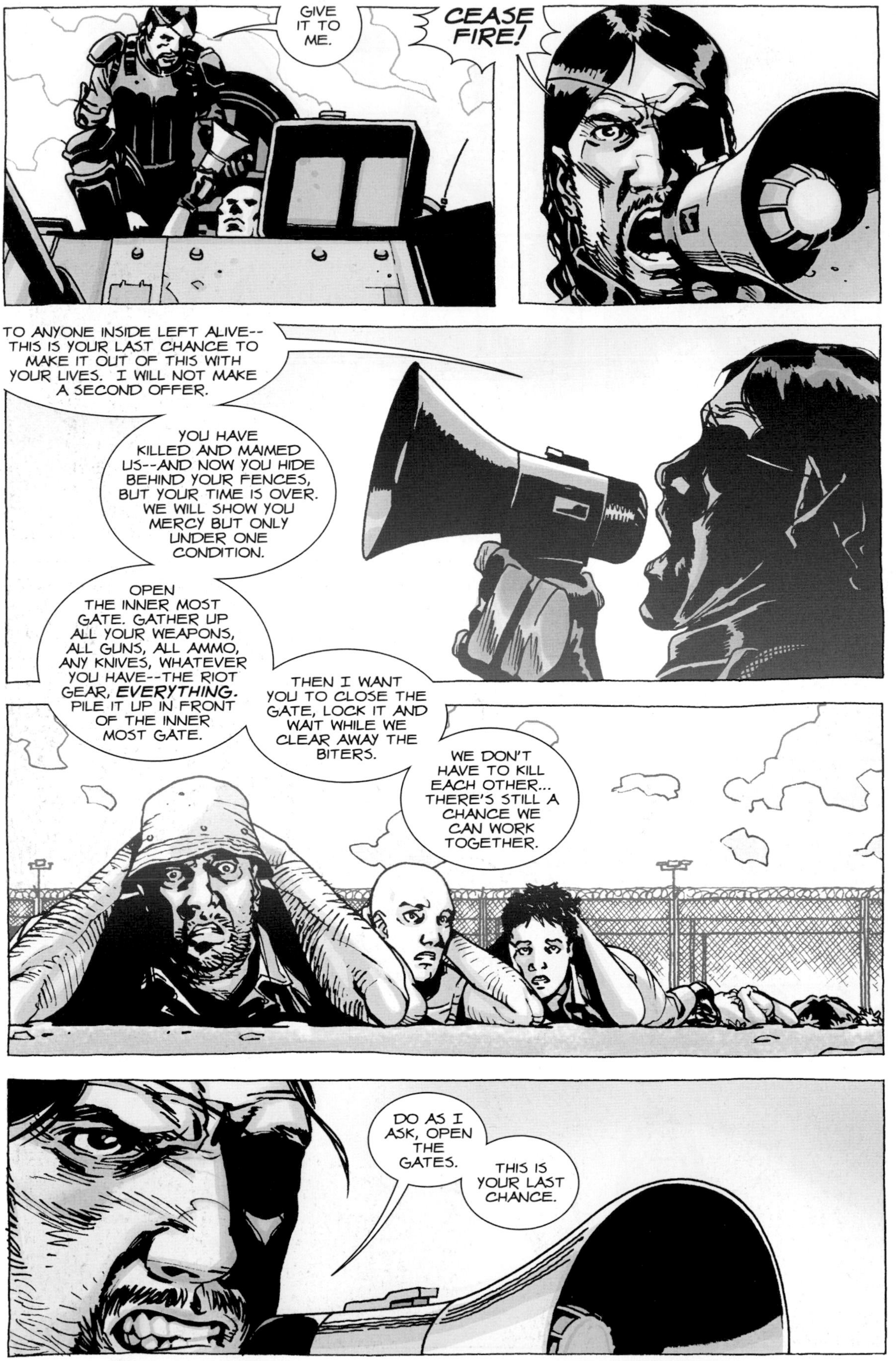
GIVE IT TO ME.
CEASE FIRE!
TO ANYONE INSIDE LEFT ALIVE-- THIS IS YOUR LAST CHANCE TO MAKE IT OUT OF THIS WITH YOUR LIVES. I WILL NOT MAKE A SECOND OFFER.
YOU HAVE KILLED AND MAIMED US--AND NOW YOU HIDE BEHIND YOUR FENCES, BUT YOUR TIME IS OVER. WE WILL SHOW YOU MERCY BUT ONLY UNDER ONE CONDITION.
OPEN THE INNER MOST GATE. GATHER UP ALL YOUR WEAPONS, ALL GUNS, ALL AMMO, ANY KNIVES, WHATEVER YOU HAVE--THE RIOT GEAR, EVERYTHING. PILE IT UP IN FRONT OF THE INNER MOST GATE.
THEN I WANT YOU TO CLOSE THE GATE, LOCK IT AND WAIT WHILE WE CLEAR AWAY THE BITERS.
WE DON'T HAVE TO KILL EACH OTHER... THERE'S STILL A CHANCE WE CAN WORK TOGETHER.
DO AS I ASK, OPEN THE GATES.
THIS IS YOUR LAST CHANCE.

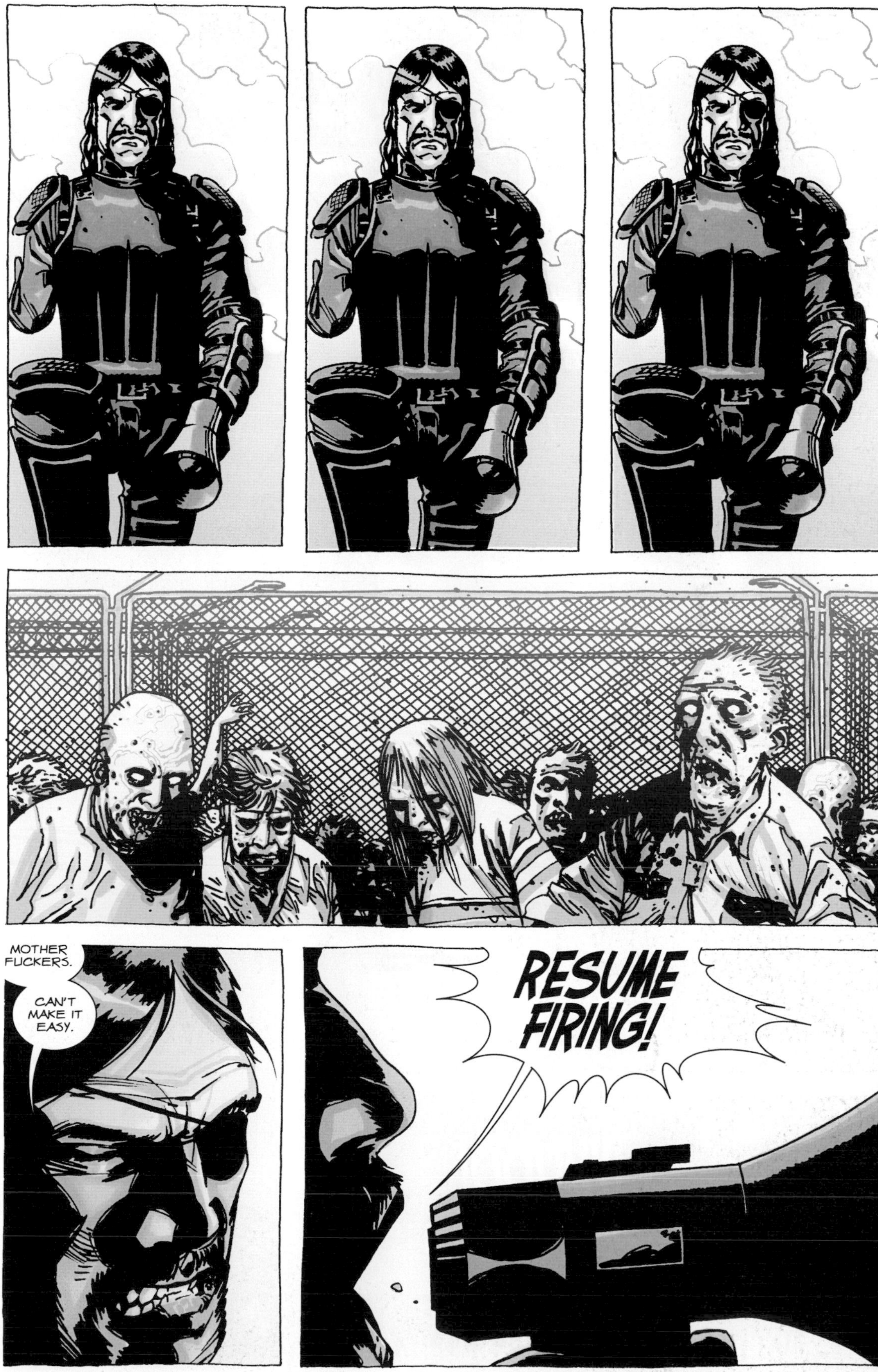
MOTHER FUCKERS.
CAN'T MAKE IT EASY.
RESUME FIRING!

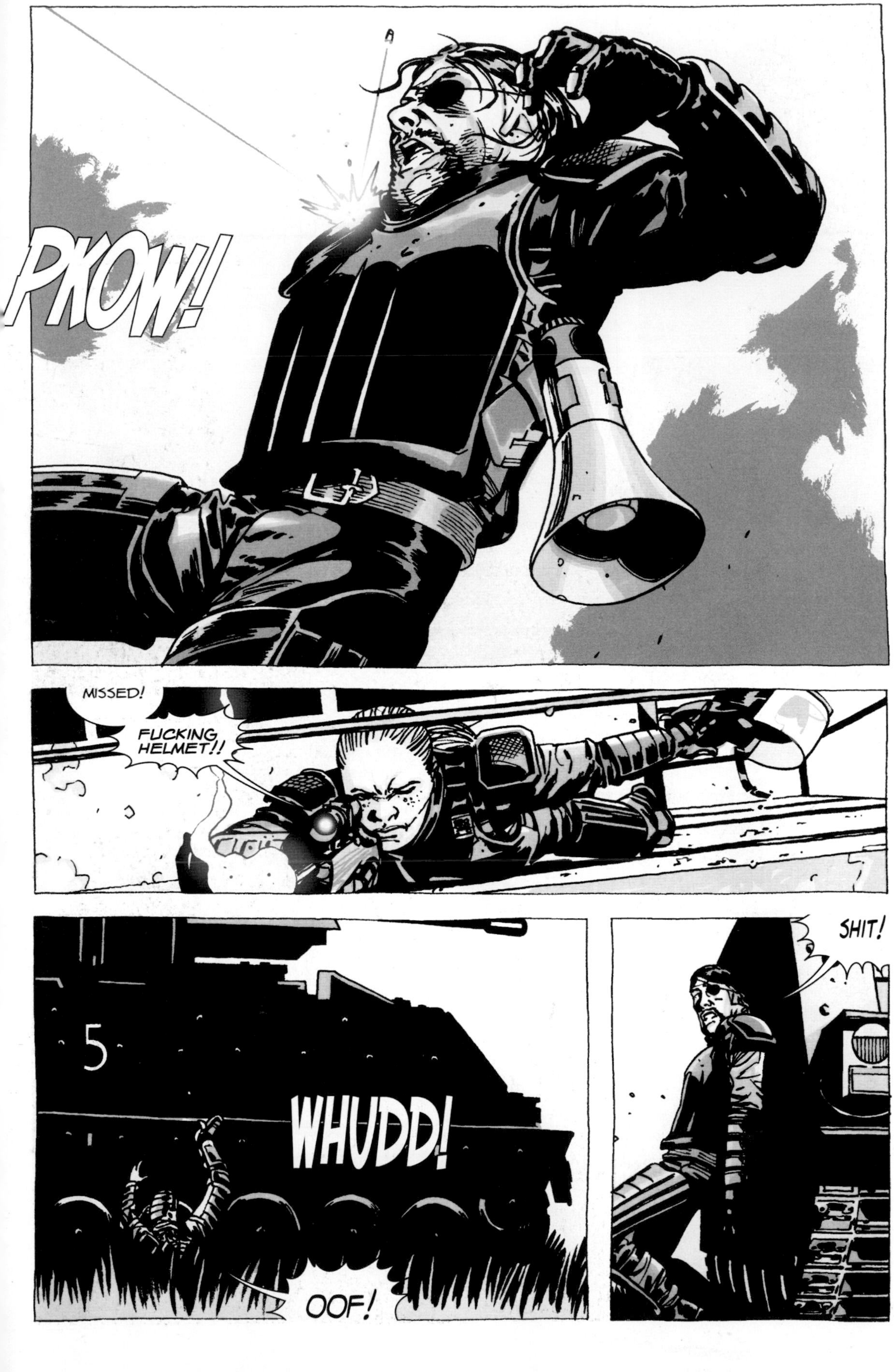
PKOW!
MISSED!
FUCKING HELMET!!
5
WHUDD!
OOF!
SHIT!

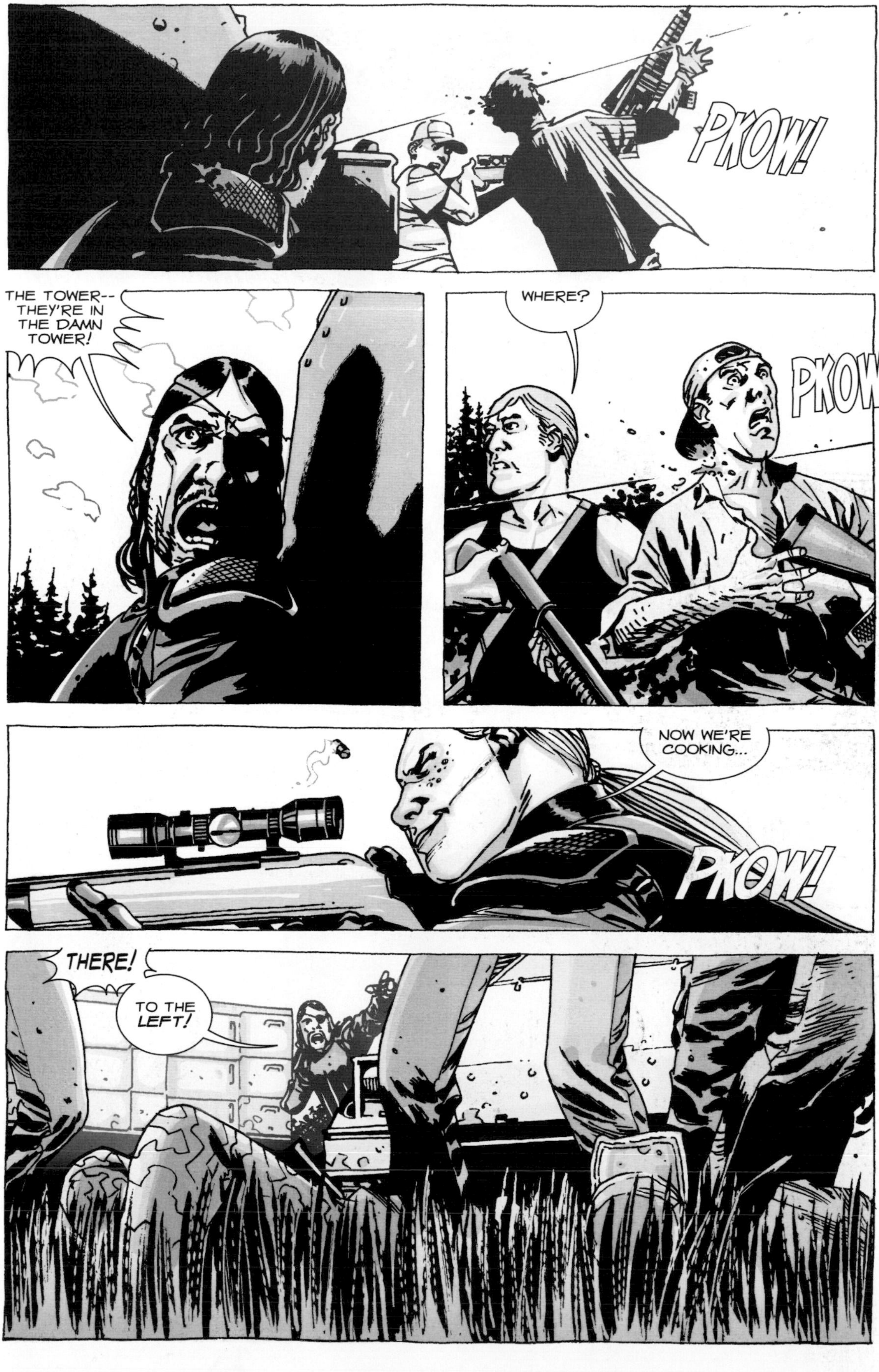
PKOW!
THE TOWER-- THEY'RE IN THE DAMN TOWER!
WHERE?
PKOW!
NOW WE'RE COOKING...
PKOW!
THERE!
TO THE LEFT!

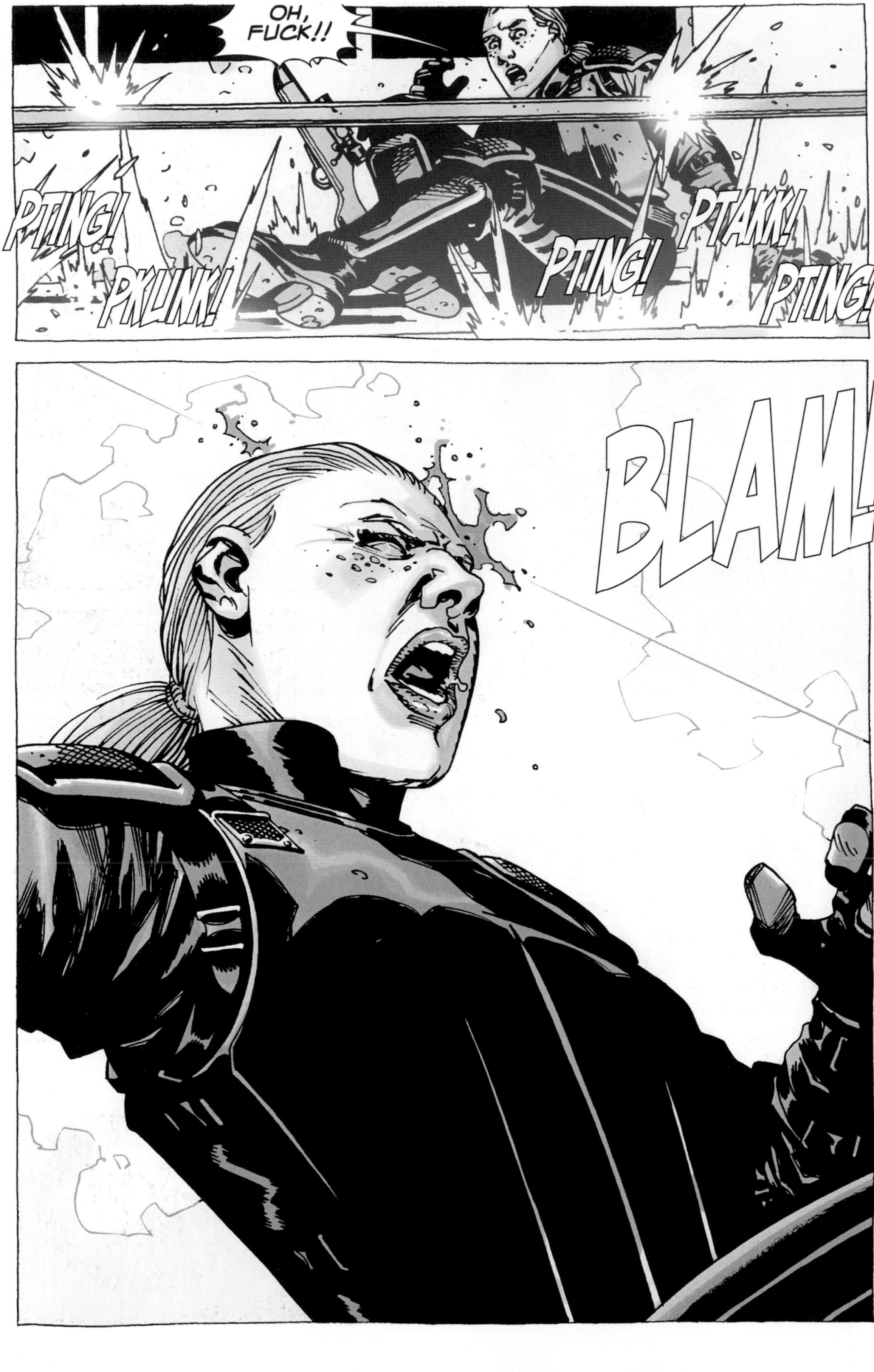
OH, FUCK!!
PTING!
PKLUNK!
PTING!
PTAKK!
PTING!
BLAM!

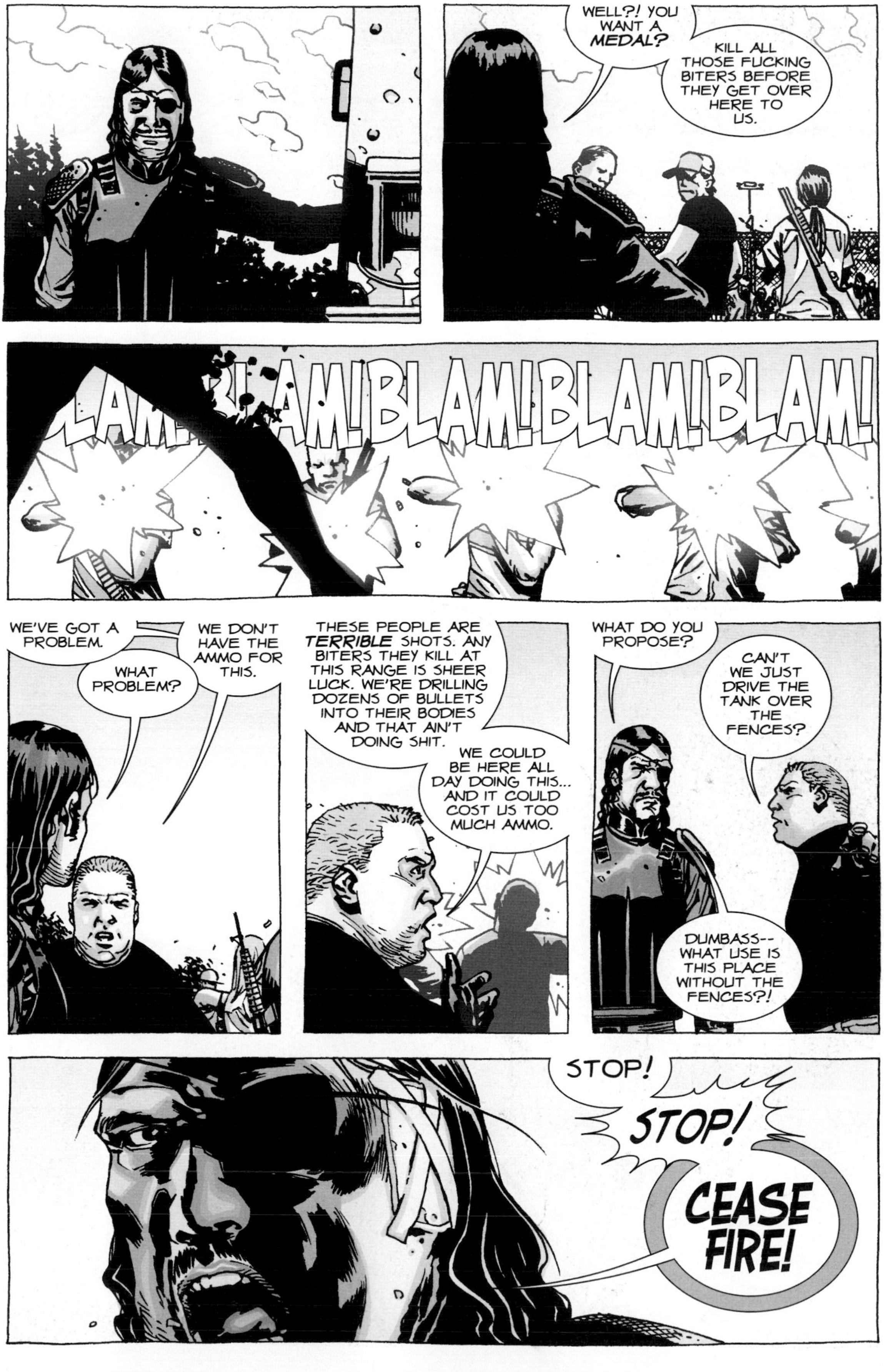
WELL?! YOU WANT A MEDAL?
KILL ALL THOSE FUCKING BITERS BEFORE THEY GET OVER HERE TO US.
BLAM! BLAM! BLAM! BLAM! BLAM!
WE'VE GOT A PROBLEM.
WHAT PROBLEM?
WE DON'T HAVE THE AMMO FOR THIS.
THESE PEOPLE ARE TERRIBLE SHOTS. ANY BITERS THEY KILL AT THIS RANGE IS SHEER LUCK. WE'RE DRILLING DOZENS OF BULLETS INTO THEIR BODIES AND THAT AIN'T DOING SHIT.
WE COULD BE HERE ALL DAY DOING THIS... AND IT COULD COST US TOO MUCH AMMO.
WHAT DO YOU PROPOSE?
CAN'T WE JUST DRIVE THE TANK OVER THE FENCES?
DUMBASS-- WHAT USE IS THIS PLACE WITHOUT THE FENCES?!
STOP!
STOP!
CEASE FIRE!

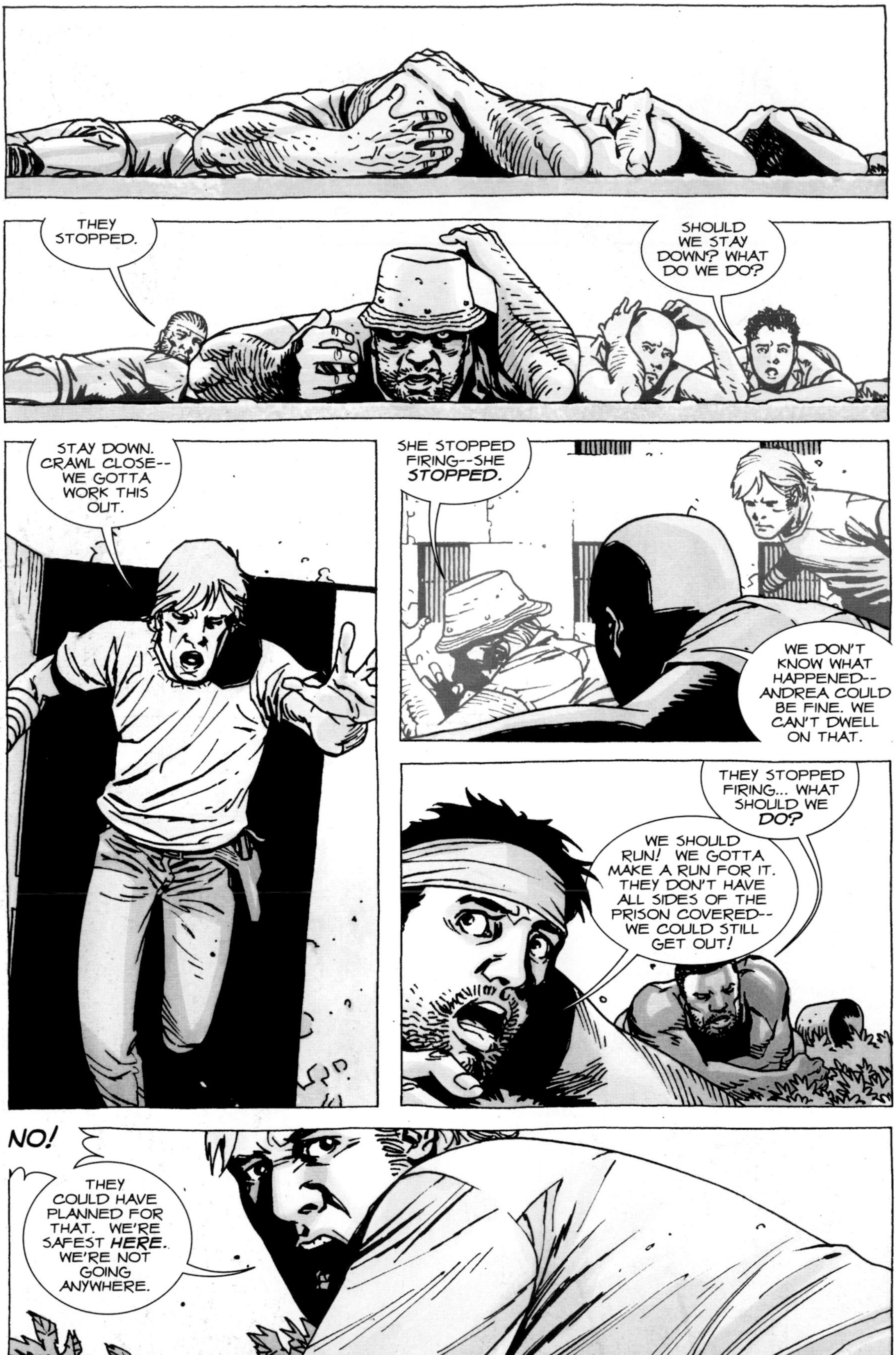

THEY STOPPED.
SHOULD WE STAY DOWN? WHAT DO WE DO?
STAY DOWN. CRAWL CLOSE-- WE GOTTA WORK THIS OUT.
SHE STOPPED FIRING--SHE STOPPED.
WE DON'T KNOW WHAT HAPPENED-- ANDREA COULD BE FINE. WE CAN'T DWELL ON THAT.
THEY STOPPED FIRING... WHAT SHOULD WE DO?
WE SHOULD RUN! WE GOTTA MAKE A RUN FOR IT. THEY DON'T HAVE ALL SIDES OF THE PRISON COVERED-- WE COULD STILL GET OUT!
NO!
THEY COULD HAVE PLANNED FOR THAT. WE'RE SAFEST HERE. WE'RE NOT GOING ANYWHERE.

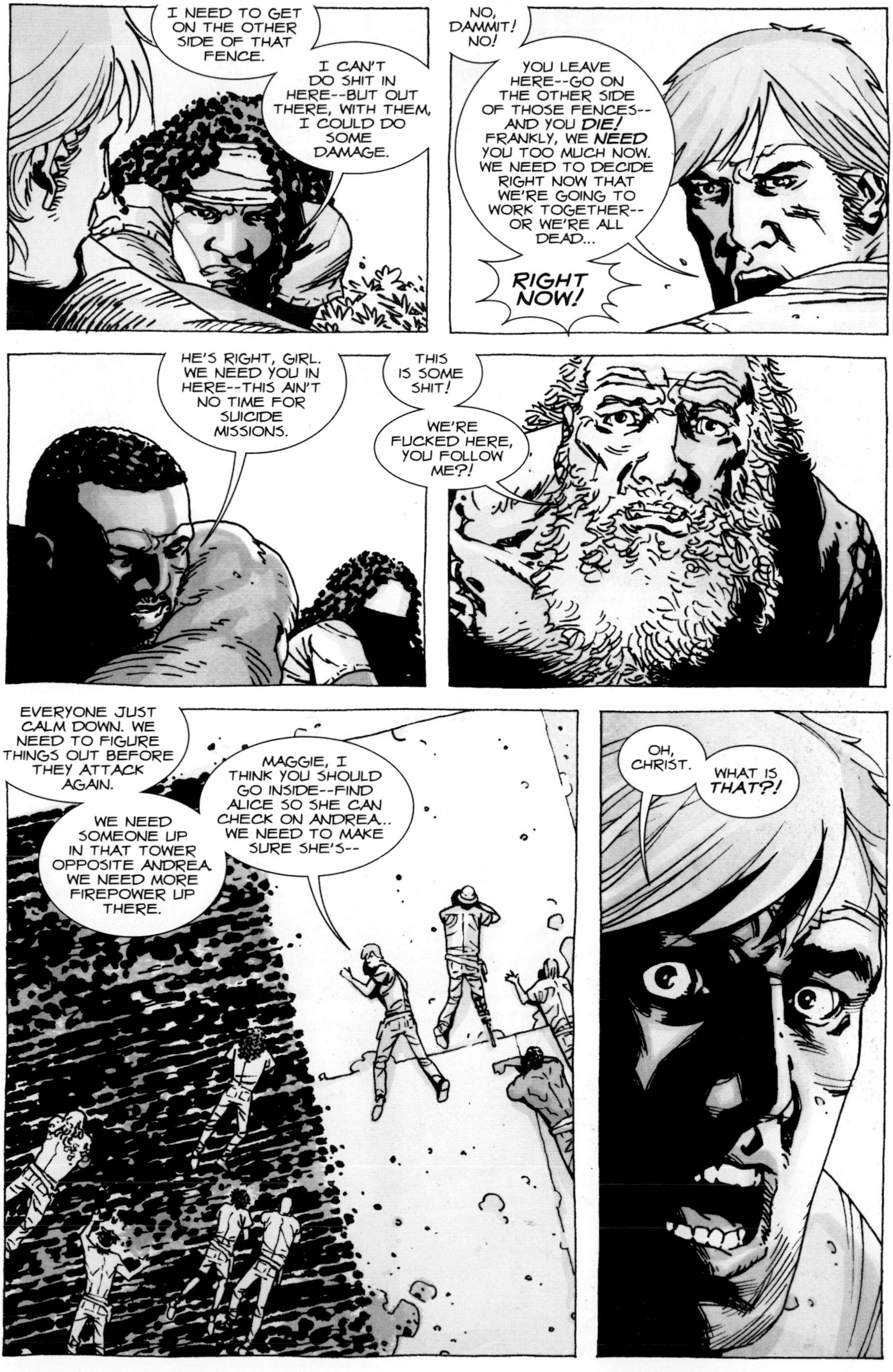
I NEED TO GET ON THE OTHER SIDE OF THAT FENCE.
I CAN'T DO SHIT IN HERE--BUT OUT THERE, WITH THEM, I COULD DO SOME DAMAGE.
NO, DAMMIT! NO!
YOU LEAVE HERE--GO ON THE OTHER SIDE OF THOSE FENCES--AND YOU DIE! FRANKLY, WE NEED YOU TOO MUCH NOW. WE NEED TO DECIDE RIGHT NOW THAT WE'RE GOING TO WORK TOGETHER--OR WE'RE ALL DEAD...
RIGHT NOW!
HE'S RIGHT, GIRL. WE NEED YOU IN HERE--THIS AIN'T NO TIME FOR SUICIDE MISSIONS.
THIS IS SOME SHIT!
WE'RE FUCKED HERE, YOU FOLLOW ME?!
EVERYONE JUST CALM DOWN. WE NEED TO FIGURE THINGS OUT BEFORE THEY ATTACK AGAIN.
WE NEED SOMEONE UP IN THAT TOWER OPPOSITE ANDREA. WE NEED MORE FIREPOWER UP THERE.
MAGGIE, I THINK YOU SHOULD GO INSIDE--FIND ALICE SO SHE CAN CHECK ON ANDREA.. WE NEED TO MAKE SURE SHE'S--
OH, CHRIST.
WHAT IS THAT?!

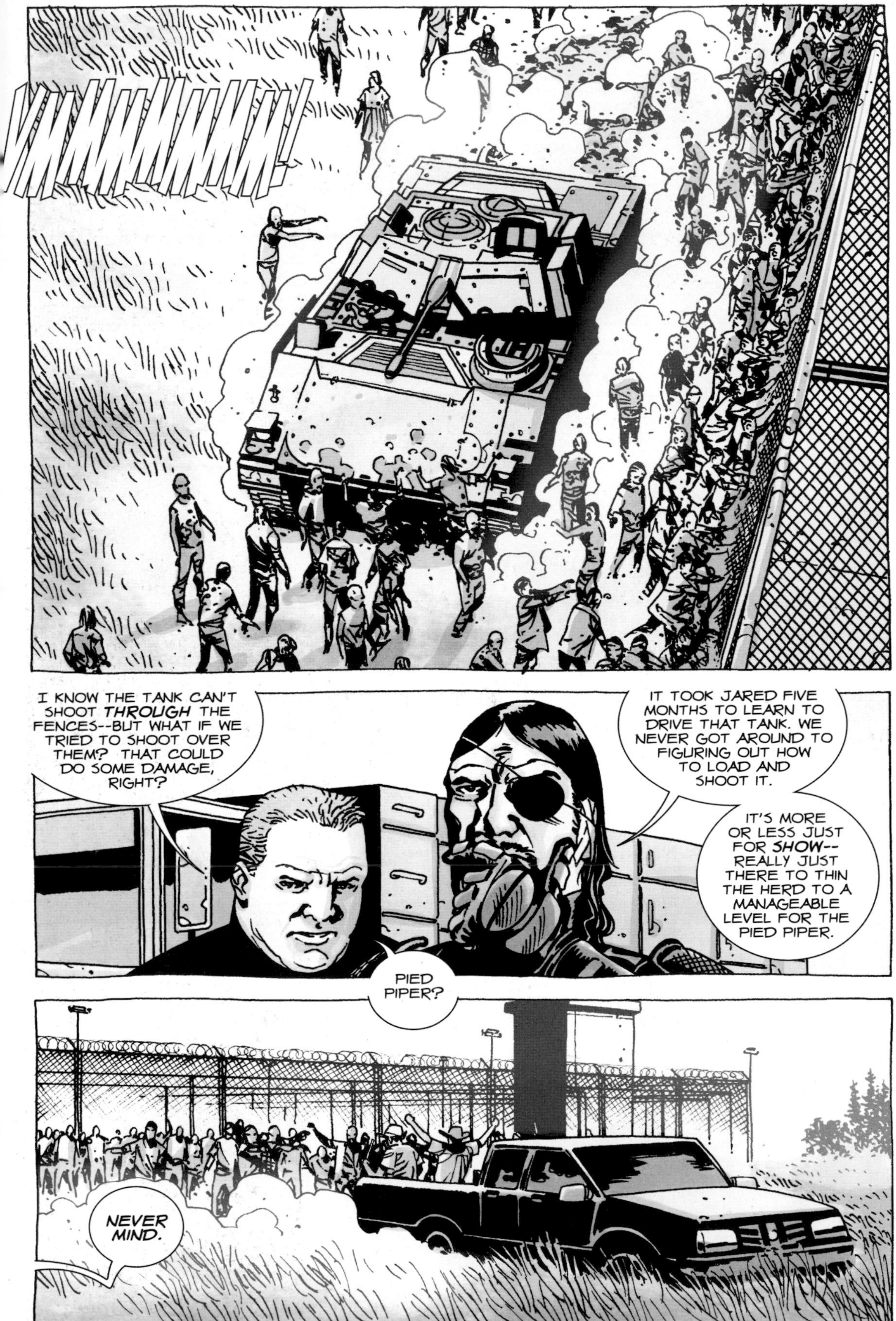
VRMMMMMMMM!
I KNOW THE TANK CAN'T SHOOT *THROUGH* THE FENCES--BUT WHAT IF WE TRIED TO SHOOT OVER THEM? THAT COULD DO SOME DAMAGE, RIGHT?
IT TOOK JARED FIVE MONTHS TO LEARN TO DRIVE THAT TANK. WE NEVER GOT AROUND TO FIGURING OUT HOW TO LOAD AND SHOOT IT.
IT'S MORE OR LESS JUST FOR *SHOW*-- REALLY JUST THERE TO THIN THE HERD TO A MANAGEABLE LEVEL FOR THE PIED PIPER.
PIED PIPER?
NEVER MIND.

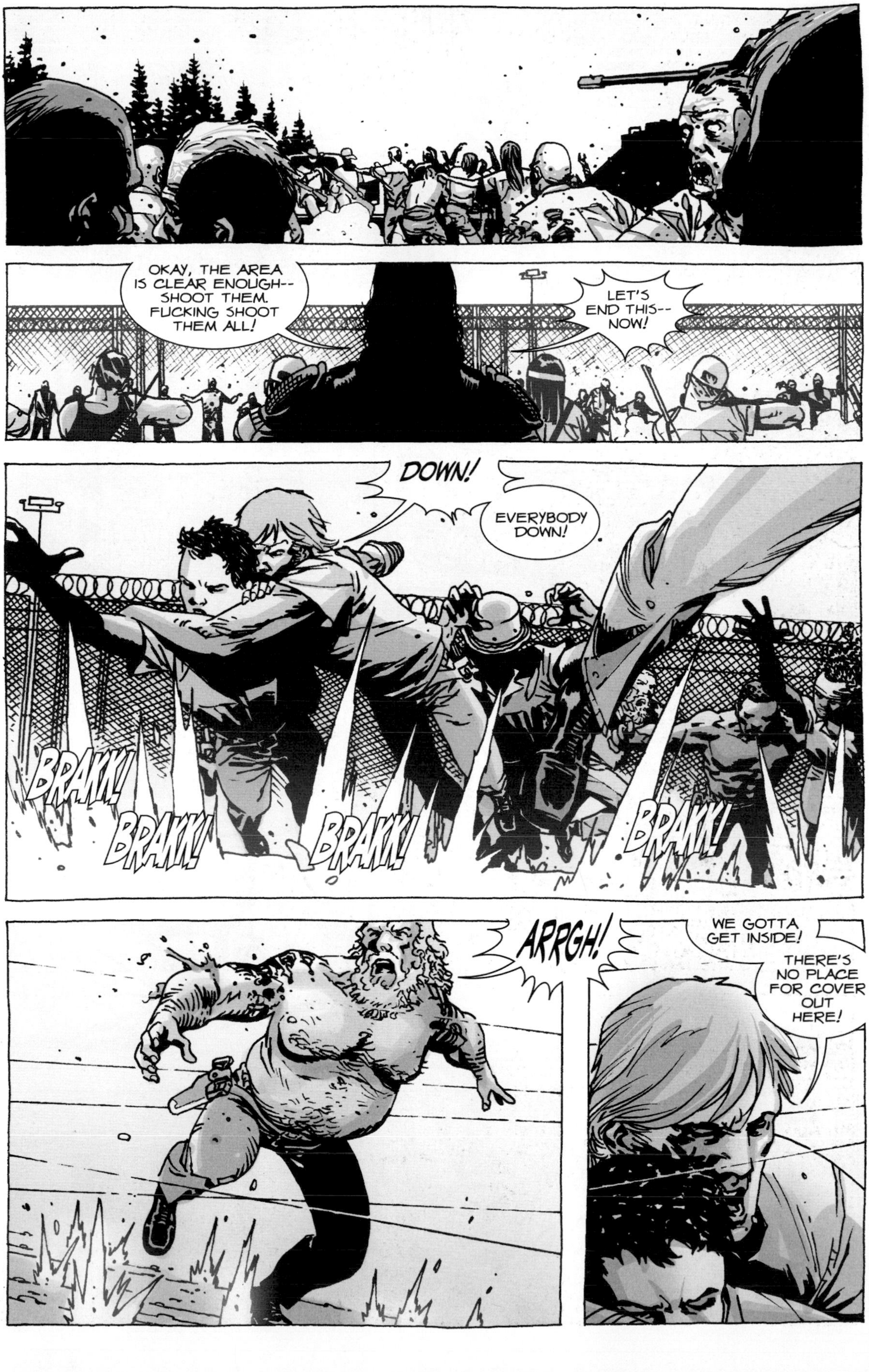
OKAY, THE AREA IS CLEAR ENOUGH-- SHOOT THEM. FUCKING SHOOT THEM ALL!
LET'S END THIS-- NOW!
DOWN!
EVERYBODY DOWN!
BRAKK!
BRAKK!
BRAKK!
BRAKK!
ARRGH!
WE GOTTA GET INSIDE!
THERE'S NO PLACE FOR COVER OUT HERE!

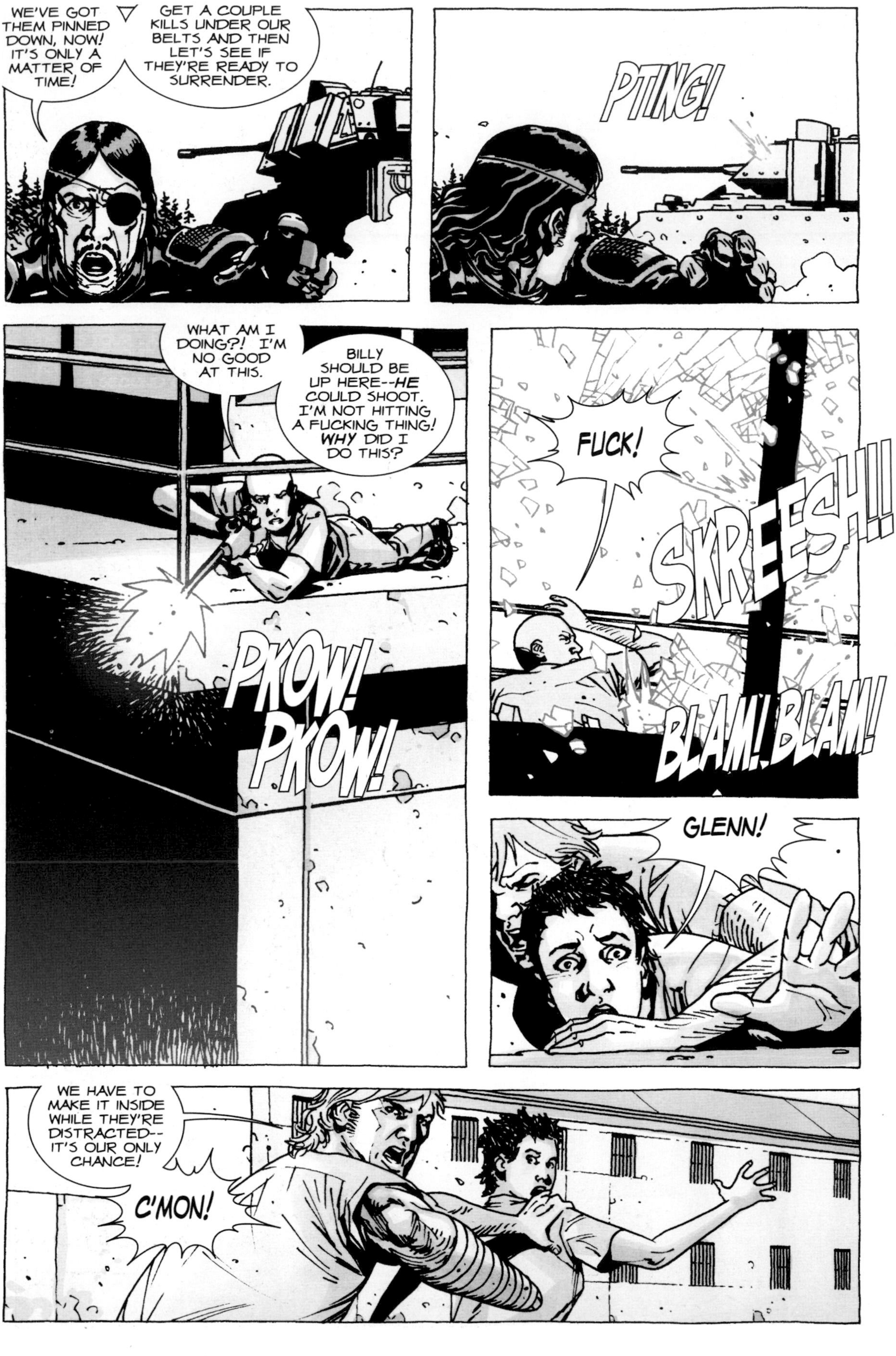
WE'VE GOT THEM PINNED DOWN, NOW! IT'S ONLY A MATTER OF TIME!
GET A COUPLE KILLS UNDER OUR BELTS AND THEN LET'S SEE IF THEY'RE READY TO SURRENDER.
PTING!
WHAT AM I DOING?! I'M NO GOOD AT THIS.
BILLY SHOULD BE UP HERE--HE COULD SHOOT. I'M NOT HITTING A FUCKING THING! WHY DID I DO THIS?
PKOW! PKOW!
FUCK!
SKREESH!!!
BLAM! BLAM!
GLENN!
WE HAVE TO MAKE IT INSIDE WHILE THEY'RE DISTRACTED-- IT'S OUR ONLY CHANCE!
C'MON!

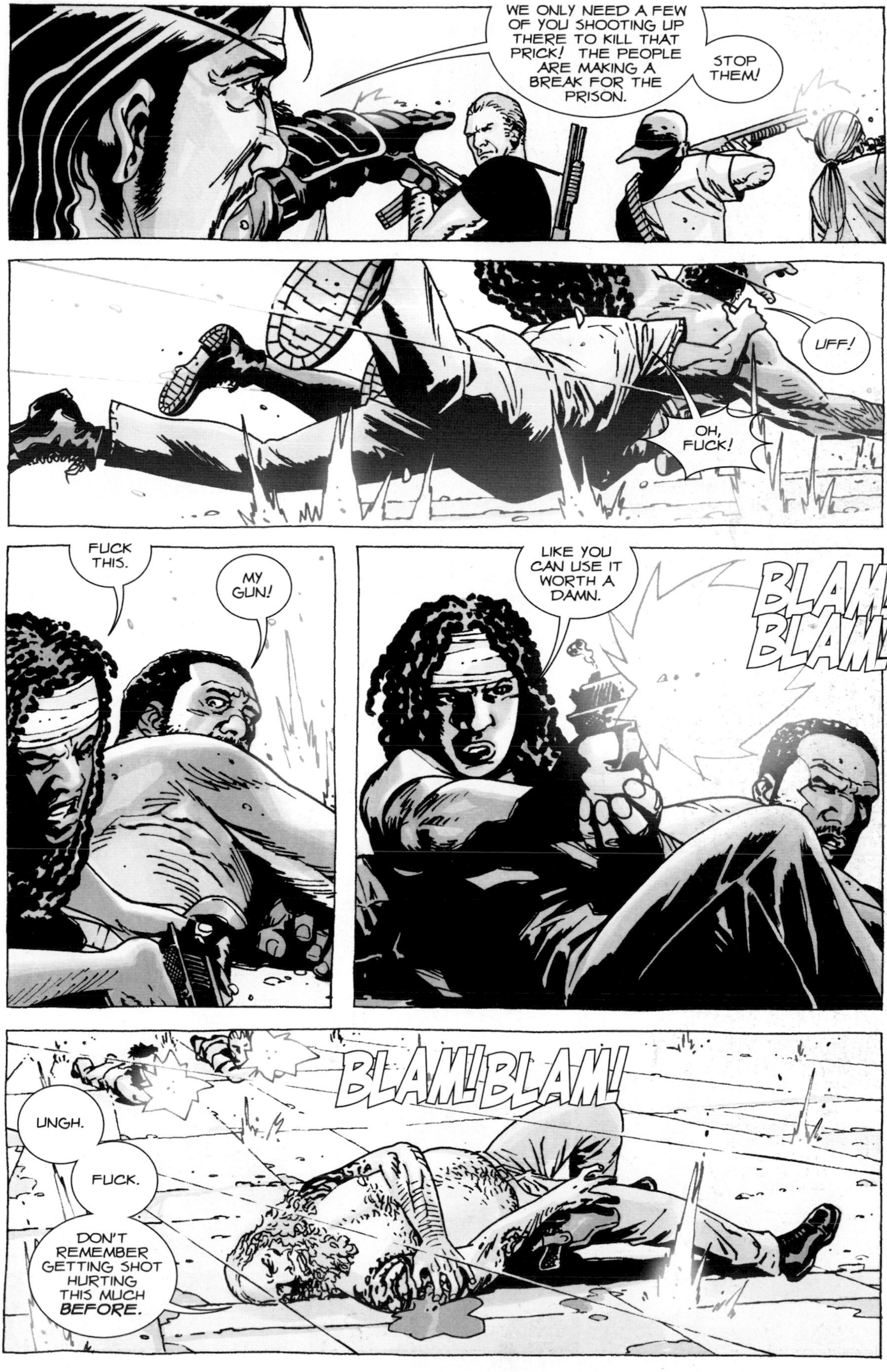
WE ONLY NEED A FEW OF YOU SHOOTING UP THERE TO KILL THAT PRICK! THE PEOPLE ARE MAKING A BREAK FOR THE PRISON.
STOP THEM!
UFF!
OH, FUCK!
FUCK THIS.
MY GUN!
LIKE YOU CAN USE IT WORTH A DAMN.
BLAM! BLAM!
BLAM! BLAM!
UNGH.
FUCK.
DON'T REMEMBER GETTING SHOT HURTING THIS MUCH BEFORE.

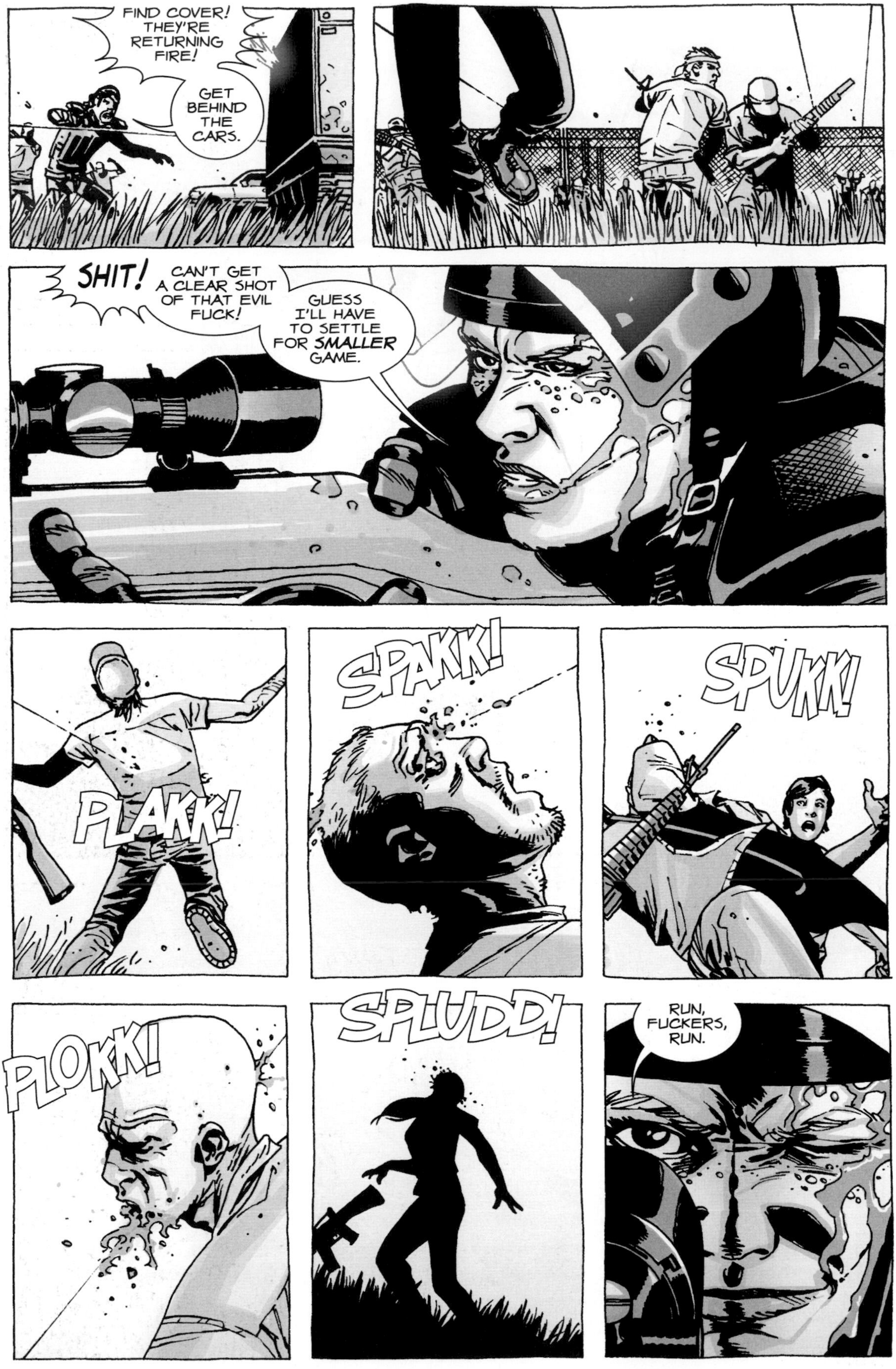
FIND COVER! THEY'RE RETURNING FIRE!
GET BEHIND THE CARS.
SHIT! CAN'T GET A CLEAR SHOT OF THAT EVIL FUCK!
GUESS I'LL HAVE TO SETTLE FOR SMALLER GAME.
PLAKK!
SPAKK!
SPUKK!
PLOKK!
SPLUDD!
RUN, FUCKERS, RUN.

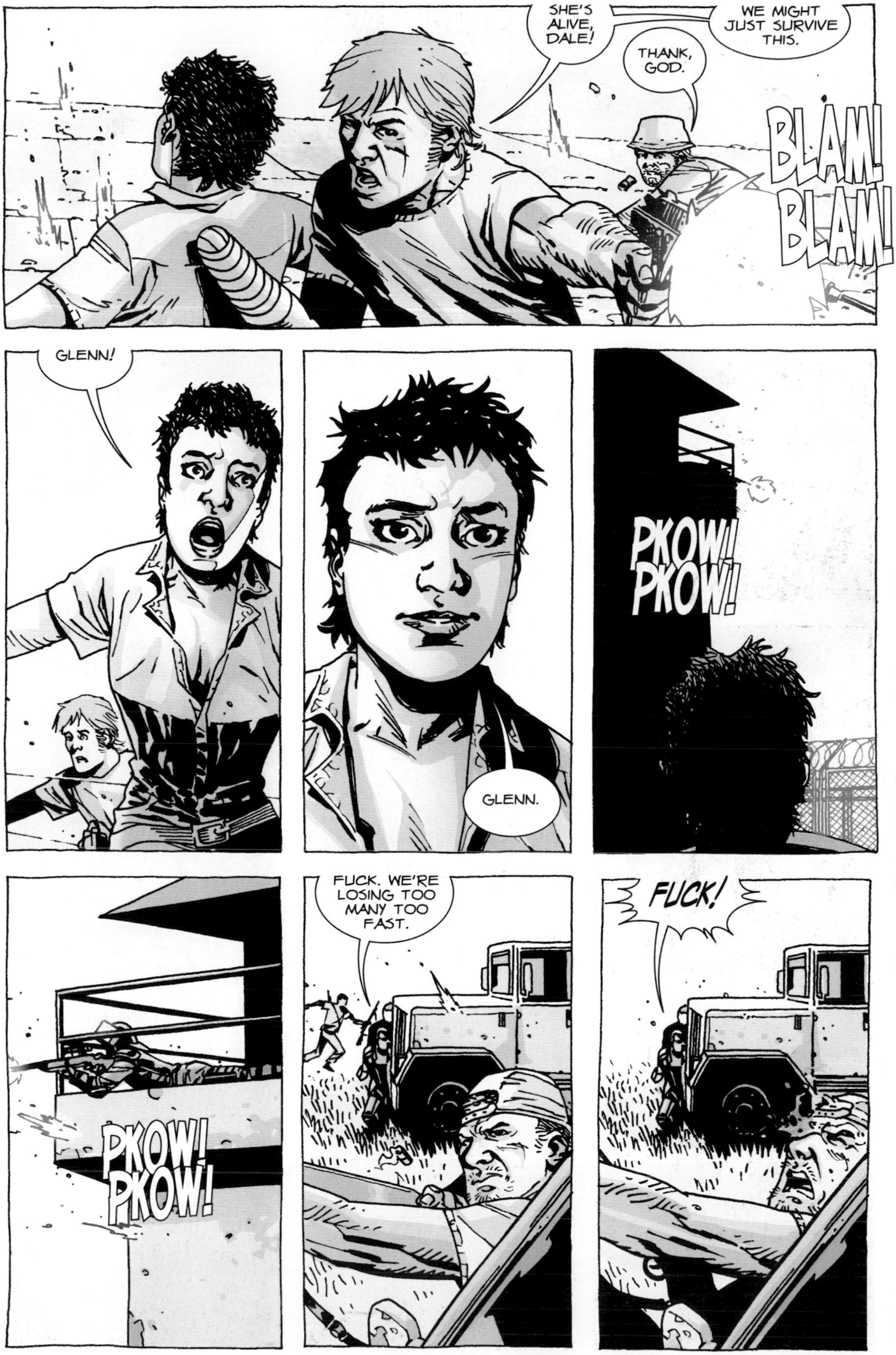
SHE'S ALIVE, DALE!
WE MIGHT JUST SURVIVE THIS.
THANK, GOD.
BLAM! BLAM!
GLENN!
GLENN.
PKOW! PKOW!
PKOW! PKOW!
FUCK. WE'RE LOSING TOO MANY TOO FAST.
FUCK!

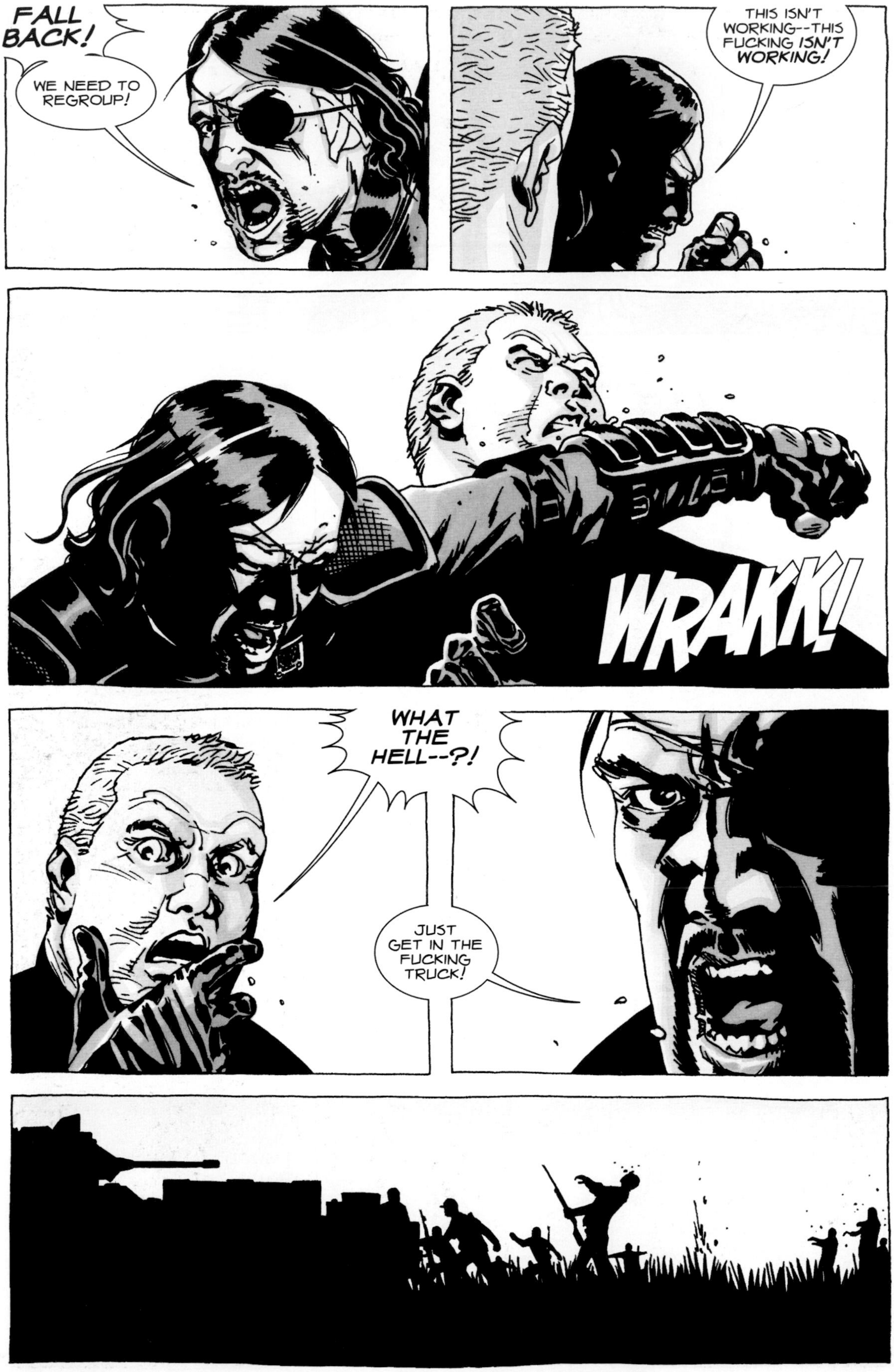
FALL BACK!
WE NEED TO REGROUP!
THIS ISN'T WORKING--THIS FUCKING ISN'T WORKING!
WRAKK!
WHAT THE HELL--?!
JUST GET IN THE FUCKING TRUCK!

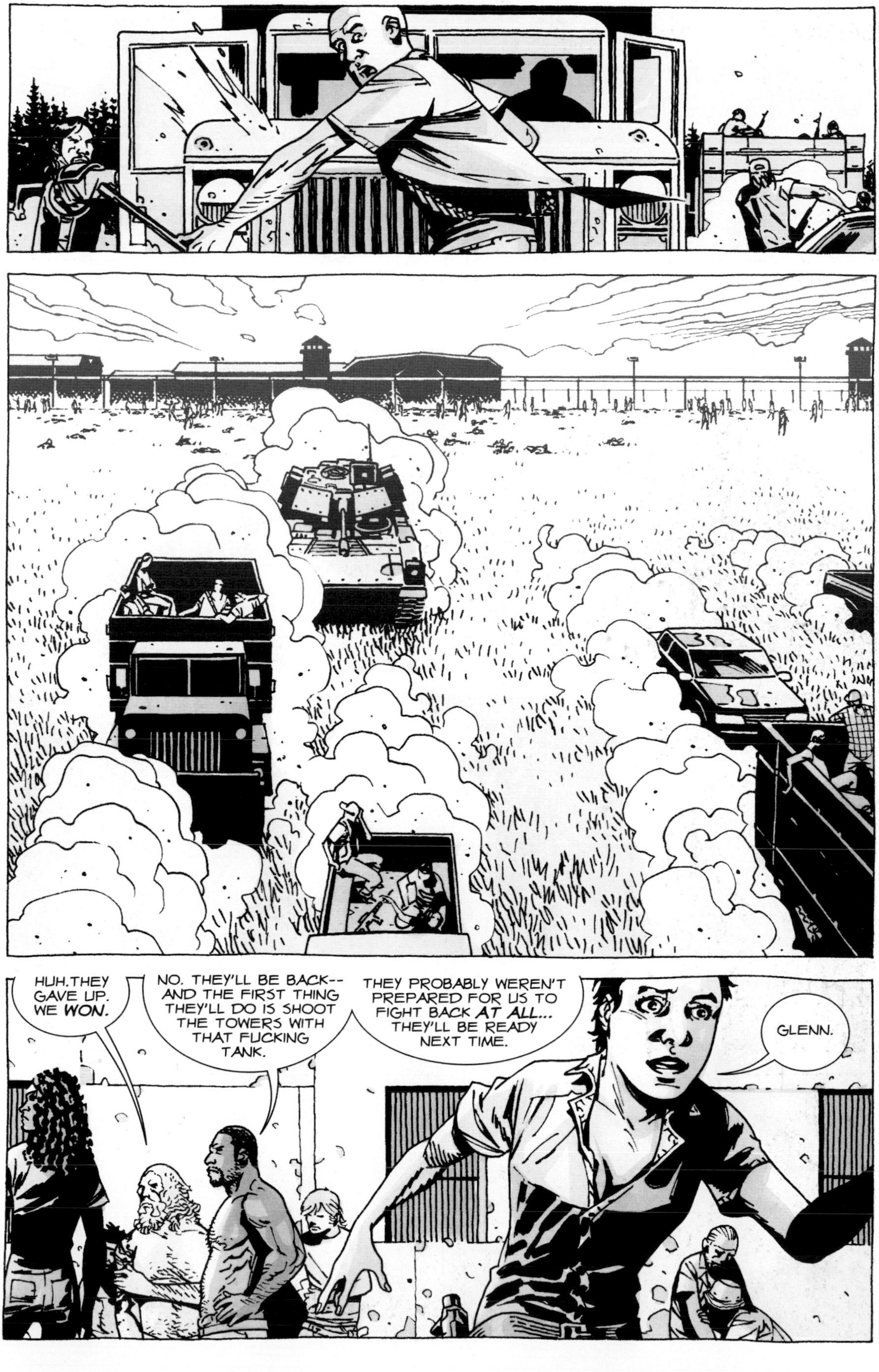
HUH. THEY GAVE UP. WE WON.
NO. THEY'LL BE BACK-- AND THE FIRST THING THEY'LL DO IS SHOOT THE TOWERS WITH THAT FUCKING TANK.
THEY PROBABLY WEREN'T PREPARED FOR US TO FIGHT BACK AT ALL... THEY'LL BE READY NEXT TIME.
GLENN.

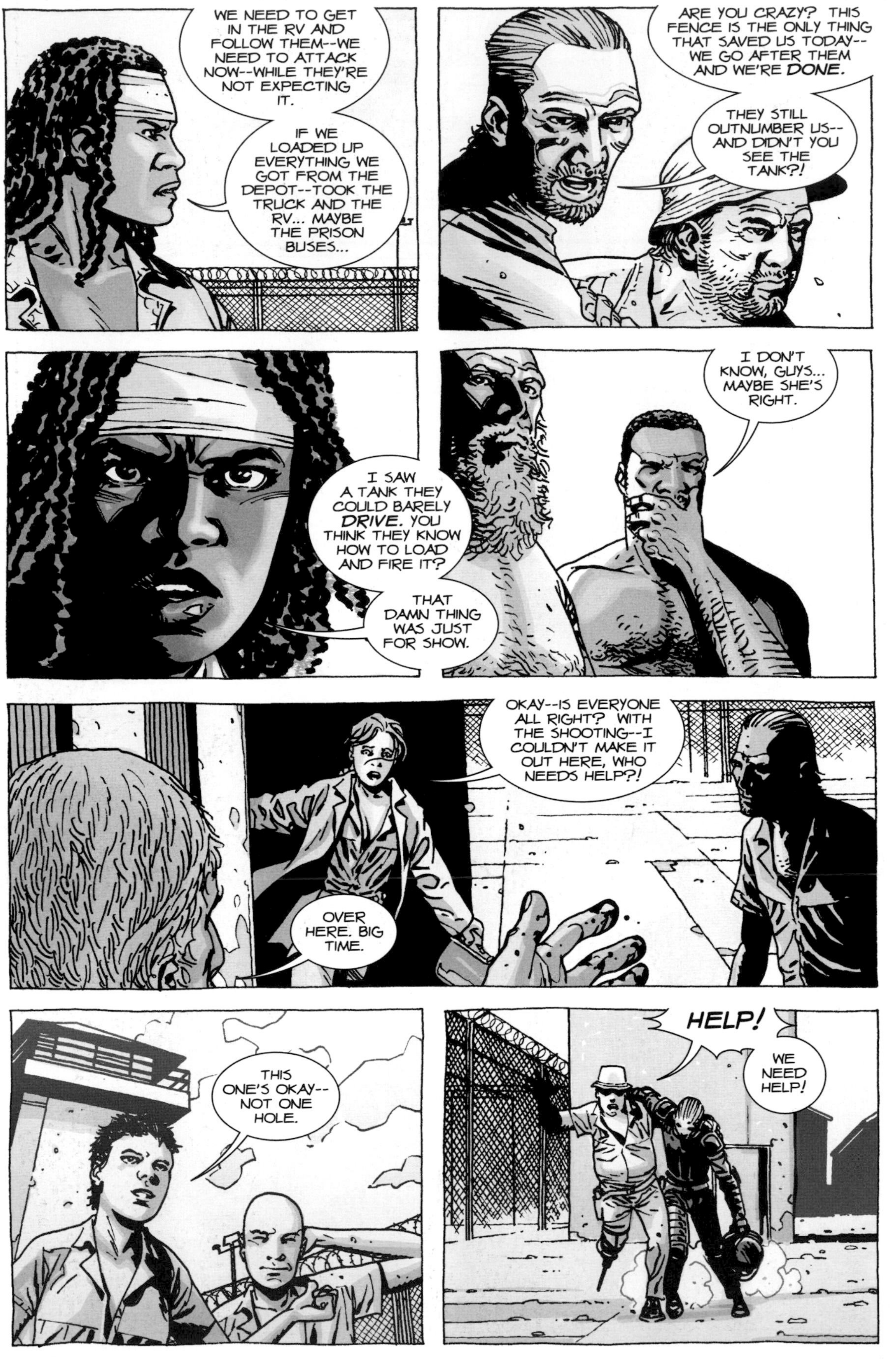

WE NEED TO GET IN THE RV AND FOLLOW THEM--WE NEED TO ATTACK NOW--WHILE THEY'RE NOT EXPECTING IT.
IF WE LOADED UP EVERYTHING WE GOT FROM THE DEPOT--TOOK THE TRUCK AND THE RV... MAYBE THE PRISON BUSES...
ARE YOU CRAZY? THIS FENCE IS THE ONLY THING THAT SAVED US TODAY--WE GO AFTER THEM AND WE'RE *DONE.*
THEY STILL OUTNUMBER US--AND DIDN'T YOU SEE THE TANK?!
I SAW A TANK THEY COULD BARELY *DRIVE.* YOU THINK THEY KNOW HOW TO LOAD AND FIRE IT?
THAT DAMN THING WAS JUST FOR SHOW.
I DON'T KNOW, GUYS... MAYBE SHE'S RIGHT.
OKAY--IS EVERYONE ALL RIGHT? WITH THE SHOOTING--I COULDN'T MAKE IT OUT HERE, WHO NEEDS HELP?!
OVER HERE. BIG TIME.
THIS ONE'S OKAY--NOT ONE HOLE.
HELP!
WE NEED HELP!

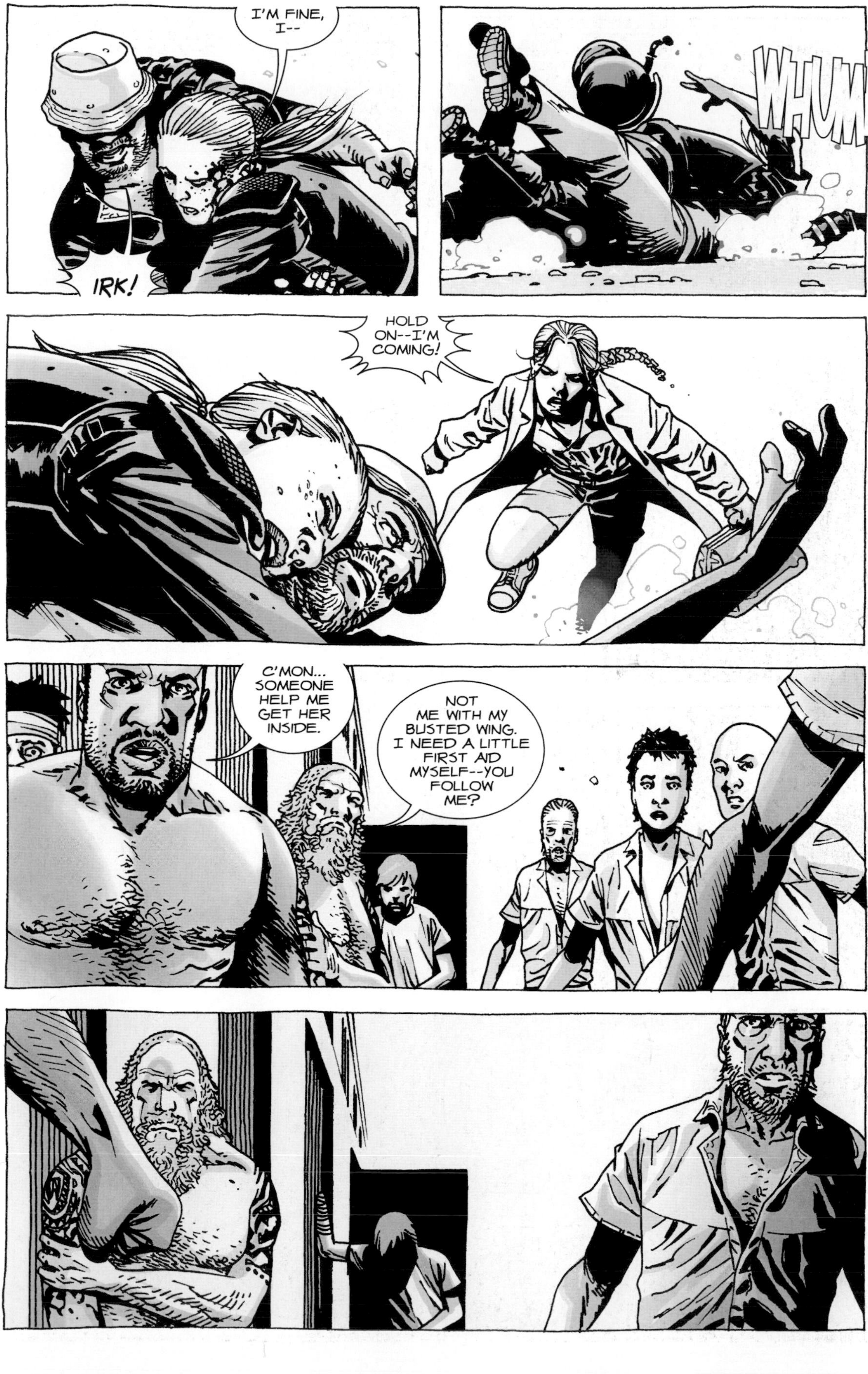
I'M FINE, I--
IRK!
WHUMP!
HOLD ON--I'M COMING!
C'MON... SOMEONE HELP ME GET HER INSIDE.
NOT ME WITH MY BUSTED WING. I NEED A LITTLE FIRST AID MYSELF--YOU FOLLOW ME?

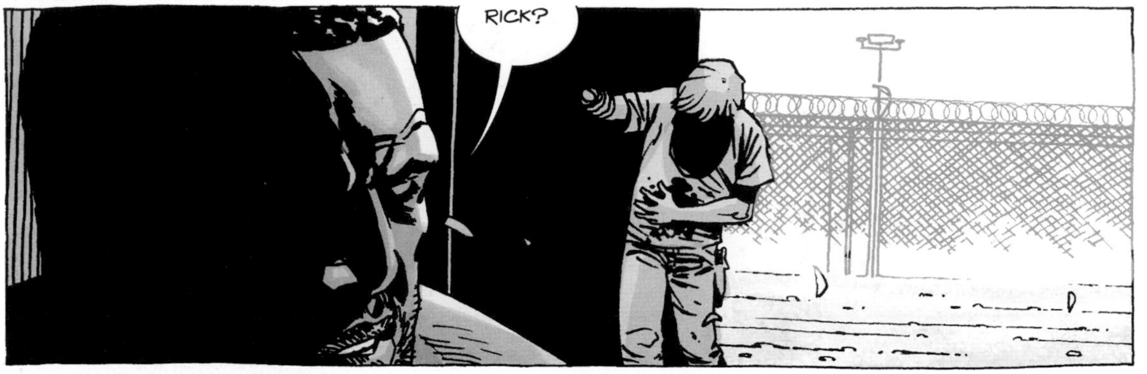
RICK?

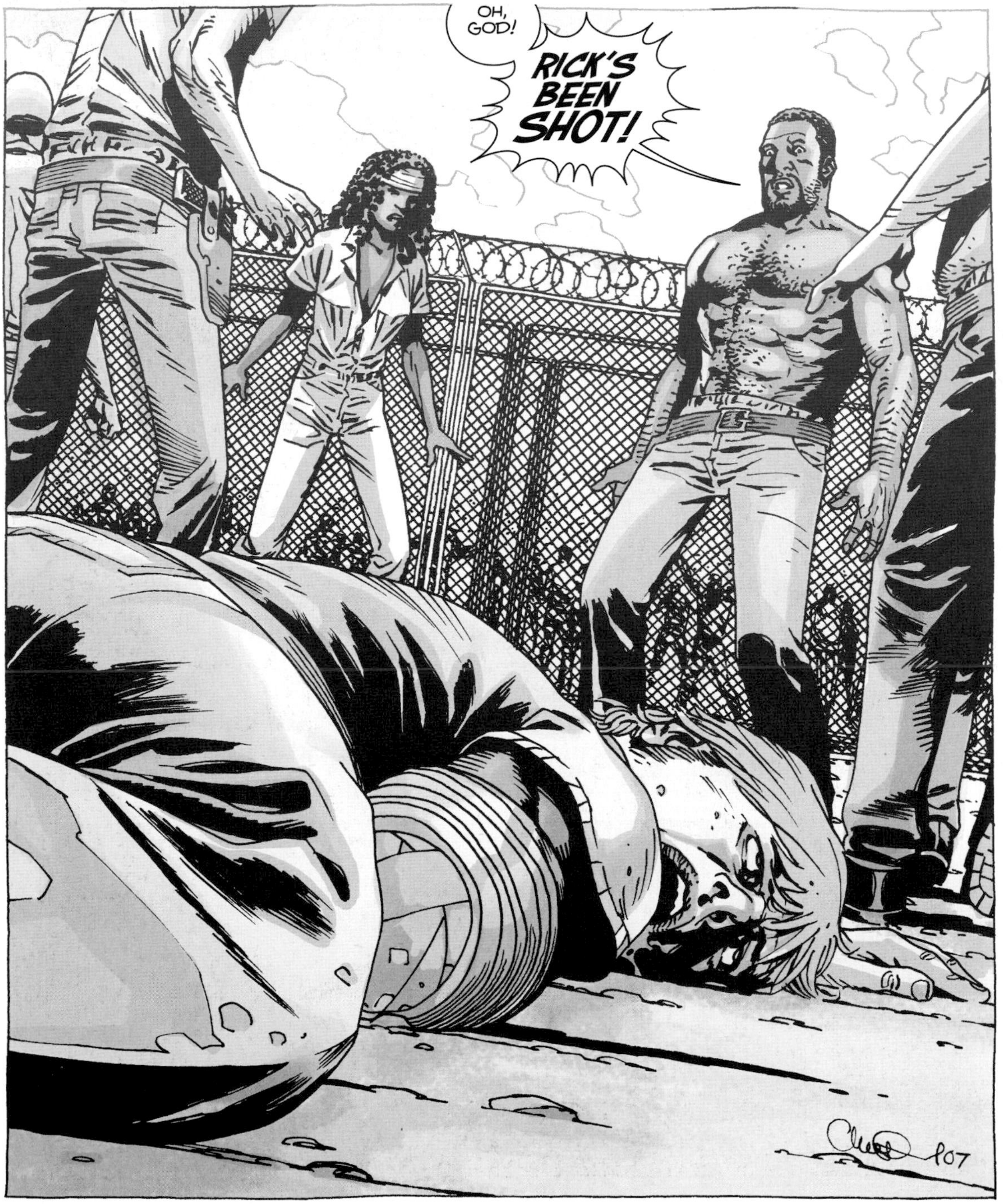
OH, GOD!
RICK'S BEEN SHOT!

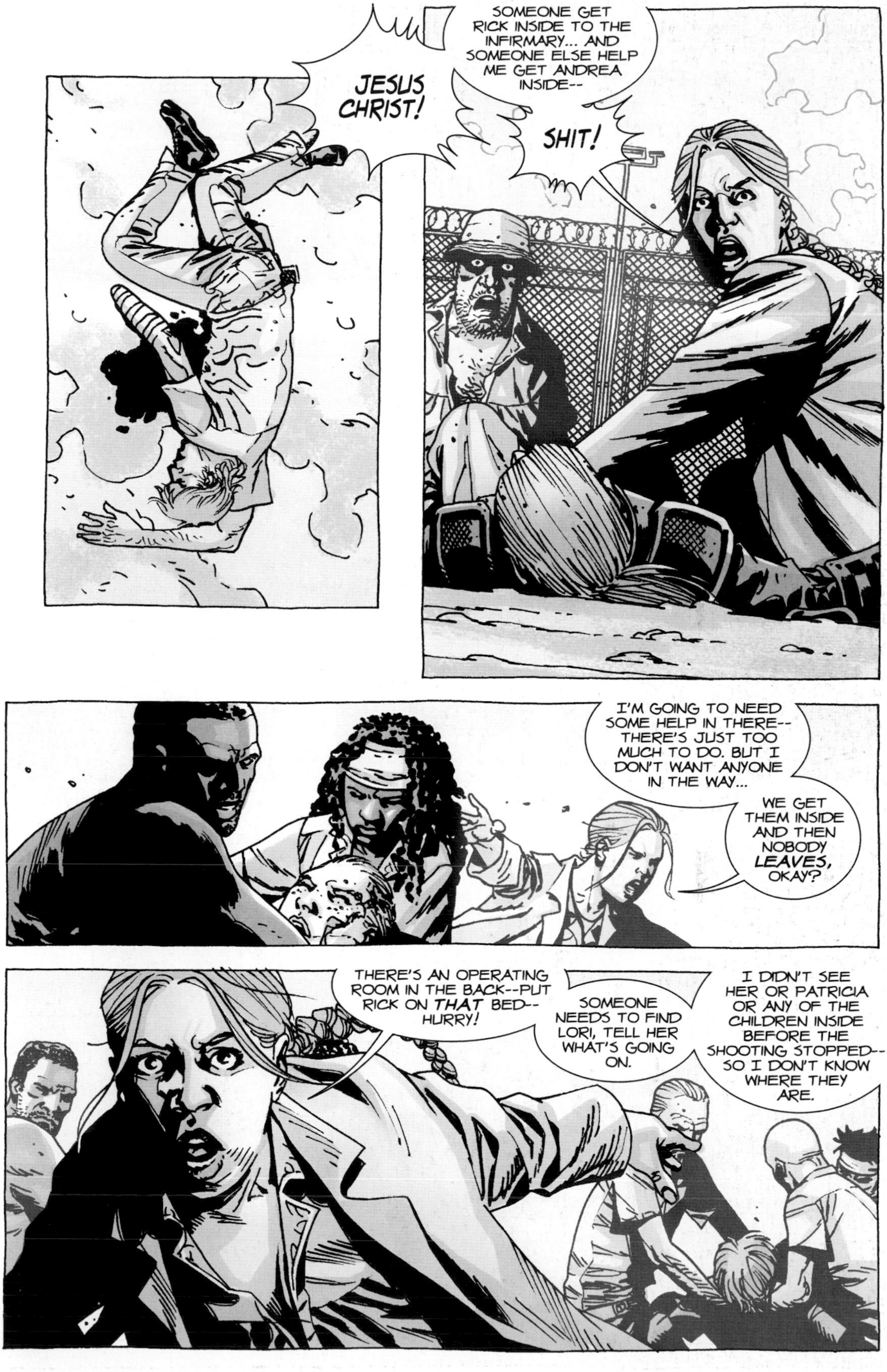
JESUS CHRIST!
SOMEONE GET RICK INSIDE TO THE INFIRMARY... AND SOMEONE ELSE HELP ME GET ANDREA INSIDE--
SHIT!
I'M GOING TO NEED SOME HELP IN THERE-- THERE'S JUST TOO MUCH TO DO. BUT I DON'T WANT ANYONE IN THE WAY...
WE GET THEM INSIDE AND THEN NOBODY LEAVES, OKAY?
THERE'S AN OPERATING ROOM IN THE BACK--PUT RICK ON THAT BED-- HURRY!
SOMEONE NEEDS TO FIND LORI, TELL HER WHAT'S GOING ON.
I DIDN'T SEE HER OR PATRICIA OR ANY OF THE CHILDREN INSIDE BEFORE THE SHOOTING STOPPED-- SO I DON'T KNOW WHERE THEY ARE.

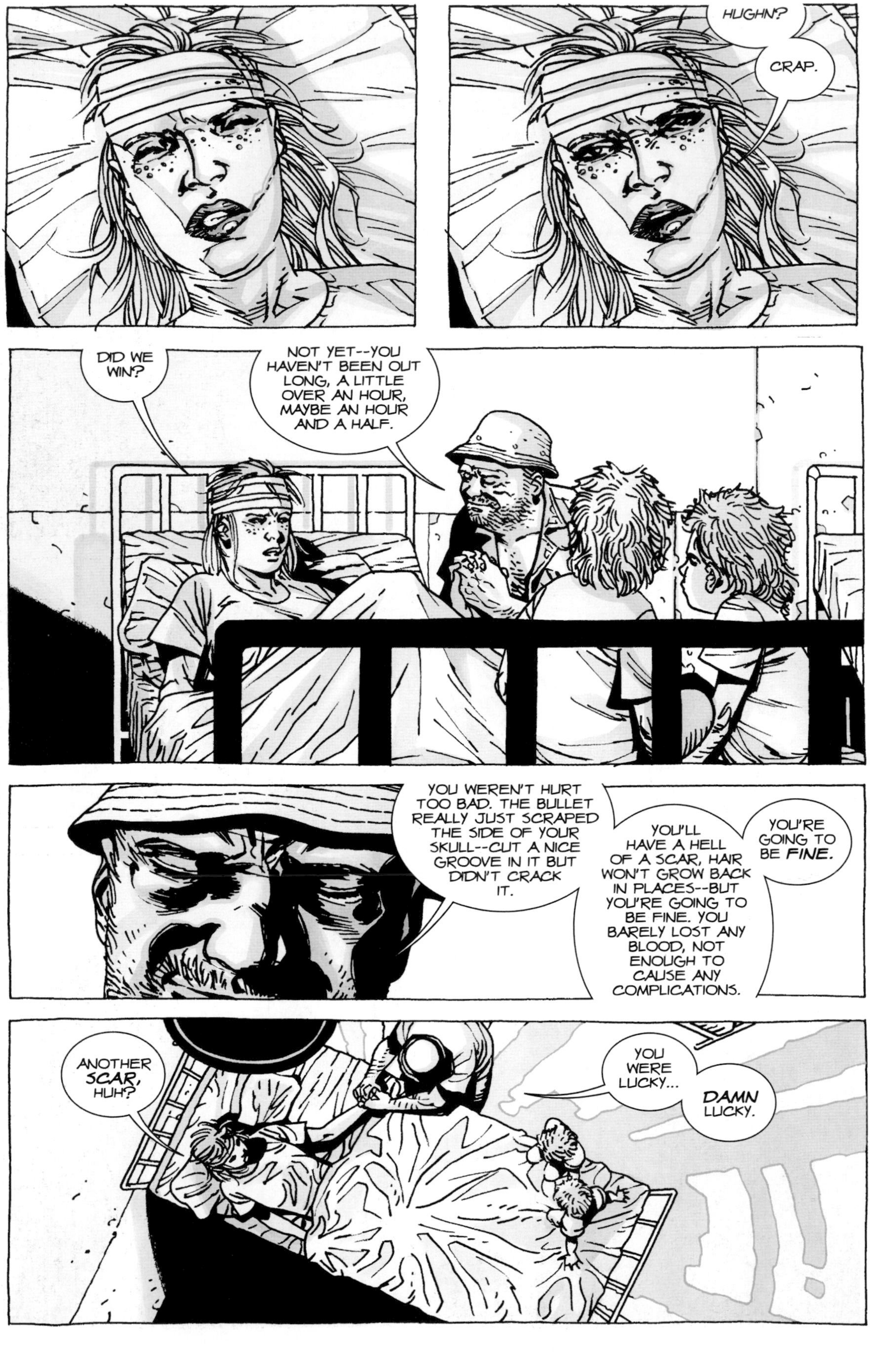
HUGHN?
CRAP.
DID WE WIN?
NOT YET--YOU HAVEN'T BEEN OUT LONG, A LITTLE OVER AN HOUR, MAYBE AN HOUR AND A HALF.
YOU WEREN'T HURT TOO BAD. THE BULLET REALLY JUST SCRAPED THE SIDE OF YOUR SKULL--CUT A NICE GROOVE IN IT BUT DIDN'T CRACK IT.
YOU'LL HAVE A HELL OF A SCAR, HAIR WON'T GROW BACK IN PLACES--BUT YOU'RE GOING TO BE FINE. YOU BARELY LOST ANY BLOOD, NOT ENOUGH TO CAUSE ANY COMPLICATIONS.
YOU'RE GOING TO BE *FINE.*
ANOTHER *SCAR,* HUH?
YOU WERE LUCKY...
DAMN LUCKY.

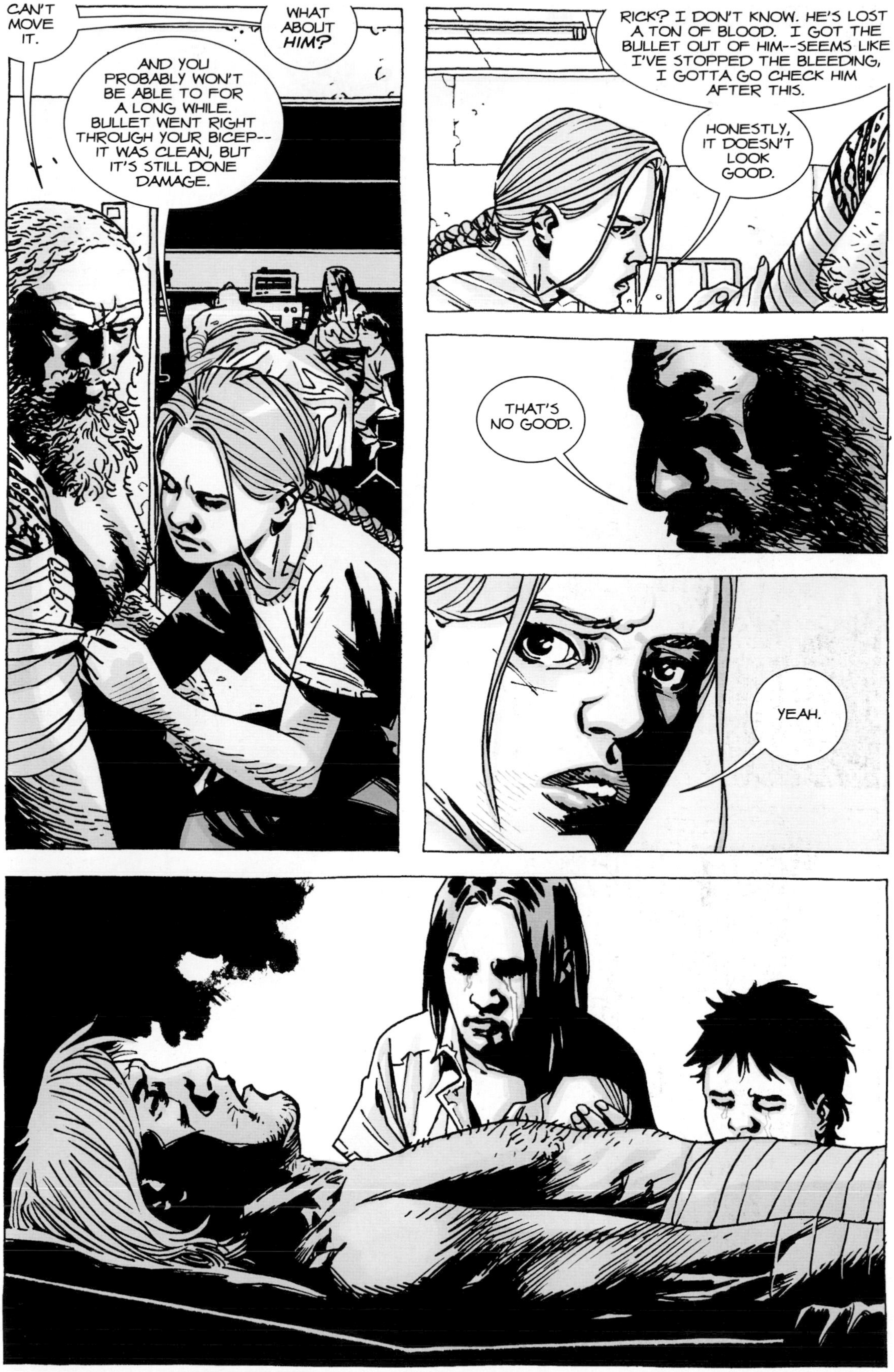
CAN'T MOVE IT.
AND YOU PROBABLY WON'T BE ABLE TO FOR A LONG WHILE. BULLET WENT RIGHT THROUGH YOUR BICEP-- IT WAS CLEAN, BUT IT'S STILL DONE DAMAGE.
WHAT ABOUT HIM?
RICK? I DON'T KNOW. HE'S LOST A TON OF BLOOD. I GOT THE BULLET OUT OF HIM--SEEMS LIKE I'VE STOPPED THE BLEEDING, I GOTTA GO CHECK HIM AFTER THIS.
HONESTLY, IT DOESN'T LOOK GOOD.
THAT'S NO GOOD.
YEAH.

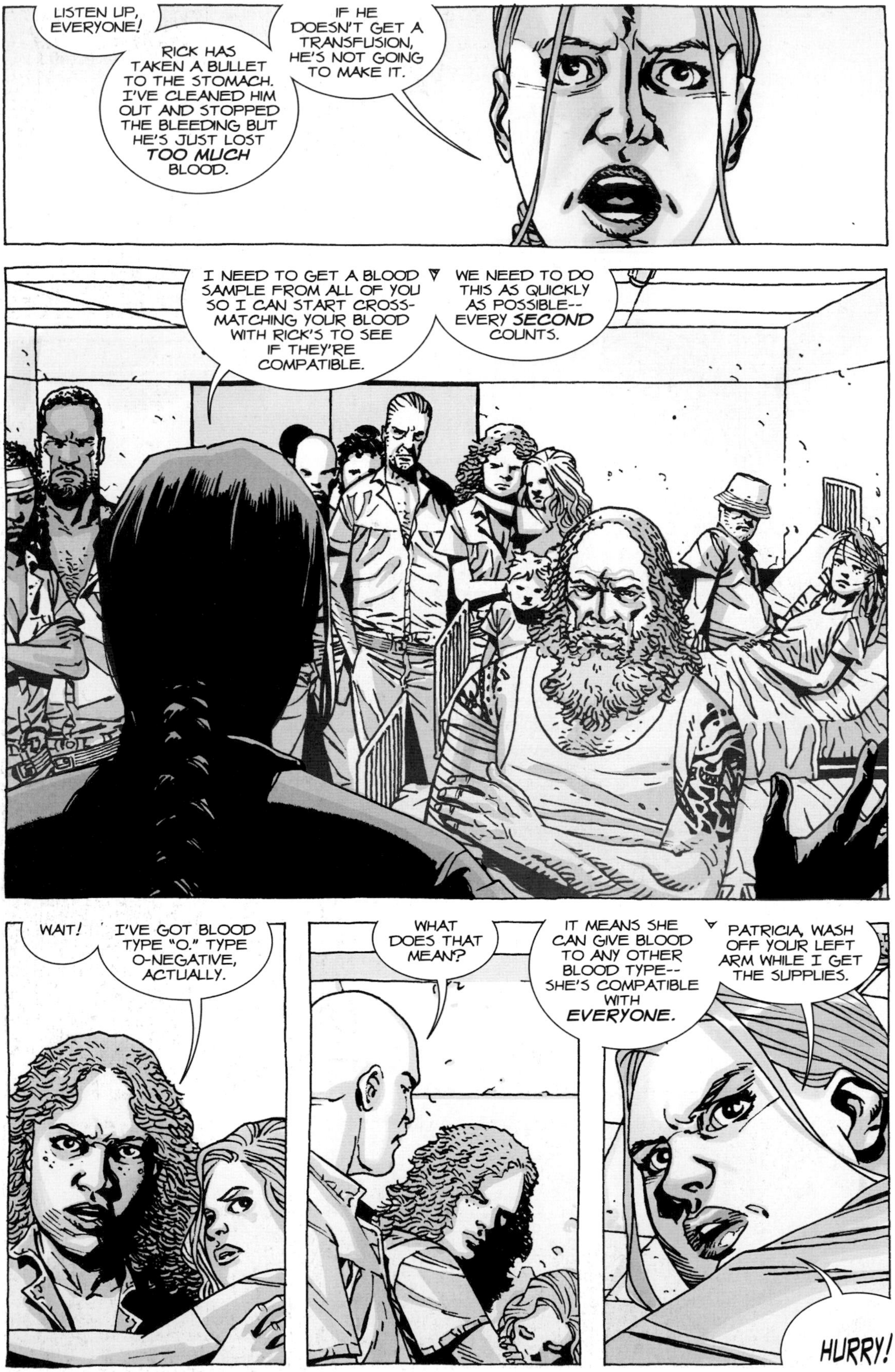
LISTEN UP, EVERYONE!
RICK HAS TAKEN A BULLET TO THE STOMACH. I'VE CLEANED HIM OUT AND STOPPED THE BLEEDING BUT HE'S JUST LOST TOO MUCH BLOOD.
IF HE DOESN'T GET A TRANSFUSION, HE'S NOT GOING TO MAKE IT.
I NEED TO GET A BLOOD SAMPLE FROM ALL OF YOU SO I CAN START CROSS-MATCHING YOUR BLOOD WITH RICK'S TO SEE IF THEY'RE COMPATIBLE.
WE NEED TO DO THIS AS QUICKLY AS POSSIBLE-- EVERY SECOND COUNTS.
WAIT!
I'VE GOT BLOOD TYPE "O." TYPE O-NEGATIVE, ACTUALLY.
WHAT DOES THAT MEAN?
IT MEANS SHE CAN GIVE BLOOD TO ANY OTHER BLOOD TYPE-- SHE'S COMPATIBLE WITH EVERYONE.
PATRICIA, WASH OFF YOUR LEFT ARM WHILE I GET THE SUPPLIES.
HURRY!

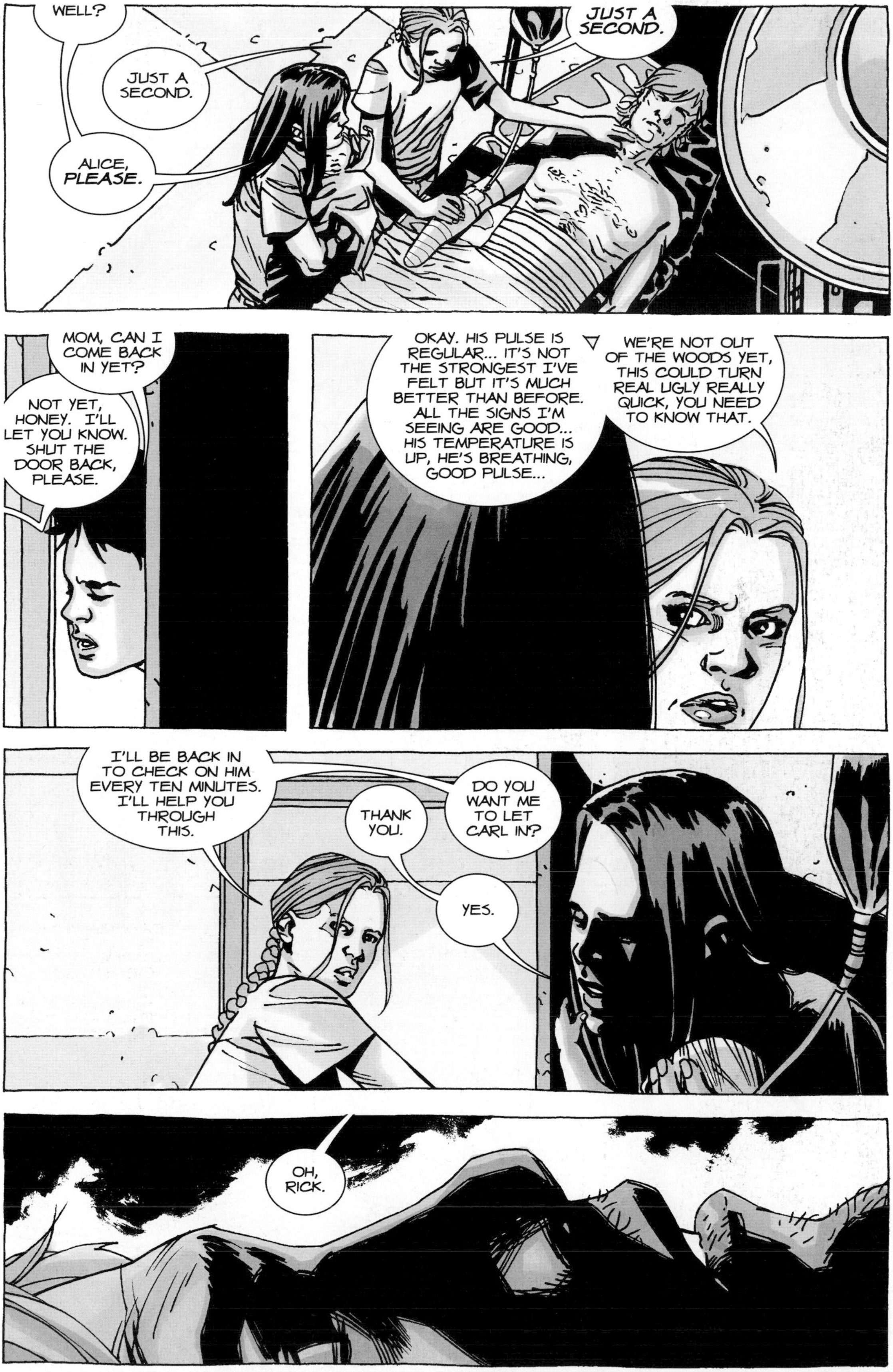
WELL?
JUST A SECOND.
JUST A SECOND.
ALICE, PLEASE.
MOM, CAN I COME BACK IN YET?
NOT YET, HONEY. I'LL LET YOU KNOW. SHUT THE DOOR BACK, PLEASE.
OKAY. HIS PULSE IS REGULAR... IT'S NOT THE STRONGEST I'VE FELT BUT IT'S MUCH BETTER THAN BEFORE. ALL THE SIGNS I'M SEEING ARE GOOD... HIS TEMPERATURE IS UP, HE'S BREATHING, GOOD PULSE...
WE'RE NOT OUT OF THE WOODS YET, THIS COULD TURN REAL UGLY REALLY QUICK, YOU NEED TO KNOW THAT.
I'LL BE BACK IN TO CHECK ON HIM EVERY TEN MINUTES. I'LL HELP YOU THROUGH THIS.
THANK YOU.
DO YOU WANT ME TO LET CARL IN?
YES.
OH, RICK.

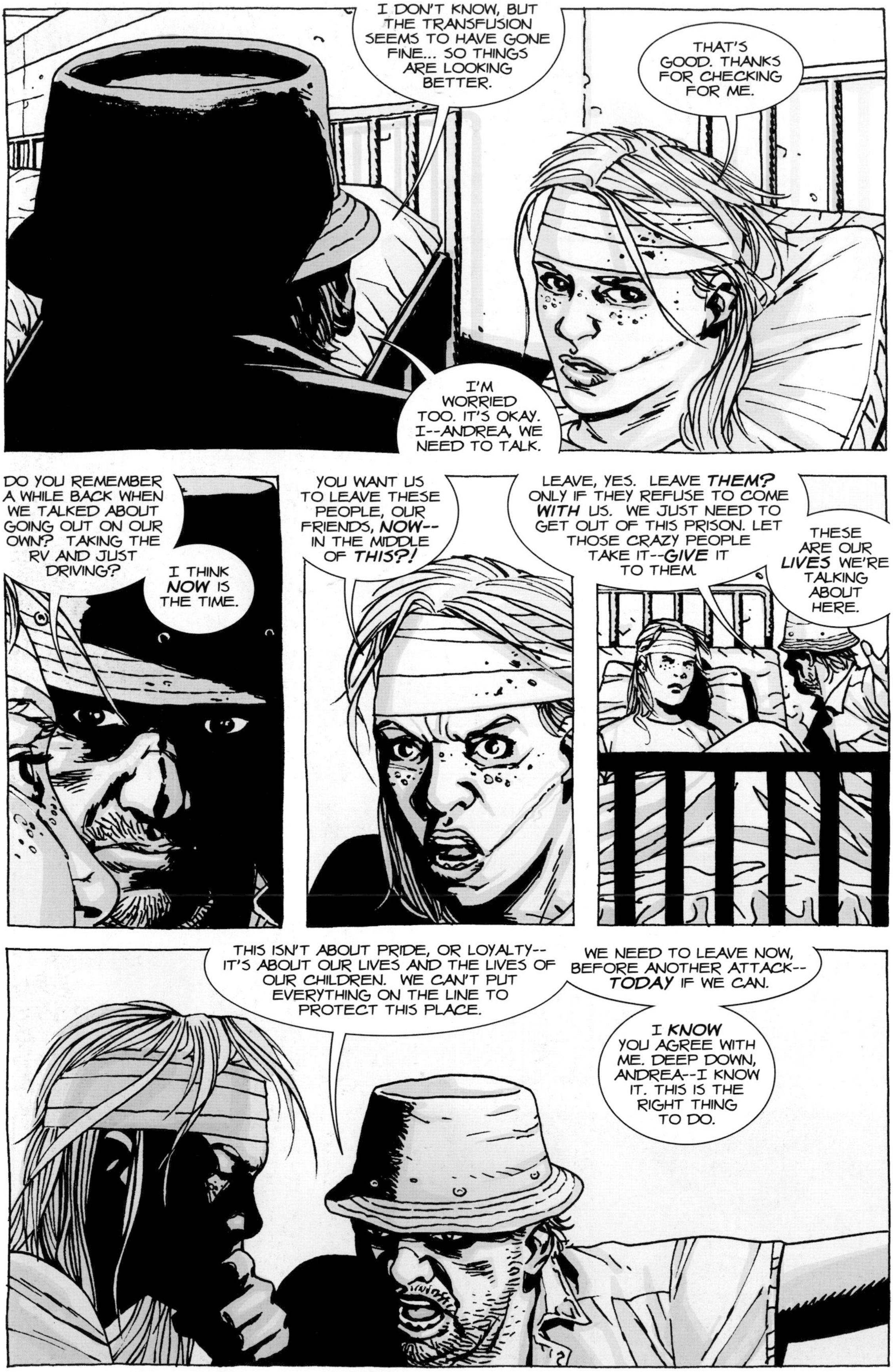
I DON'T KNOW, BUT THE TRANSFUSION SEEMS TO HAVE GONE FINE... SO THINGS ARE LOOKING BETTER.
THAT'S GOOD. THANKS FOR CHECKING FOR ME.
I'M WORRIED TOO. IT'S OKAY. I--ANDREA, WE NEED TO TALK.
DO YOU REMEMBER A WHILE BACK WHEN WE TALKED ABOUT GOING OUT ON OUR OWN? TAKING THE RV AND JUST DRIVING?
I THINK NOW IS THE TIME.
YOU WANT US TO LEAVE THESE PEOPLE, OUR FRIENDS, NOW-- IN THE MIDDLE OF THIS?!
LEAVE, YES. LEAVE THEM? ONLY IF THEY REFUSE TO COME WITH US. WE JUST NEED TO GET OUT OF THIS PRISON. LET THOSE CRAZY PEOPLE TAKE IT--GIVE IT TO THEM.
THESE ARE OUR LIVES WE'RE TALKING ABOUT HERE.
THIS ISN'T ABOUT PRIDE, OR LOYALTY-- IT'S ABOUT OUR LIVES AND THE LIVES OF OUR CHILDREN. WE CAN'T PUT EVERYTHING ON THE LINE TO PROTECT THIS PLACE.
WE NEED TO LEAVE NOW, BEFORE ANOTHER ATTACK-- TODAY IF WE CAN.
I KNOW YOU AGREE WITH ME. DEEP DOWN, ANDREA--I KNOW IT. THIS IS THE RIGHT THING TO DO.

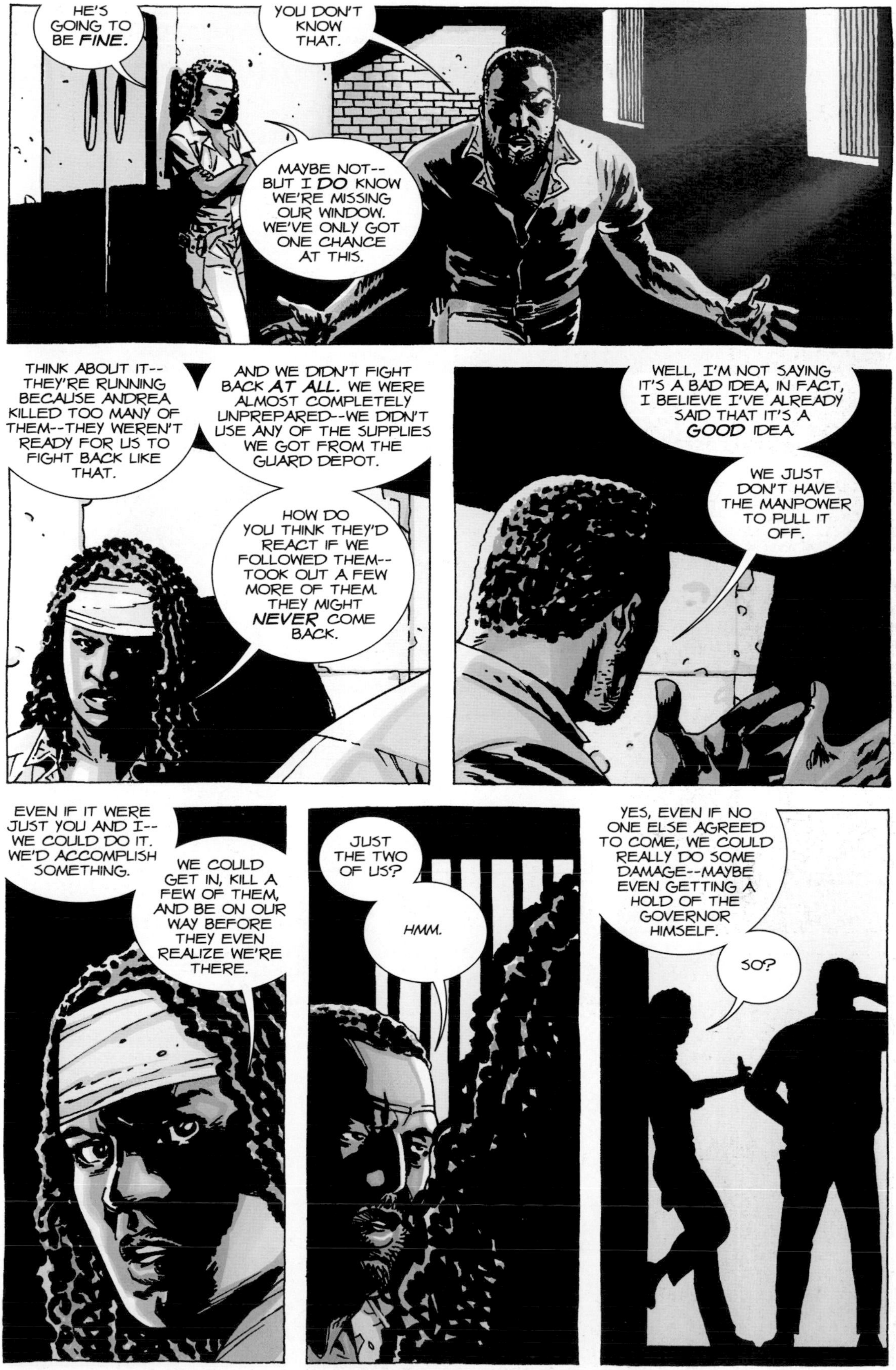
HE'S GOING TO BE *FINE.*
YOU DON'T KNOW THAT.
MAYBE NOT-- BUT I *DO* KNOW WE'RE MISSING OUR WINDOW. WE'VE ONLY GOT ONE CHANCE AT THIS.
THINK ABOUT IT-- THEY'RE RUNNING BECAUSE ANDREA KILLED TOO MANY OF THEM--THEY WEREN'T READY FOR US TO FIGHT BACK LIKE THAT.
AND WE DIDN'T FIGHT BACK *AT ALL.* WE WERE ALMOST COMPLETELY UNPREPARED--WE DIDN'T USE ANY OF THE SUPPLIES WE GOT FROM THE GUARD DEPOT.
HOW DO YOU THINK THEY'D REACT IF WE FOLLOWED THEM-- TOOK OUT A FEW MORE OF THEM. THEY MIGHT *NEVER* COME BACK.
WELL, I'M NOT SAYING IT'S A BAD IDEA. IN FACT, I BELIEVE I'VE ALREADY SAID THAT IT'S A *GOOD* IDEA.
WE JUST DON'T HAVE THE MANPOWER TO PULL IT OFF.
EVEN IF IT WERE JUST YOU AND I-- WE COULD DO IT. WE'D ACCOMPLISH SOMETHING.
WE COULD GET IN, KILL A FEW OF THEM, AND BE ON OUR WAY BEFORE THEY EVEN REALIZE WE'RE THERE.
JUST THE TWO OF US?
HMM.
YES, EVEN IF NO ONE ELSE AGREED TO COME, WE COULD REALLY DO SOME DAMAGE--MAYBE EVEN GETTING A HOLD OF THE GOVERNOR HIMSELF.
SO?

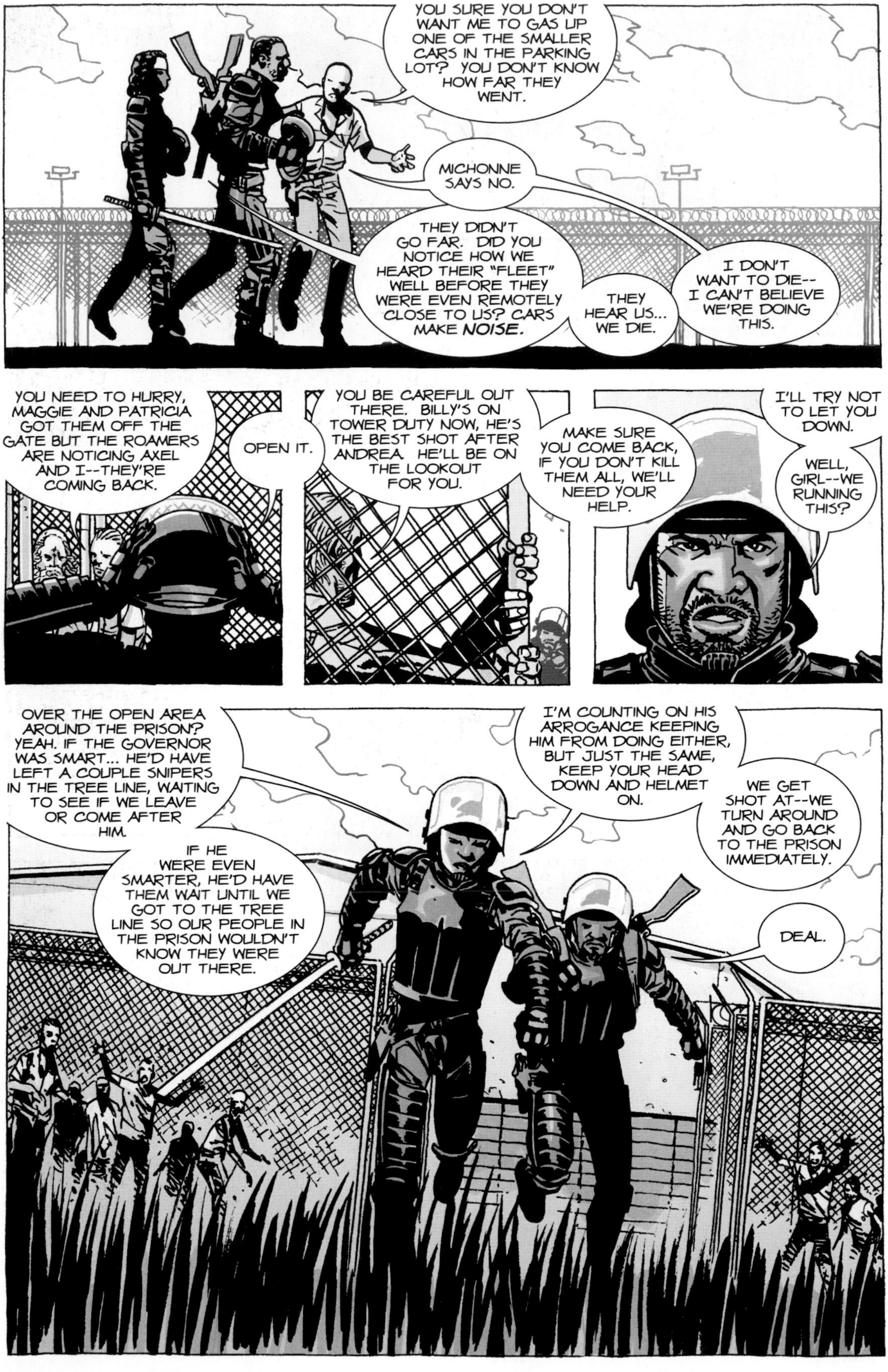
YOU SURE YOU DON'T WANT ME TO GAS UP ONE OF THE SMALLER CARS IN THE PARKING LOT? YOU DON'T KNOW HOW FAR THEY WENT.
MICHONNE SAYS NO.
THEY DIDN'T GO FAR. DID YOU NOTICE HOW WE HEARD THEIR "FLEET" WELL BEFORE THEY WERE EVEN REMOTELY CLOSE TO US? CARS MAKE NOISE.
THEY HEAR US... WE DIE.
I DON'T WANT TO DIE-- I CAN'T BELIEVE WE'RE DOING THIS.
YOU NEED TO HURRY, MAGGIE AND PATRICIA GOT THEM OFF THE GATE BUT THE ROAMERS ARE NOTICING AXEL AND I--THEY'RE COMING BACK.
OPEN IT.
YOU BE CAREFUL OUT THERE. BILLY'S ON TOWER DUTY NOW, HE'S THE BEST SHOT AFTER ANDREA. HE'LL BE ON THE LOOKOUT FOR YOU.
MAKE SURE YOU COME BACK, IF YOU DON'T KILL THEM ALL, WE'LL NEED YOUR HELP.
I'LL TRY NOT TO LET YOU DOWN.
WELL, GIRL--WE RUNNING THIS?
OVER THE OPEN AREA AROUND THE PRISON? YEAH. IF THE GOVERNOR WAS SMART... HE'D HAVE LEFT A COUPLE SNIPERS IN THE TREE LINE, WAITING TO SEE IF WE LEAVE OR COME AFTER HIM.
IF HE WERE EVEN SMARTER, HE'D HAVE THEM WAIT UNTIL WE GOT TO THE TREE LINE SO OUR PEOPLE IN THE PRISON WOULDN'T KNOW THEY WERE OUT THERE.
I'M COUNTING ON HIS ARROGANCE KEEPING HIM FROM DOING EITHER, BUT JUST THE SAME, KEEP YOUR HEAD DOWN AND HELMET ON.
WE GET SHOT AT--WE TURN AROUND AND GO BACK TO THE PRISON IMMEDIATELY.
DEAL.

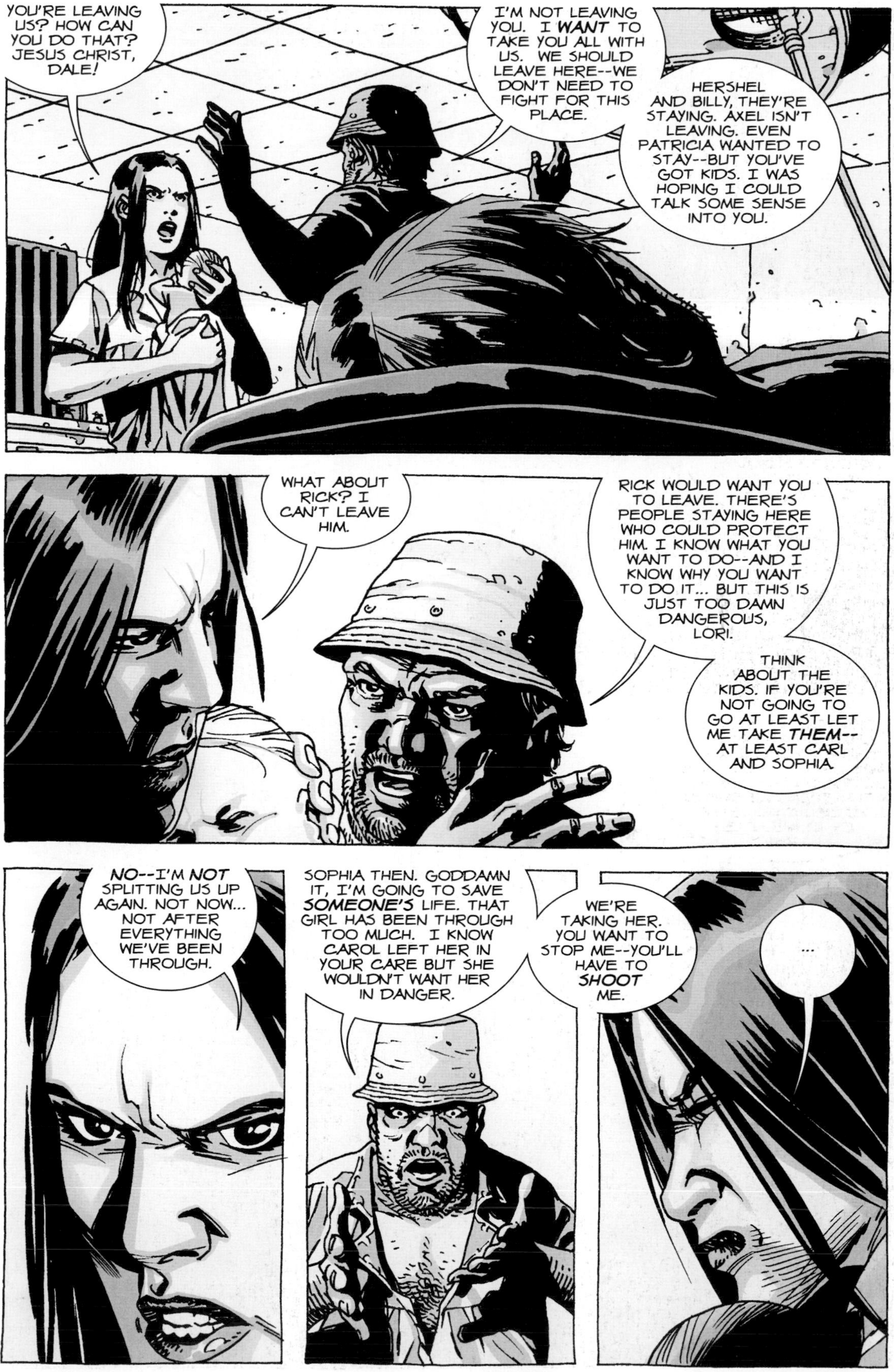
YOU'RE LEAVING US? HOW CAN YOU DO THAT? JESUS CHRIST, DALE!
I'M NOT LEAVING YOU. I WANT TO TAKE YOU ALL WITH US. WE SHOULD LEAVE HERE--WE DON'T NEED TO FIGHT FOR THIS PLACE.
HERSHEL AND BILLY, THEY'RE STAYING. AXEL ISN'T LEAVING. EVEN PATRICIA WANTED TO STAY--BUT YOU'VE GOT KIDS. I WAS HOPING I COULD TALK SOME SENSE INTO YOU.
WHAT ABOUT RICK? I CAN'T LEAVE HIM.
RICK WOULD WANT YOU TO LEAVE. THERE'S PEOPLE STAYING HERE WHO COULD PROTECT HIM. I KNOW WHAT YOU WANT TO DO--AND I KNOW WHY YOU WANT TO DO IT... BUT THIS IS JUST TOO DAMN DANGEROUS, LORI.
THINK ABOUT THE KIDS. IF YOU'RE NOT GOING TO GO AT LEAST LET ME TAKE THEM--AT LEAST CARL AND SOPHIA.
NO--I'M NOT SPLITTING US UP AGAIN. NOT NOW... NOT AFTER EVERYTHING WE'VE BEEN THROUGH.
SOPHIA THEN. GODDAMN IT, I'M GOING TO SAVE SOMEONE'S LIFE. THAT GIRL HAS BEEN THROUGH TOO MUCH. I KNOW CAROL LEFT HER IN YOUR CARE BUT SHE WOULDN'T WANT HER IN DANGER.
WE'RE TAKING HER. YOU WANT TO STOP ME--YOU'LL HAVE TO SHOOT ME.
...

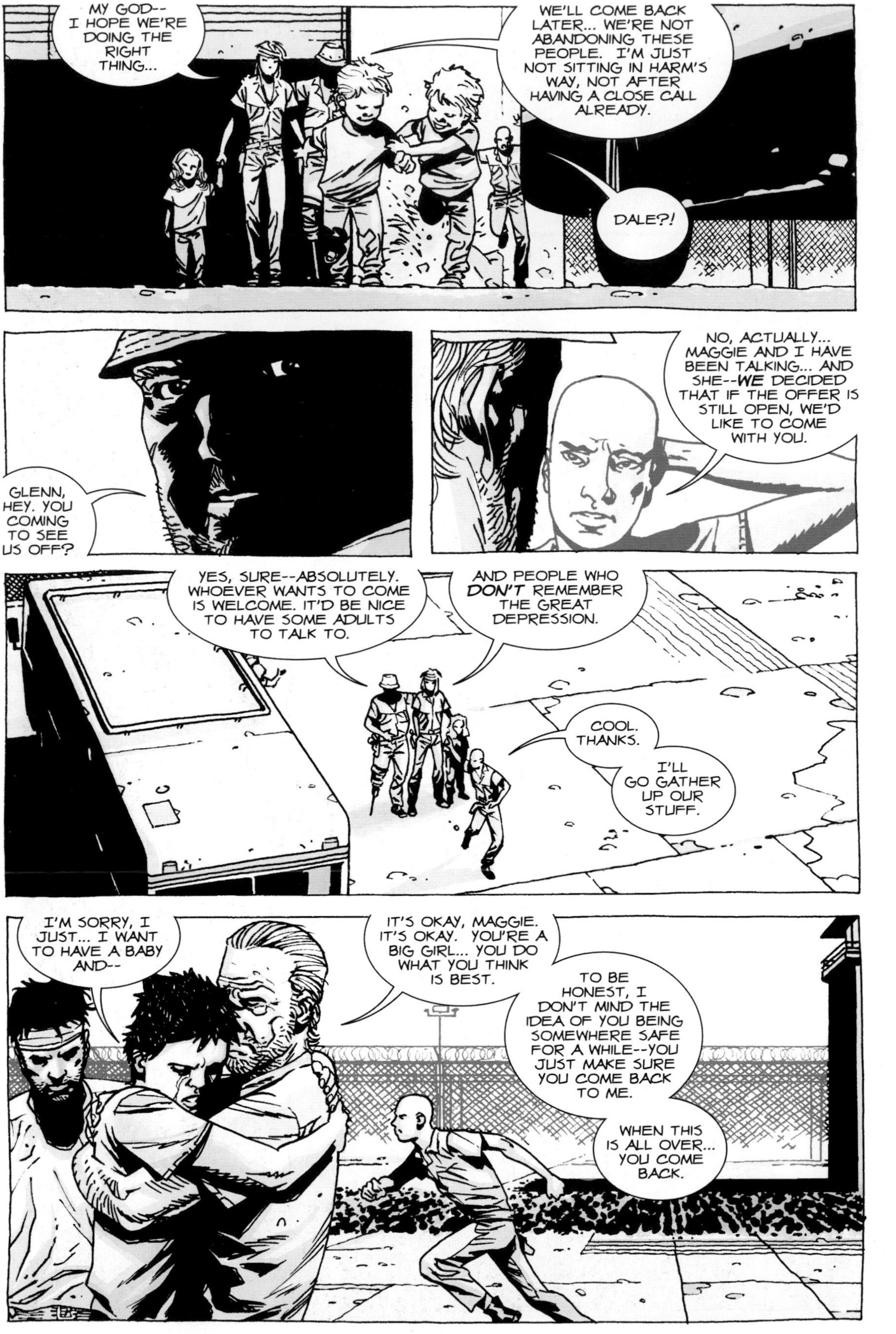

MY GOD-- I HOPE WE'RE DOING THE RIGHT THING...
WE'LL COME BACK LATER... WE'RE NOT ABANDONING THESE PEOPLE. I'M JUST NOT SITTING IN HARM'S WAY, NOT AFTER HAVING A CLOSE CALL ALREADY.
DALE?!
GLENN, HEY. YOU COMING TO SEE US OFF?
NO, ACTUALLY... MAGGIE AND I HAVE BEEN TALKING... AND SHE--*WE* DECIDED THAT IF THE OFFER IS STILL OPEN, WE'D LIKE TO COME WITH YOU.
YES, SURE--ABSOLUTELY. WHOEVER WANTS TO COME IS WELCOME. IT'D BE NICE TO HAVE SOME ADULTS TO TALK TO.
AND PEOPLE WHO *DON'T* REMEMBER THE GREAT DEPRESSION.
COOL. THANKS.
I'LL GO GATHER UP OUR STUFF.
I'M SORRY, I JUST... I WANT TO HAVE A BABY AND--
IT'S OKAY, MAGGIE. IT'S OKAY. YOU'RE A BIG GIRL... YOU DO WHAT YOU THINK IS BEST.
TO BE HONEST, I DON'T MIND THE IDEA OF YOU BEING SOMEWHERE SAFE FOR A WHILE--YOU JUST MAKE SURE YOU COME BACK TO ME.
WHEN THIS IS ALL OVER... YOU COME BACK.

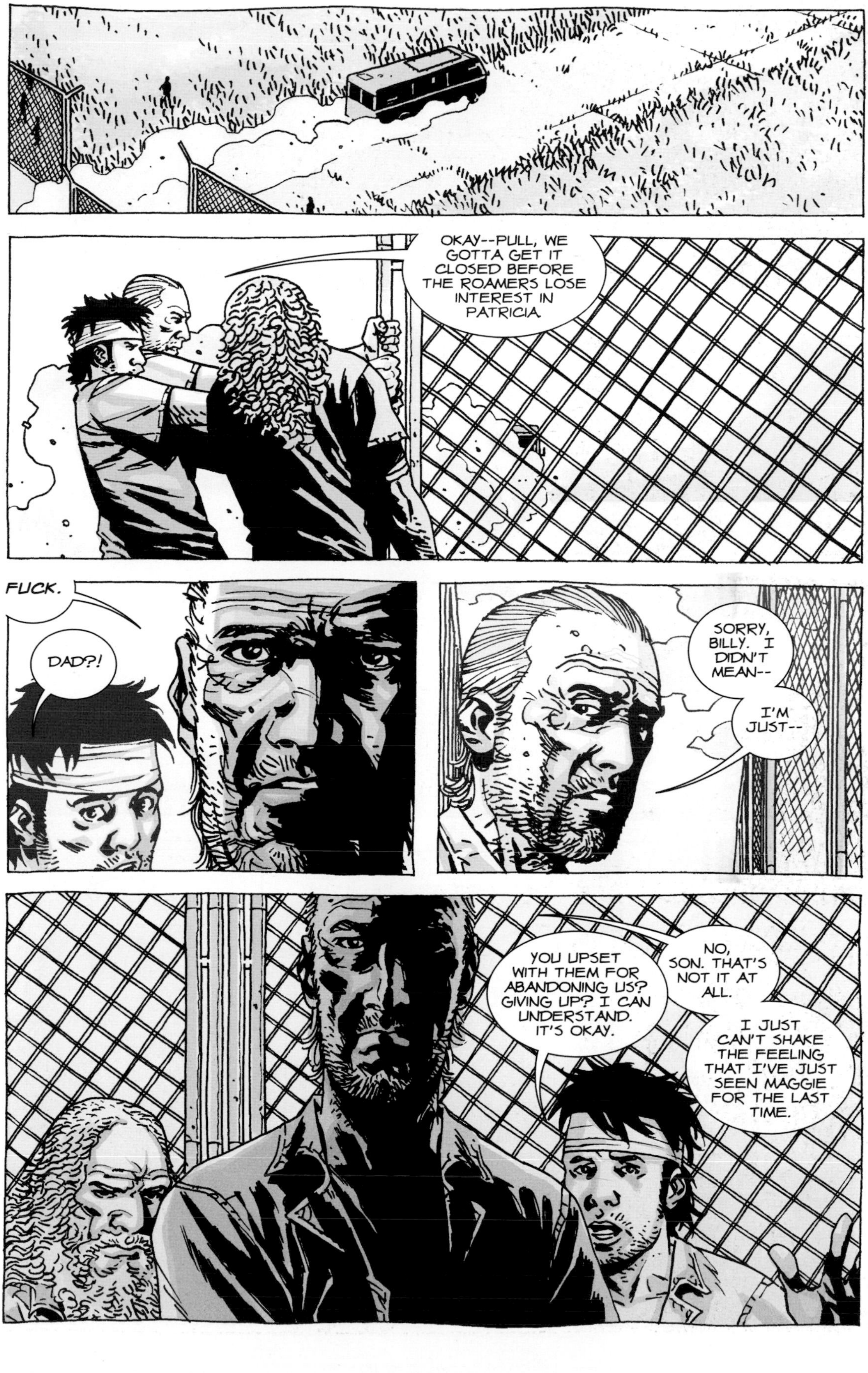
OKAY--PULL, WE GOTTA GET IT CLOSED BEFORE THE ROAMERS LOSE INTEREST IN PATRICIA.
FUCK.
DAD?!
SORRY, BILLY. I DIDN'T MEAN--
I'M JUST--
YOU UPSET WITH THEM FOR ABANDONING US? GIVING UP? I CAN UNDERSTAND. IT'S OKAY.
NO, SON. THAT'S NOT IT AT ALL.
I JUST CAN'T SHAKE THE FEELING THAT I'VE JUST SEEN MAGGIE FOR THE LAST TIME.

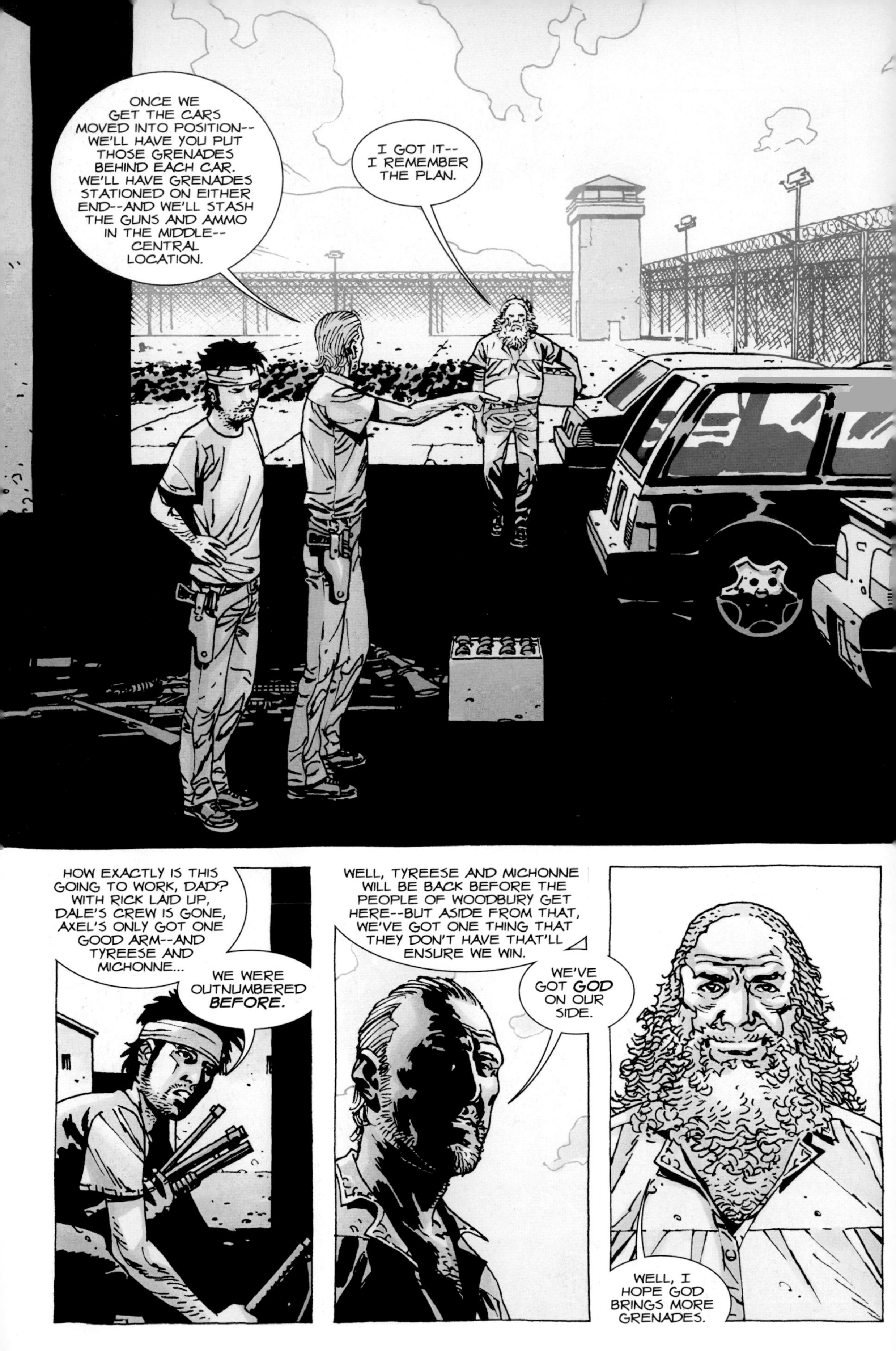
ONCE WE GET THE CARS MOVED INTO POSITION-- WE'LL HAVE YOU PUT THOSE GRENADES BEHIND EACH CAR. WE'LL HAVE GRENADES STATIONED ON EITHER END--AND WE'LL STASH THE GUNS AND AMMO IN THE MIDDLE-- CENTRAL LOCATION.
I GOT IT-- I REMEMBER THE PLAN.
HOW EXACTLY IS THIS GOING TO WORK, DAD? WITH RICK LAID UP, DALE'S CREW IS GONE, AXEL'S ONLY GOT ONE GOOD ARM--AND TYREESE AND MICHONNE...
WE WERE OUTNUMBERED BEFORE.
WELL, TYREESE AND MICHONNE WILL BE BACK BEFORE THE PEOPLE OF WOODBURY GET HERE--BUT ASIDE FROM THAT, WE'VE GOT ONE THING THAT THEY DON'T HAVE THAT'LL ENSURE WE WIN.
WE'VE GOT GOD ON OUR SIDE.
WELL, I HOPE GOD BRINGS MORE GRENADES.

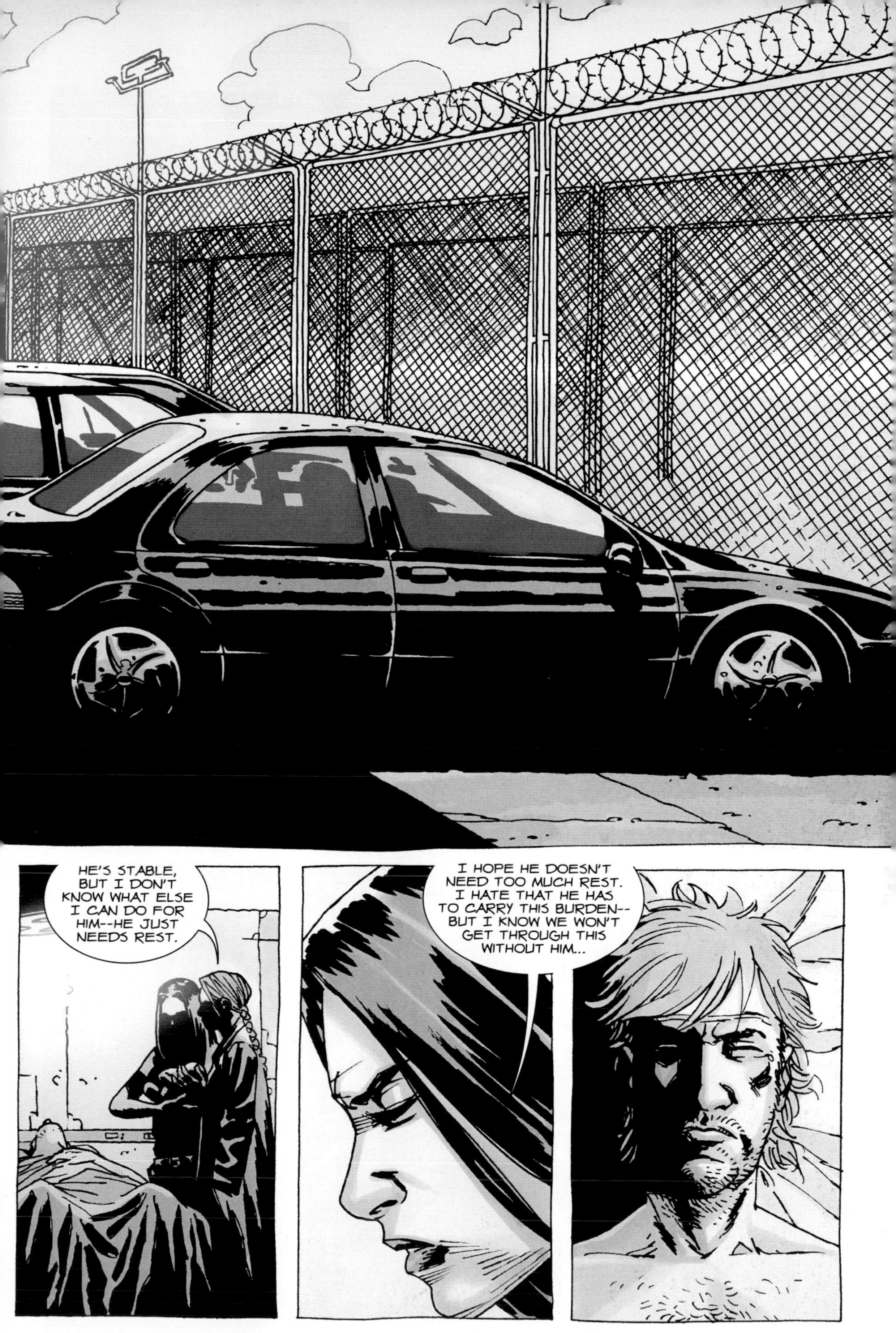
HE'S STABLE, BUT I DON'T KNOW WHAT ELSE I CAN DO FOR HIM--HE JUST NEEDS REST.
I HOPE HE DOESN'T NEED TOO MUCH REST. I HATE THAT HE HAS TO CARRY THIS BURDEN-- BUT I KNOW WE WON'T GET THROUGH THIS WITHOUT HIM...

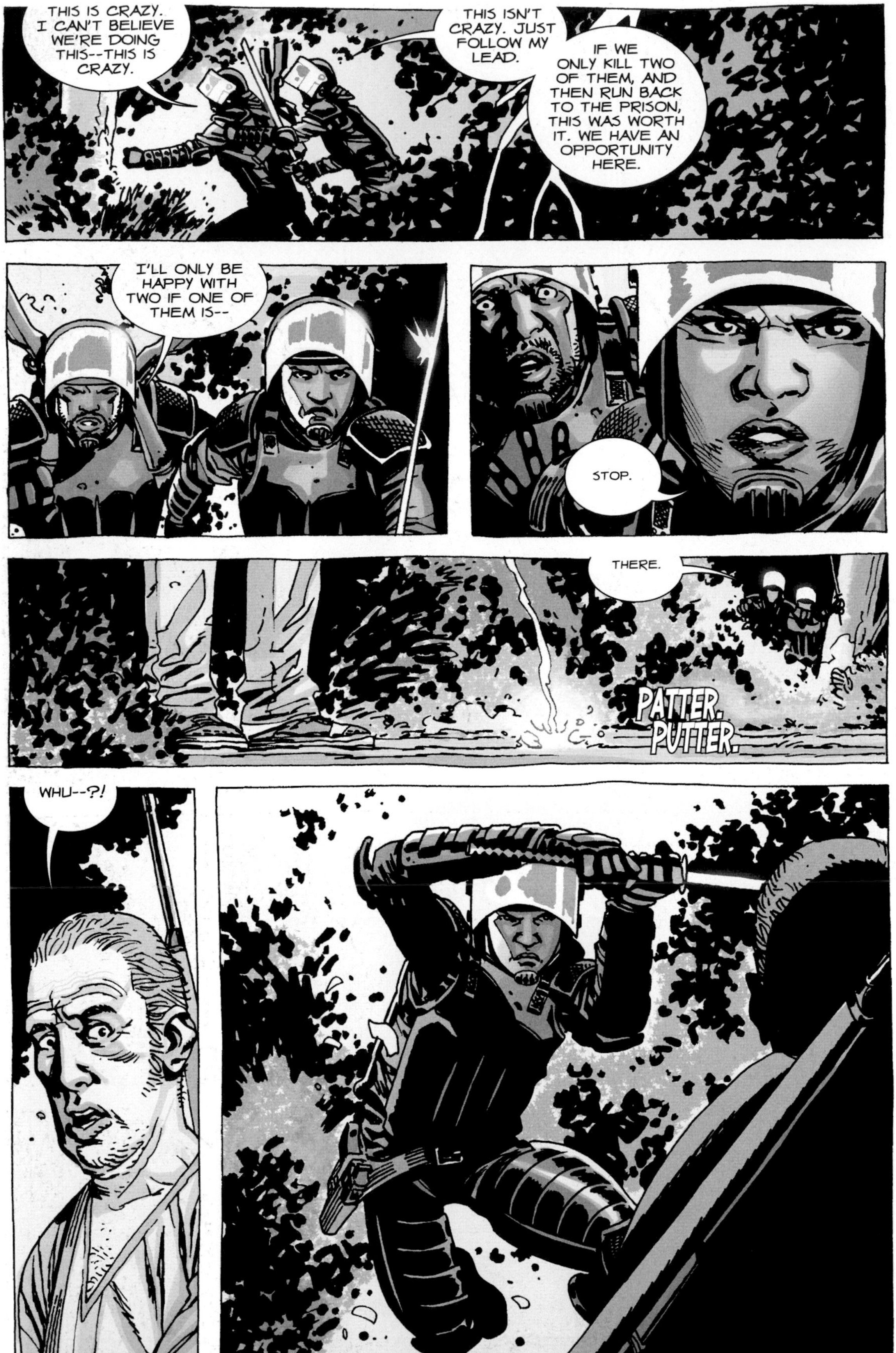
THIS IS CRAZY. I CAN'T BELIEVE WE'RE DOING THIS--THIS IS CRAZY.
THIS ISN'T CRAZY. JUST FOLLOW MY LEAD.
IF WE ONLY KILL TWO OF THEM, AND THEN RUN BACK TO THE PRISON, THIS WAS WORTH IT. WE HAVE AN OPPORTUNITY HERE.
I'LL ONLY BE HAPPY WITH TWO IF ONE OF THEM IS--
STOP.
THERE.
PATTER. PUTTER.
WHU--?!

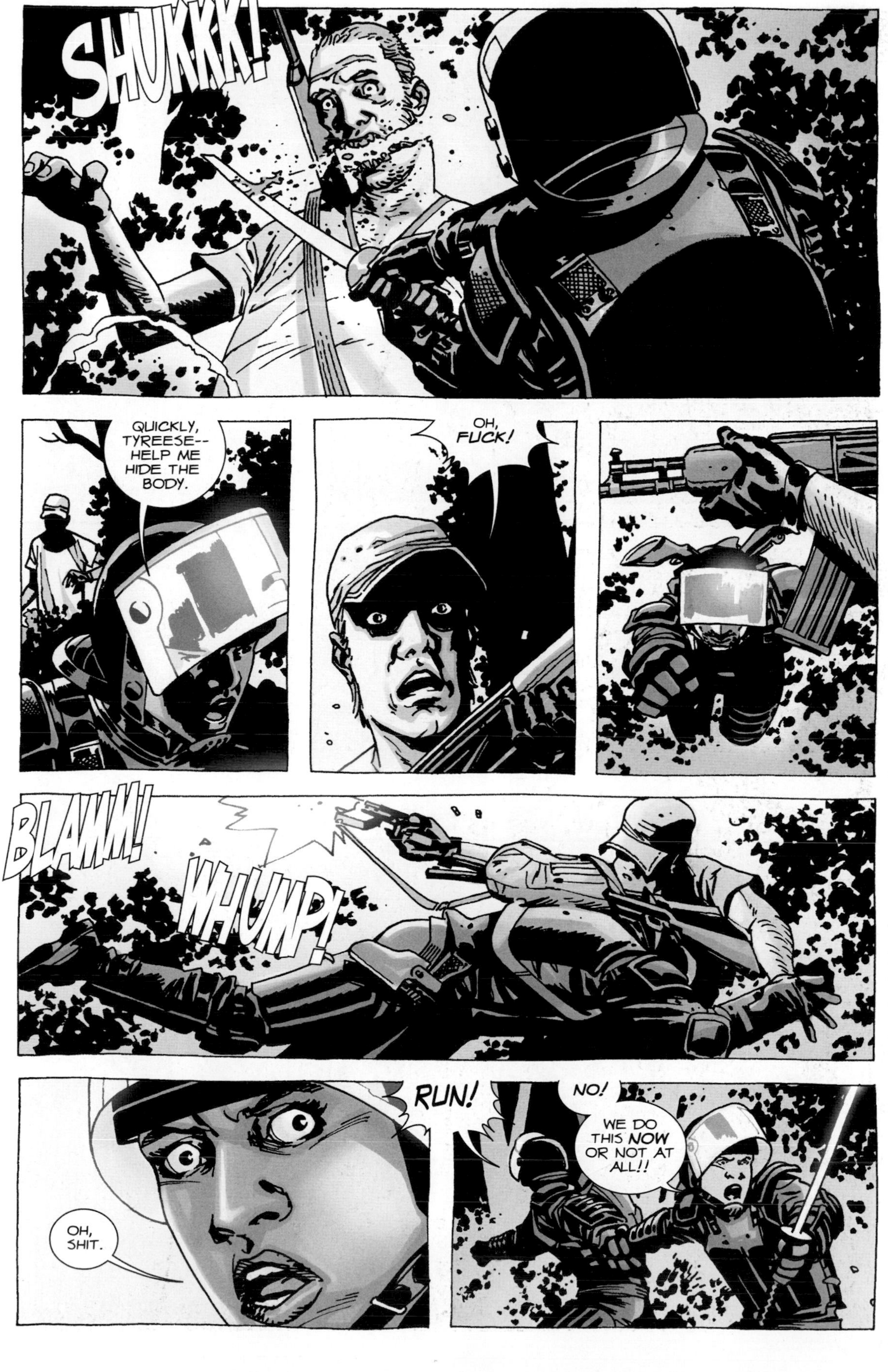
SHUKKK!
QUICKLY, TYREESE-- HELP ME HIDE THE BODY.
OH, FUCK!
BLAMM!
WHUMP!
OH, SHIT.
RUN!
NO!
WE DO THIS NOW OR NOT AT ALL!!

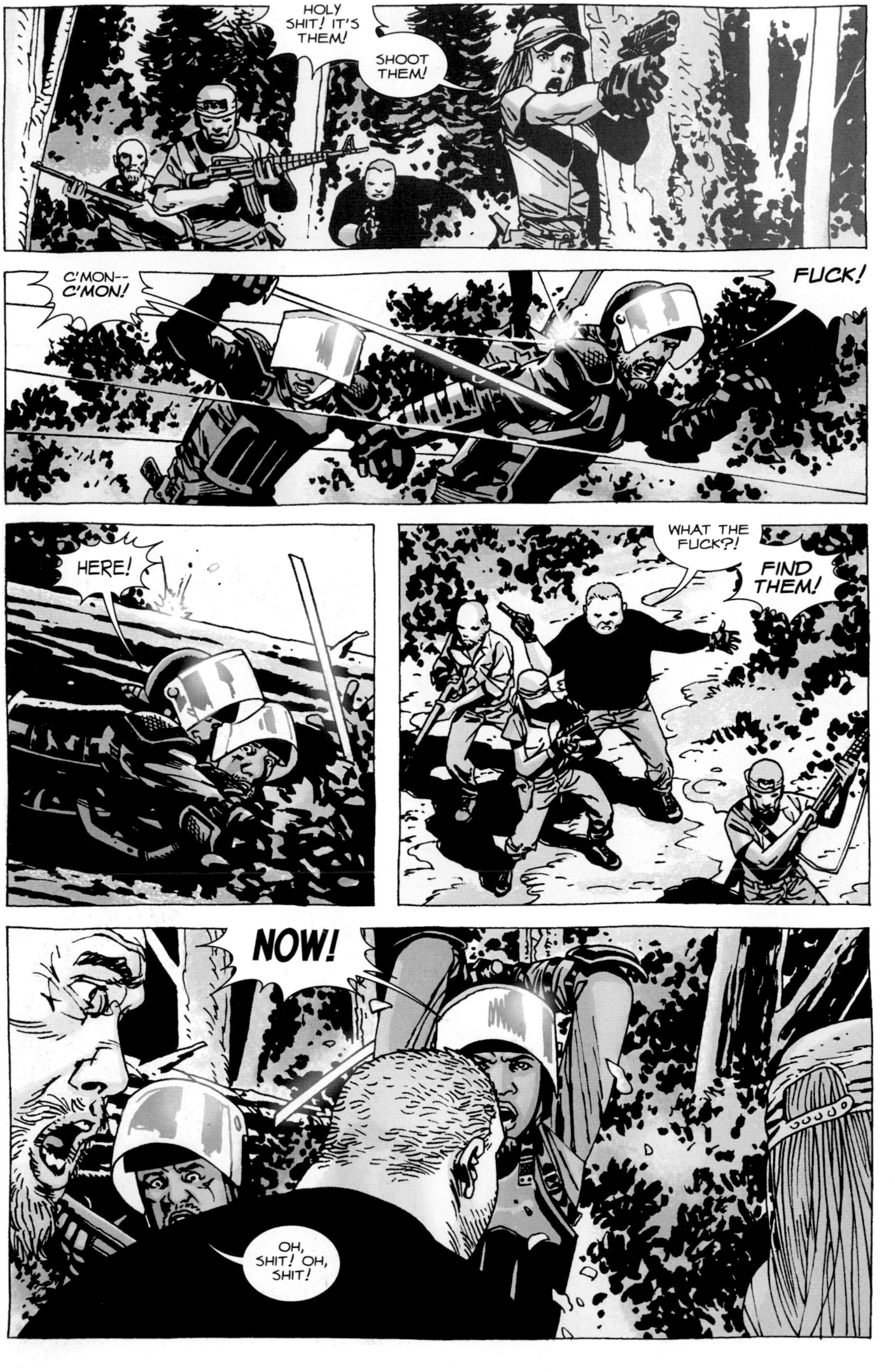
HOLY SHIT! IT'S THEM!
SHOOT THEM!
C'MON-- C'MON!
FUCK!
HERE!
WHAT THE FUCK?!
FIND THEM!
NOW!
OH, SHIT! OH, SHIT!

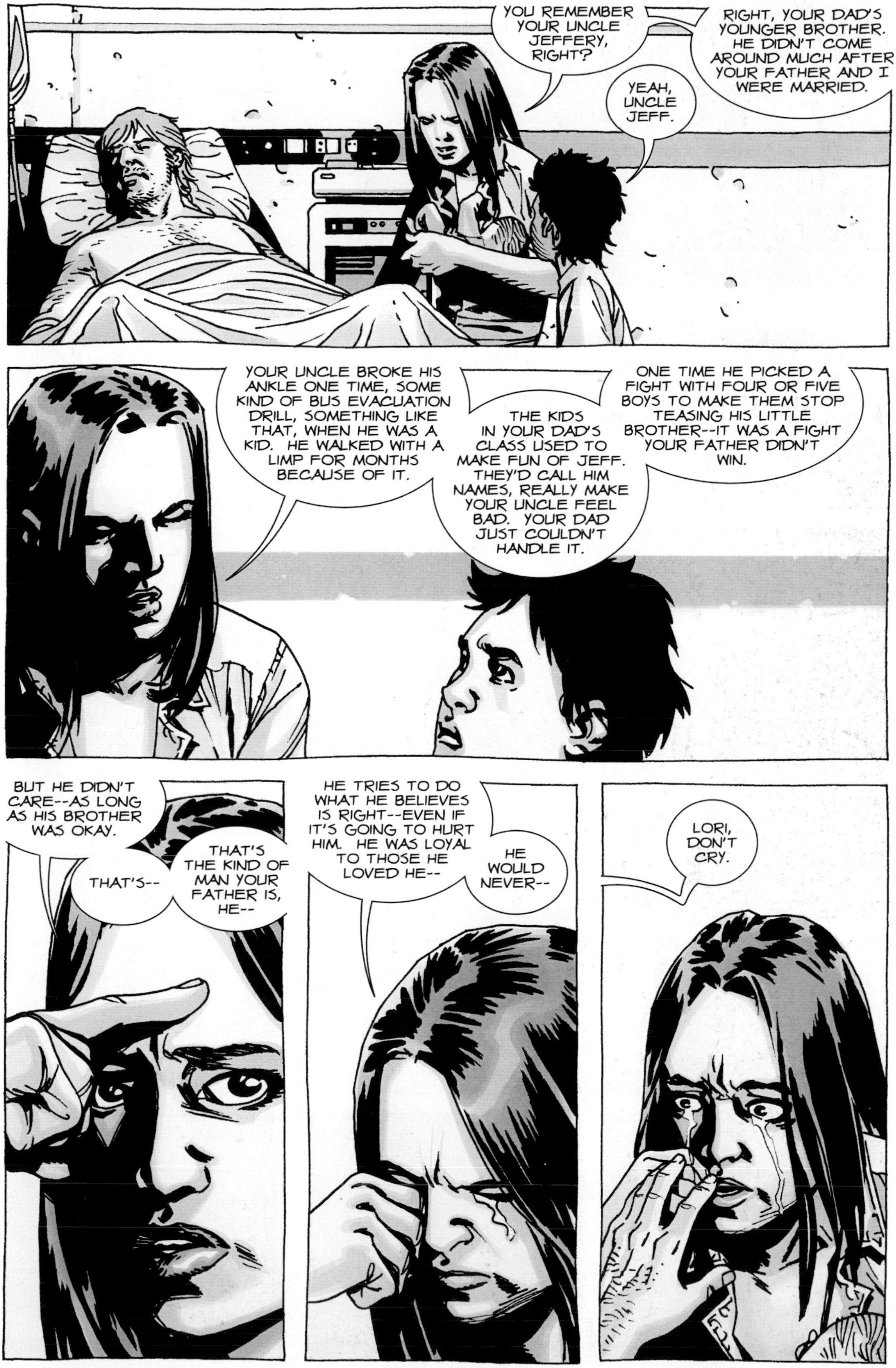
YOU REMEMBER YOUR UNCLE JEFFERY, RIGHT?
YEAH, UNCLE JEFF.
RIGHT, YOUR DAD'S YOUNGER BROTHER. HE DIDN'T COME AROUND MUCH AFTER YOUR FATHER AND I WERE MARRIED.
YOUR UNCLE BROKE HIS ANKLE ONE TIME, SOME KIND OF BUS EVACUATION DRILL, SOMETHING LIKE THAT, WHEN HE WAS A KID. HE WALKED WITH A LIMP FOR MONTHS BECAUSE OF IT.
THE KIDS IN YOUR DAD'S CLASS USED TO MAKE FUN OF JEFF. THEY'D CALL HIM NAMES, REALLY MAKE YOUR UNCLE FEEL BAD. YOUR DAD JUST COULDN'T HANDLE IT.
ONE TIME HE PICKED A FIGHT WITH FOUR OR FIVE BOYS TO MAKE THEM STOP TEASING HIS LITTLE BROTHER--IT WAS A FIGHT YOUR FATHER DIDN'T WIN.
BUT HE DIDN'T CARE--AS LONG AS HIS BROTHER WAS OKAY.
THAT'S--
THAT'S THE KIND OF MAN YOUR FATHER IS, HE--
HE TRIES TO DO WHAT HE BELIEVES IS RIGHT--EVEN IF IT'S GOING TO HURT HIM. HE WAS LOYAL TO THOSE HE LOVED HE--
HE WOULD NEVER--
LORI, DON'T CRY.

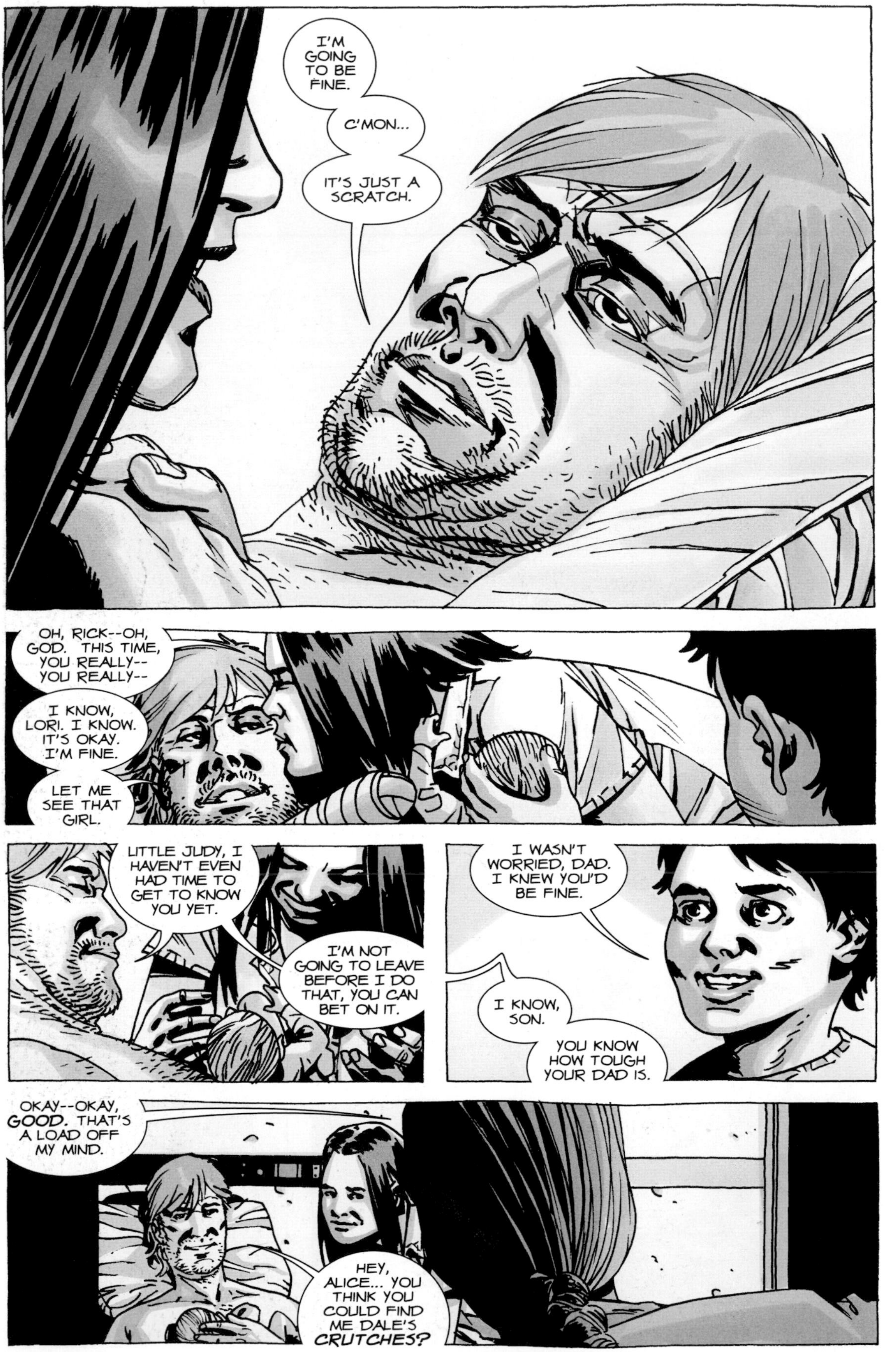
I'M GOING TO BE FINE.
C'MON...
IT'S JUST A SCRATCH.
OH, RICK--OH, GOD. THIS TIME, YOU REALLY-- YOU REALLY--
I KNOW, LORI. I KNOW. IT'S OKAY. I'M FINE.
LET ME SEE THAT GIRL.
LITTLE JUDY, I HAVEN'T EVEN HAD TIME TO GET TO KNOW YOU YET.
I'M NOT GOING TO LEAVE BEFORE I DO THAT, YOU CAN BET ON IT.
I WASN'T WORRIED, DAD. I KNEW YOU'D BE FINE.
I KNOW, SON.
YOU KNOW HOW TOUGH YOUR DAD IS.
OKAY--OKAY, **GOOD.** THAT'S A LOAD OFF MY MIND.
HEY, ALICE... YOU THINK YOU COULD FIND ME DALE'S ***CRUTCHES?***

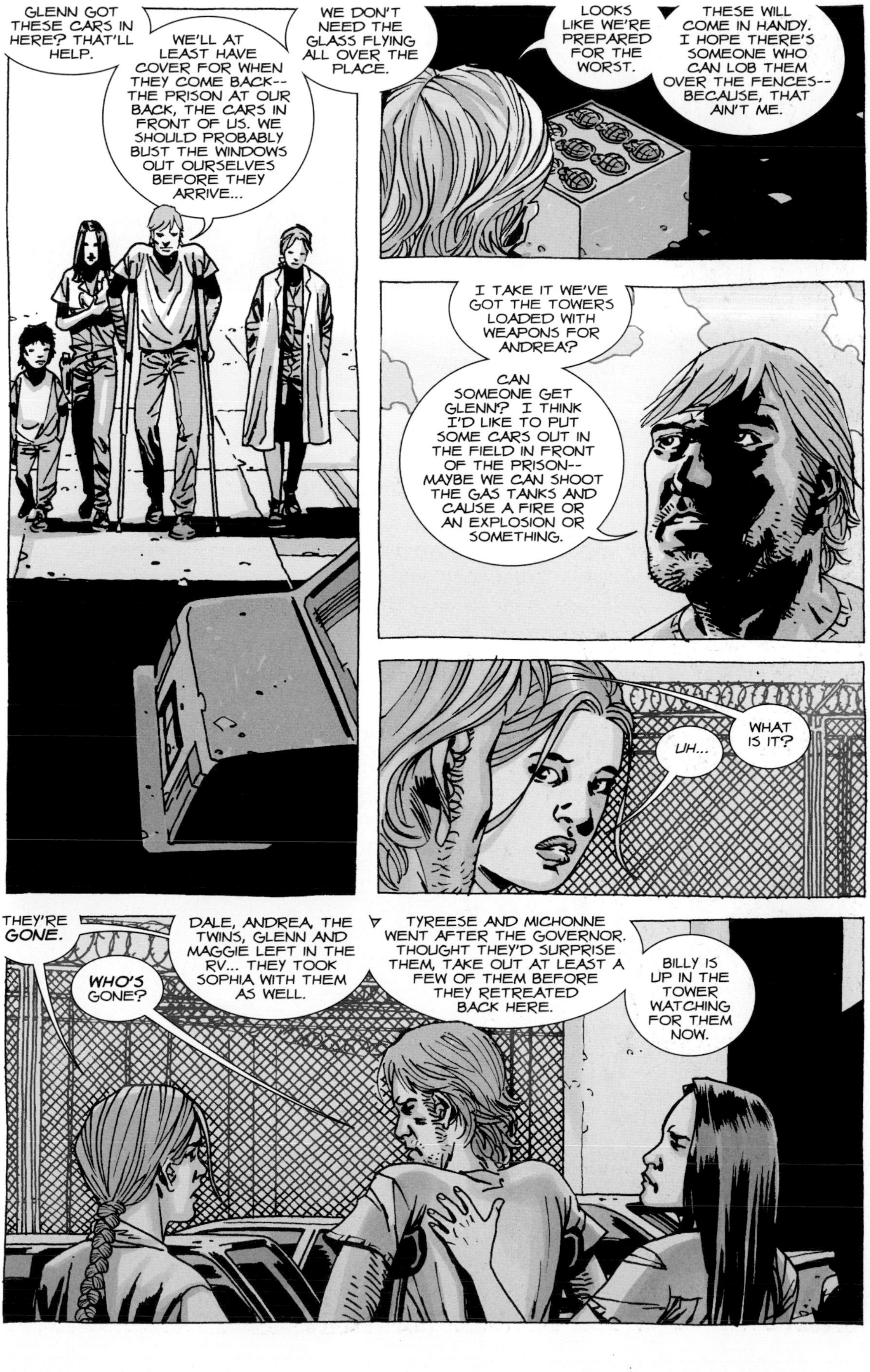
GLENN GOT THESE CARS IN HERE? THAT'LL HELP.
WE'LL AT LEAST HAVE COVER FOR WHEN THEY COME BACK-- THE PRISON AT OUR BACK, THE CARS IN FRONT OF US. WE SHOULD PROBABLY BUST THE WINDOWS OUT OURSELVES BEFORE THEY ARRIVE...
WE DON'T NEED THE GLASS FLYING ALL OVER THE PLACE.
LOOKS LIKE WE'RE PREPARED FOR THE WORST.
THESE WILL COME IN HANDY. I HOPE THERE'S SOMEONE WHO CAN LOB THEM OVER THE FENCES-- BECAUSE, THAT AIN'T ME.
I TAKE IT WE'VE GOT THE TOWERS LOADED WITH WEAPONS FOR ANDREA?
CAN SOMEONE GET GLENN? I THINK I'D LIKE TO PUT SOME CARS OUT IN THE FIELD IN FRONT OF THE PRISON-- MAYBE WE CAN SHOOT THE GAS TANKS AND CAUSE A FIRE OR AN EXPLOSION OR SOMETHING.
WHAT IS IT?
UH...
THEY'RE GONE.
WHO'S GONE?
DALE, ANDREA, THE TWINS, GLENN AND MAGGIE LEFT IN THE RV... THEY TOOK SOPHIA WITH THEM AS WELL.
TYREESE AND MICHONNE WENT AFTER THE GOVERNOR. THOUGHT THEY'D SURPRISE THEM, TAKE OUT AT LEAST A FEW OF THEM BEFORE THEY RETREATED BACK HERE.
BILLY IS UP IN THE TOWER WATCHING FOR THEM NOW.

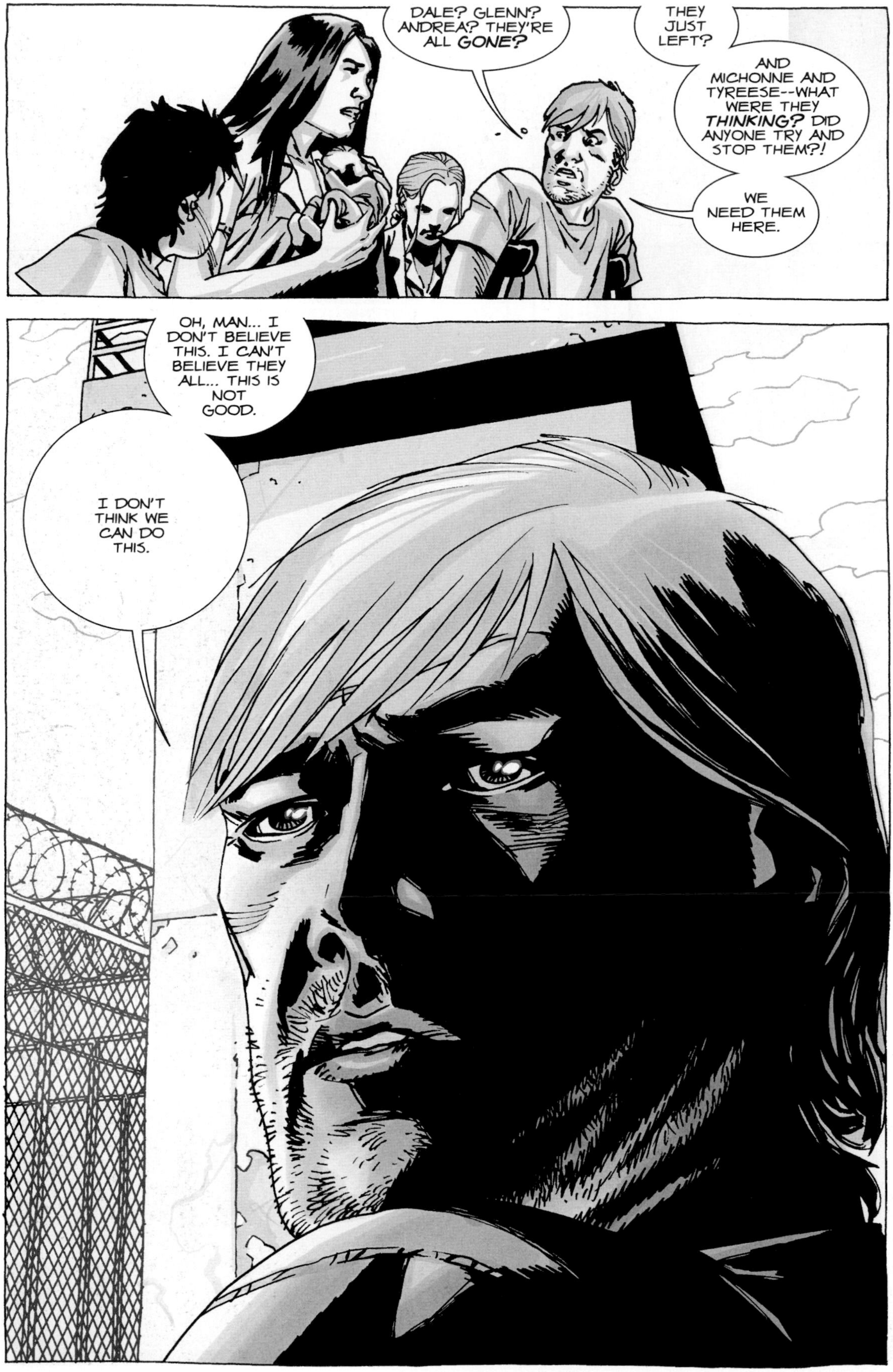
DALE? GLENN? ANDREA? THEY'RE ALL GONE?
THEY JUST LEFT?
AND MICHONNE AND TYREESE--WHAT WERE THEY THINKING? DID ANYONE TRY AND STOP THEM?!
WE NEED THEM HERE.
OH, MAN... I DON'T BELIEVE THIS. I CAN'T BELIEVE THEY ALL... THIS IS NOT GOOD.
I DON'T THINK WE CAN DO THIS.

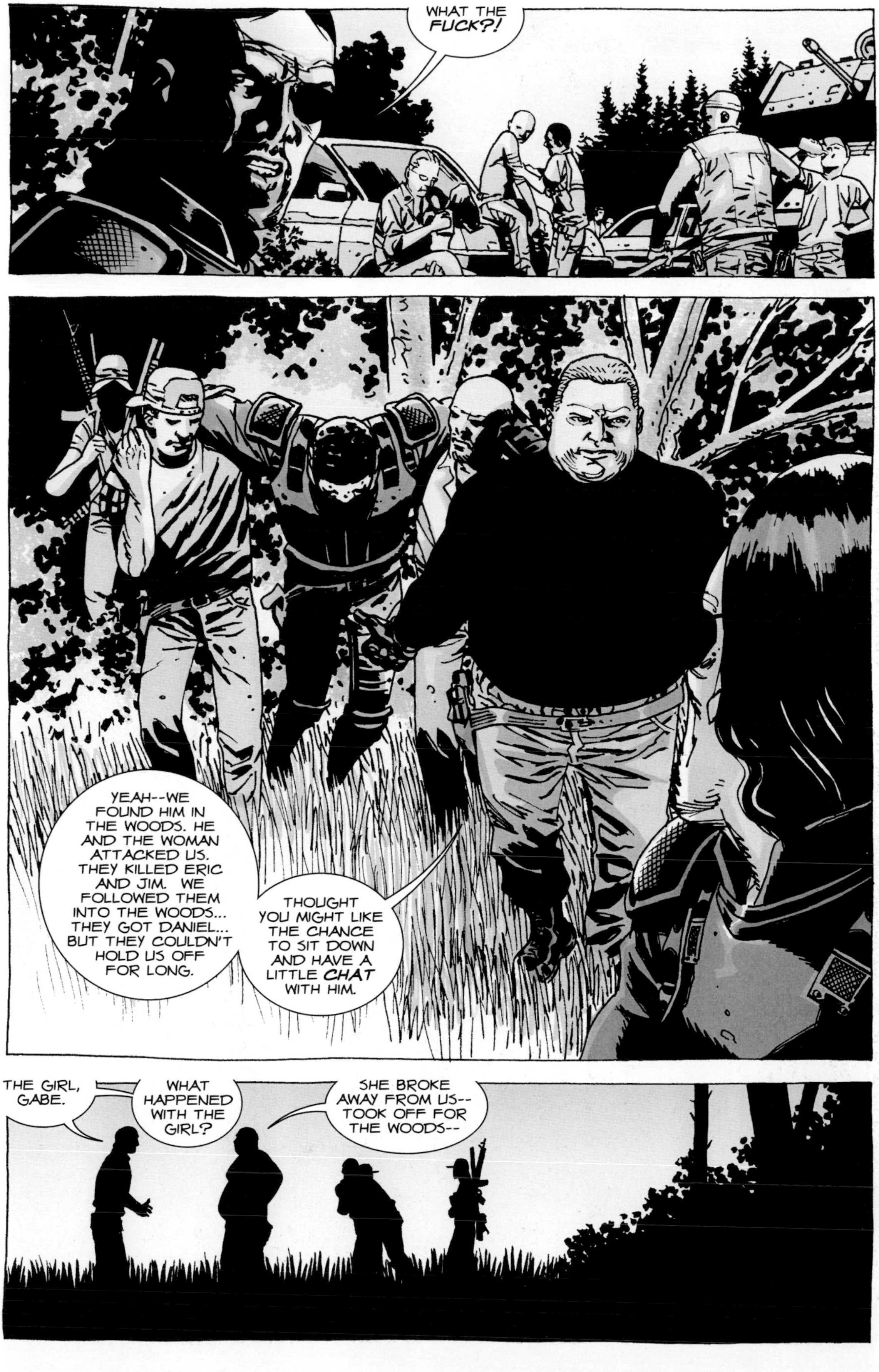
WHAT THE FUCK?!
YEAH--WE FOUND HIM IN THE WOODS. HE AND THE WOMAN ATTACKED US. THEY KILLED ERIC AND JIM. WE FOLLOWED THEM INTO THE WOODS... THEY GOT DANIEL... BUT THEY COULDN'T HOLD US OFF FOR LONG.
THOUGHT YOU MIGHT LIKE THE CHANCE TO SIT DOWN AND HAVE A LITTLE CHAT WITH HIM.
THE GIRL, GABE.
WHAT HAPPENED WITH THE GIRL?
SHE BROKE AWAY FROM US-- TOOK OFF FOR THE WOODS--

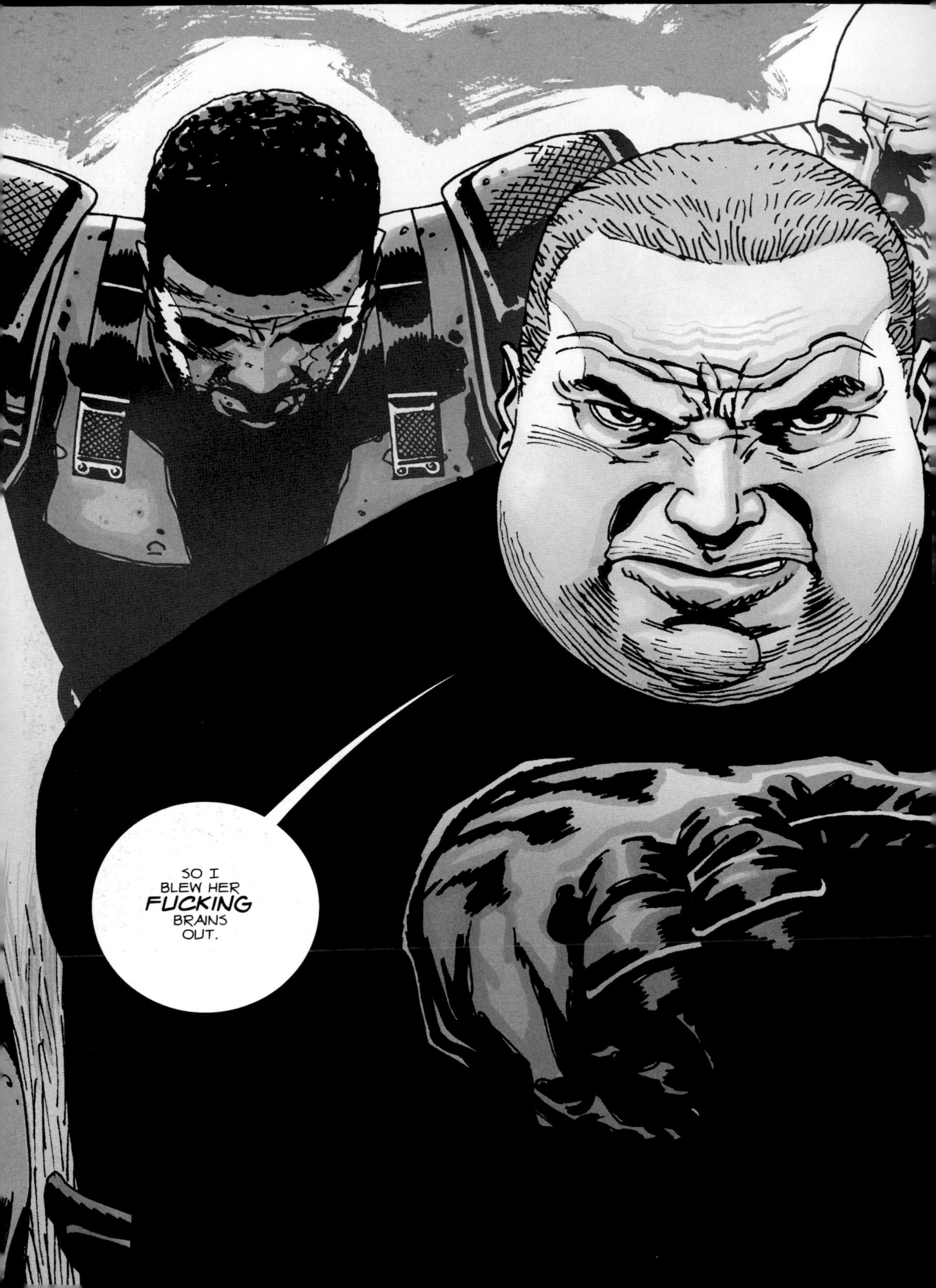
SO I BLEW HER FUCKING BRAINS OUT.

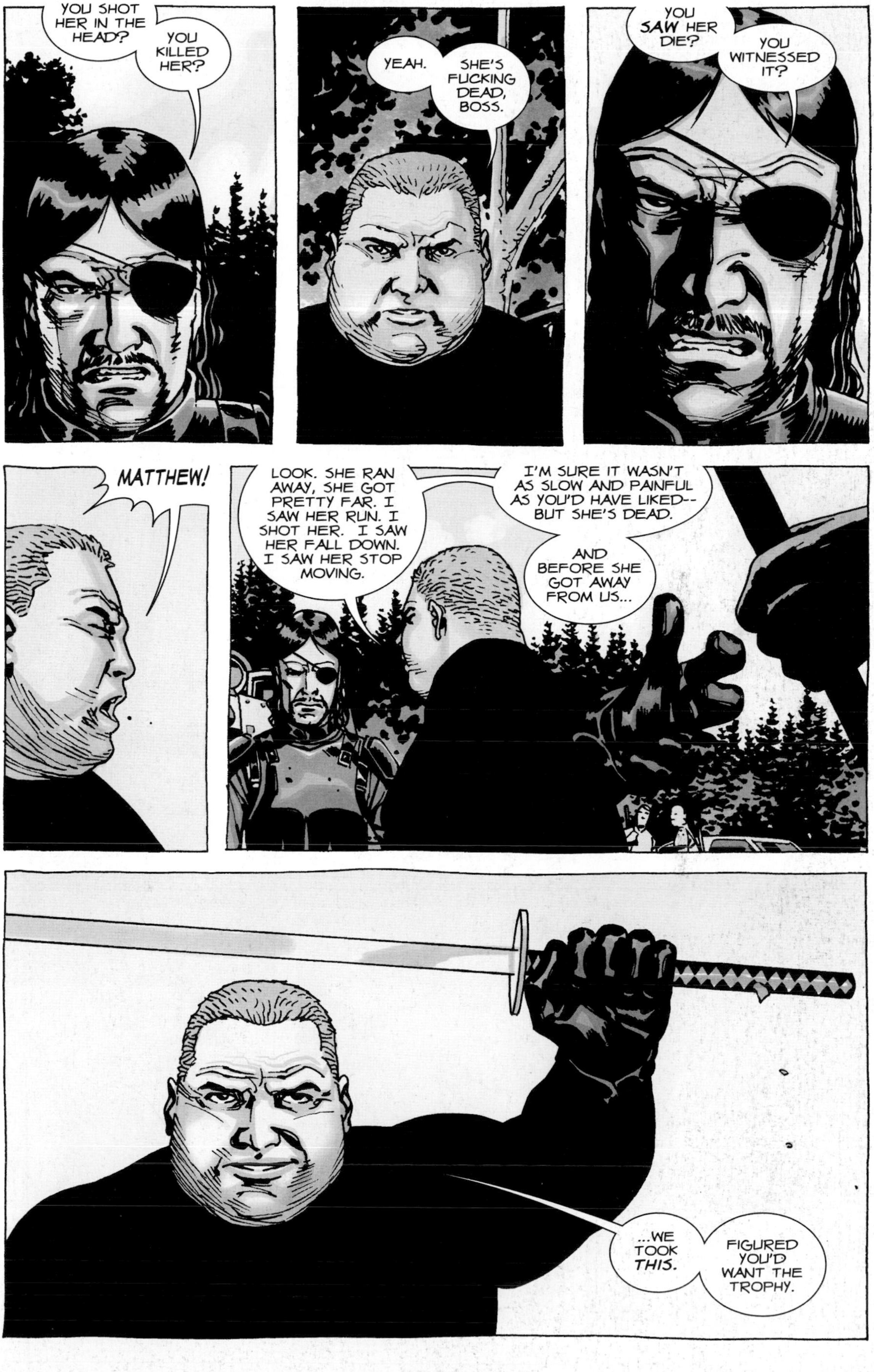
YOU SHOT HER IN THE HEAD?
YOU KILLED HER?
YEAH.
SHE'S FUCKING DEAD, BOSS.
YOU SAW HER DIE?
YOU WITNESSED IT?
MATTHEW!
LOOK. SHE RAN AWAY, SHE GOT PRETTY FAR. I SAW HER RUN. I SHOT HER. I SAW HER FALL DOWN. I SAW HER STOP MOVING.
I'M SURE IT WASN'T AS SLOW AND PAINFUL AS YOU'D HAVE LIKED-- BUT SHE'S DEAD.
AND BEFORE SHE GOT AWAY FROM US...
...WE TOOK THIS.
FIGURED YOU'D WANT THE TROPHY.

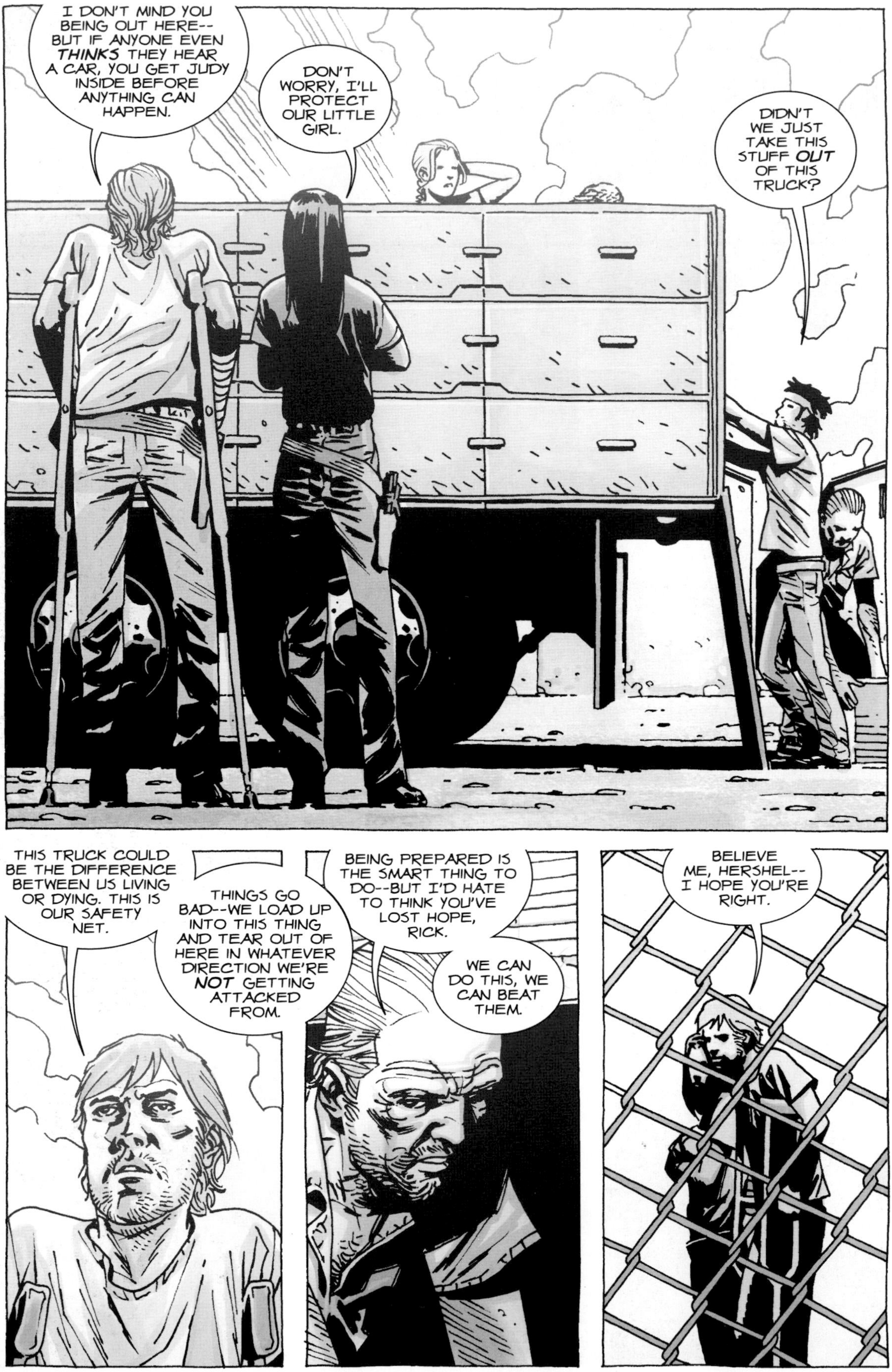
I DON'T MIND YOU BEING OUT HERE-- BUT IF ANYONE EVEN THINKS THEY HEAR A CAR, YOU GET JUDY INSIDE BEFORE ANYTHING CAN HAPPEN.
DON'T WORRY, I'LL PROTECT OUR LITTLE GIRL.
DIDN'T WE JUST TAKE THIS STUFF OUT OF THIS TRUCK?
THIS TRUCK COULD BE THE DIFFERENCE BETWEEN US LIVING OR DYING. THIS IS OUR SAFETY NET.
THINGS GO BAD--WE LOAD UP INTO THIS THING AND TEAR OUT OF HERE IN WHATEVER DIRECTION WE'RE NOT GETTING ATTACKED FROM.
BEING PREPARED IS THE SMART THING TO DO--BUT I'D HATE TO THINK YOU'VE LOST HOPE, RICK.
WE CAN DO THIS, WE CAN BEAT THEM.
BELIEVE ME, HERSHEL-- I HOPE YOU'RE RIGHT.

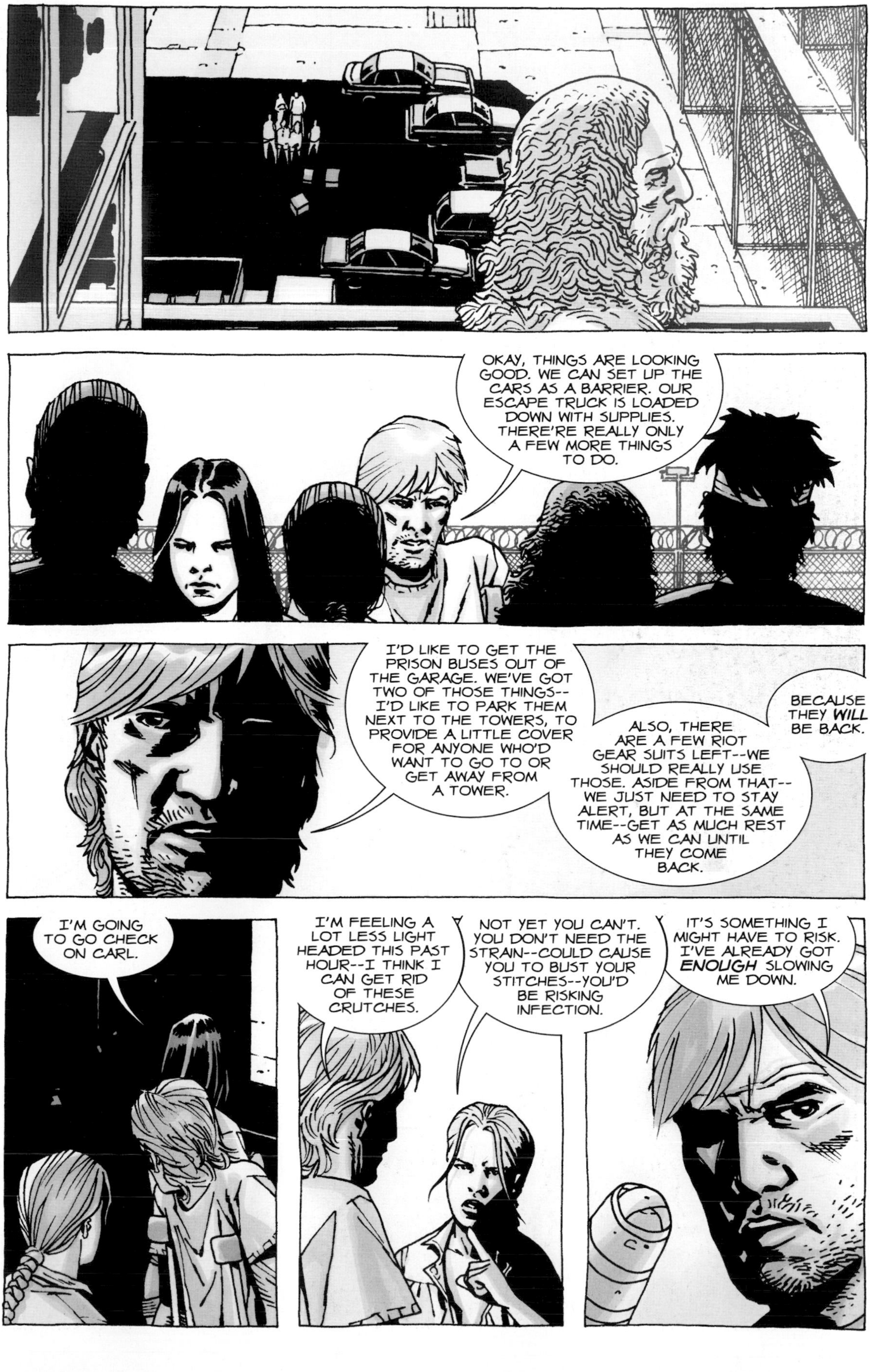
OKAY, THINGS ARE LOOKING GOOD. WE CAN SET UP THE CARS AS A BARRIER. OUR ESCAPE TRUCK IS LOADED DOWN WITH SUPPLIES. THERE'RE REALLY ONLY A FEW MORE THINGS TO DO.
I'D LIKE TO GET THE PRISON BUSES OUT OF THE GARAGE. WE'VE GOT TWO OF THOSE THINGS-- I'D LIKE TO PARK THEM NEXT TO THE TOWERS, TO PROVIDE A LITTLE COVER FOR ANYONE WHO'D WANT TO GO TO OR GET AWAY FROM A TOWER.
ALSO, THERE ARE A FEW RIOT GEAR SUITS LEFT--WE SHOULD REALLY USE THOSE. ASIDE FROM THAT-- WE JUST NEED TO STAY ALERT, BUT AT THE SAME TIME--GET AS MUCH REST AS WE CAN UNTIL THEY COME BACK.
BECAUSE THEY *WILL* BE BACK.
I'M GOING TO GO CHECK ON CARL.
I'M FEELING A LOT LESS LIGHT HEADED THIS PAST HOUR--I THINK I CAN GET RID OF THESE CRUTCHES.
NOT YET YOU CAN'T. YOU DON'T NEED THE STRAIN--COULD CAUSE YOU TO BUST YOUR STITCHES--YOU'D BE RISKING INFECTION.
IT'S SOMETHING I MIGHT HAVE TO RISK. I'VE ALREADY GOT *ENOUGH* SLOWING ME DOWN.

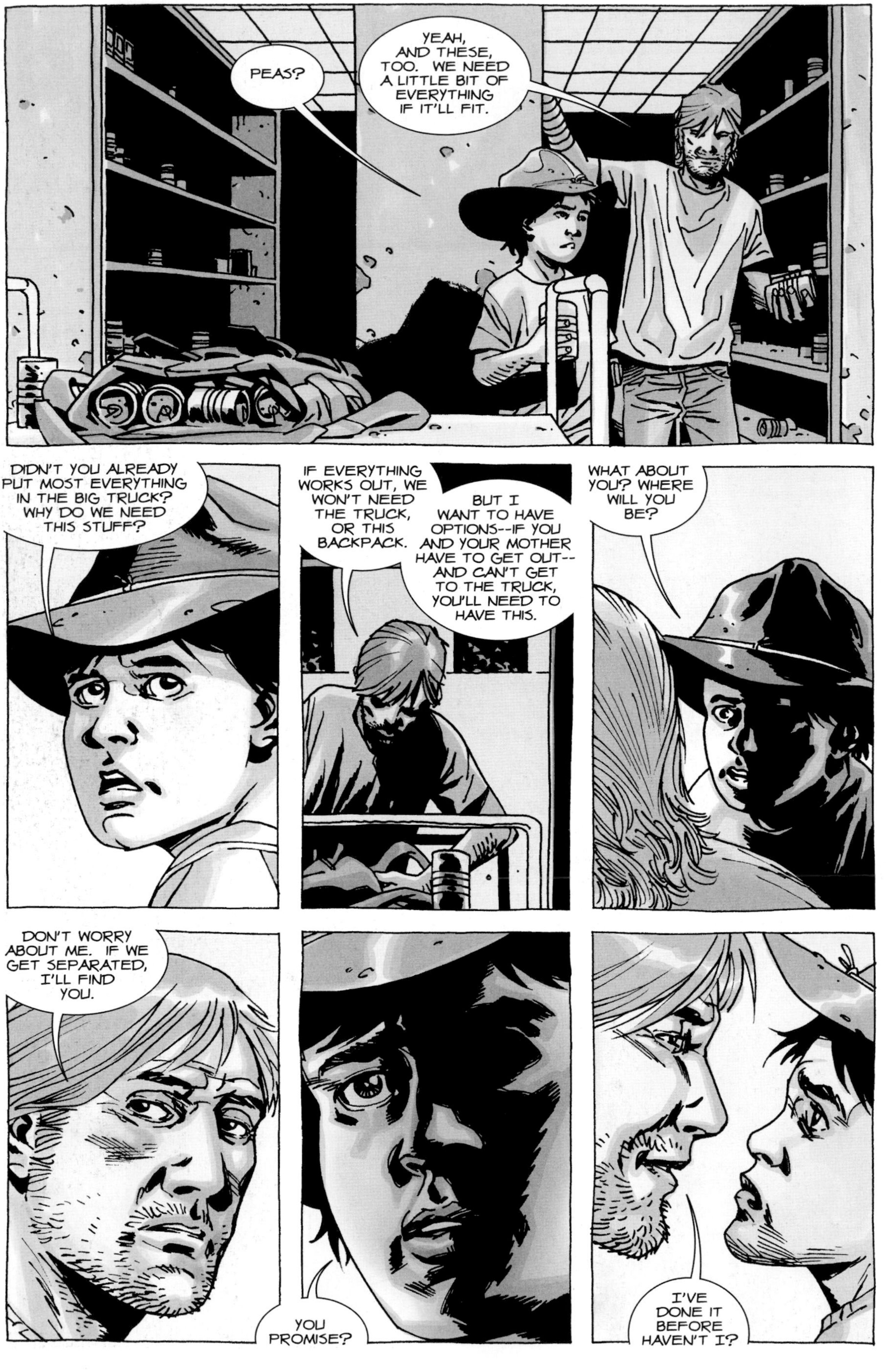
PEAS?
YEAH, AND THESE, TOO. WE NEED A LITTLE BIT OF EVERYTHING IF IT'LL FIT.
DIDN'T YOU ALREADY PUT MOST EVERYTHING IN THE BIG TRUCK? WHY DO WE NEED THIS STUFF?
IF EVERYTHING WORKS OUT, WE WON'T NEED THE TRUCK, OR THIS BACKPACK.
BUT I WANT TO HAVE OPTIONS--IF YOU AND YOUR MOTHER HAVE TO GET OUT--AND CAN'T GET TO THE TRUCK, YOU'LL NEED TO HAVE THIS.
WHAT ABOUT YOU? WHERE WILL YOU BE?
DON'T WORRY ABOUT ME. IF WE GET SEPARATED, I'LL FIND YOU.
YOU PROMISE?
I'VE DONE IT BEFORE HAVEN'T I?

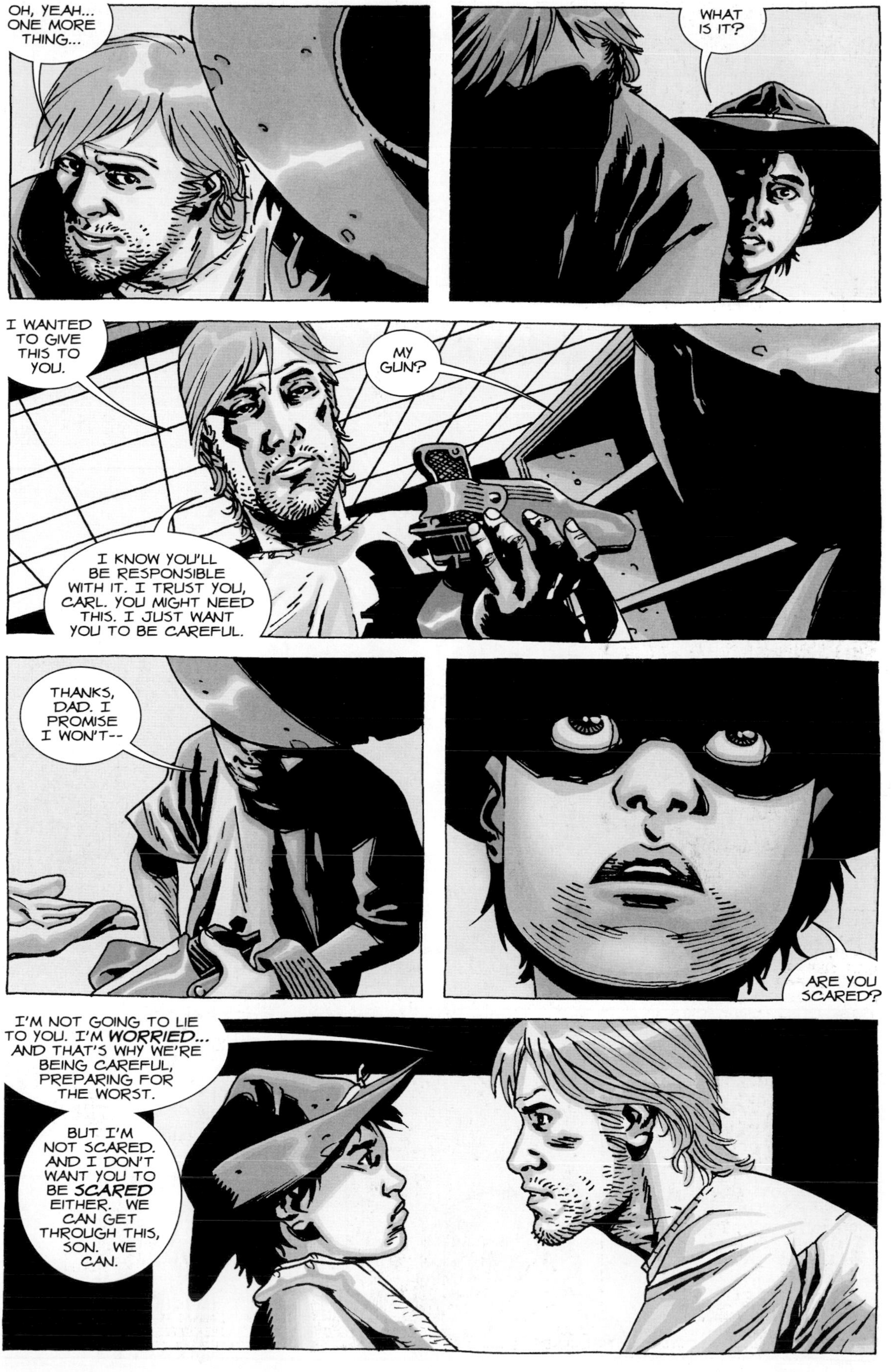
OH, YEAH... ONE MORE THING...
WHAT IS IT?
I WANTED TO GIVE THIS TO YOU.
MY GUN?
I KNOW YOU'LL BE RESPONSIBLE WITH IT. I TRUST YOU, CARL. YOU MIGHT NEED THIS. I JUST WANT YOU TO BE CAREFUL.
THANKS, DAD. I PROMISE I WON'T--
ARE YOU SCARED?
I'M NOT GOING TO LIE TO YOU. I'M WORRIED... AND THAT'S WHY WE'RE BEING CAREFUL, PREPARING FOR THE WORST.
BUT I'M NOT SCARED. AND I DON'T WANT YOU TO BE SCARED EITHER. WE CAN GET THROUGH THIS, SON. WE CAN.

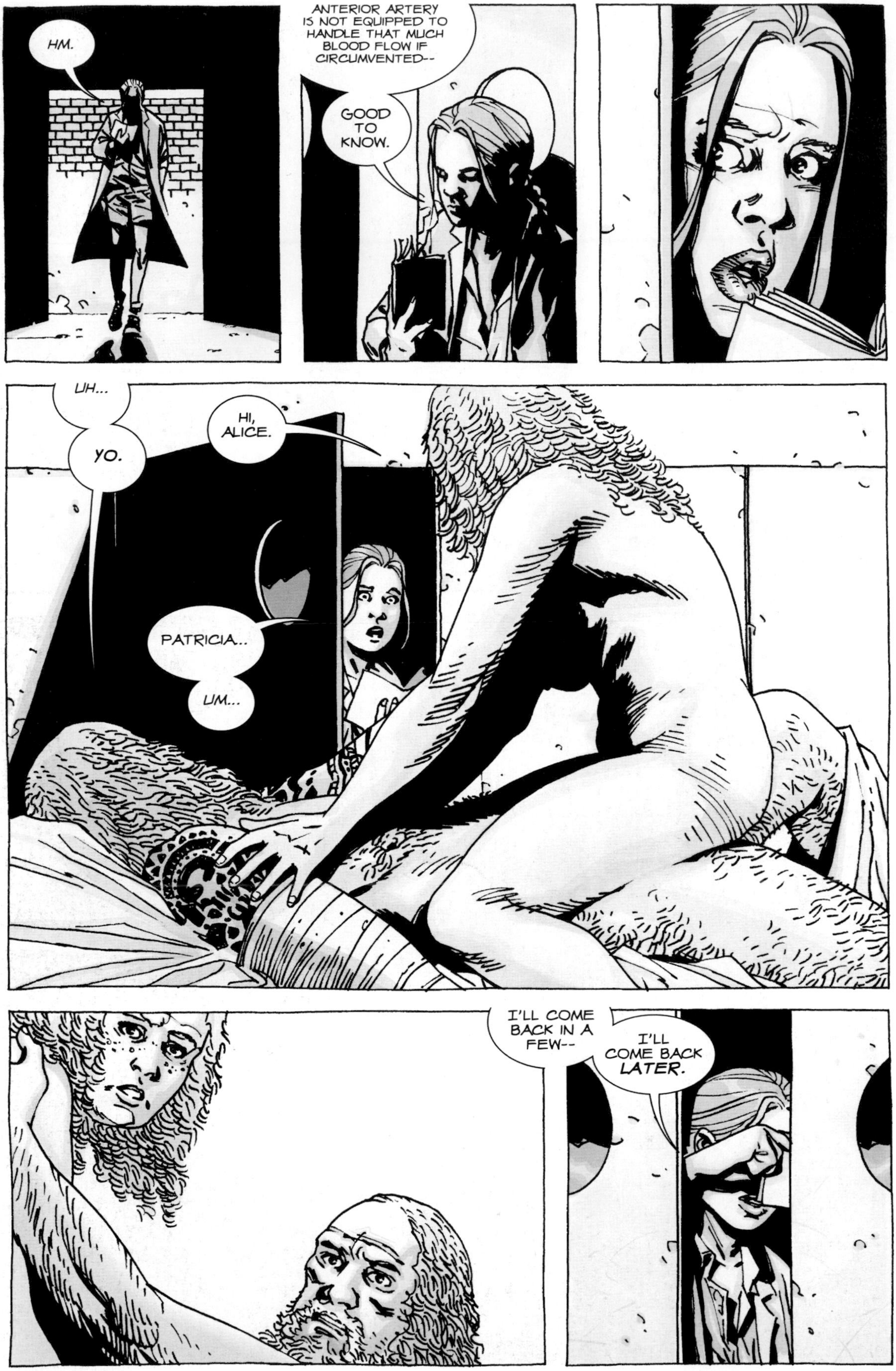
HM.
ANTERIOR ARTERY IS NOT EQUIPPED TO HANDLE THAT MUCH BLOOD FLOW IF CIRCUMVENTED--
GOOD TO KNOW.
UH...
YO.
HI, ALICE.
PATRICIA..
UM...
I'LL COME BACK IN A FEW--
I'LL COME BACK LATER.

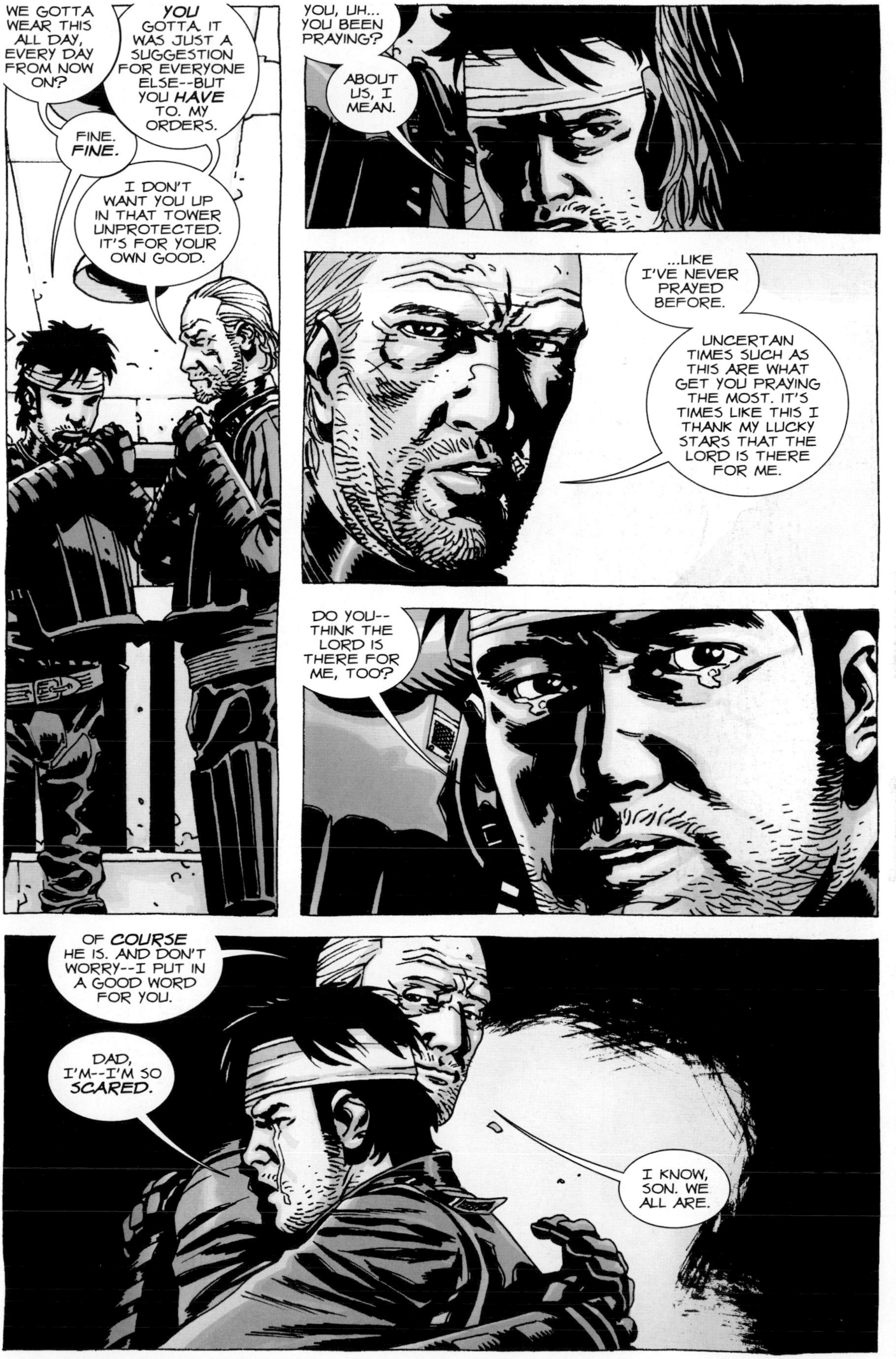
WE GOTTA WEAR THIS ALL DAY, EVERY DAY FROM NOW ON?
YOU GOTTA. IT WAS JUST A SUGGESTION FOR EVERYONE ELSE--BUT YOU *HAVE* TO. MY ORDERS.
FINE. *FINE.*
I DON'T WANT YOU UP IN THAT TOWER UNPROTECTED. IT'S FOR YOUR OWN GOOD.
YOU, UH... YOU BEEN PRAYING?
ABOUT US, I MEAN.
...LIKE I'VE NEVER PRAYED BEFORE.
UNCERTAIN TIMES SUCH AS THIS ARE WHAT GET YOU PRAYING THE MOST. IT'S TIMES LIKE THIS I THANK MY LUCKY STARS THAT THE LORD IS THERE FOR ME.
DO YOU--THINK THE LORD IS THERE FOR ME, TOO?
OF *COURSE* HE IS. AND DON'T WORRY--I PUT IN A GOOD WORD FOR YOU.
DAD, I'M--I'M SO *SCARED.*
I KNOW, SON. WE ALL ARE.

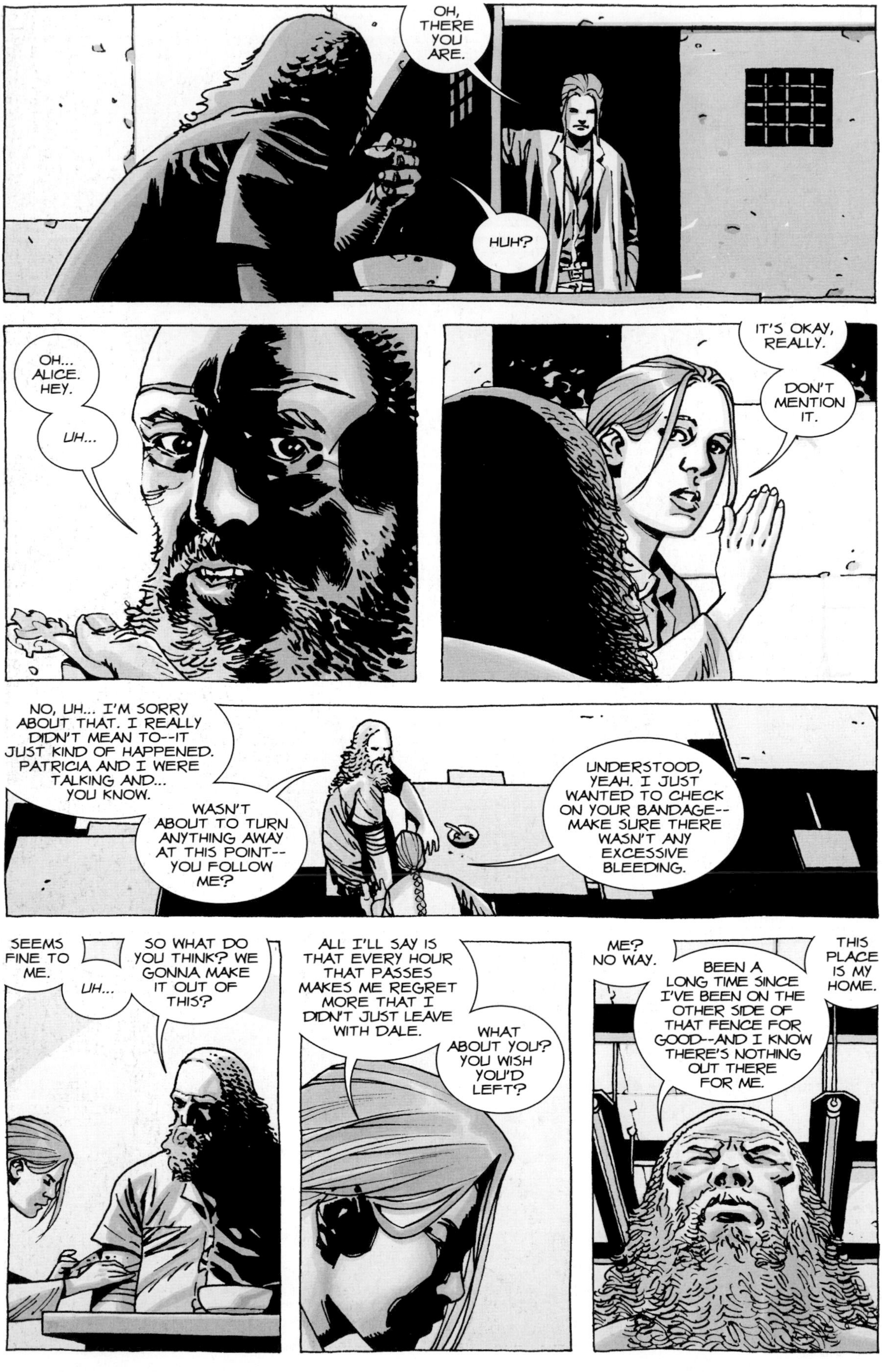
OH, THERE YOU ARE.
HUH?
OH... ALICE. HEY.
UH...
IT'S OKAY, REALLY.
DON'T MENTION IT.
NO, UH... I'M SORRY ABOUT THAT. I REALLY DIDN'T MEAN TO--IT JUST KIND OF HAPPENED. PATRICIA AND I WERE TALKING AND... YOU KNOW.
WASN'T ABOUT TO TURN ANYTHING AWAY AT THIS POINT-- YOU FOLLOW ME?
UNDERSTOOD, YEAH. I JUST WANTED TO CHECK ON YOUR BANDAGE-- MAKE SURE THERE WASN'T ANY EXCESSIVE BLEEDING.
SEEMS FINE TO ME.
UH...
SO WHAT DO YOU THINK? WE GONNA MAKE IT OUT OF THIS?
ALL I'LL SAY IS THAT EVERY HOUR THAT PASSES MAKES ME REGRET MORE THAT I DIDN'T JUST LEAVE WITH DALE.
WHAT ABOUT YOU? YOU WISH YOU'D LEFT?
ME? NO WAY.
THIS PLACE IS MY HOME.
BEEN A LONG TIME SINCE I'VE BEEN ON THE OTHER SIDE OF THAT FENCE FOR GOOD--AND I KNOW THERE'S NOTHING OUT THERE FOR ME.

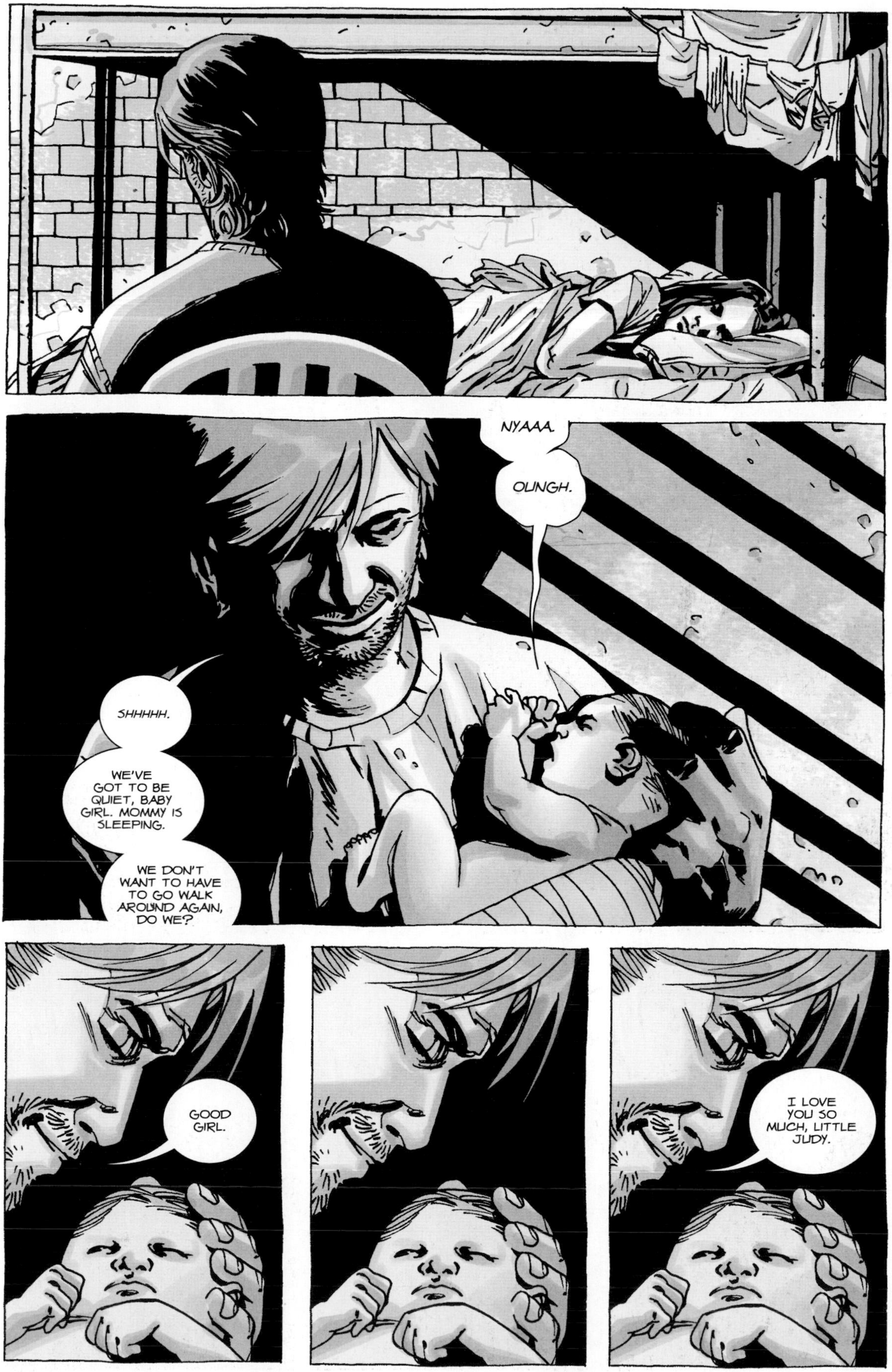
NYAAA.
OUNGH.
SHHHHH.
WE'VE GOT TO BE QUIET, BABY GIRL. MOMMY IS SLEEPING.
WE DON'T WANT TO HAVE TO GO WALK AROUND AGAIN, DO WE?
GOOD GIRL.
I LOVE YOU SO MUCH, LITTLE JUDY.

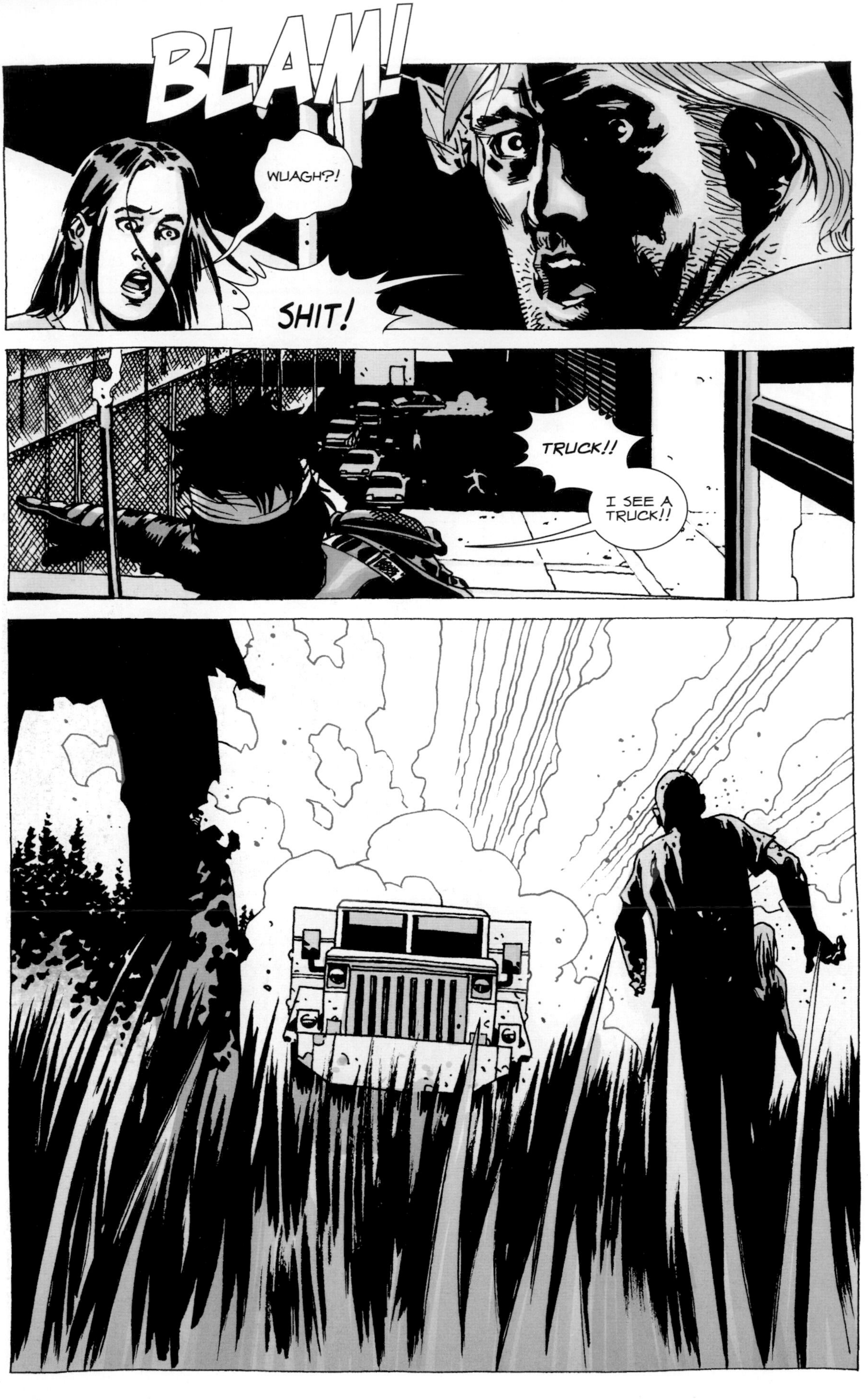
BLAM!
WUAGH?!
SHIT!
TRUCK!!
I SEE A TRUCK!!

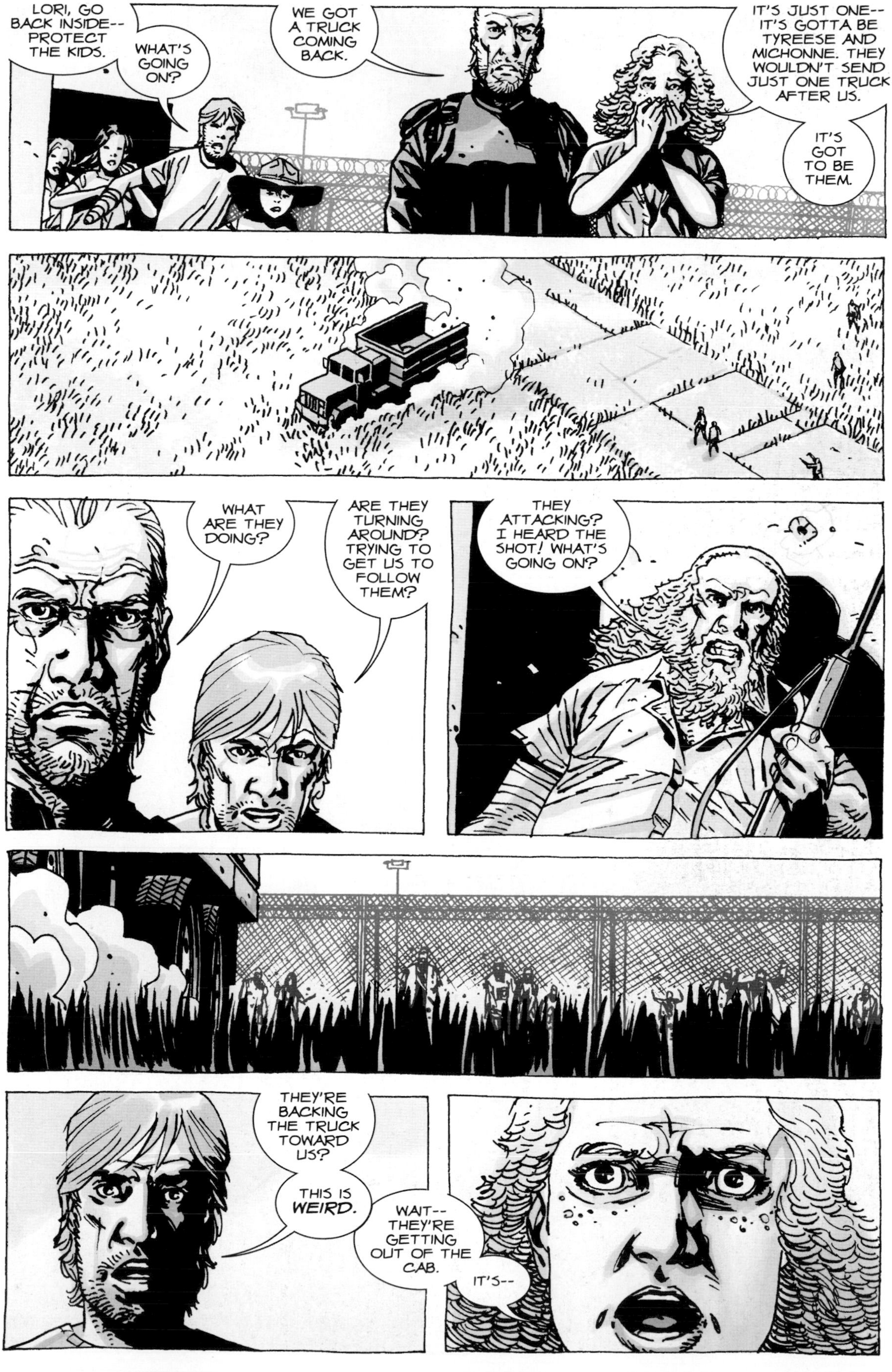
LORI, GO BACK INSIDE-- PROTECT THE KIDS.
WHAT'S GOING ON?
WE GOT A TRUCK COMING BACK.
IT'S JUST ONE-- IT'S GOTTA BE TYREESE AND MICHONNE. THEY WOULDN'T SEND JUST ONE TRUCK AFTER US.
IT'S GOT TO BE THEM.
WHAT ARE THEY DOING?
ARE THEY TURNING AROUND? TRYING TO GET US TO FOLLOW THEM?
THEY ATTACKING? I HEARD THE SHOT! WHAT'S GOING ON?
THEY'RE BACKING THE TRUCK TOWARD US?
THIS IS WEIRD.
WAIT-- THEY'RE GETTING OUT OF THE CAB.
IT'S--

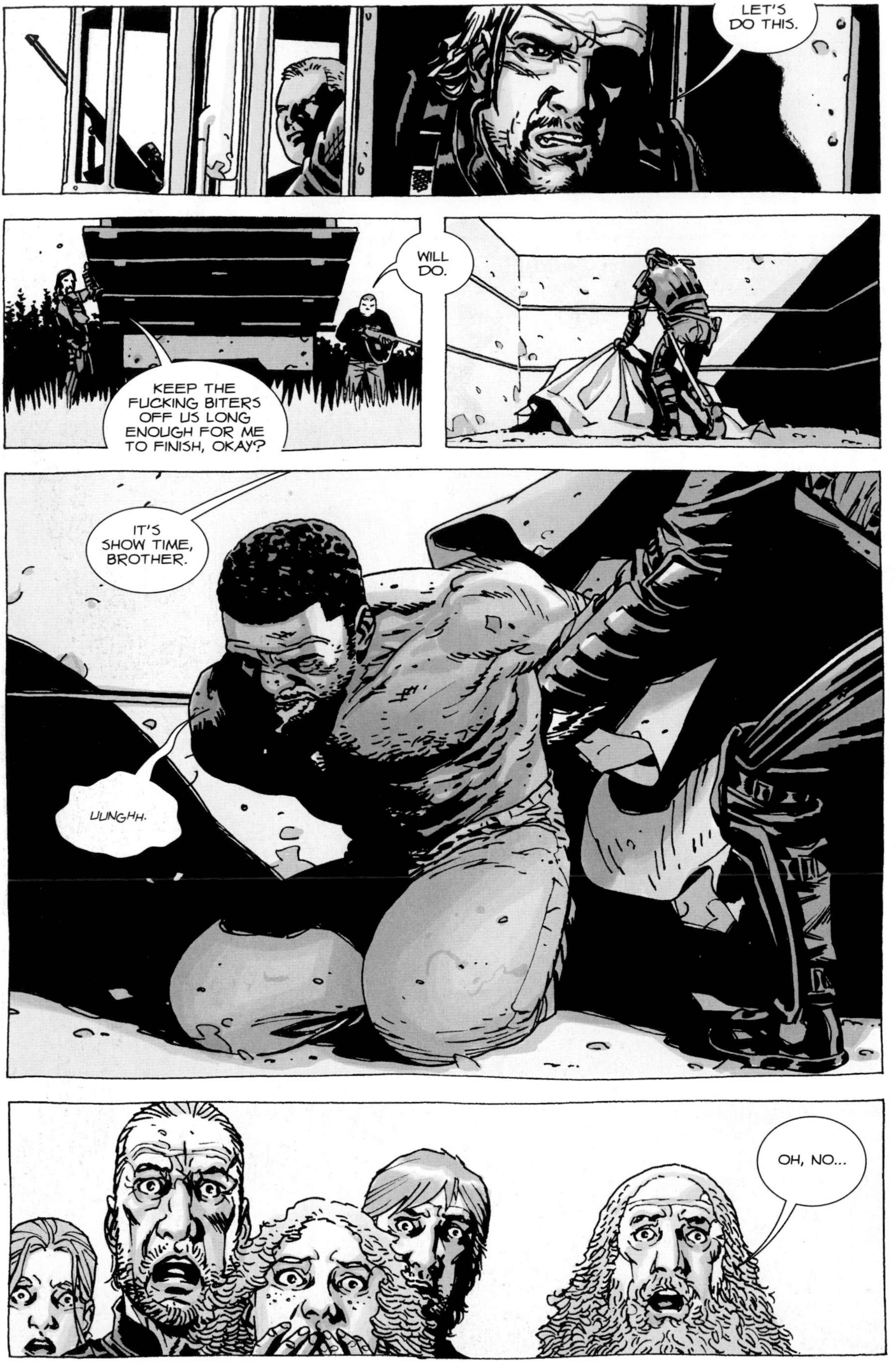
LET'S DO THIS.
KEEP THE FUCKING BITERS OFF US LONG ENOUGH FOR ME TO FINISH, OKAY?
WILL DO.
IT'S SHOW TIME, BROTHER.
UUNGHH.
OH, NO...

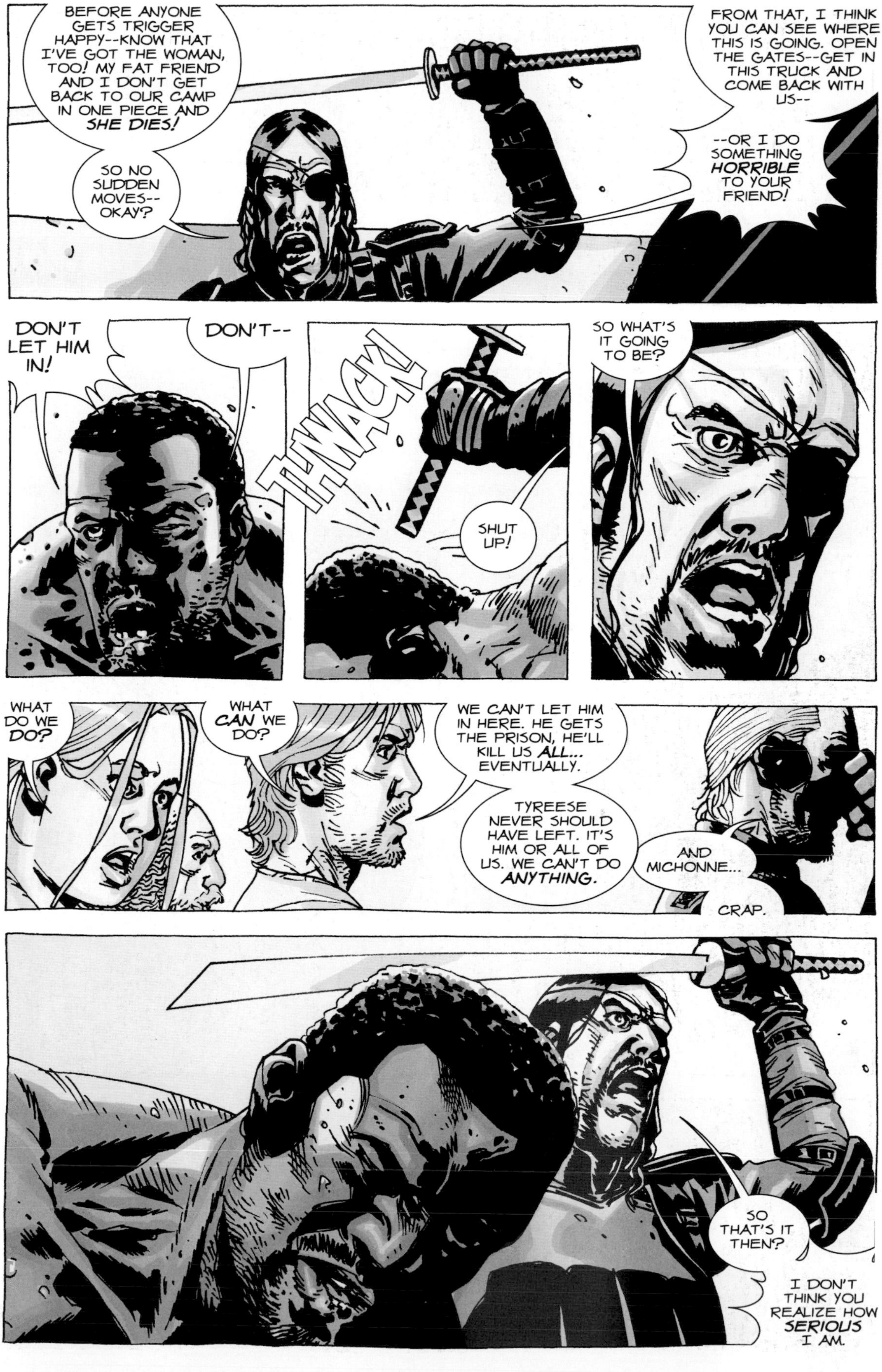
BEFORE ANYONE GETS TRIGGER HAPPY--KNOW THAT I'VE GOT THE WOMAN, TOO! MY FAT FRIEND AND I DON'T GET BACK TO OUR CAMP IN ONE PIECE AND SHE DIES!
SO NO SUDDEN MOVES-- OKAY?
FROM THAT, I THINK YOU CAN SEE WHERE THIS IS GOING. OPEN THE GATES--GET IN THIS TRUCK AND COME BACK WITH US--
--OR I DO SOMETHING HORRIBLE TO YOUR FRIEND!
DON'T LET HIM IN!
DON'T--
THWACK!
SHUT UP!
SO WHAT'S IT GOING TO BE?
WHAT DO WE DO?
WHAT CAN WE DO?
WE CAN'T LET HIM IN HERE. HE GETS THE PRISON, HE'LL KILL US ALL... EVENTUALLY.
TYREESE NEVER SHOULD HAVE LEFT. IT'S HIM OR ALL OF US. WE CAN'T DO ANYTHING.
AND MICHONNE...
CRAP.
SO THAT'S IT THEN?
I DON'T THINK YOU REALIZE HOW SERIOUS I AM.

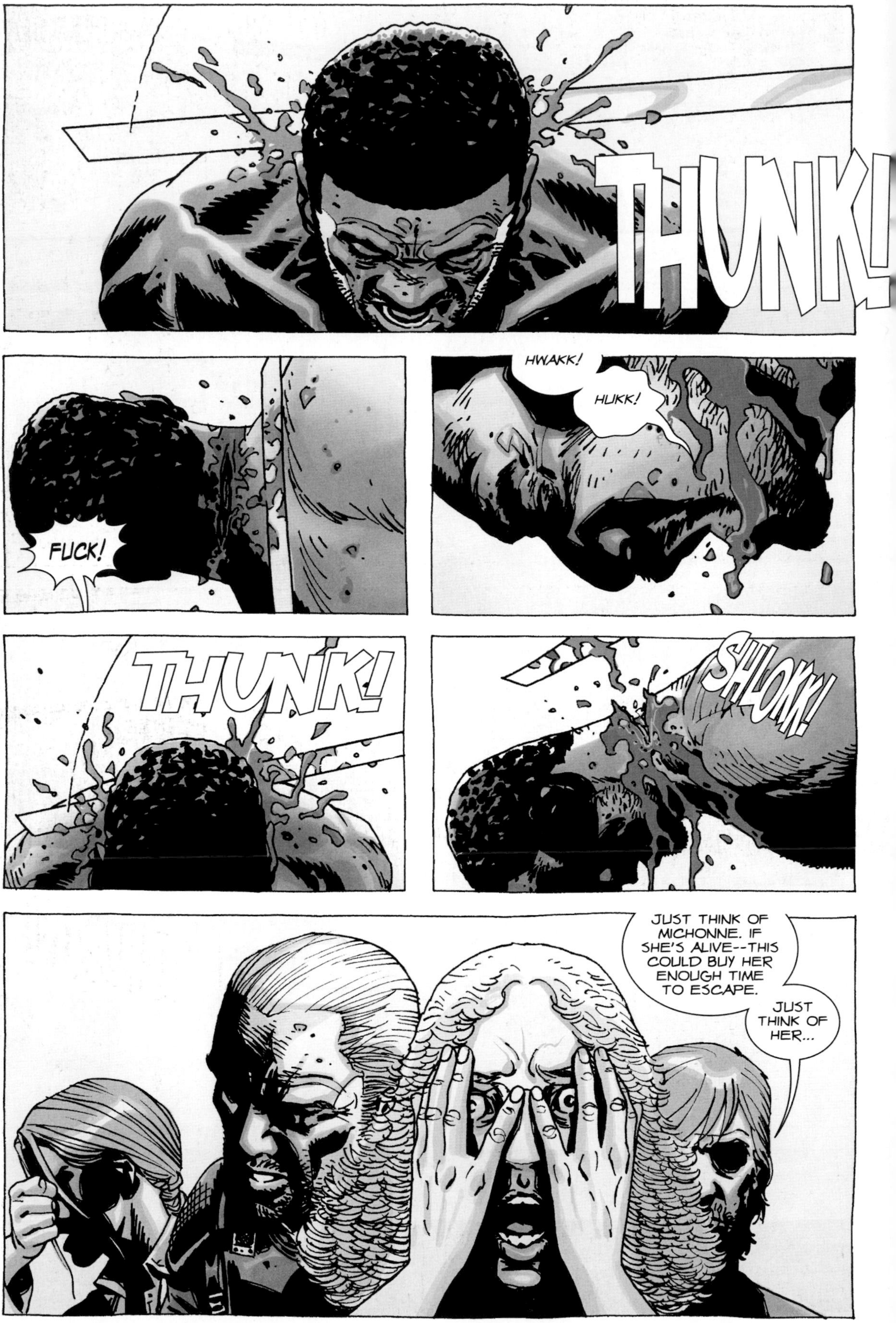
THUNK!
FUCK!
HWAKK!
HUKK!
THUNK!
SHLOKK!
JUST THINK OF MICHONNE. IF SHE'S ALIVE--THIS COULD BUY HER ENOUGH TIME TO ESCAPE.
JUST THINK OF HER...

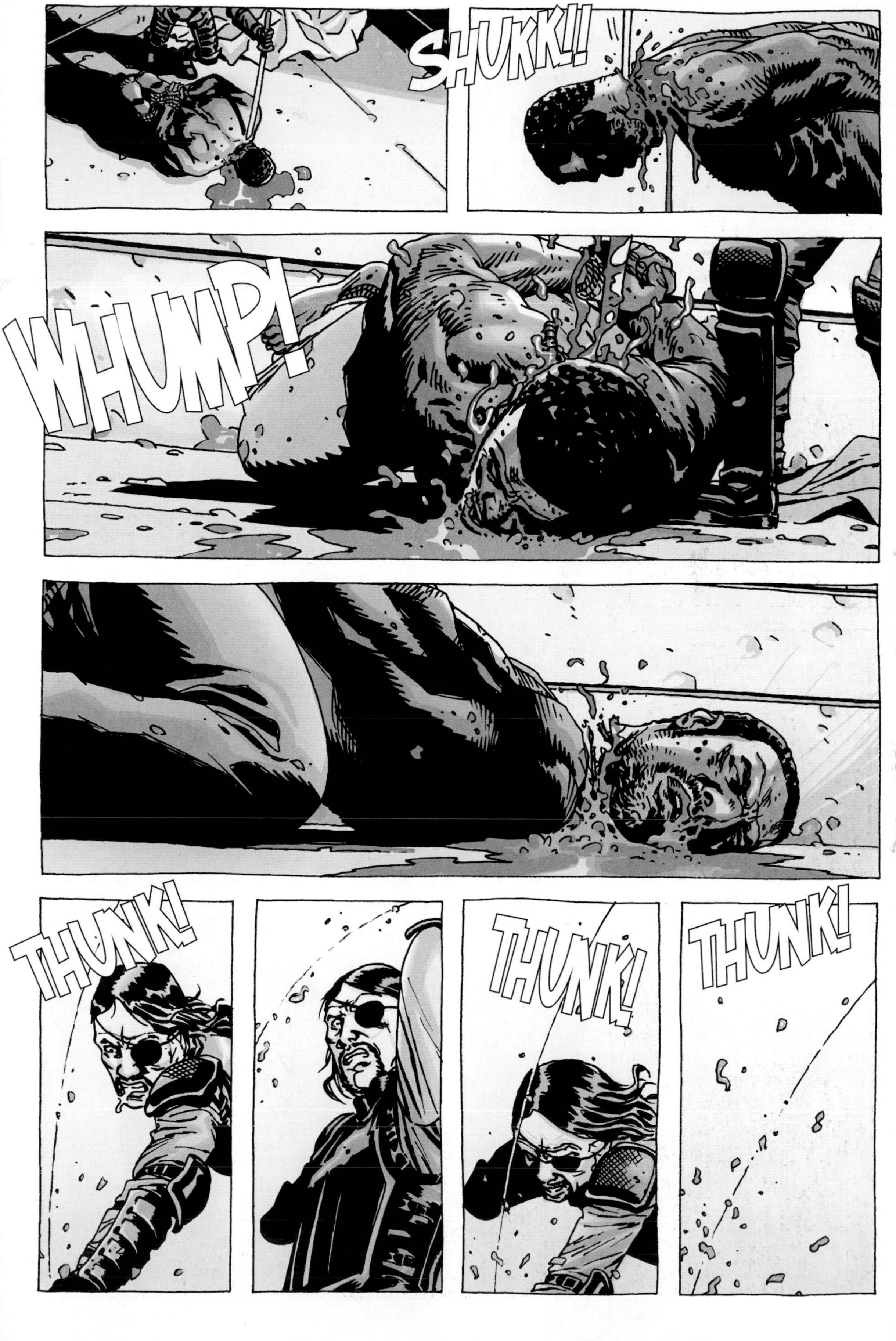
SHUKK!!
WHUMP!
THUNK!
THUNK!
THUNK!

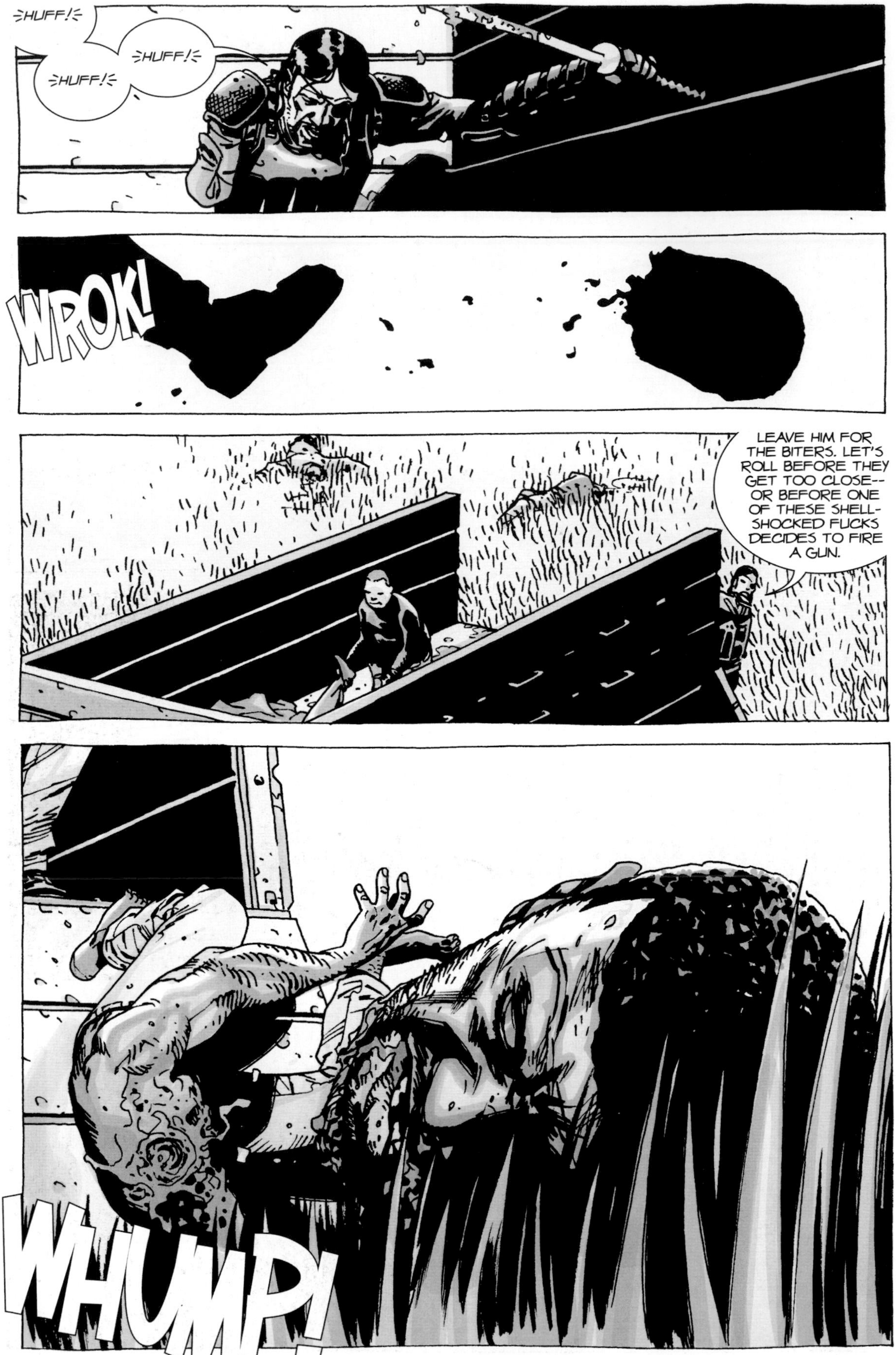

HUFF!
HUFF!
HUFF!
WROK!
LEAVE HIM FOR THE BITERS. LET'S ROLL BEFORE THEY GET TOO CLOSE-- OR BEFORE ONE OF THESE SHELL-SHOCKED FUCKS DECIDES TO FIRE A GUN.
WHUMP!

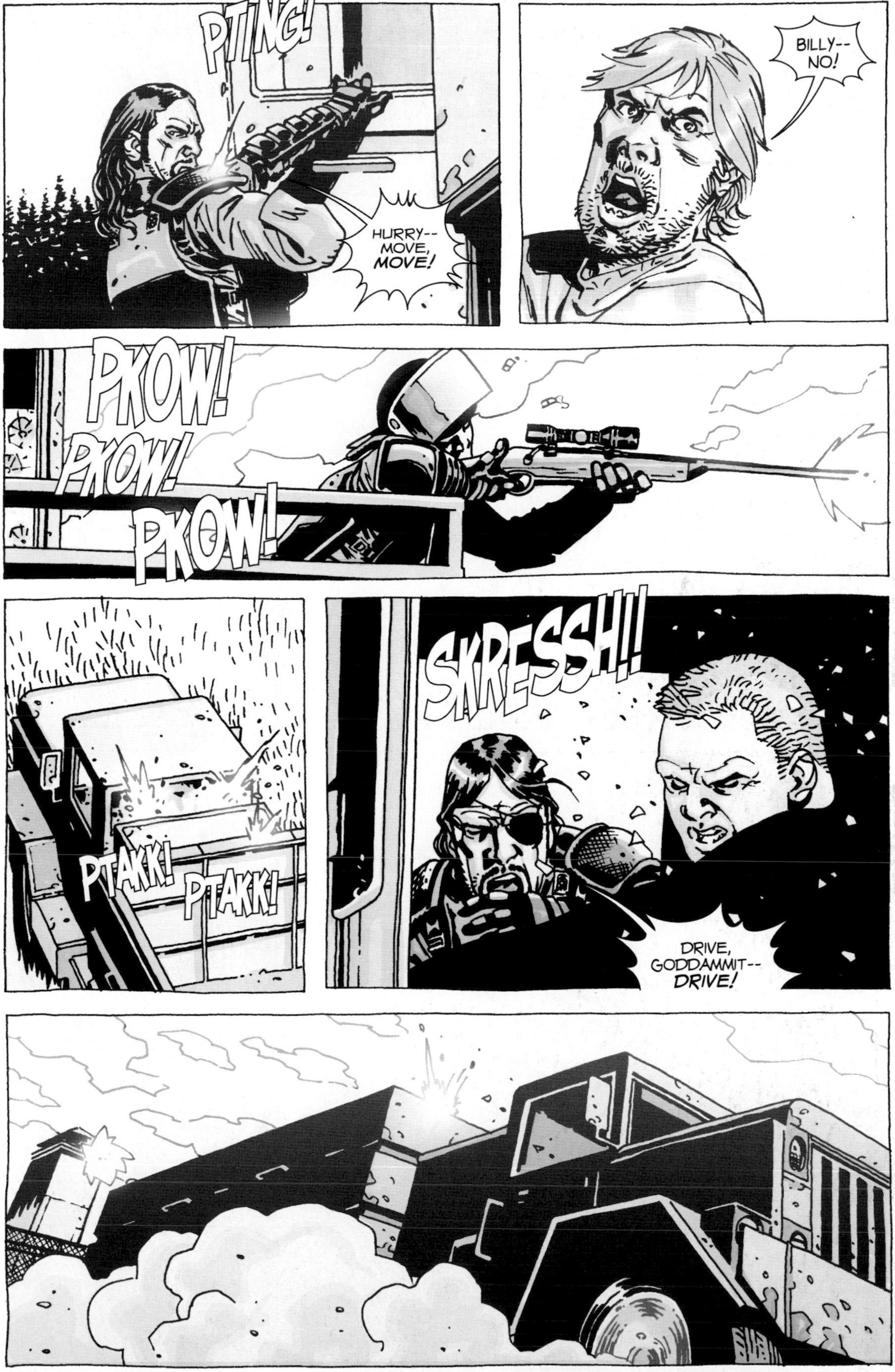
PTING!
HURRY-- MOVE, MOVE!
BILLY-- NO!
PKOW!
PKOW!
PKOW!
PTAKK!
PTAKK!
SKRESSH!!
DRIVE, GODDAMMIT-- DRIVE!

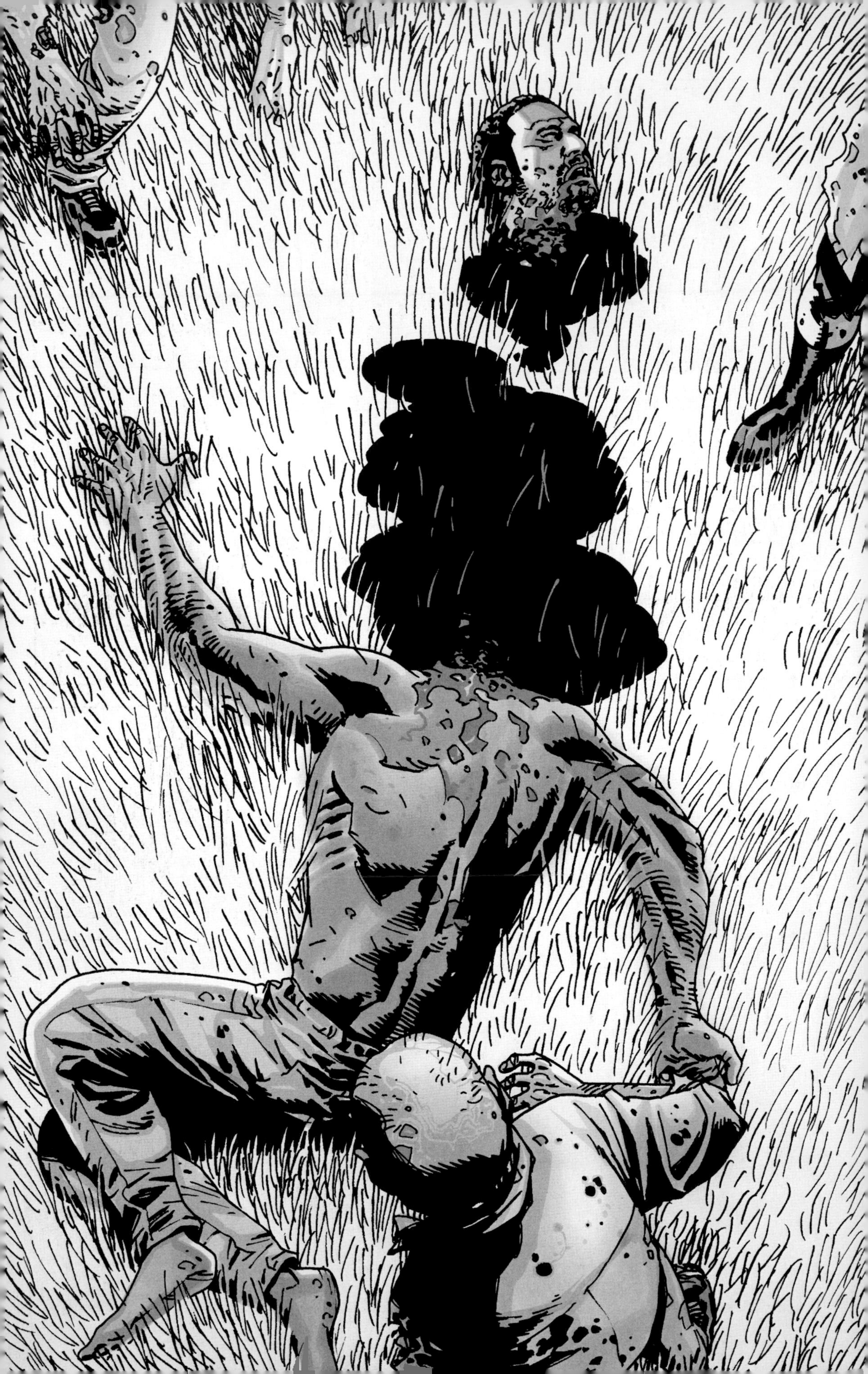

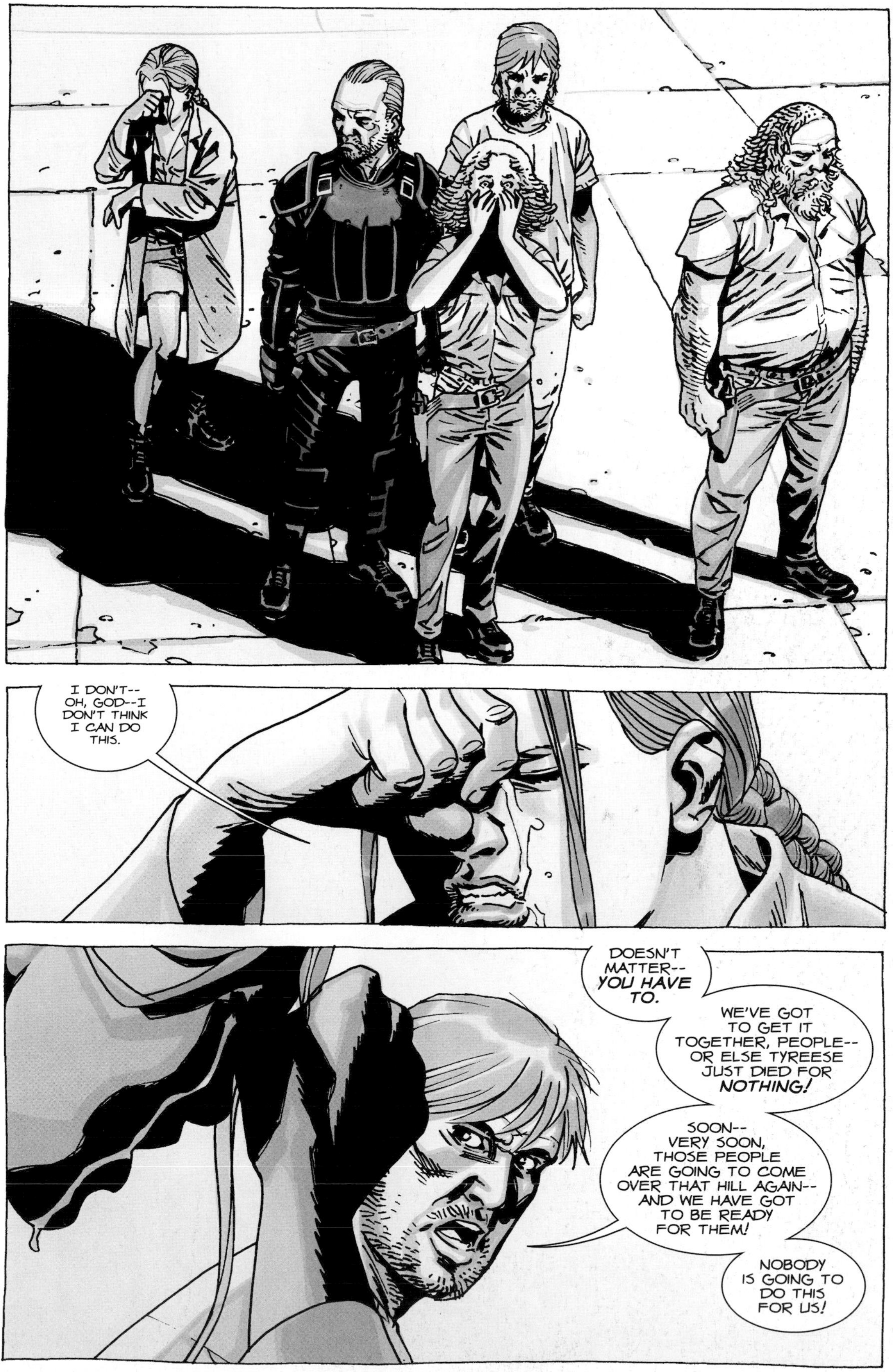
I DON'T-- OH, GOD--I DON'T THINK I CAN DO THIS.
DOESN'T MATTER-- *YOU HAVE TO.*
WE'VE GOT TO GET IT TOGETHER, PEOPLE-- OR ELSE TYREESE JUST DIED FOR *NOTHING!*
SOON-- VERY SOON, THOSE PEOPLE ARE GOING TO COME OVER THAT HILL AGAIN-- AND WE HAVE GOT TO BE READY FOR THEM!
NOBODY IS GOING TO DO THIS FOR US!

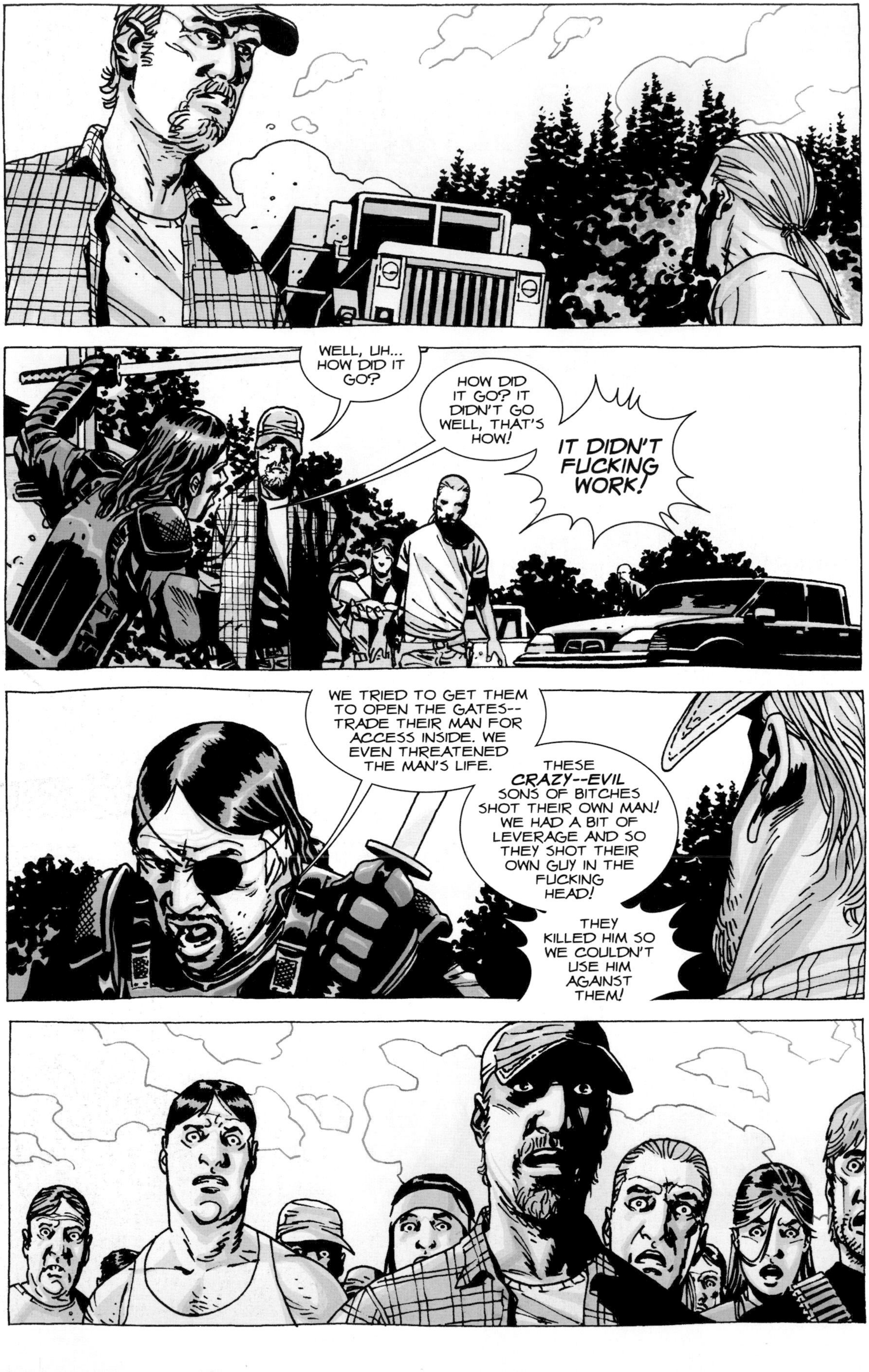
WELL, UH... HOW DID IT GO?
HOW DID IT GO? IT DIDN'T GO WELL, THAT'S HOW!
IT DIDN'T FUCKING WORK!
WE TRIED TO GET THEM TO OPEN THE GATES-- TRADE THEIR MAN FOR ACCESS INSIDE. WE EVEN THREATENED THE MAN'S LIFE.
THESE CRAZY--EVIL SONS OF BITCHES SHOT THEIR OWN MAN! WE HAD A BIT OF LEVERAGE AND SO THEY SHOT THEIR OWN GUY IN THE FUCKING HEAD!
THEY KILLED HIM SO WE COULDN'T USE HIM AGAINST THEM!

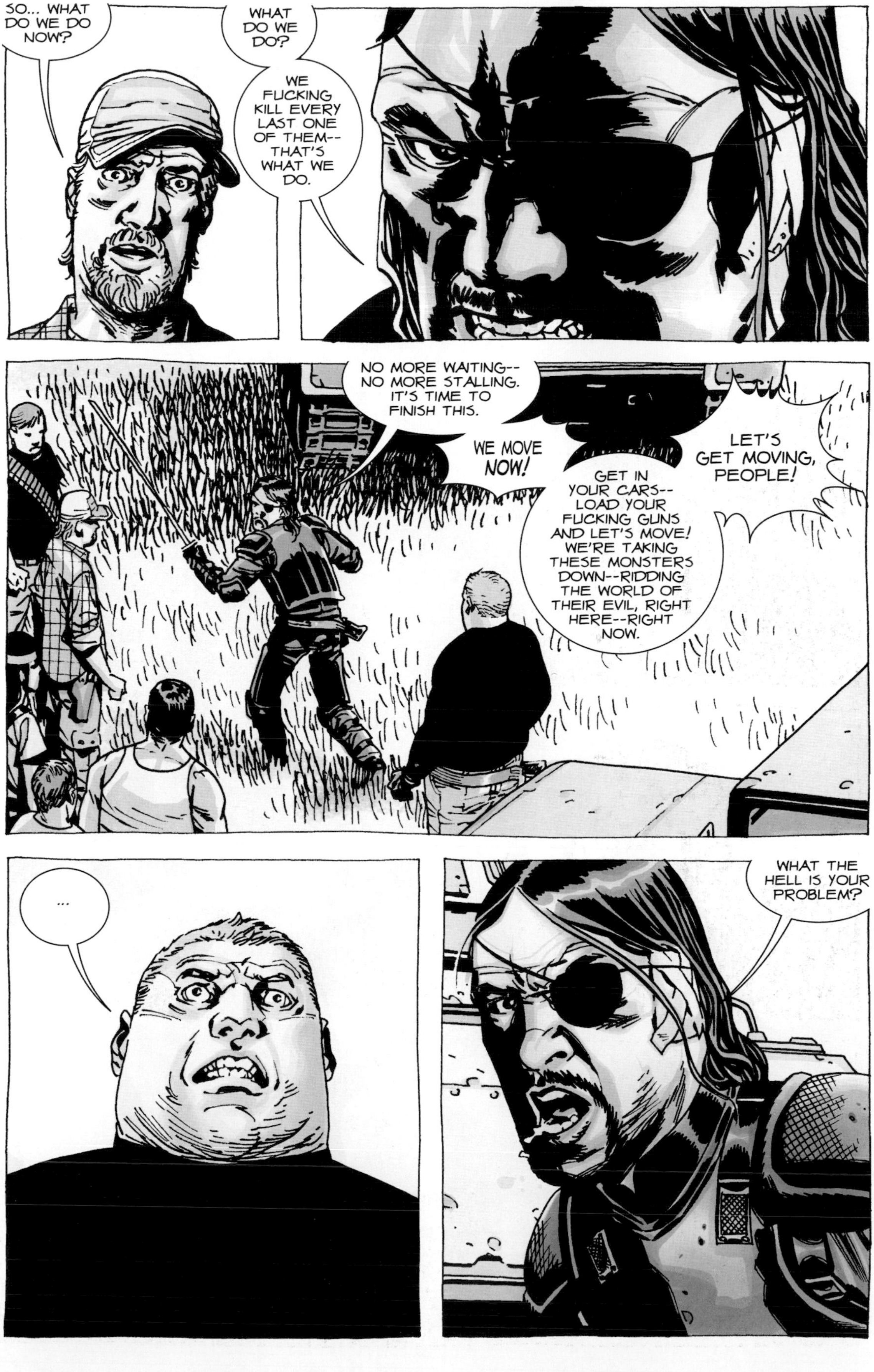
SO... WHAT DO WE DO NOW?
WHAT DO WE DO?
WE FUCKING KILL EVERY LAST ONE OF THEM--THAT'S WHAT WE DO.
NO MORE WAITING--NO MORE STALLING. IT'S TIME TO FINISH THIS.
WE MOVE NOW!
GET IN YOUR CARS--LOAD YOUR FUCKING GUNS AND LET'S MOVE! WE'RE TAKING THESE MONSTERS DOWN--RIDDING THE WORLD OF THEIR EVIL, RIGHT HERE--RIGHT NOW.
LET'S GET MOVING, PEOPLE!
...
WHAT THE HELL IS YOUR PROBLEM?

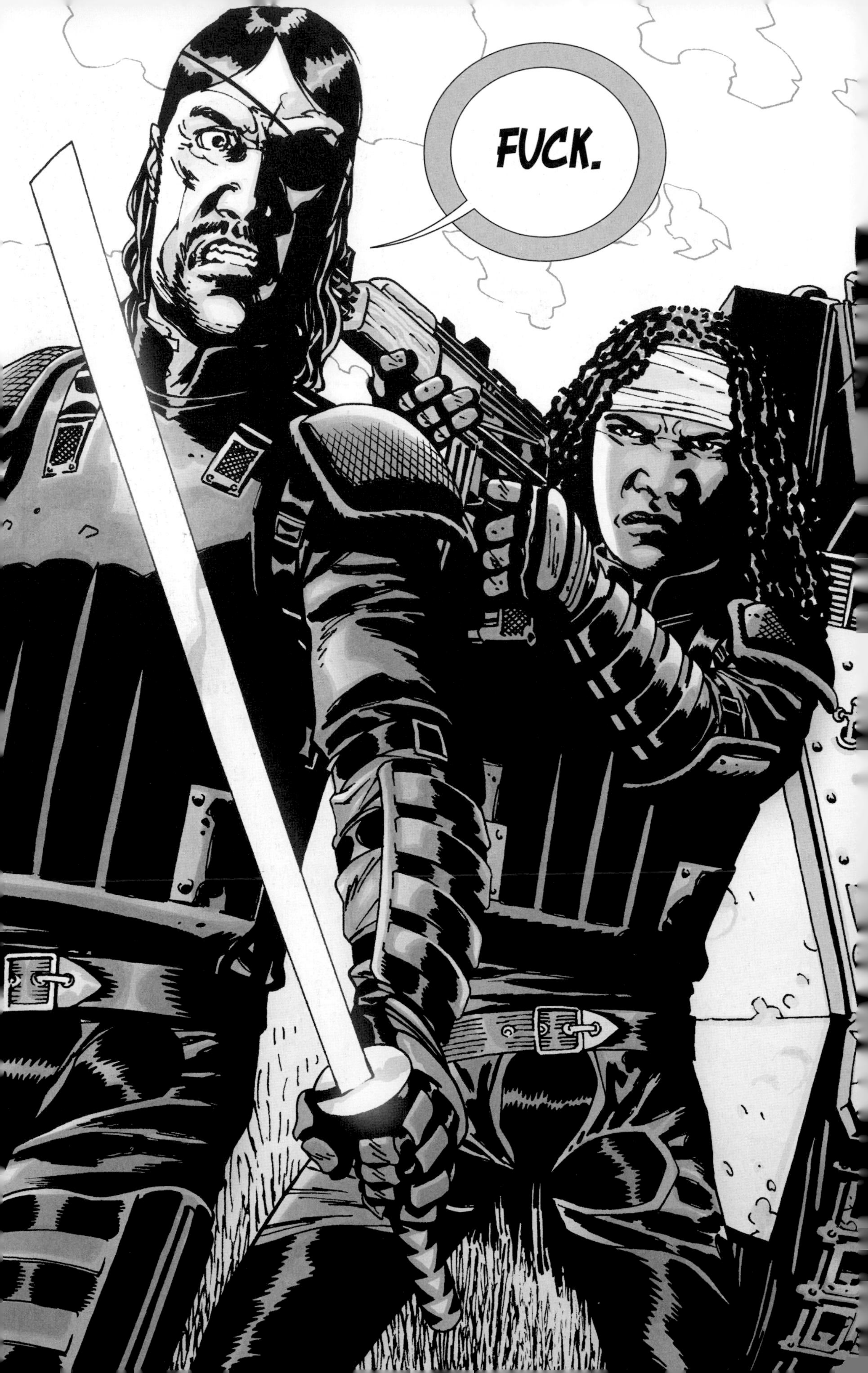
FUCK.

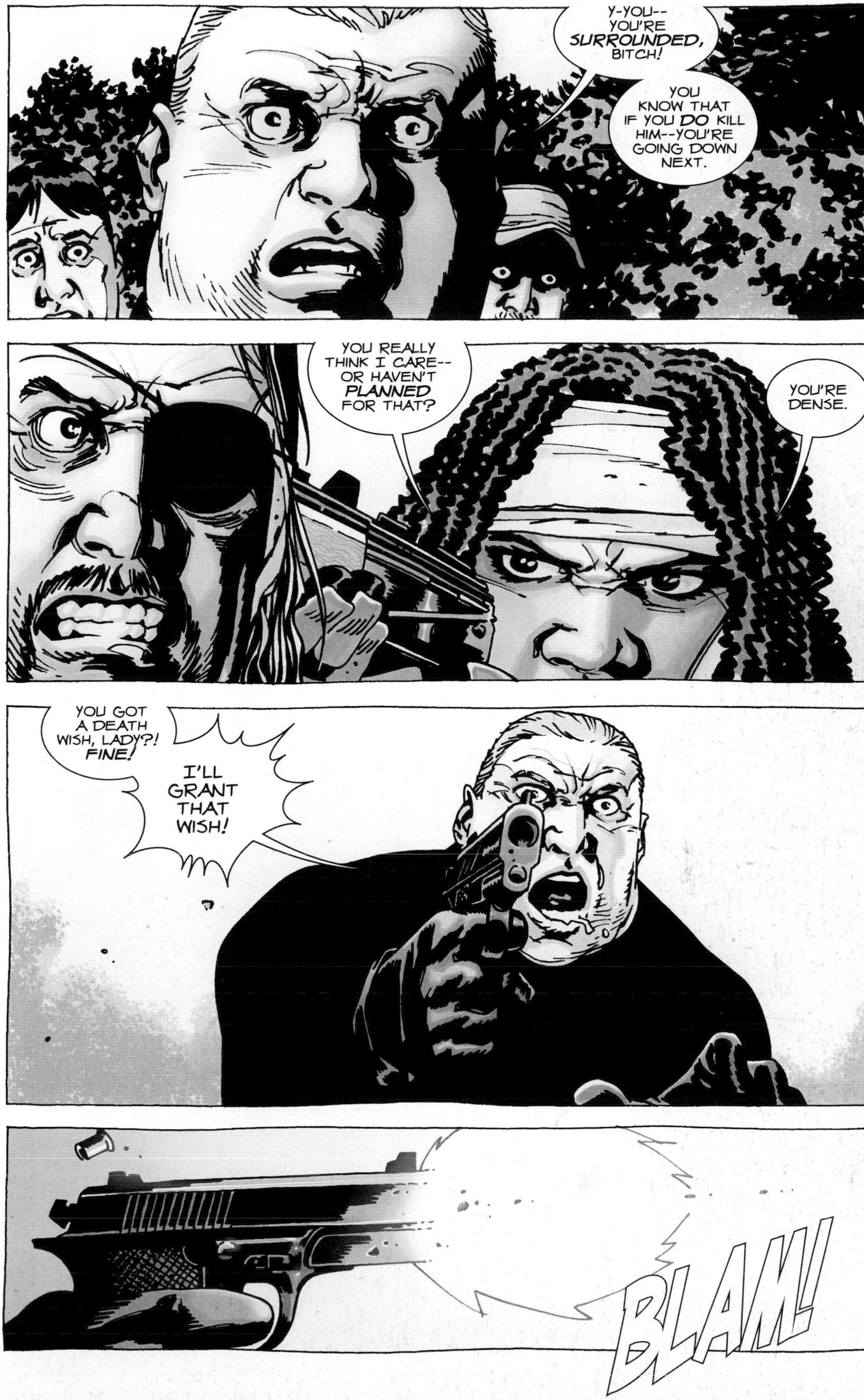
Y-YOU-- YOU'RE SURROUNDED, BITCH!
YOU KNOW THAT IF YOU DO KILL HIM--YOU'RE GOING DOWN NEXT.
YOU REALLY THINK I CARE-- OR HAVEN'T PLANNED FOR THAT?
YOU'RE DENSE.
YOU GOT A DEATH WISH, LADY?! FINE!
I'LL GRANT THAT WISH!
BLAM!

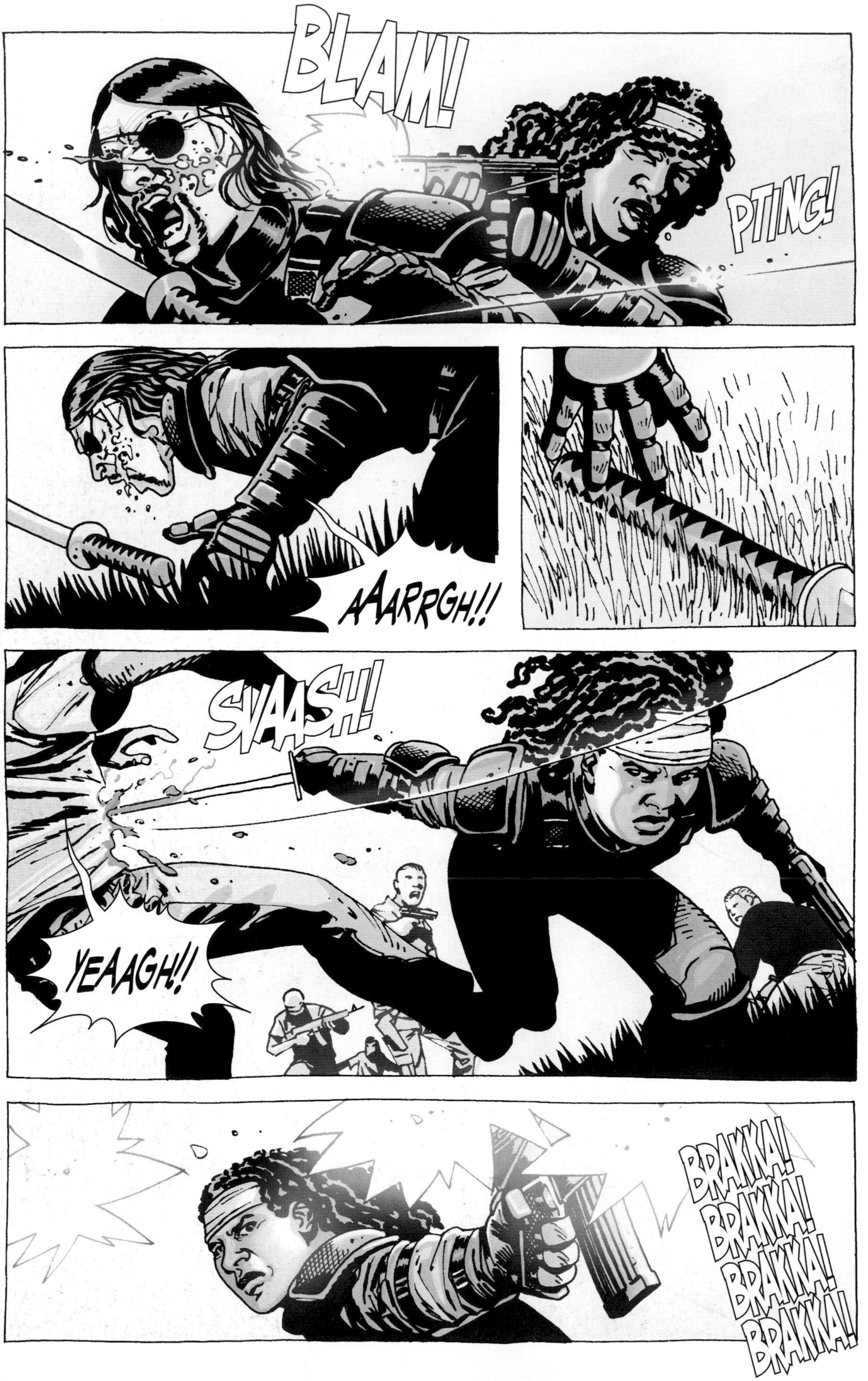
BLAM!
PTING!
AAARRGH!!
SVAASH!
YEAAGH!!
BRAKKA!
BRAKKA!
BRAKKA!
BRAKKA!
BRAKKA!

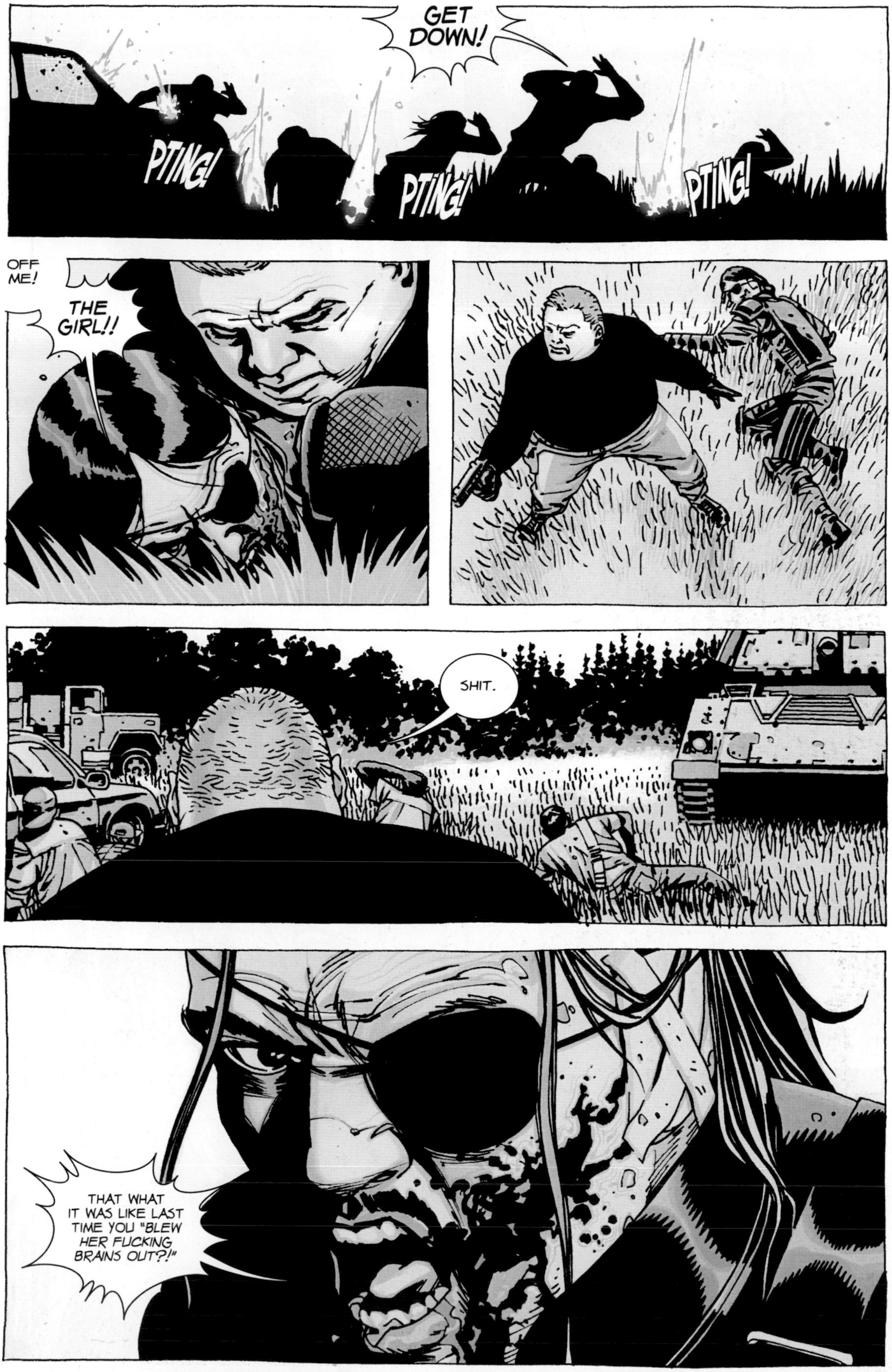
GET DOWN!
PTING!
PTING!
PTING!
OFF ME!
THE GIRL!!
SHIT.
THAT WHAT IT WAS LIKE LAST TIME YOU "BLEW HER FUCKING BRAINS OUT?!"

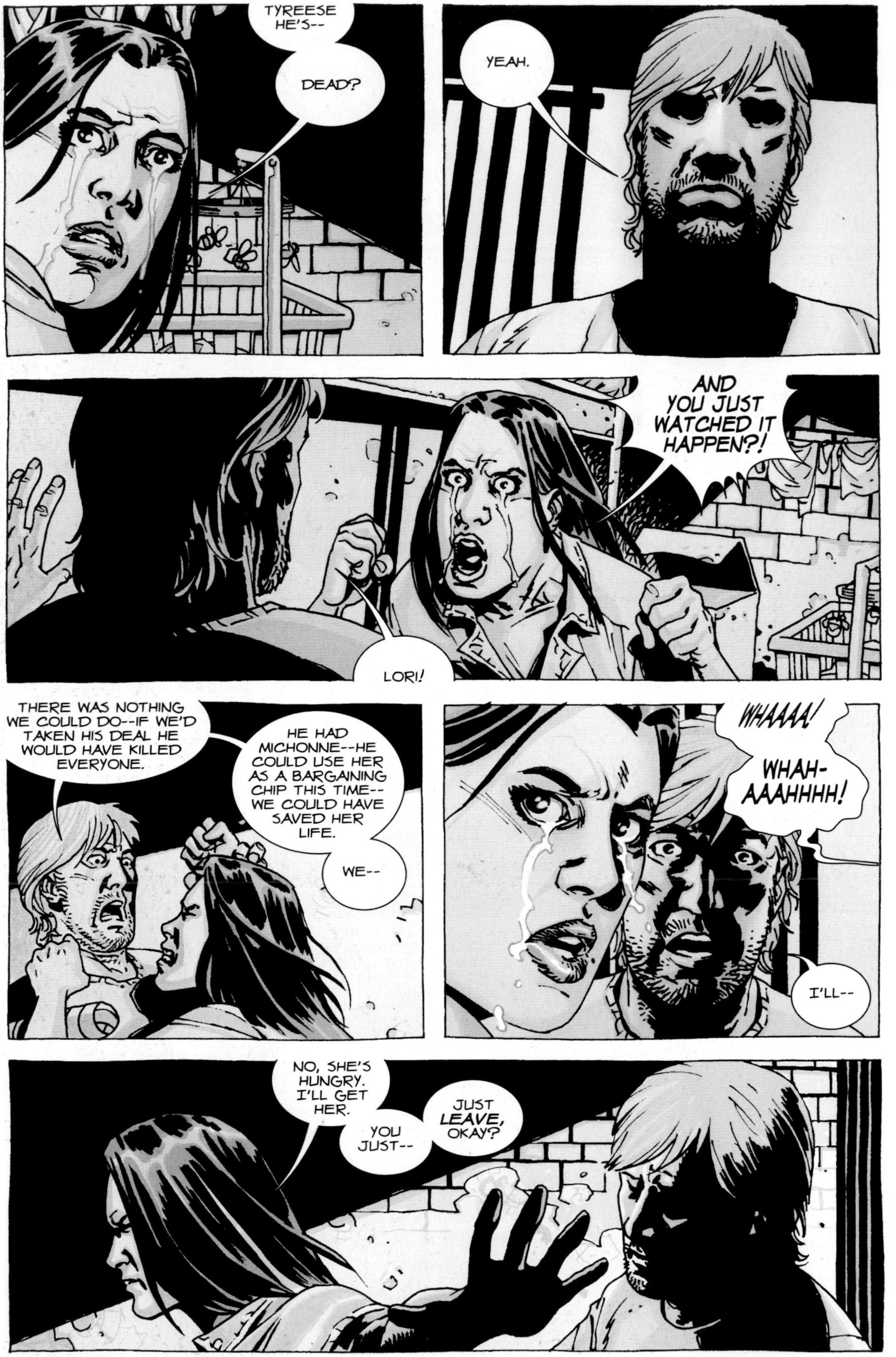
TYREESE HE'S--
DEAD?
YEAH.
AND YOU JUST WATCHED IT HAPPEN?!
LORI!
THERE WAS NOTHING WE COULD DO--IF WE'D TAKEN HIS DEAL HE WOULD HAVE KILLED EVERYONE.
HE HAD MICHONNE--HE COULD USE HER AS A BARGAINING CHIP THIS TIME--WE COULD HAVE SAVED HER LIFE.
WE--
WHAAAA!
WHAH-AAAHHHH!
I'LL--
NO, SHE'S HUNGRY. I'LL GET HER.
YOU JUST--
JUST LEAVE, OKAY?

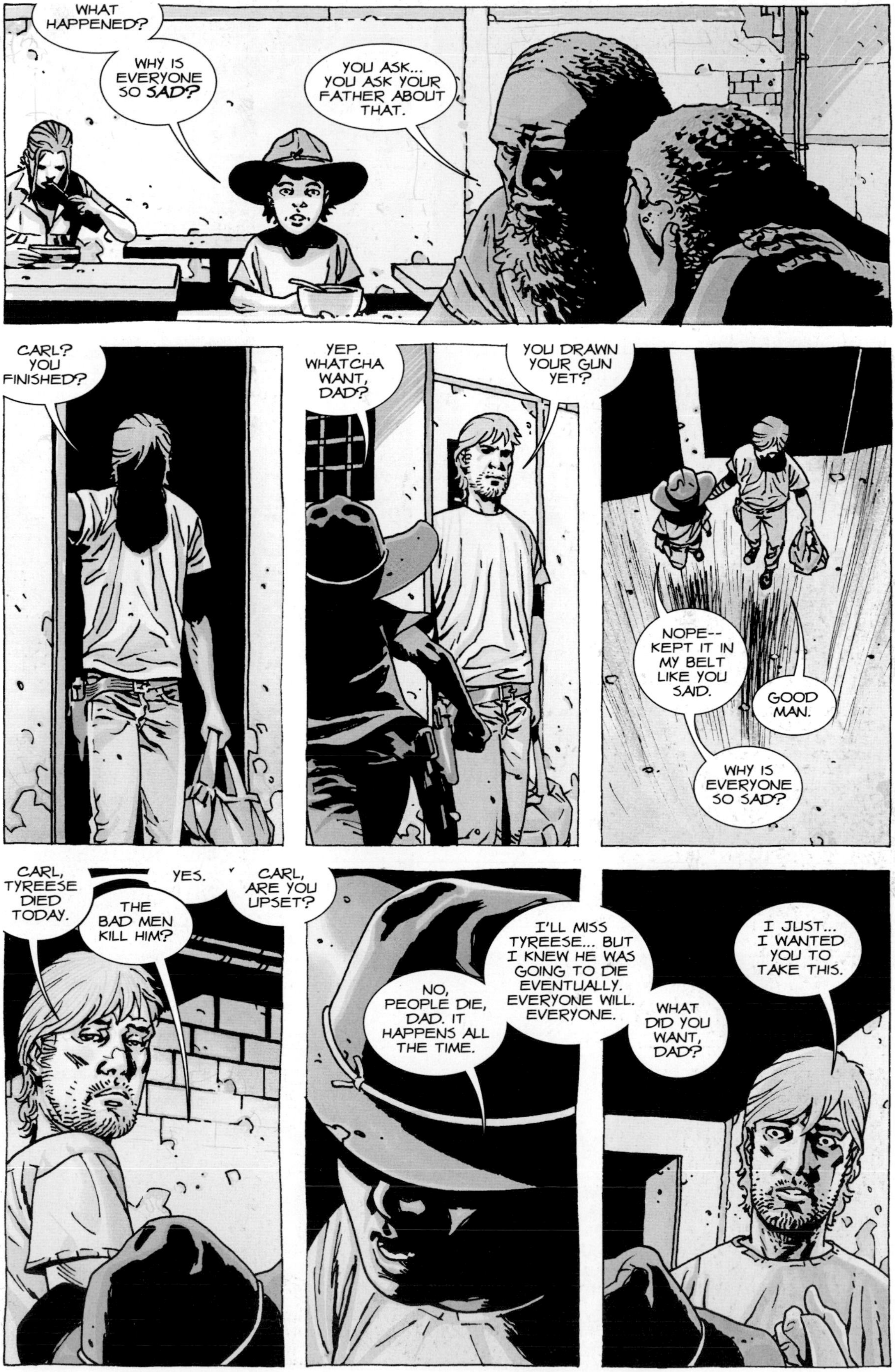
WHAT HAPPENED?
WHY IS EVERYONE SO SAD?
YOU ASK... YOU ASK YOUR FATHER ABOUT THAT.
CARL? YOU FINISHED?
YEP. WHATCHA WANT, DAD?
YOU DRAWN YOUR GUN YET?
NOPE-- KEPT IT IN MY BELT LIKE YOU SAID.
GOOD MAN.
WHY IS EVERYONE SO SAD?
CARL, TYREESE DIED TODAY.
THE BAD MEN KILL HIM?
YES.
CARL, ARE YOU UPSET?
NO, PEOPLE DIE, DAD. IT HAPPENS ALL THE TIME.
I'LL MISS TYREESE... BUT I KNEW HE WAS GOING TO DIE EVENTUALLY. EVERYONE WILL. EVERYONE.
WHAT DID YOU WANT, DAD?
I JUST... I WANTED YOU TO TAKE THIS.

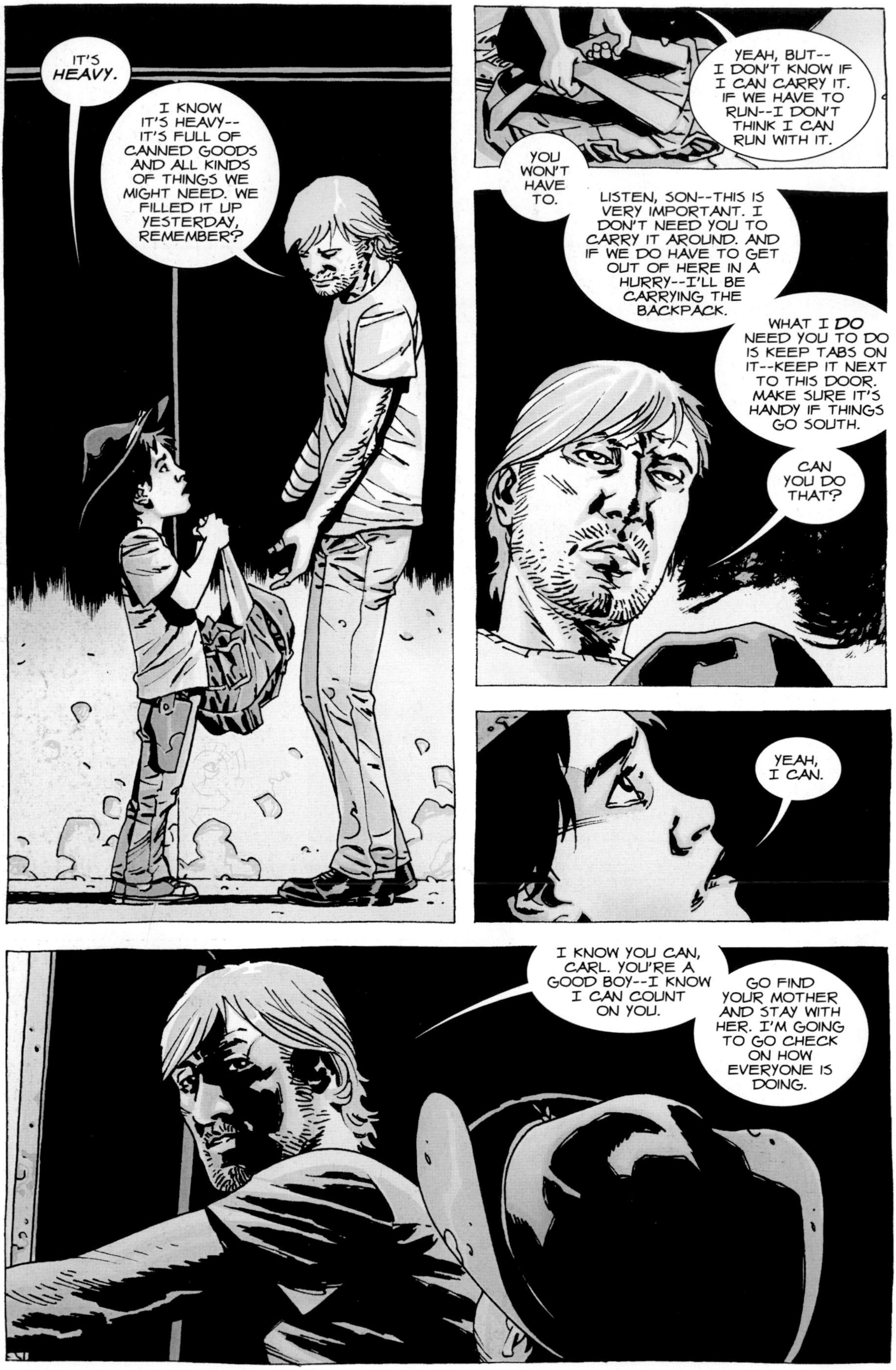
IT'S HEAVY.
I KNOW IT'S HEAVY-- IT'S FULL OF CANNED GOODS AND ALL KINDS OF THINGS WE MIGHT NEED. WE FILLED IT UP YESTERDAY, REMEMBER?
YEAH, BUT-- I DON'T KNOW IF I CAN CARRY IT. IF WE HAVE TO RUN--I DON'T THINK I CAN RUN WITH IT.
YOU WON'T HAVE TO.
LISTEN, SON--THIS IS VERY IMPORTANT. I DON'T NEED YOU TO CARRY IT AROUND. AND IF WE DO HAVE TO GET OUT OF HERE IN A HURRY--I'LL BE CARRYING THE BACKPACK.
WHAT I DO NEED YOU TO DO IS KEEP TABS ON IT--KEEP IT NEXT TO THIS DOOR. MAKE SURE IT'S HANDY IF THINGS GO SOUTH.
CAN YOU DO THAT?
YEAH, I CAN.
I KNOW YOU CAN, CARL. YOU'RE A GOOD BOY--I KNOW I CAN COUNT ON YOU.
GO FIND YOUR MOTHER AND STAY WITH HER. I'M GOING TO GO CHECK ON HOW EVERYONE IS DOING.

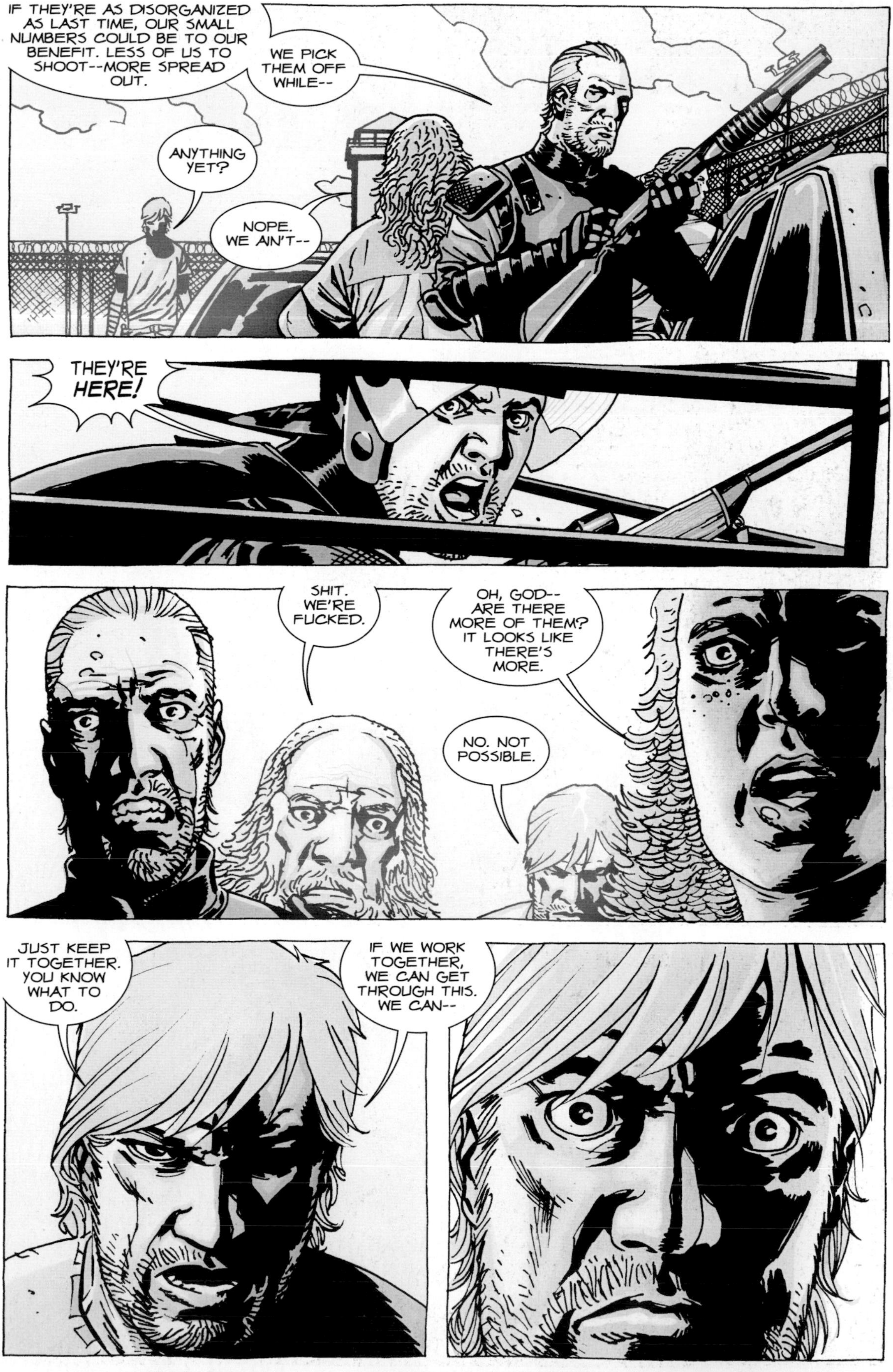
IF THEY'RE AS DISORGANIZED AS LAST TIME, OUR SMALL NUMBERS COULD BE TO OUR BENEFIT. LESS OF US TO SHOOT--MORE SPREAD OUT.
WE PICK THEM OFF WHILE--
ANYTHING YET?
NOPE. WE AIN'T--
THEY'RE HERE!
SHIT. WE'RE FUCKED.
OH, GOD--ARE THERE MORE OF THEM? IT LOOKS LIKE THERE'S MORE.
NO. NOT POSSIBLE.
JUST KEEP IT TOGETHER. YOU KNOW WHAT TO DO.
IF WE WORK TOGETHER, WE CAN GET THROUGH THIS. WE CAN--

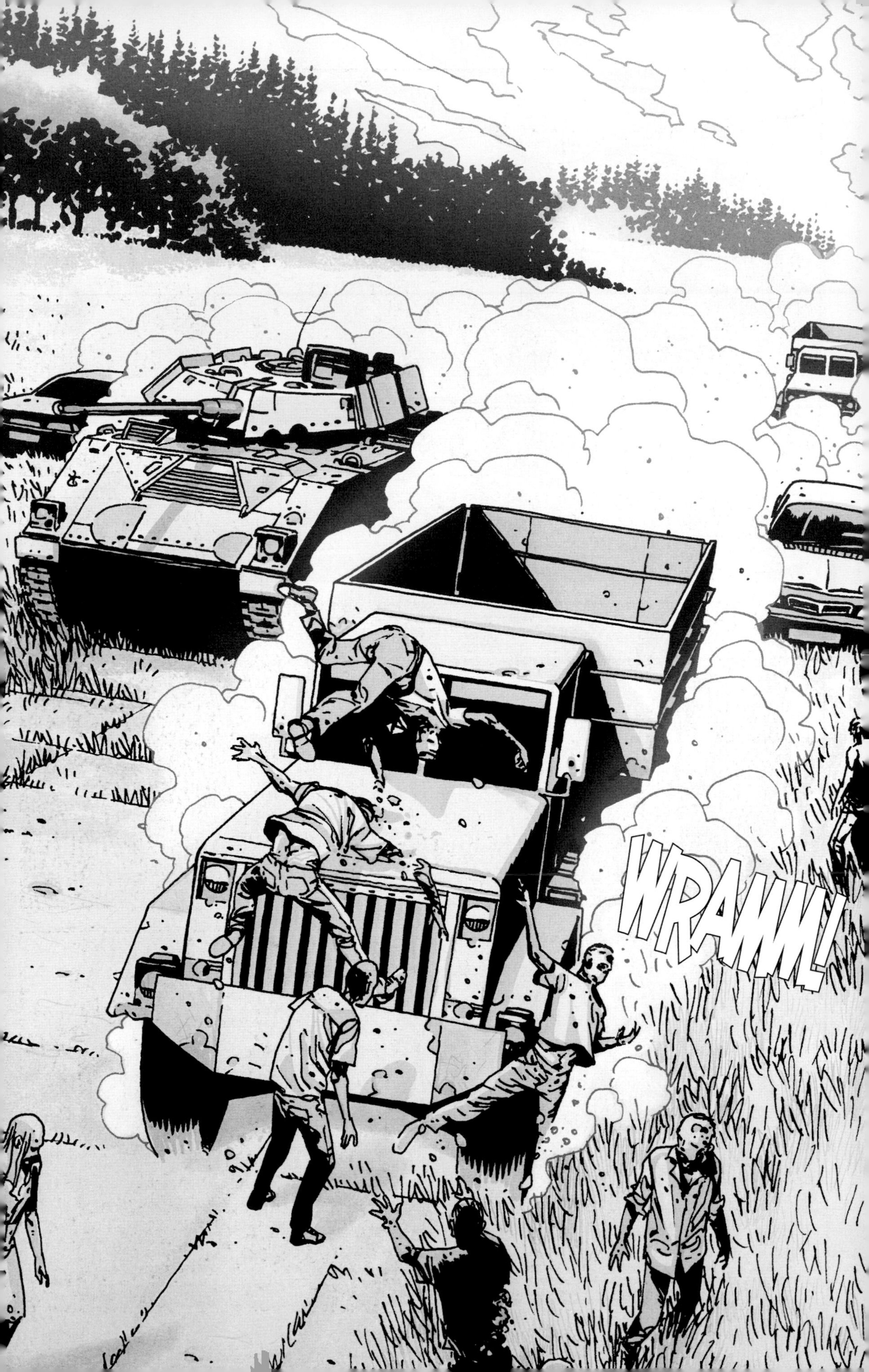
WRAMM!

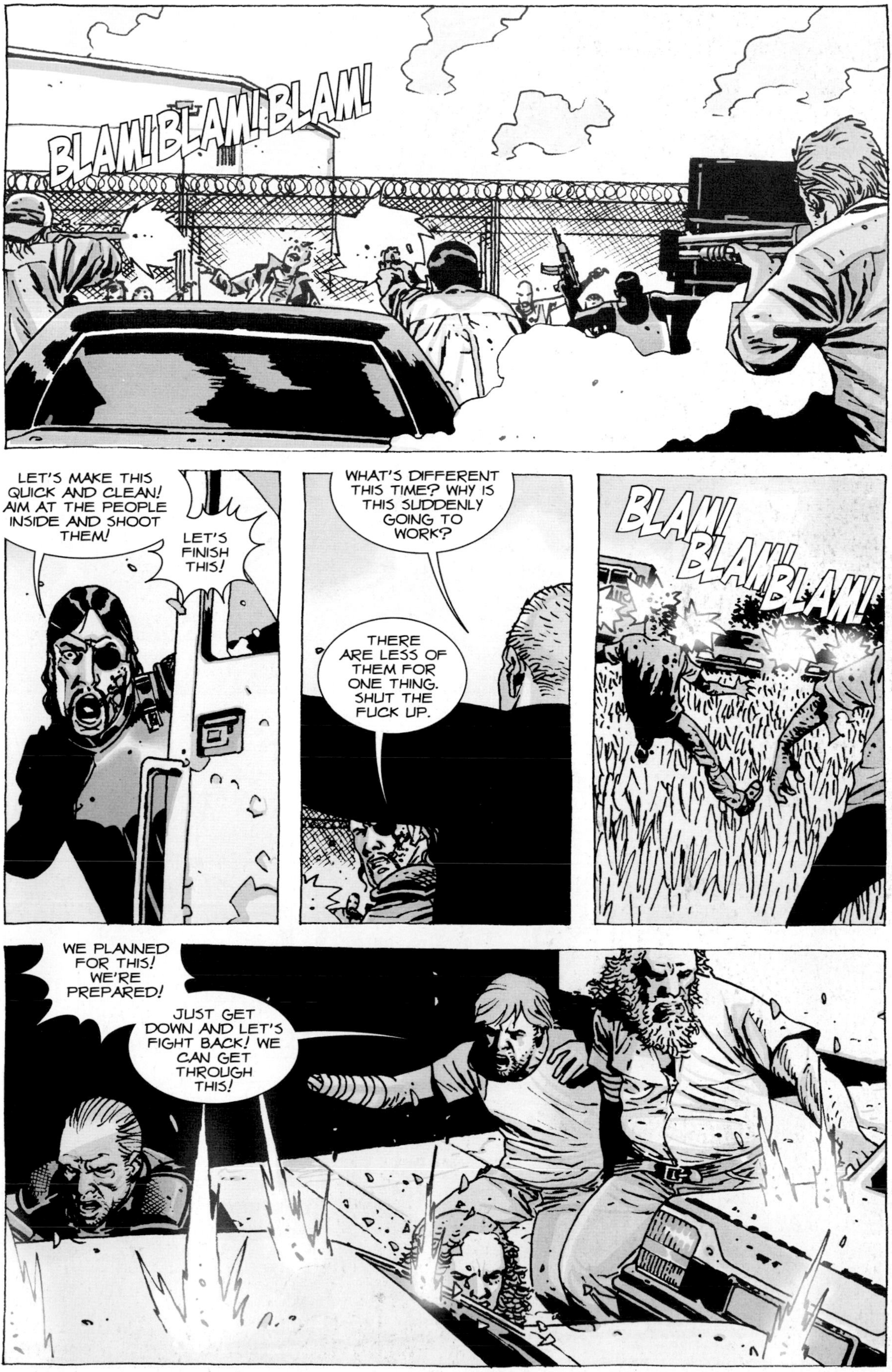
BLAM! BLAM! BLAM!
LET'S MAKE THIS QUICK AND CLEAN! AIM AT THE PEOPLE INSIDE AND SHOOT THEM!
LET'S FINISH THIS!
WHAT'S DIFFERENT THIS TIME? WHY IS THIS SUDDENLY GOING TO WORK?
THERE ARE LESS OF THEM FOR ONE THING. SHUT THE FUCK UP.
BLAM! BLAM! BLAM!
WE PLANNED FOR THIS! WE'RE PREPARED!
JUST GET DOWN AND LET'S FIGHT BACK! WE CAN GET THROUGH THIS!

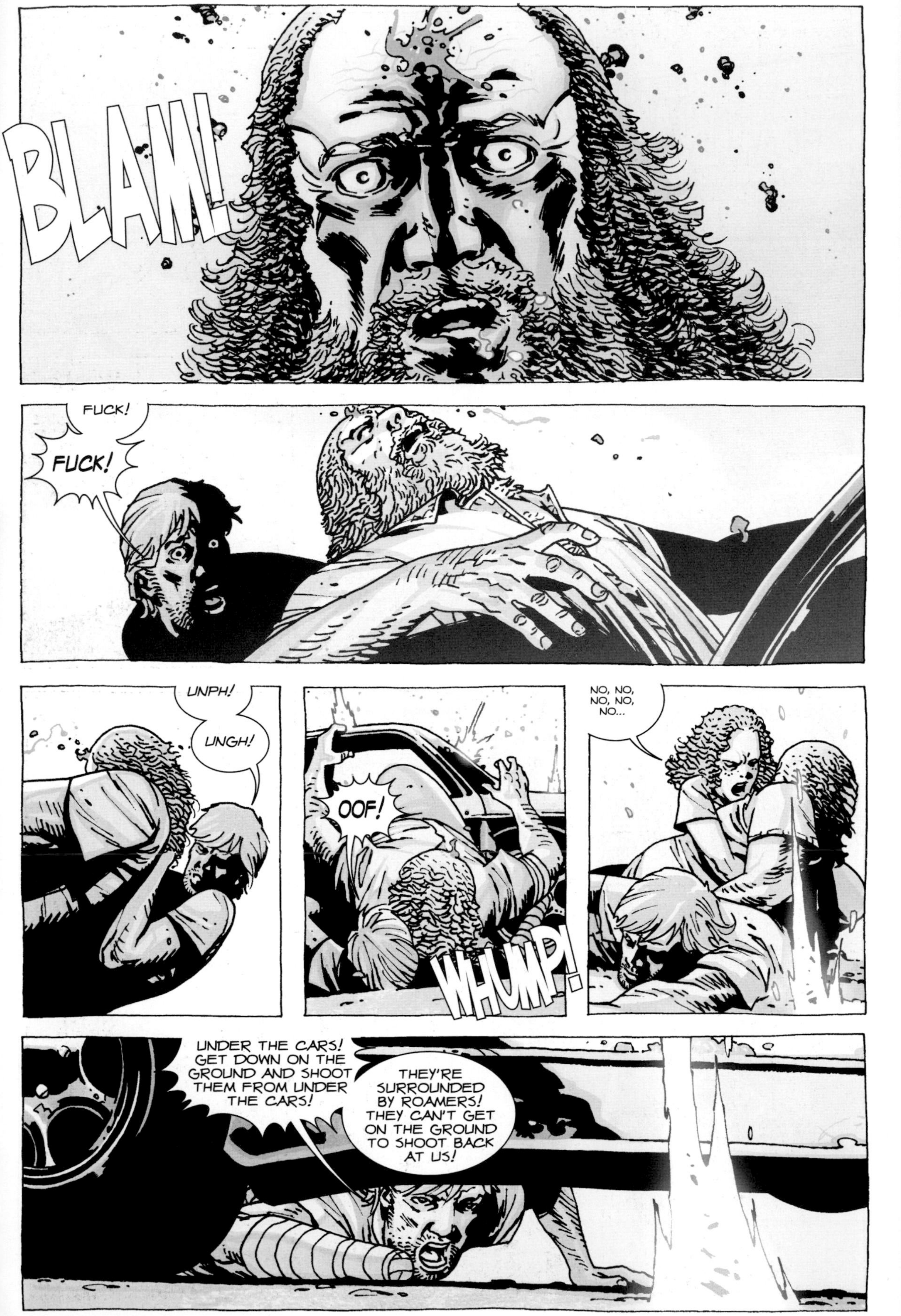
BLAM!
FUCK!
FUCK!
UNPH!
UNGH!
OOF!
WHUMP!
NO, NO, NO, NO, NO...
UNDER THE CARS! GET DOWN ON THE GROUND AND SHOOT THEM FROM UNDER THE CARS!
THEY'RE SURROUNDED BY ROAMERS! THEY CAN'T GET ON THE GROUND TO SHOOT BACK AT US!

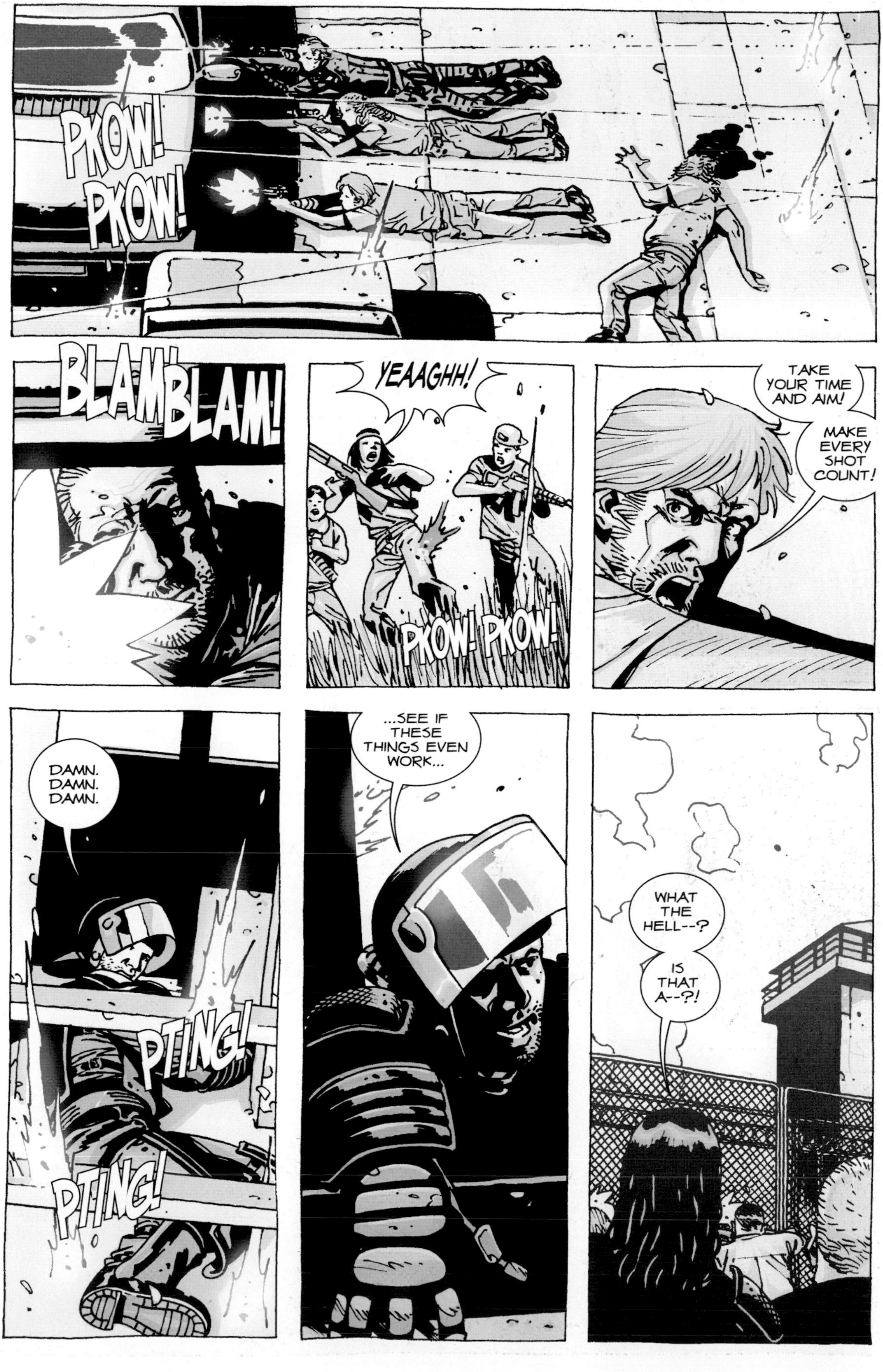
PKOW!
PKOW!
BLAM!
BLAM!
YEAAGHH!
PKOW! PKOW!
TAKE YOUR TIME AND AIM!
MAKE EVERY SHOT COUNT!
DAMN. DAMN. DAMN.
PTING!
PTING!
...SEE IF THESE THINGS EVEN WORK...
WHAT THE HELL--?
IS THAT A--?!

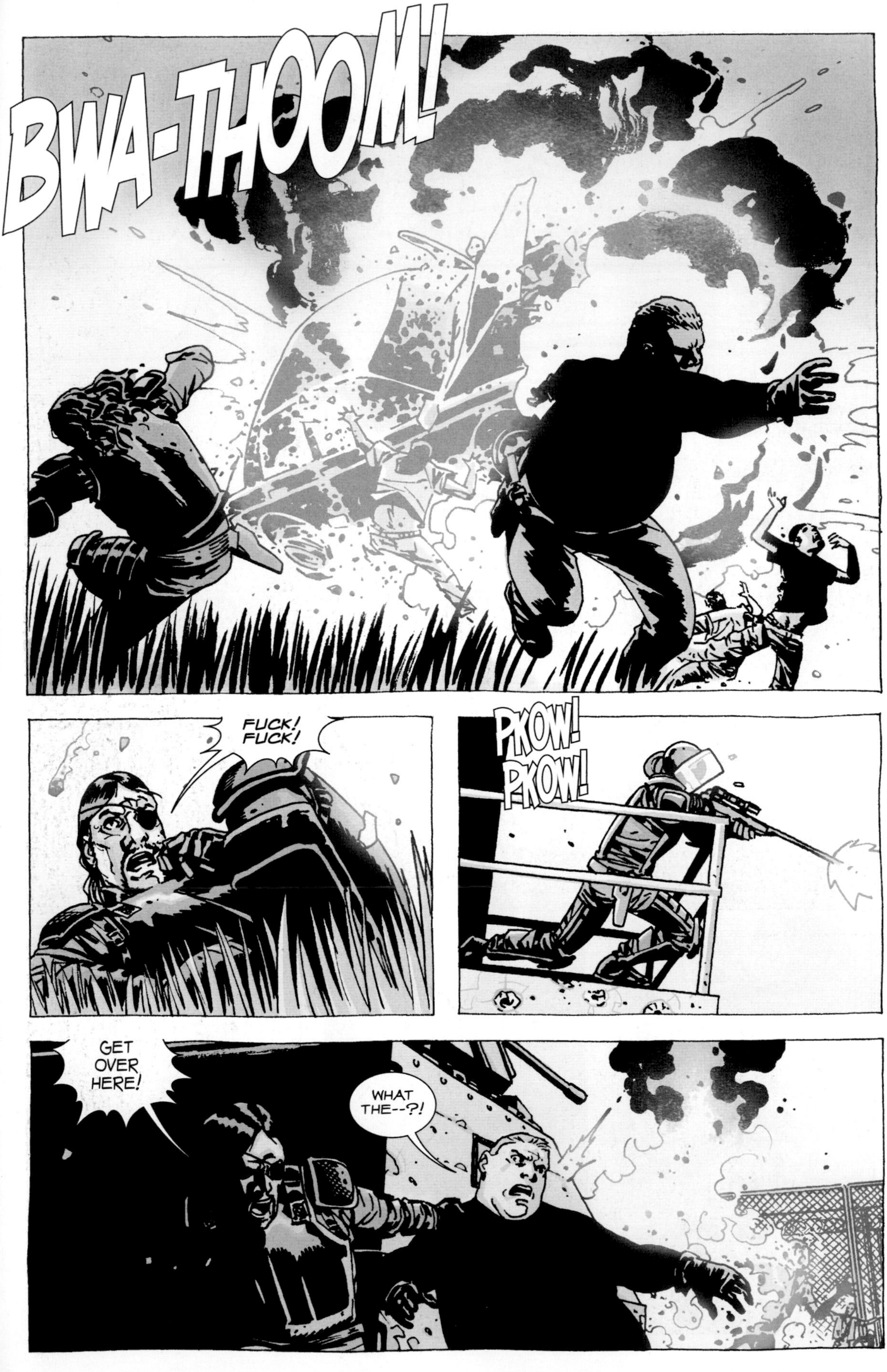
BWA-THOOM!
FUCK! FUCK!
PKOW! PKOW!
GET OVER HERE!
WHAT THE--?!

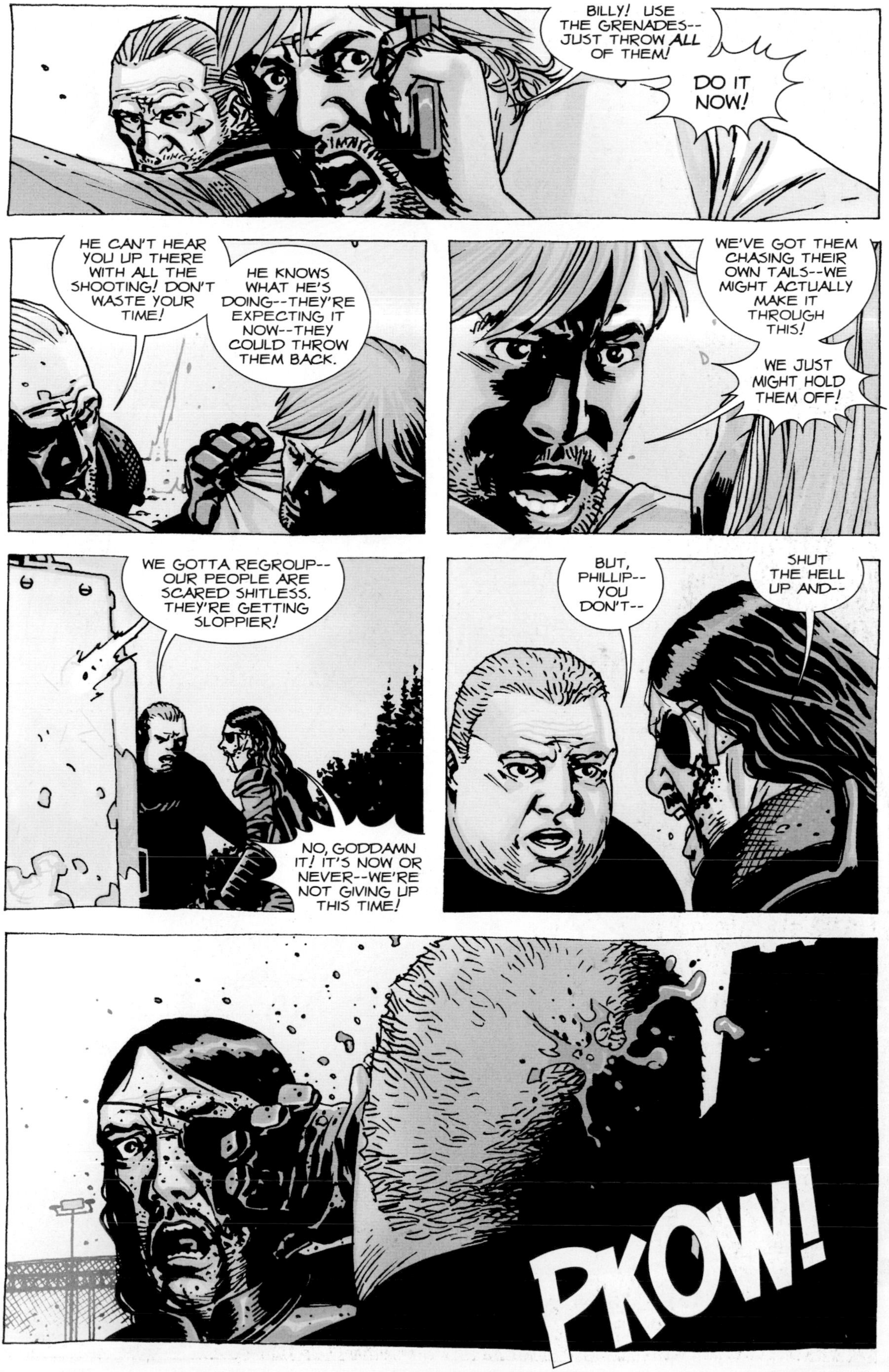
BILLY! USE THE GRENADES-- JUST THROW ALL OF THEM!
DO IT NOW!
HE CAN'T HEAR YOU UP THERE WITH ALL THE SHOOTING! DON'T WASTE YOUR TIME!
HE KNOWS WHAT HE'S DOING--THEY'RE EXPECTING IT NOW--THEY COULD THROW THEM BACK.
WE'VE GOT THEM CHASING THEIR OWN TAILS--WE MIGHT ACTUALLY MAKE IT THROUGH THIS!
WE JUST MIGHT HOLD THEM OFF!
WE GOTTA REGROUP-- OUR PEOPLE ARE SCARED SHITLESS. THEY'RE GETTING SLOPPIER!
NO, GODDAMN IT! IT'S NOW OR NEVER--WE'RE NOT GIVING UP THIS TIME!
BUT, PHILLIP-- YOU DON'T--
SHUT THE HELL UP AND--
PKOW!

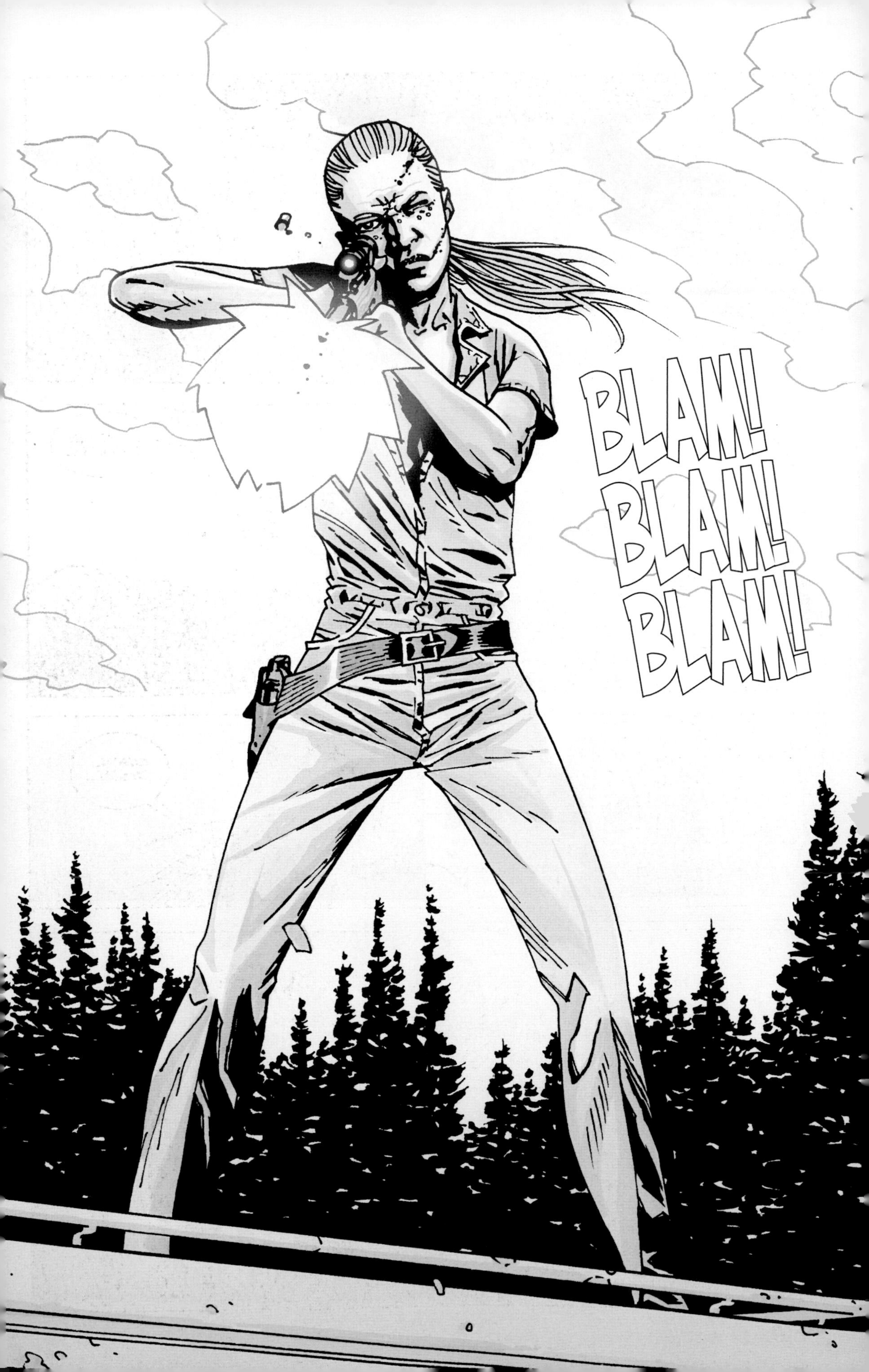
BLAM!
BLAM!
BLAM!

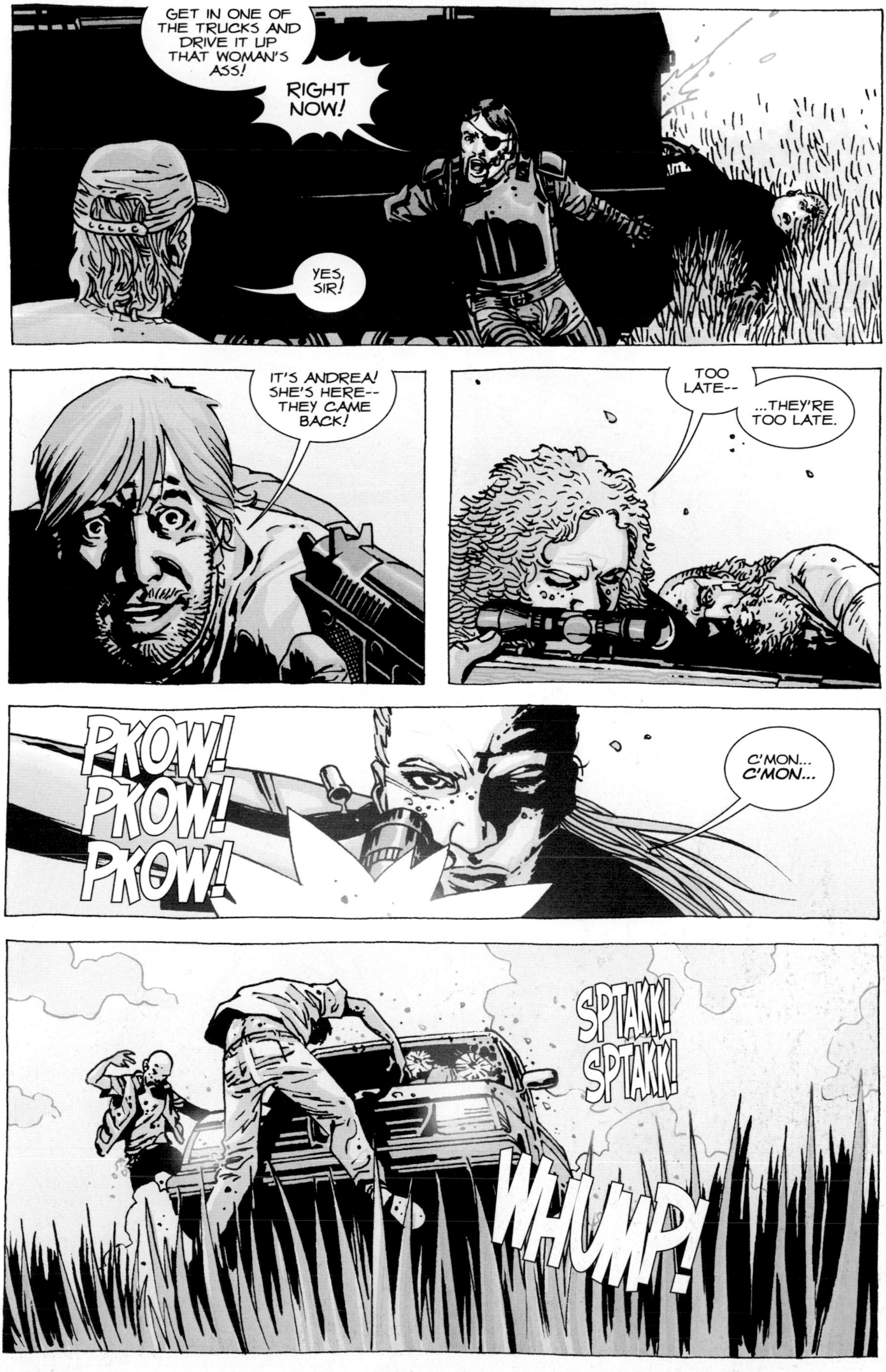
GET IN ONE OF THE TRUCKS AND DRIVE IT UP THAT WOMAN'S ASS!
RIGHT NOW!
YES, SIR!
IT'S ANDREA! SHE'S HERE-- THEY CAME BACK!
TOO LATE--
...THEY'RE TOO LATE.
PKOW! PKOW! PKOW!
C'MON... C'MON...
SPTAKK! SPTAKK!
WHUMP!

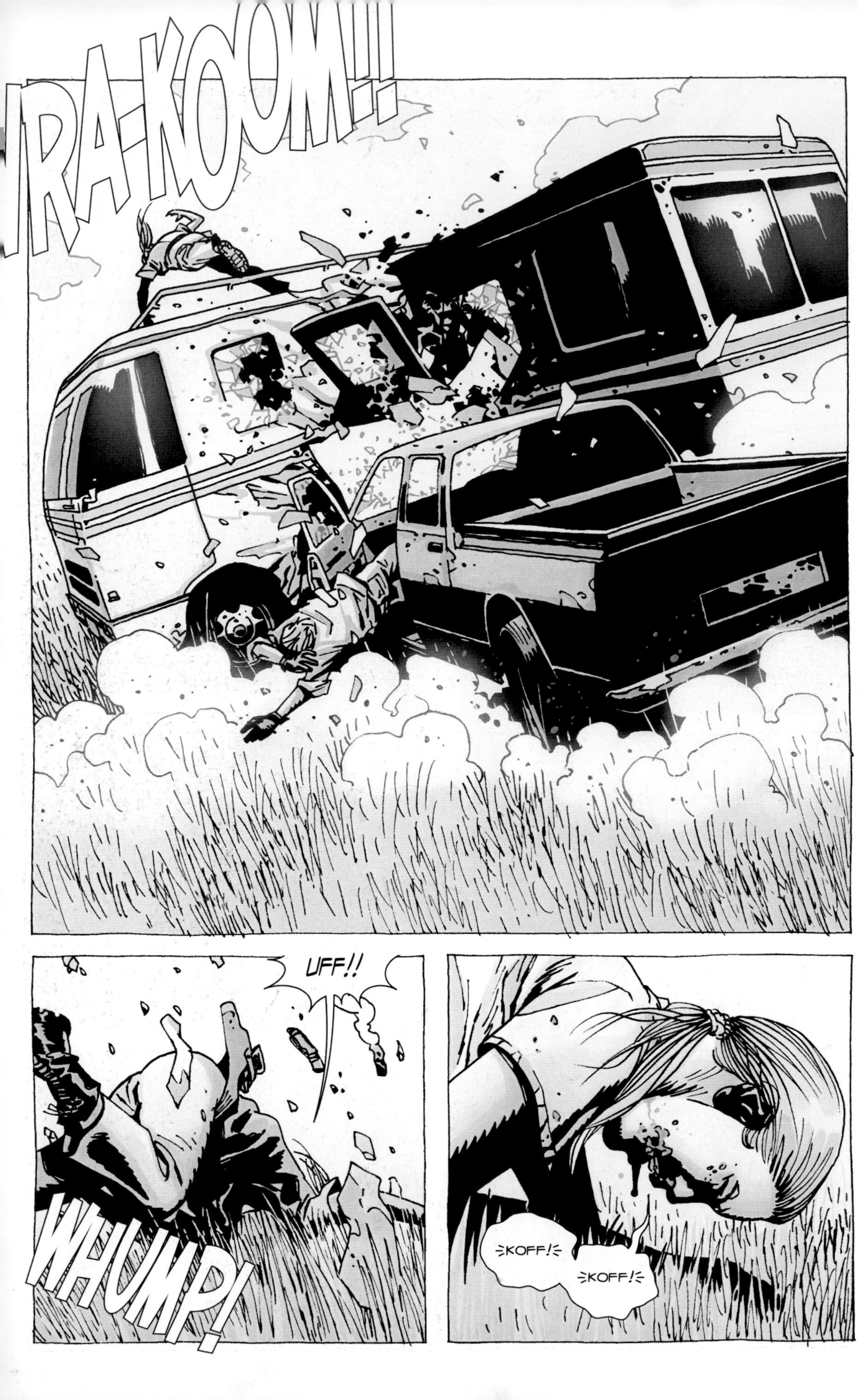
RA-KOOM!!!
UFF!!
WHUMP!
KOFF!
KOFF!

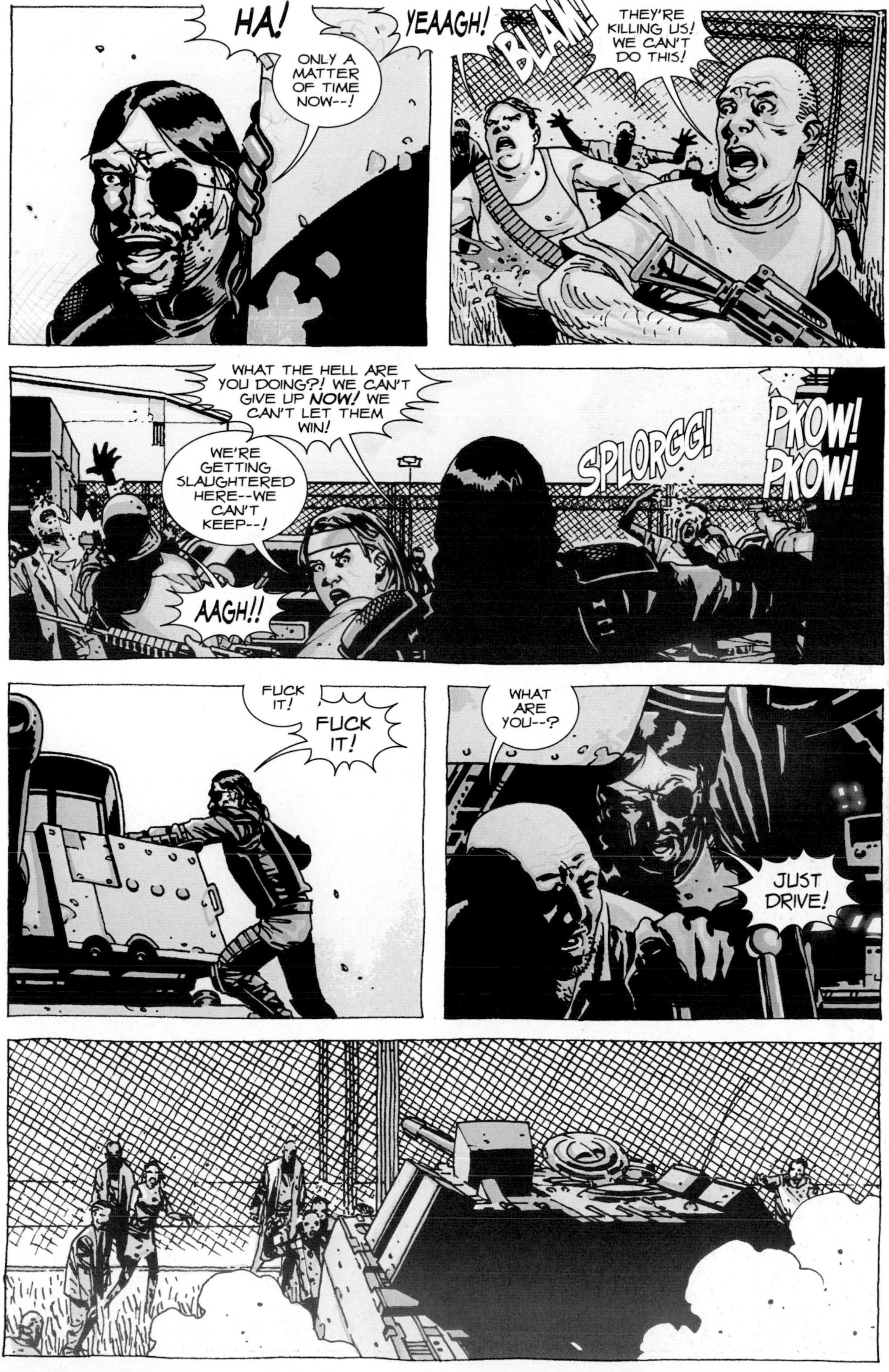
HA!
YEAAGH!
ONLY A MATTER OF TIME NOW--!
BLAM!
THEY'RE KILLING US! WE CAN'T DO THIS!
WHAT THE HELL ARE YOU DOING?! WE CAN'T GIVE UP NOW! WE CAN'T LET THEM WIN!
WE'RE GETTING SLAUGHTERED HERE--WE CAN'T KEEP--!
AAGH!!
SPLORGG!
PKOW! PKOW!
FUCK IT!
FUCK IT!
WHAT ARE YOU--?
JUST DRIVE!

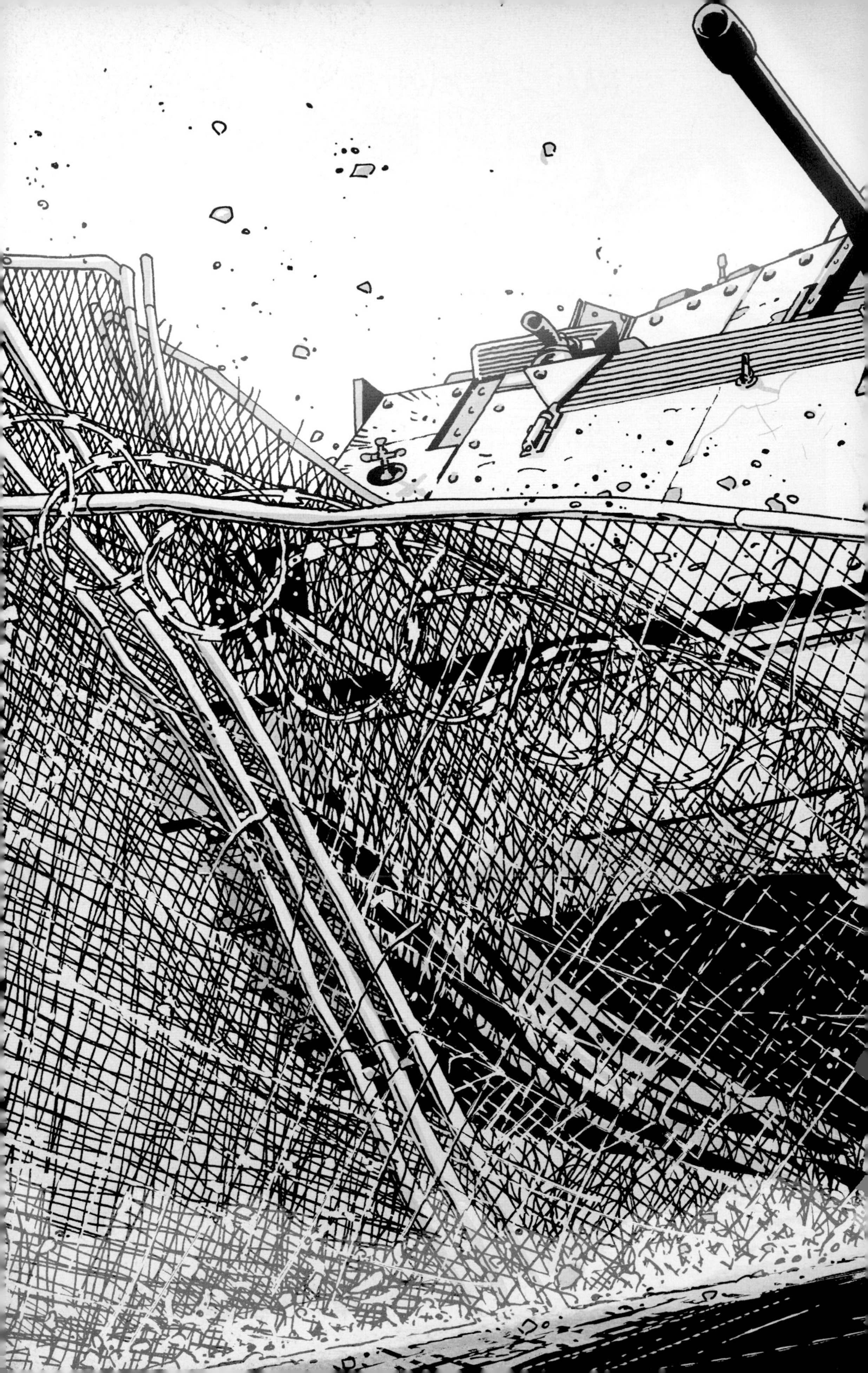

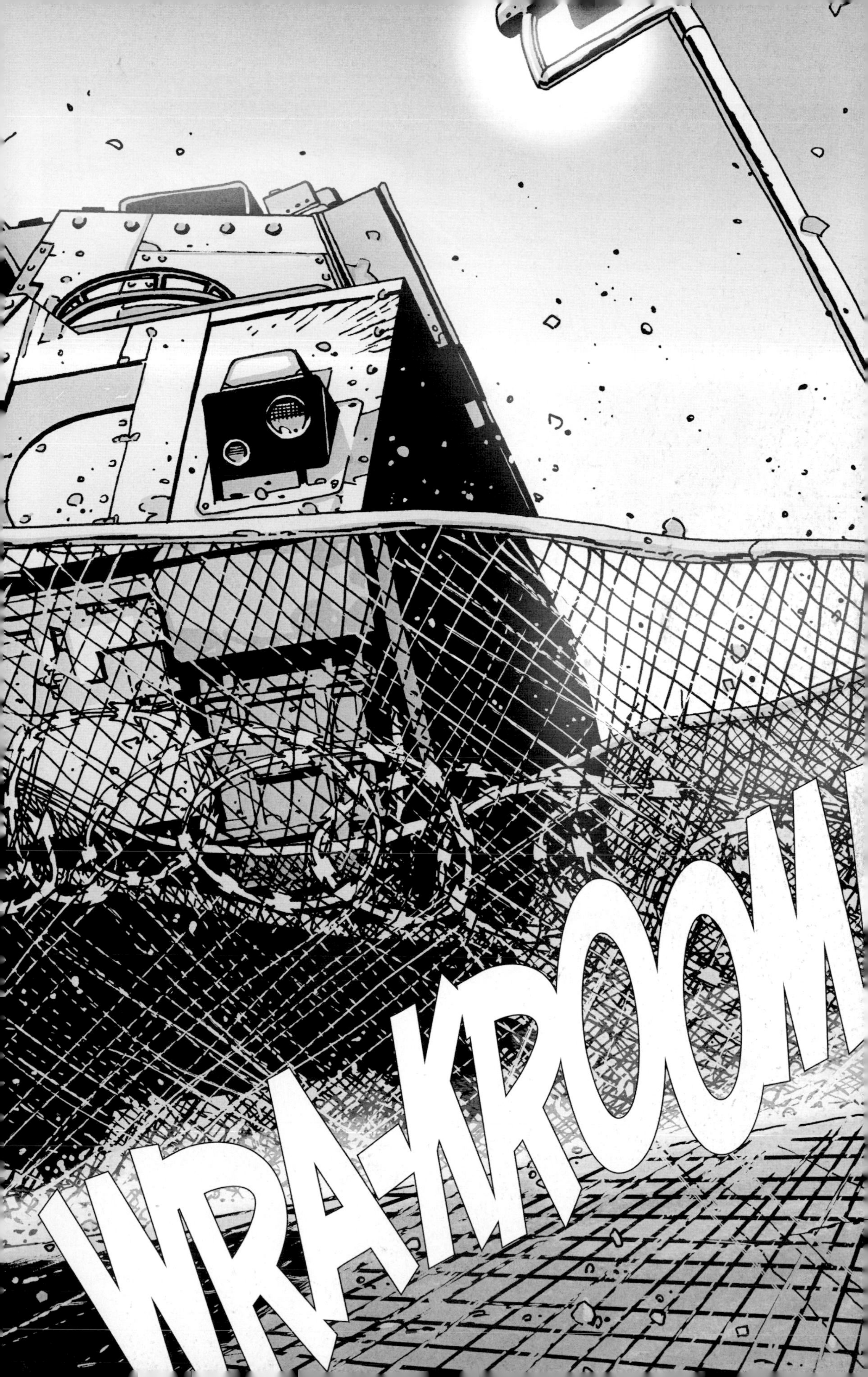
WRA-KROOM

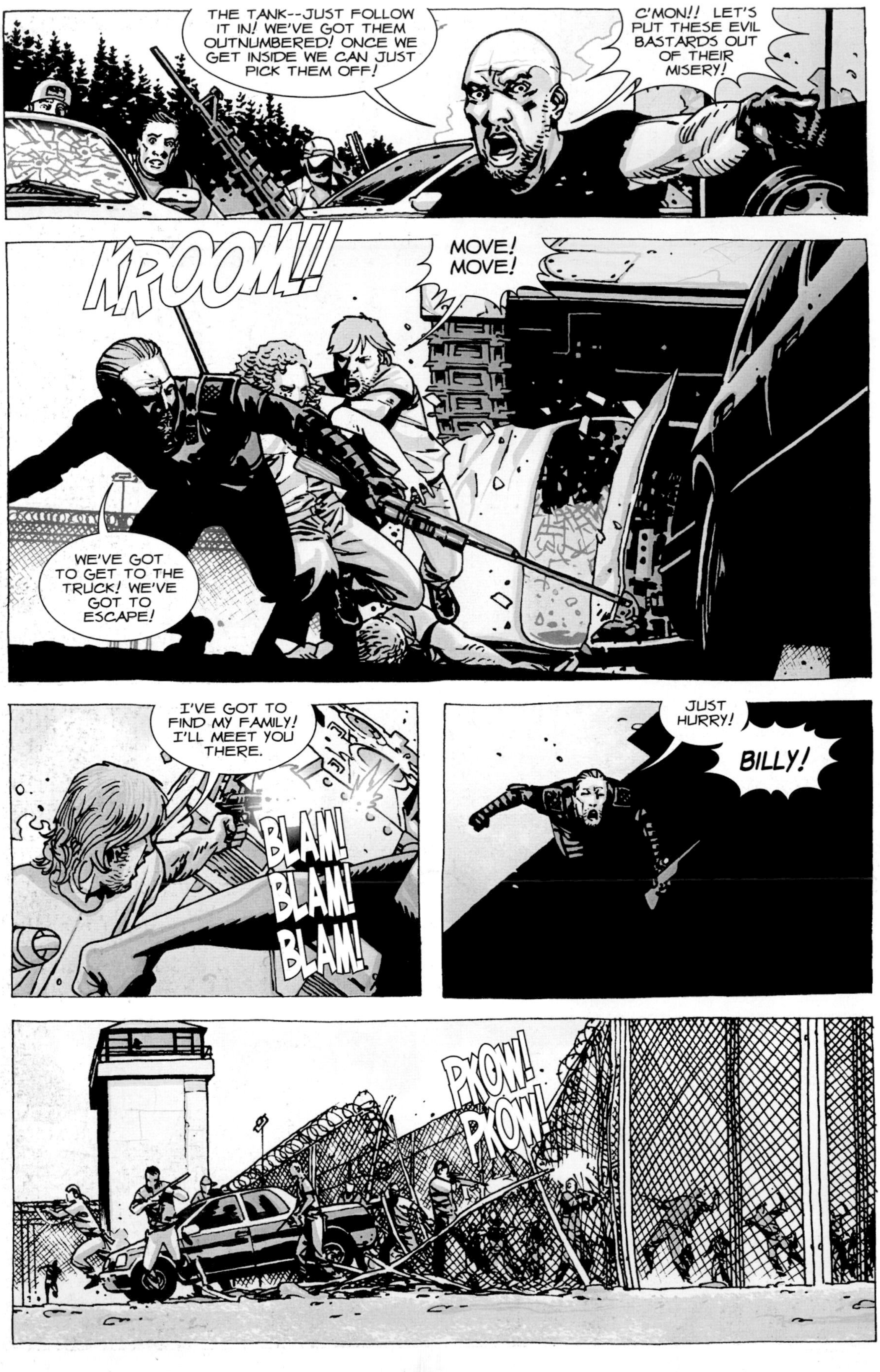

THE TANK--JUST FOLLOW IT IN! WE'VE GOT THEM OUTNUMBERED! ONCE WE GET INSIDE WE CAN JUST PICK THEM OFF!
C'MON!! LET'S PUT THESE EVIL BASTARDS OUT OF THEIR MISERY!
KROOM!!
MOVE! MOVE!
WE'VE GOT TO GET TO THE TRUCK! WE'VE GOT TO ESCAPE!
I'VE GOT TO FIND MY FAMILY! I'LL MEET YOU THERE.
BLAM! BLAM! BLAM!
JUST HURRY!
BILLY!
PKOW! PKOW!

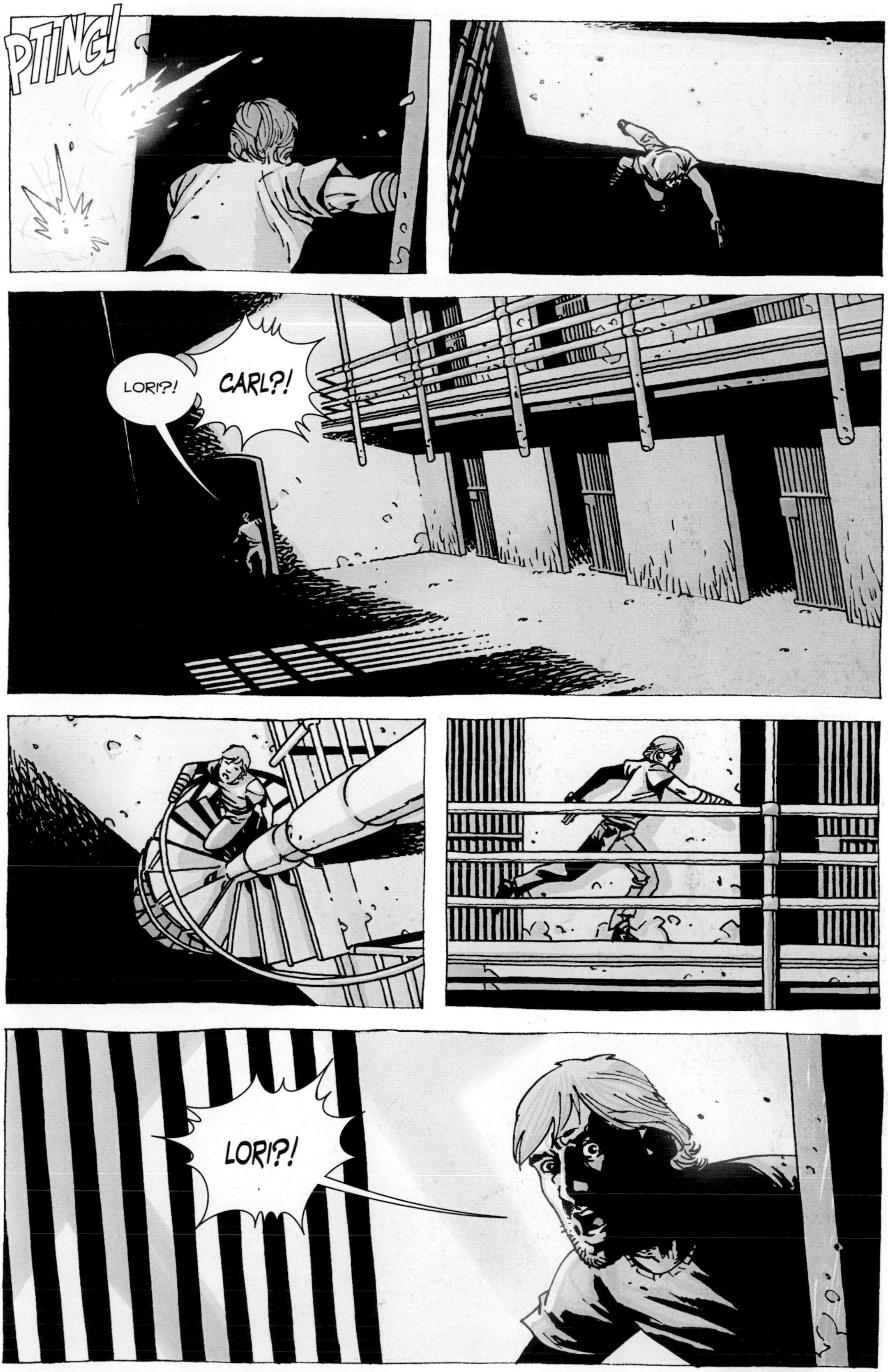
PTING!
LORI?!
CARL?!
LORI?!

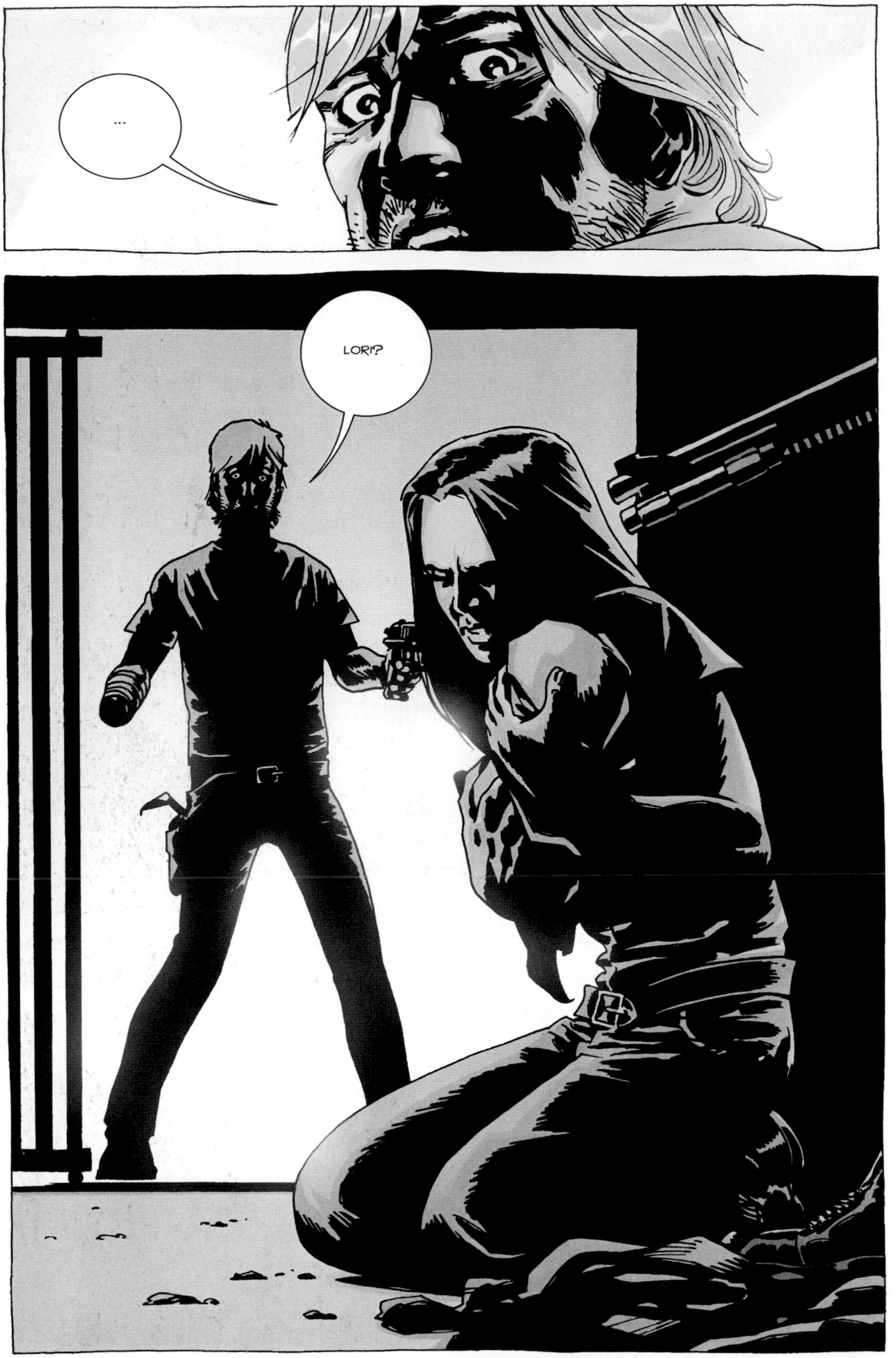
...
LORI?

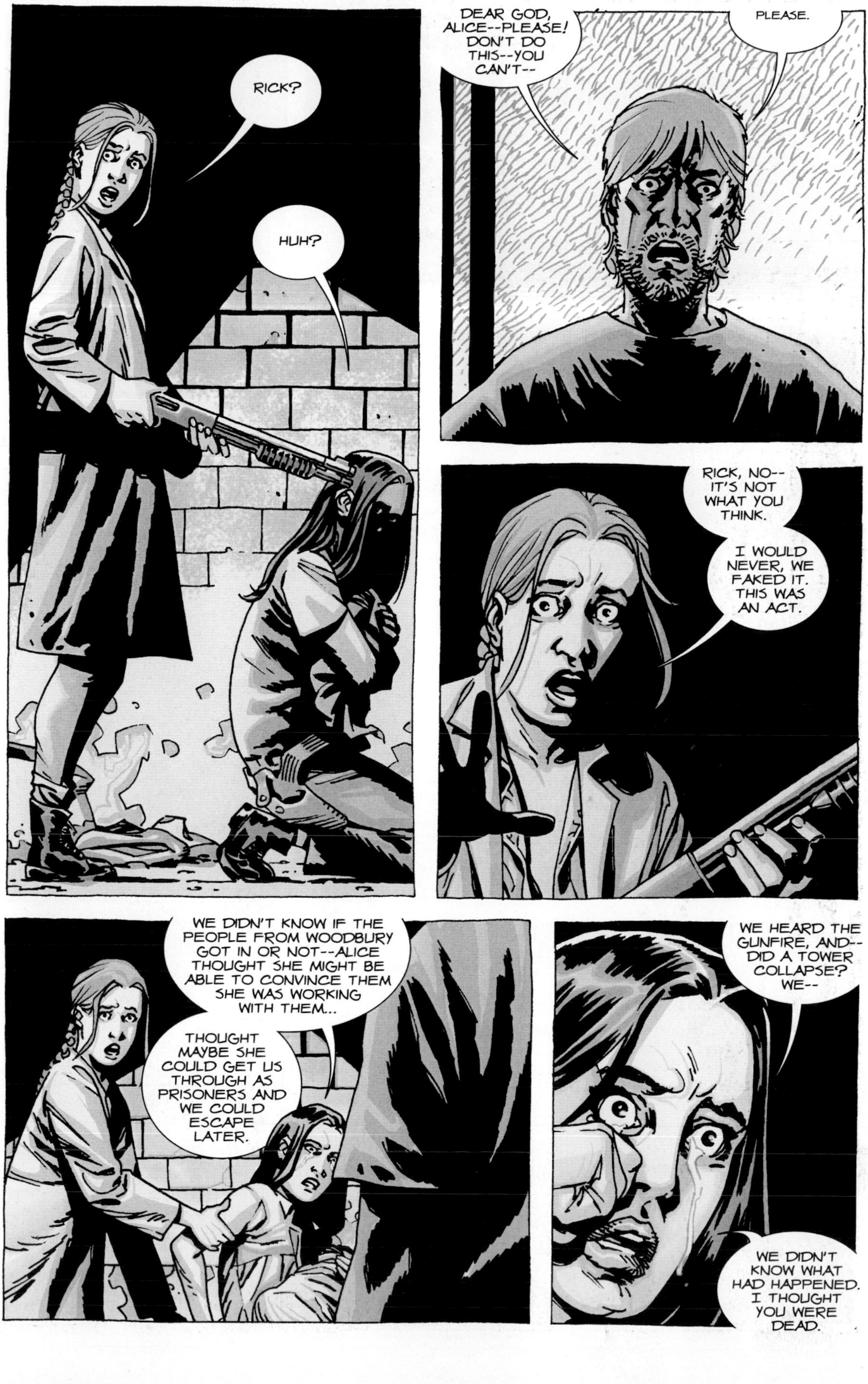
RICK?
HUH?
DEAR GOD, ALICE--PLEASE! DON'T DO THIS--YOU CAN'T--
PLEASE.
RICK, NO-- IT'S NOT WHAT YOU THINK.
I WOULD NEVER, WE FAKED IT. THIS WAS AN ACT.
WE DIDN'T KNOW IF THE PEOPLE FROM WOODBURY GOT IN OR NOT--ALICE THOUGHT SHE MIGHT BE ABLE TO CONVINCE THEM SHE WAS WORKING WITH THEM...
THOUGHT MAYBE SHE COULD GET US THROUGH AS PRISONERS AND WE COULD ESCAPE LATER.
WE HEARD THE GUNFIRE, AND-- DID A TOWER COLLAPSE? WE--
WE DIDN'T KNOW WHAT HAD HAPPENED. I THOUGHT YOU WERE DEAD.

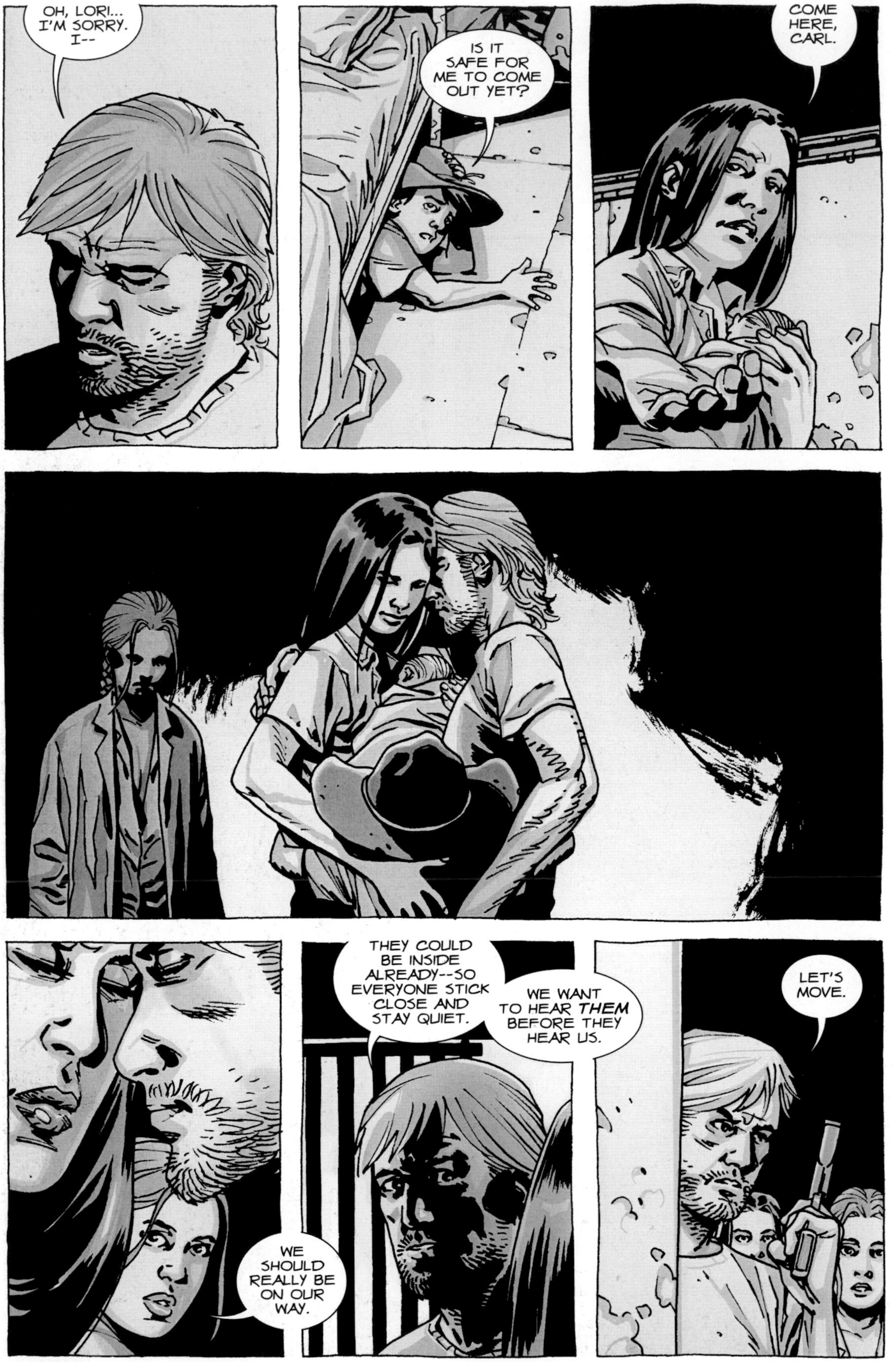
OH, LORI... I'M SORRY. I--
IS IT SAFE FOR ME TO COME OUT YET?
COME HERE, CARL.
WE SHOULD REALLY BE ON OUR WAY.
THEY COULD BE INSIDE ALREADY--SO EVERYONE STICK CLOSE AND STAY QUIET.
WE WANT TO HEAR *THEM* BEFORE THEY HEAR US.
LET'S MOVE.

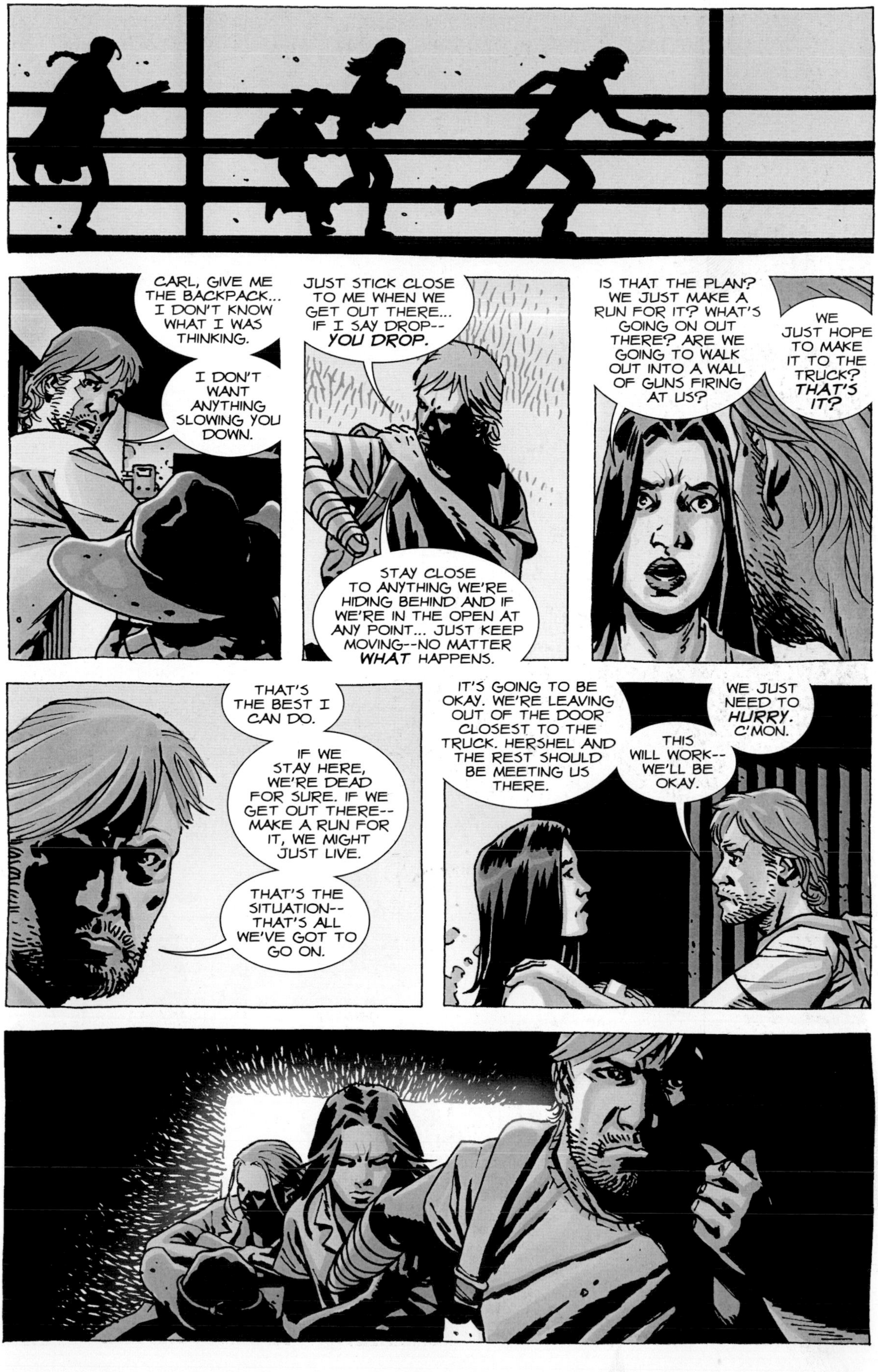
CARL, GIVE ME THE BACKPACK... I DON'T KNOW WHAT I WAS THINKING.
I DON'T WANT ANYTHING SLOWING YOU DOWN.
JUST STICK CLOSE TO ME WHEN WE GET OUT THERE... IF I SAY DROP-- YOU DROP.
STAY CLOSE TO ANYTHING WE'RE HIDING BEHIND AND IF WE'RE IN THE OPEN AT ANY POINT... JUST KEEP MOVING--NO MATTER WHAT HAPPENS.
IS THAT THE PLAN? WE JUST MAKE A RUN FOR IT? WHAT'S GOING ON OUT THERE? ARE WE GOING TO WALK OUT INTO A WALL OF GUNS FIRING AT US?
WE JUST HOPE TO MAKE IT TO THE TRUCK? THAT'S IT?
THAT'S THE BEST I CAN DO.
IF WE STAY HERE, WE'RE DEAD FOR SURE. IF WE GET OUT THERE-- MAKE A RUN FOR IT, WE MIGHT JUST LIVE.
THAT'S THE SITUATION-- THAT'S ALL WE'VE GOT TO GO ON.
IT'S GOING TO BE OKAY. WE'RE LEAVING OUT OF THE DOOR CLOSEST TO THE TRUCK. HERSHEL AND THE REST SHOULD BE MEETING US THERE.
THIS WILL WORK-- WE'LL BE OKAY.
WE JUST NEED TO HURRY. C'MON.

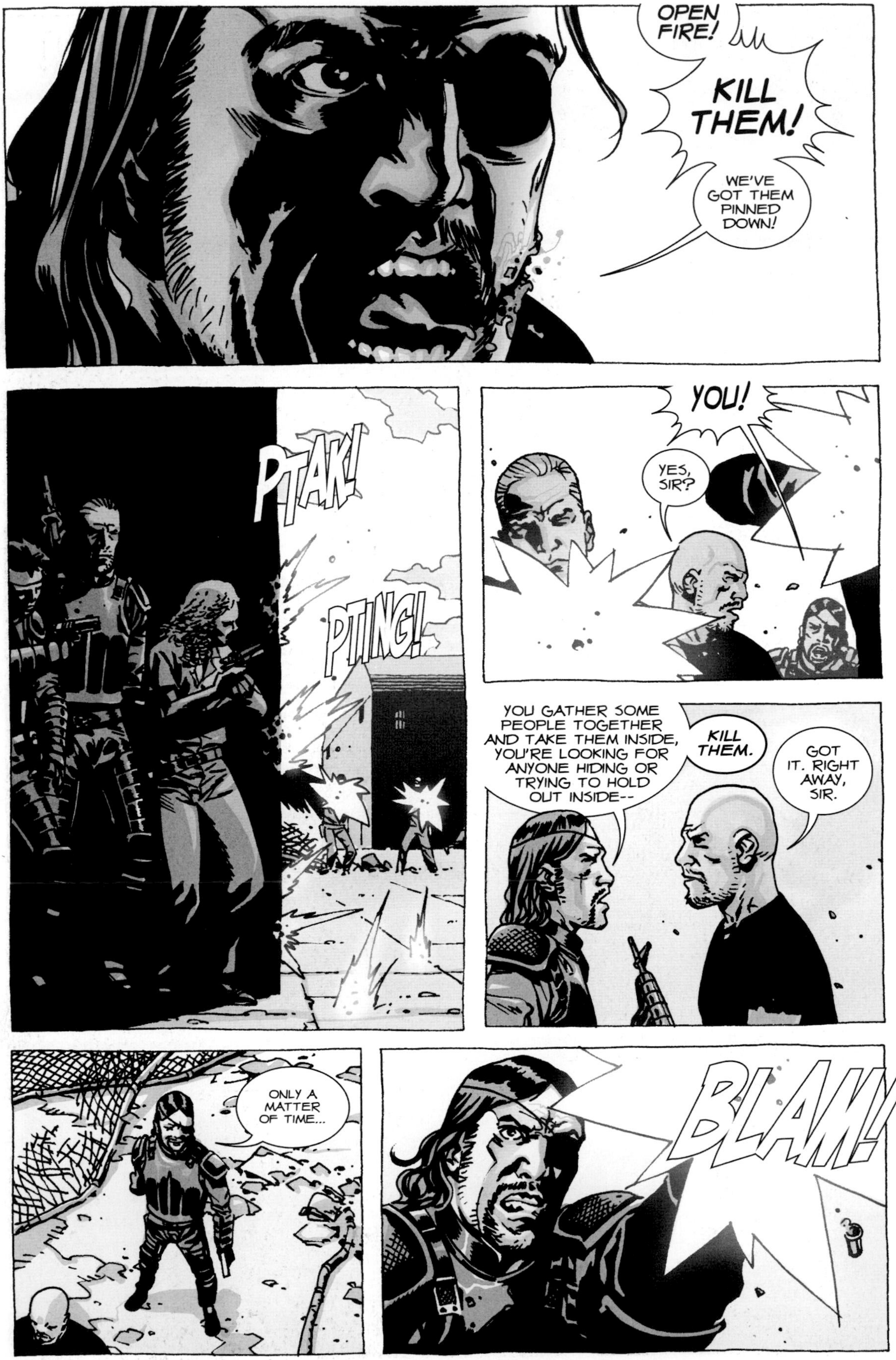
OPEN FIRE!
KILL THEM!
WE'VE GOT THEM PINNED DOWN!
PTAK!
PTING!
YOU!
YES, SIR?
YOU GATHER SOME PEOPLE TOGETHER AND TAKE THEM INSIDE, YOU'RE LOOKING FOR ANYONE HIDING OR TRYING TO HOLD OUT INSIDE--
KILL THEM.
GOT IT. RIGHT AWAY, SIR.
ONLY A MATTER OF TIME...
BLAM!

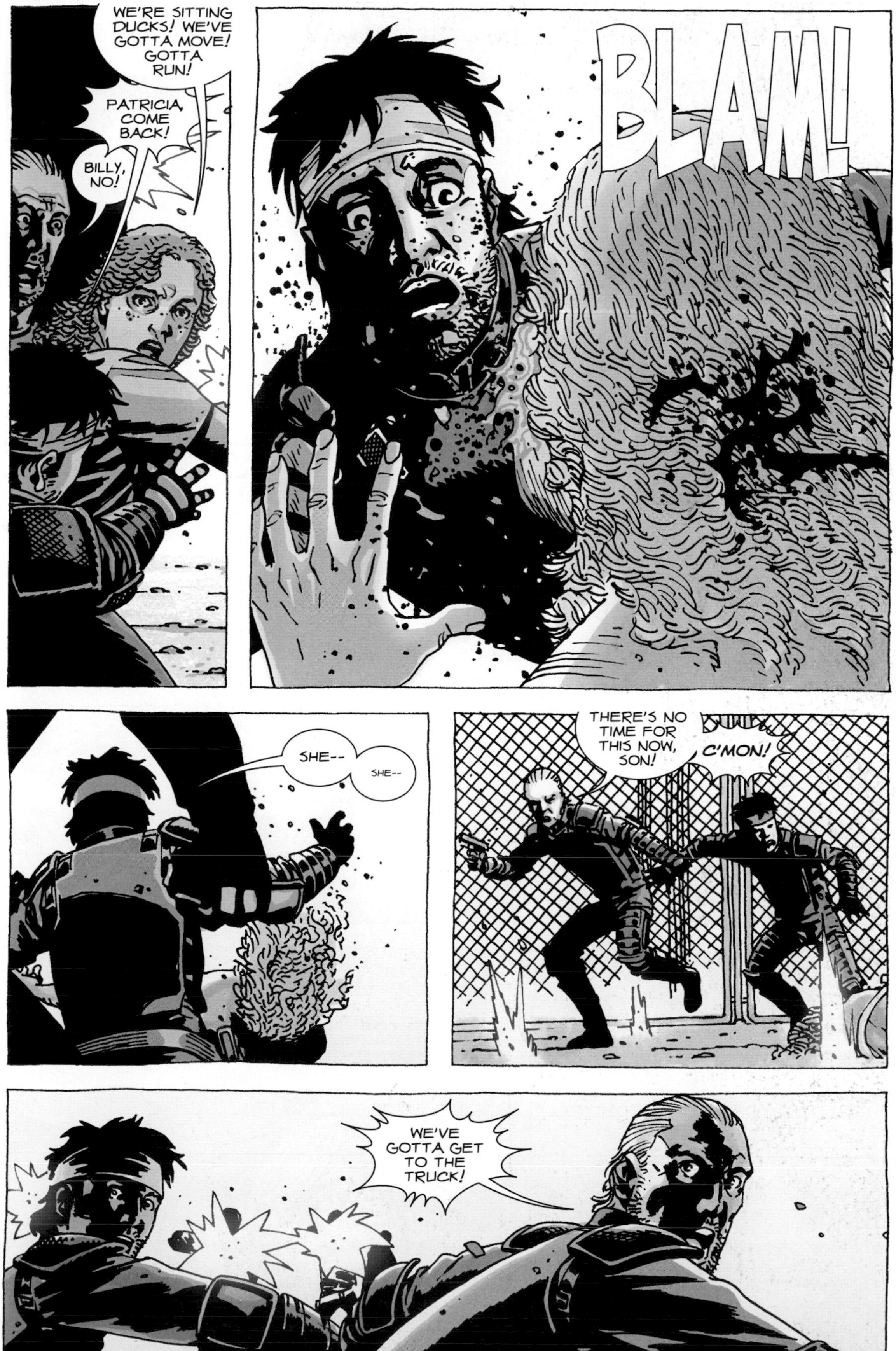
WE'RE SITTING DUCKS! WE'VE GOTTA MOVE! GOTTA RUN!
PATRICIA, COME BACK!
BILLY, NO!
BLAM!
SHE--
SHE--
THERE'S NO TIME FOR THIS NOW, SON!
C'MON!
WE'VE GOTTA GET TO THE TRUCK!

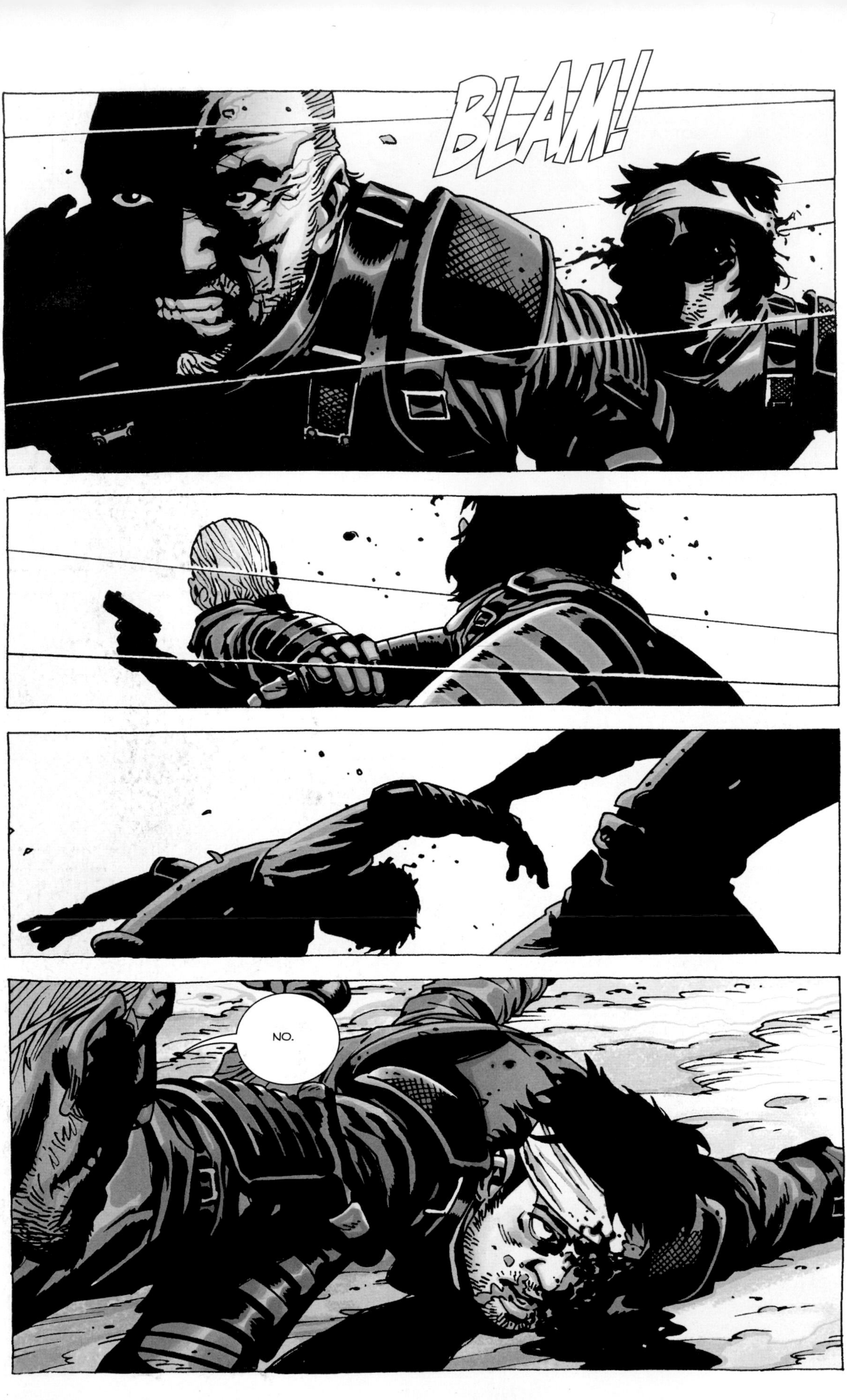
BLAM!
NO.

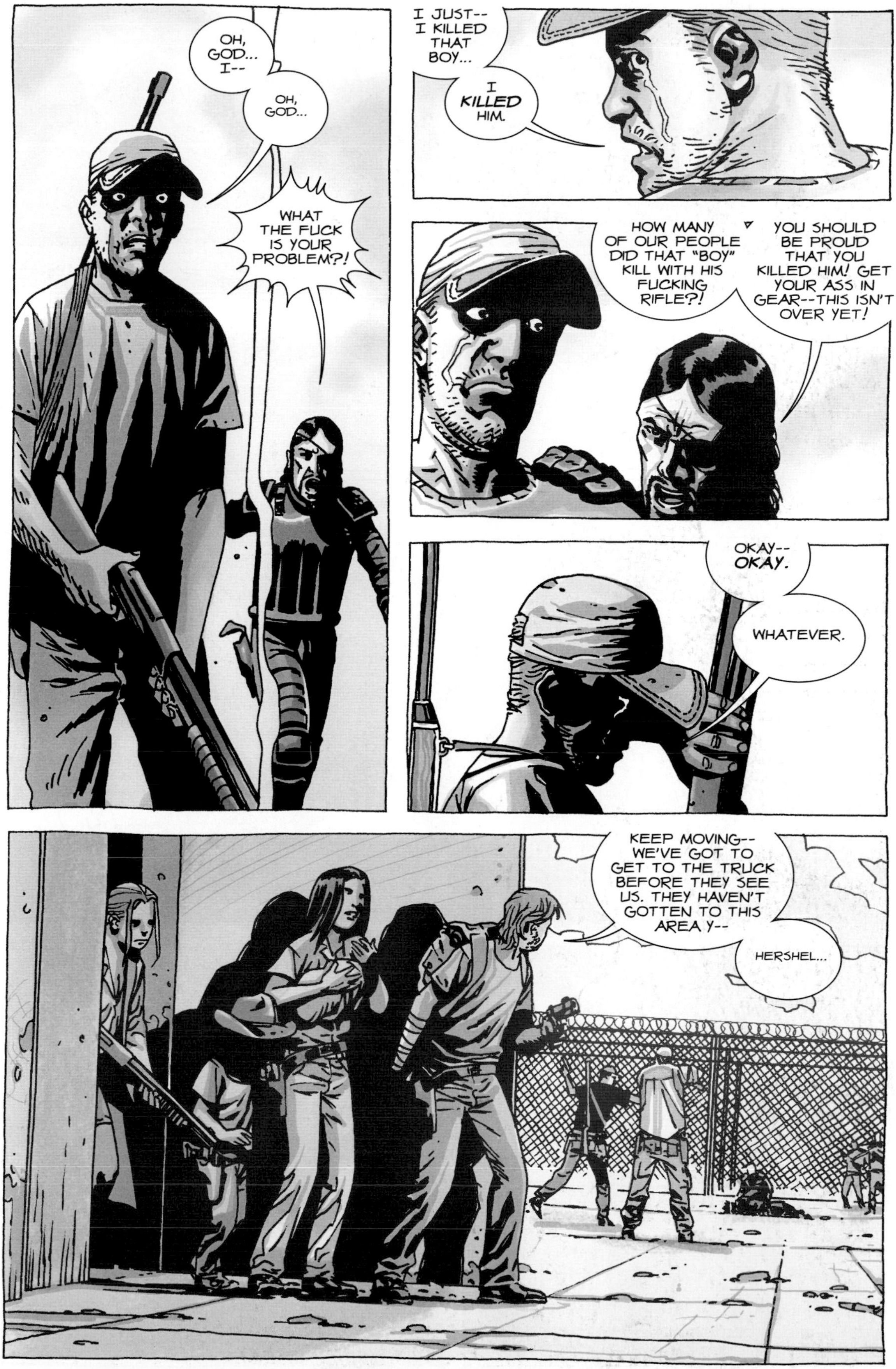
OH, GOD... I--
OH, GOD...
WHAT THE FUCK IS YOUR PROBLEM?!
I JUST-- I KILLED THAT BOY...
I KILLED HIM.
HOW MANY OF OUR PEOPLE DID THAT "BOY" KILL WITH HIS FUCKING RIFLE?!
YOU SHOULD BE PROUD THAT YOU KILLED HIM! GET YOUR ASS IN GEAR--THIS ISN'T OVER YET!
OKAY-- OKAY.
WHATEVER.
KEEP MOVING-- WE'VE GOT TO GET TO THE TRUCK BEFORE THEY SEE US. THEY HAVEN'T GOTTEN TO THIS AREA Y--
HERSHEL...

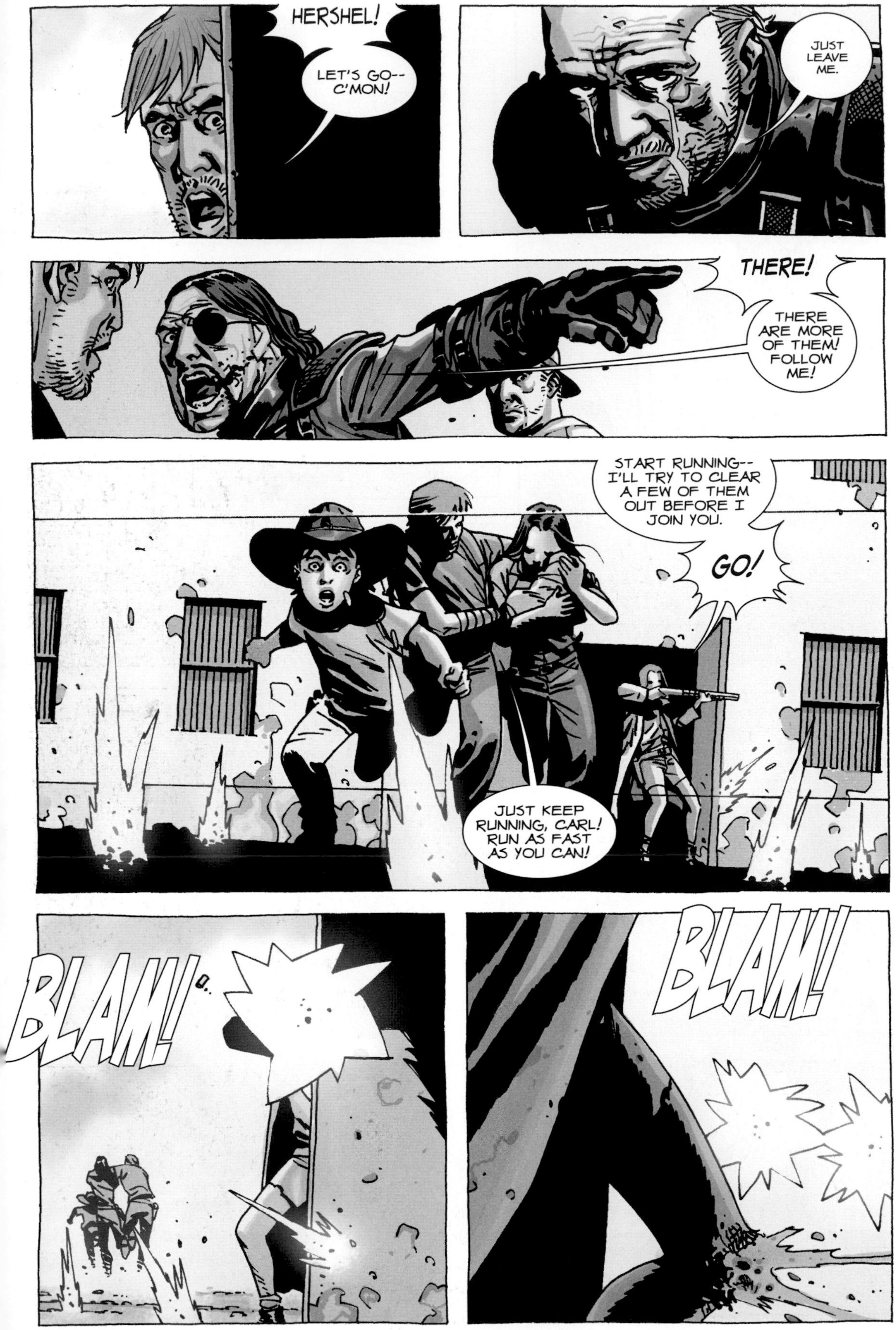
HERSHEL!
LET'S GO-- C'MON!
JUST LEAVE ME.
THERE!
THERE ARE MORE OF THEM! FOLLOW ME!
START RUNNING-- I'LL TRY TO CLEAR A FEW OF THEM OUT BEFORE I JOIN YOU.
GO!
JUST KEEP RUNNING, CARL! RUN AS FAST AS YOU CAN!
BLAM!
BLAM!

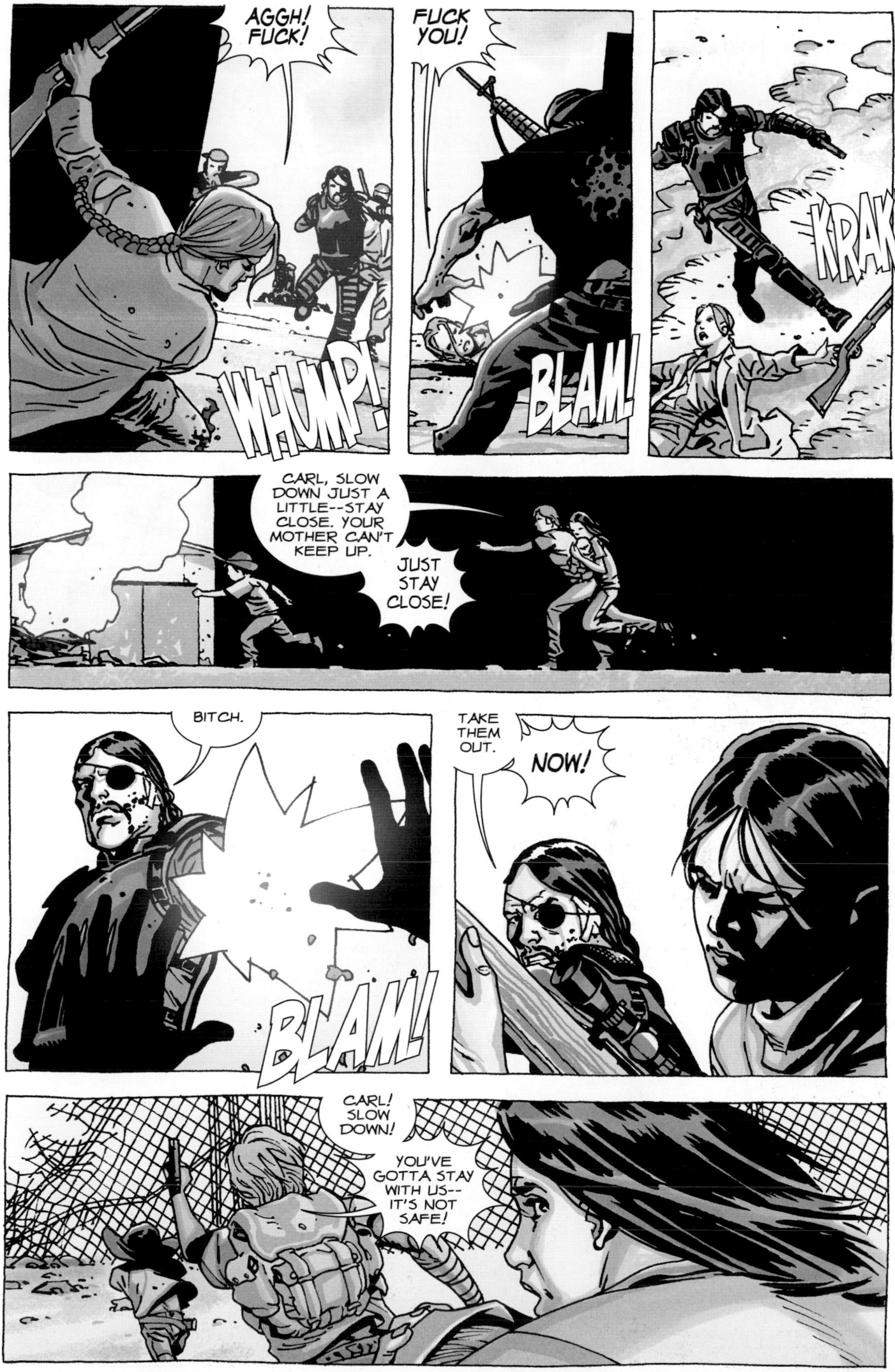
AGGH! FUCK!
WHUMP!
FUCK YOU!
BLAM!
KRAK!
CARL, SLOW DOWN JUST A LITTLE--STAY CLOSE. YOUR MOTHER CAN'T KEEP UP.
JUST STAY CLOSE!
BITCH.
BLAM!
TAKE THEM OUT.
NOW!
CARL! SLOW DOWN!
YOU'VE GOTTA STAY WITH US-- IT'S NOT SAFE!

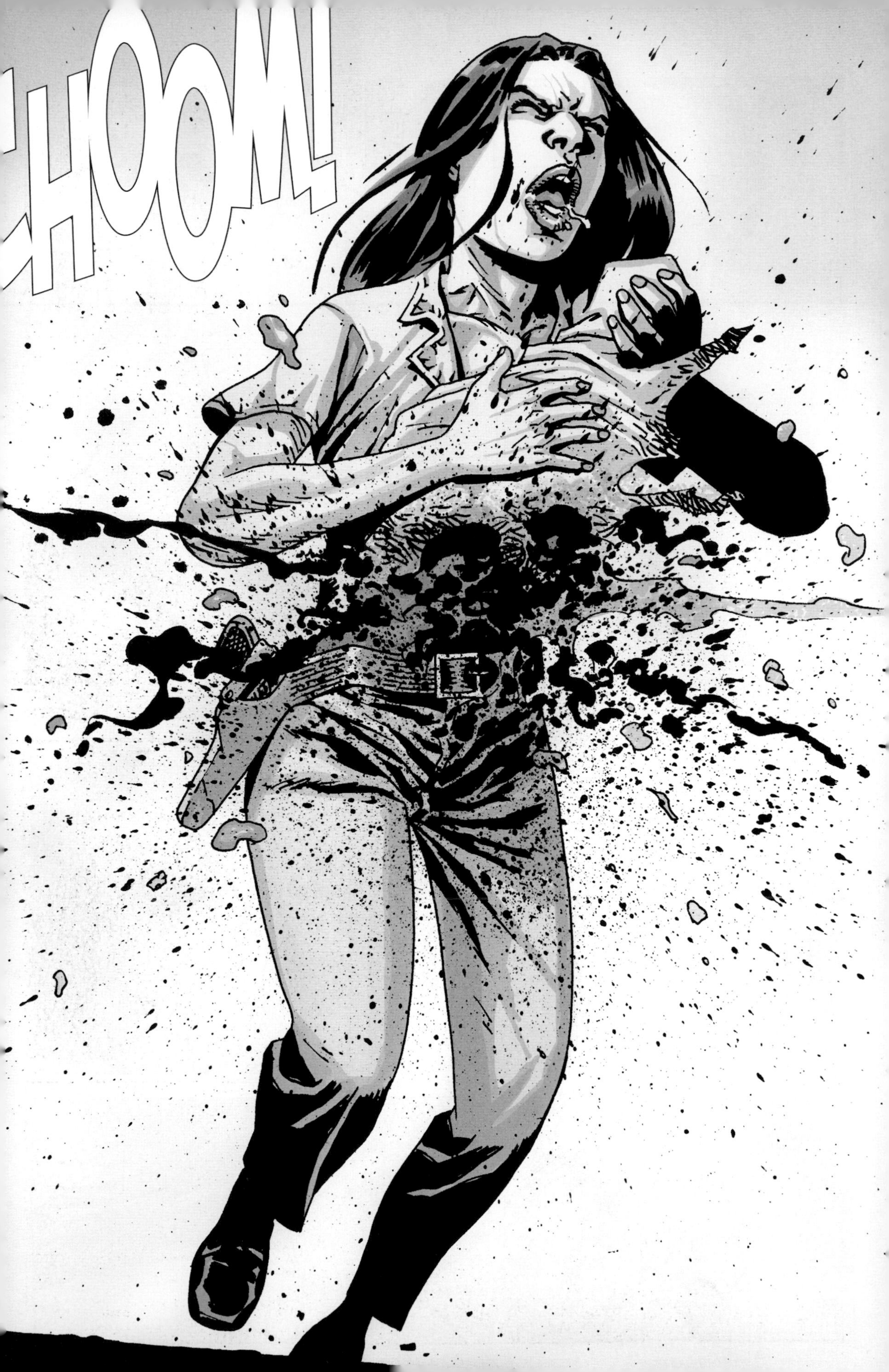
HOOM!

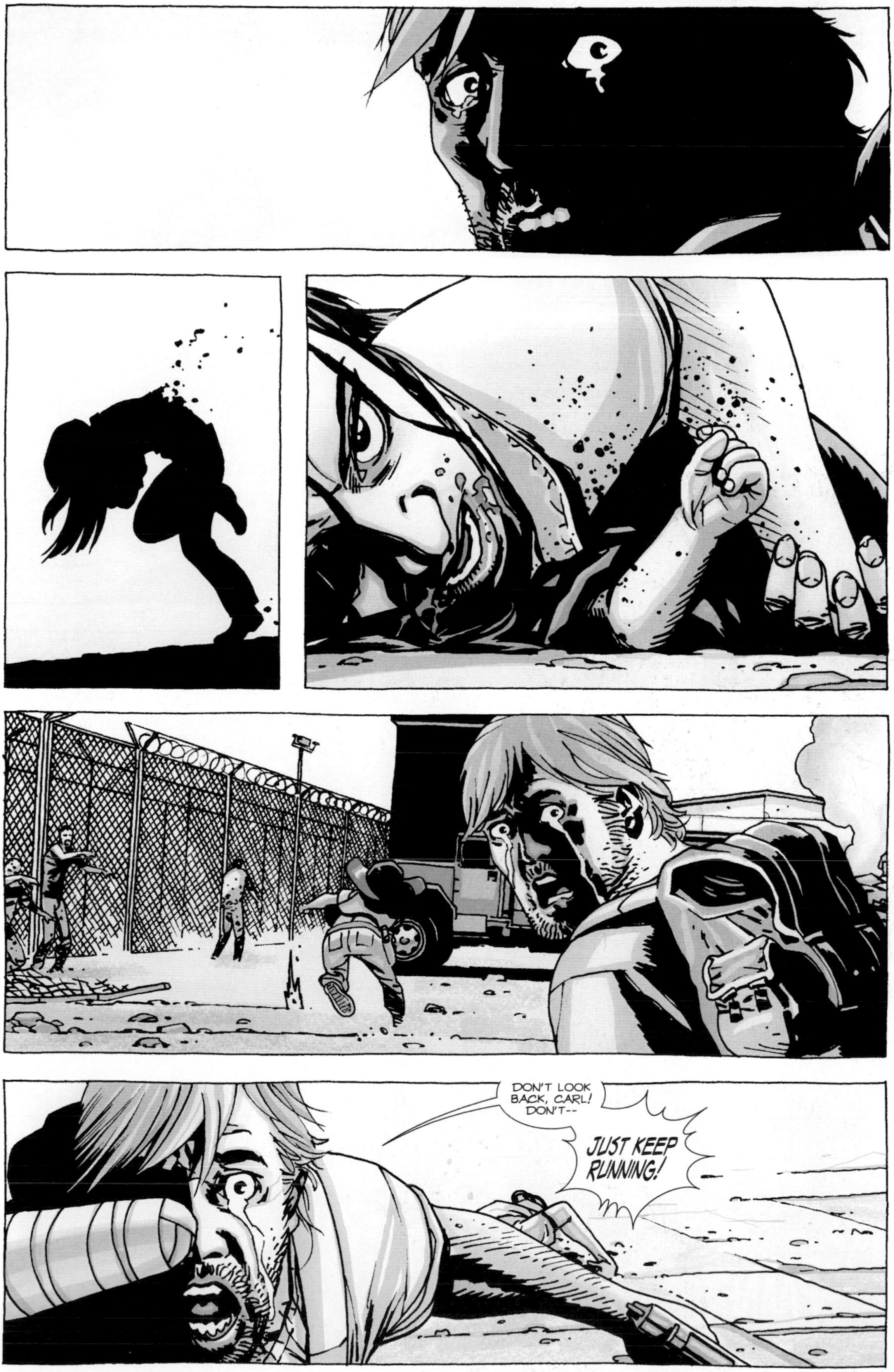

DON'T LOOK BACK, CARL! DON'T--
JUST KEEP RUNNING!

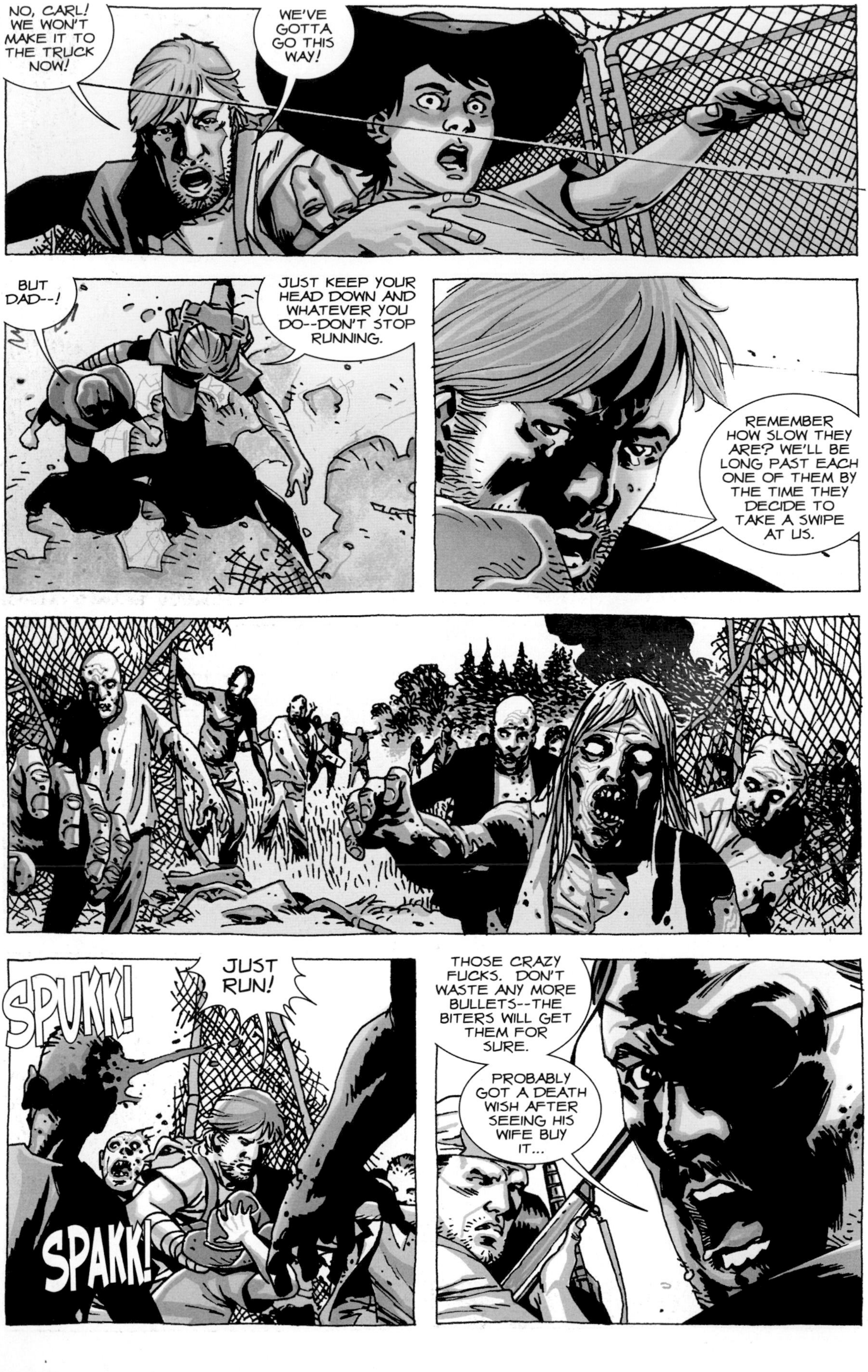
NO, CARL! WE WON'T MAKE IT TO THE TRUCK NOW!
WE'VE GOTTA GO THIS WAY!
BUT DAD--!
JUST KEEP YOUR HEAD DOWN AND WHATEVER YOU DO--DON'T STOP RUNNING.
REMEMBER HOW SLOW THEY ARE? WE'LL BE LONG PAST EACH ONE OF THEM BY THE TIME THEY DECIDE TO TAKE A SWIPE AT US.
SPUKK!
JUST RUN!
SPAKK!
THOSE CRAZY FUCKS. DON'T WASTE ANY MORE BULLETS--THE BITERS WILL GET THEM FOR SURE.
PROBABLY GOT A DEATH WISH AFTER SEEING HIS WIFE BUY IT...

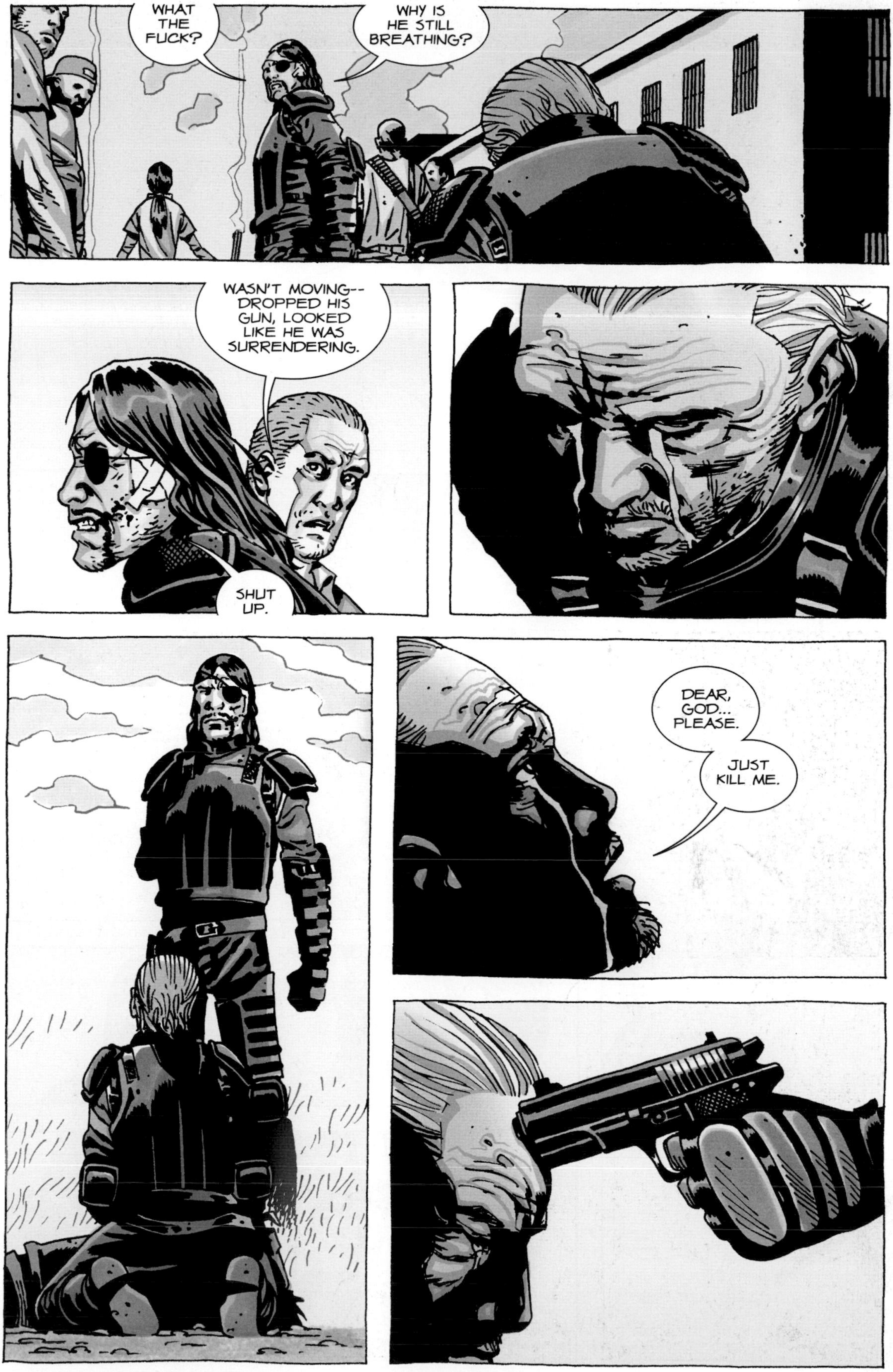
WHAT THE FUCK?
WHY IS HE STILL BREATHING?
WASN'T MOVING-- DROPPED HIS GUN, LOOKED LIKE HE WAS SURRENDERING.
SHUT UP.
DEAR, GOD... PLEASE.
JUST KILL ME.

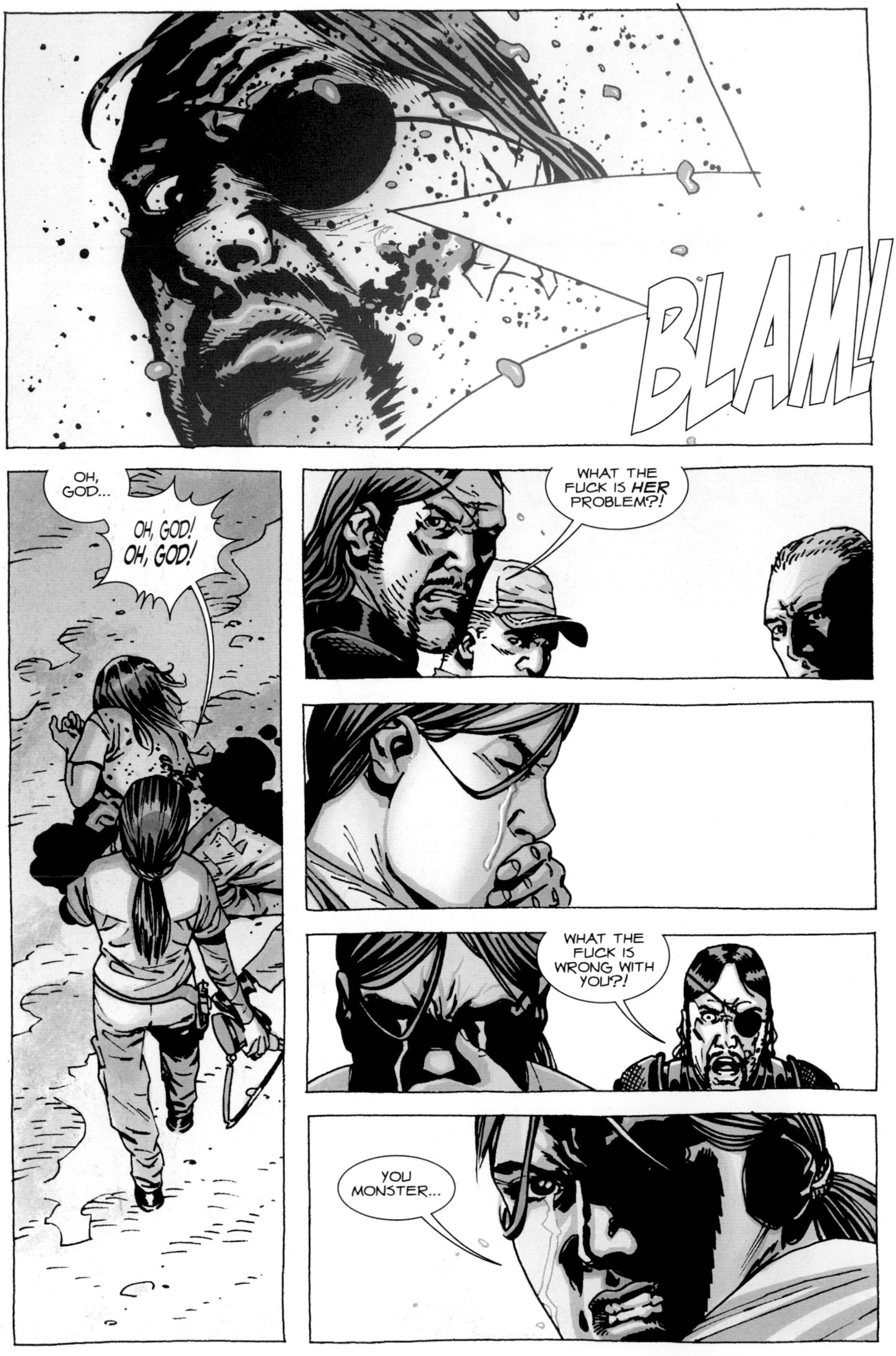
BLAM!
OH, GOD...
OH, GOD! OH, GOD!
WHAT THE FUCK IS HER PROBLEM?!
WHAT THE FUCK IS WRONG WITH YOU?!
YOU MONSTER...

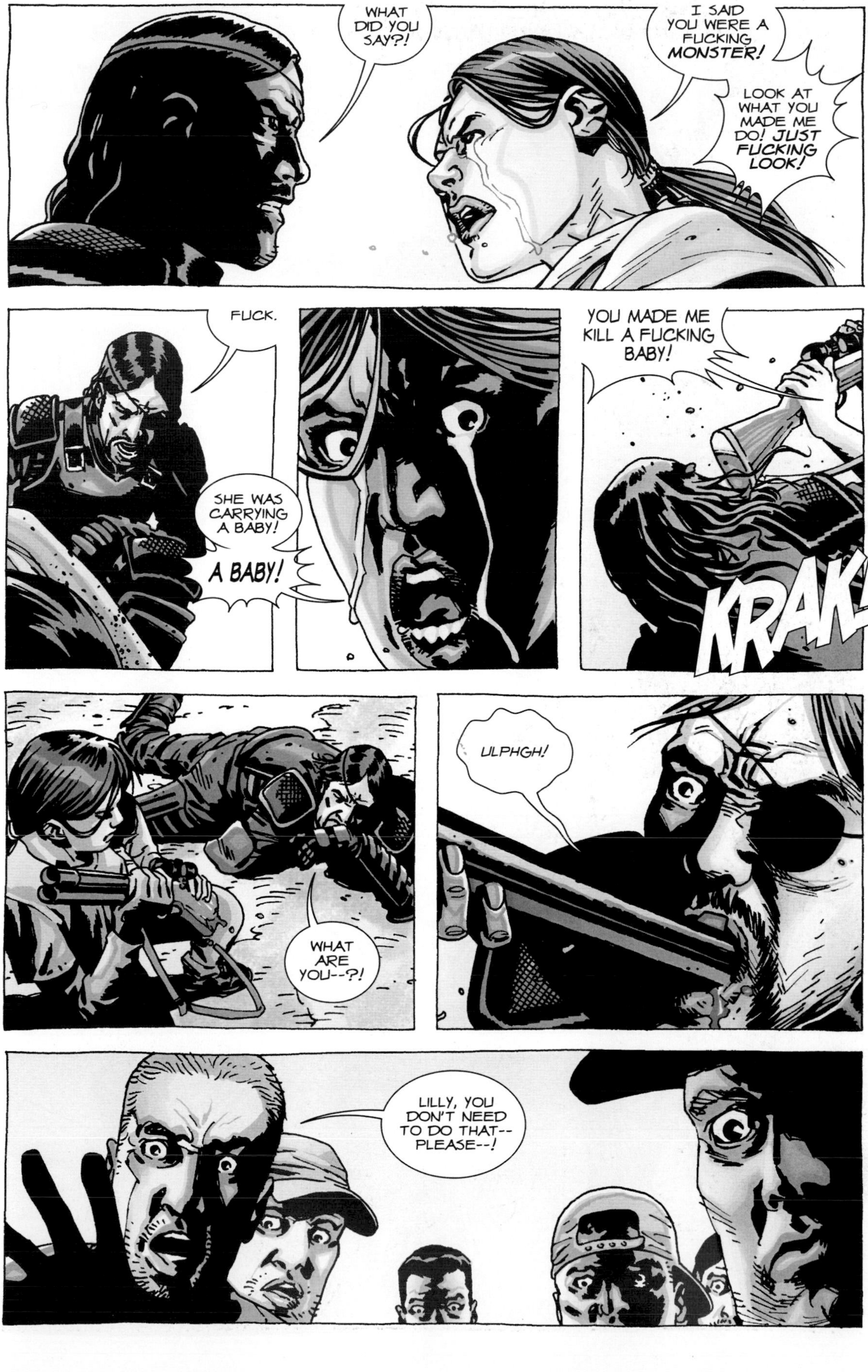
WHAT DID YOU SAY?!
I SAID YOU WERE A FUCKING MONSTER!
LOOK AT WHAT YOU MADE ME DO! JUST FUCKING LOOK!
FUCK.
SHE WAS CARRYING A BABY!
A BABY!
YOU MADE ME KILL A FUCKING BABY!
KRAK!
WHAT ARE YOU--?!
ULPHGH!
LILLY, YOU DON'T NEED TO DO THAT-- PLEASE--!

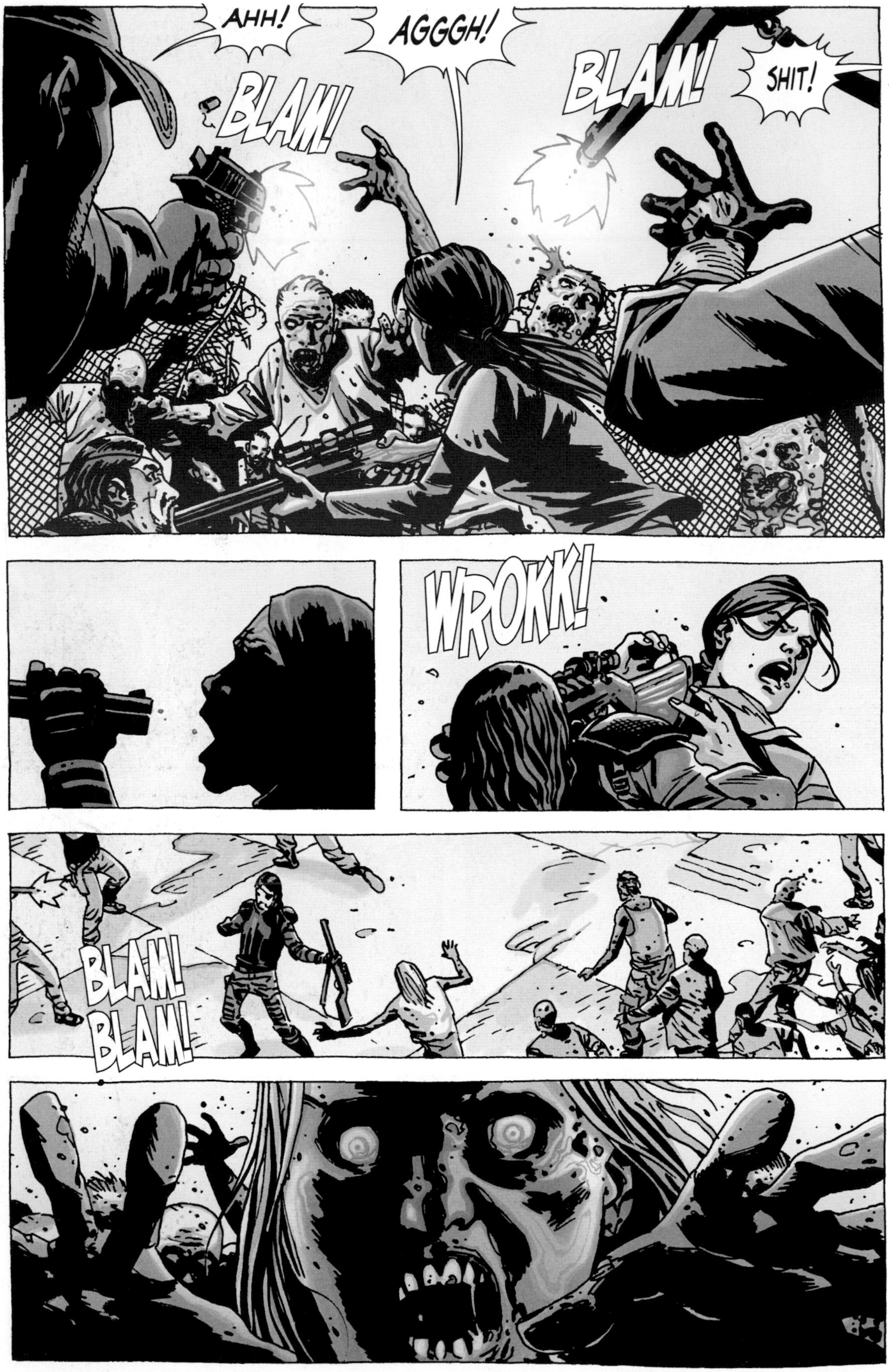
AHH!
AGGGH!
BLAM!
BLAM!
SHIT!
WROKK!
BLAM! BLAM!

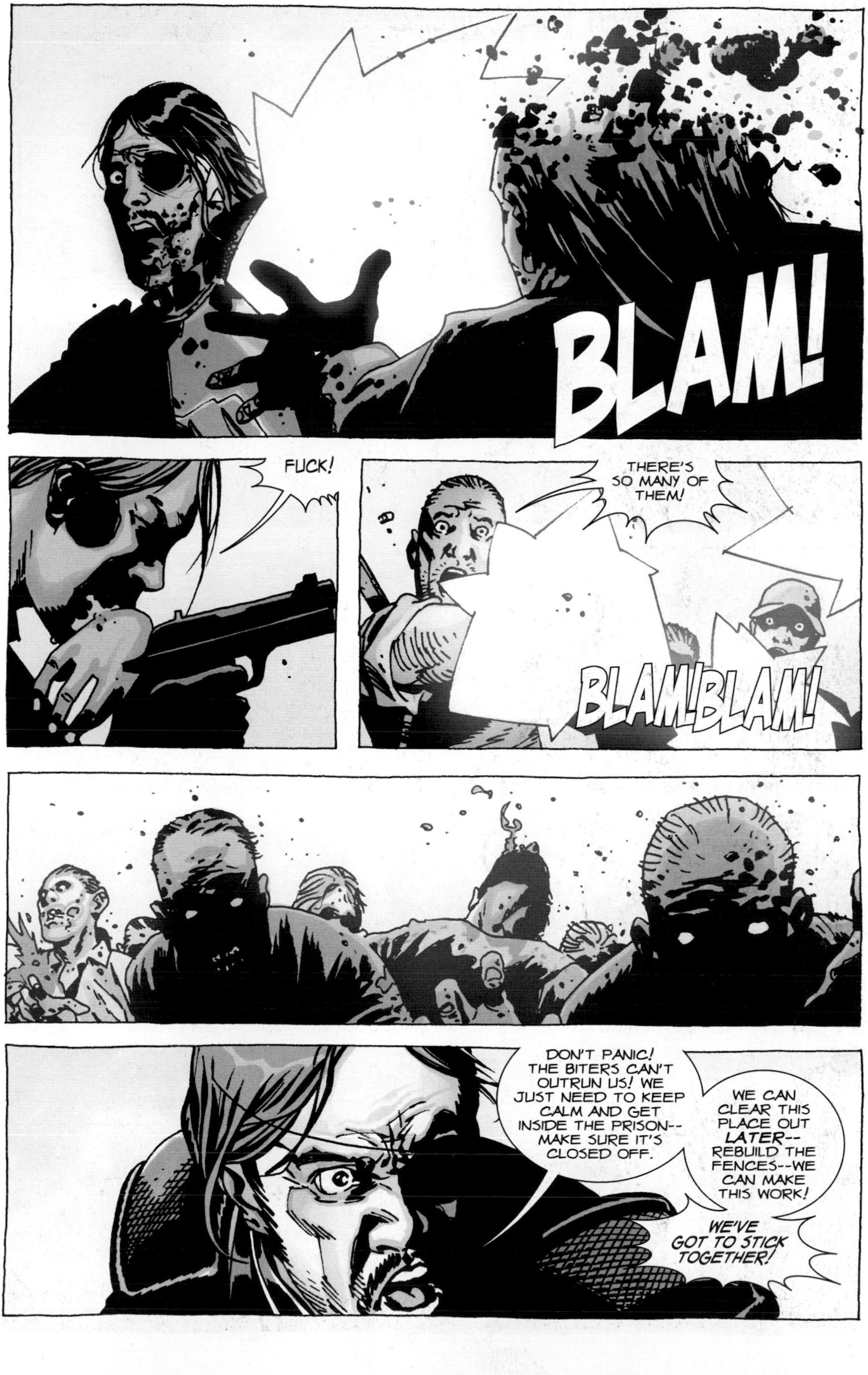
BLAM!
FUCK!
THERE'S SO MANY OF THEM!
BLAM! BLAM!
DON'T PANIC! THE BITERS CAN'T OUTRUN US! WE JUST NEED TO KEEP CALM AND GET INSIDE THE PRISON-- MAKE SURE IT'S CLOSED OFF.
WE CAN CLEAR THIS PLACE OUT *LATER*-- REBUILD THE FENCES--WE CAN MAKE THIS WORK!
WE'VE GOT TO STICK TOGETHER!

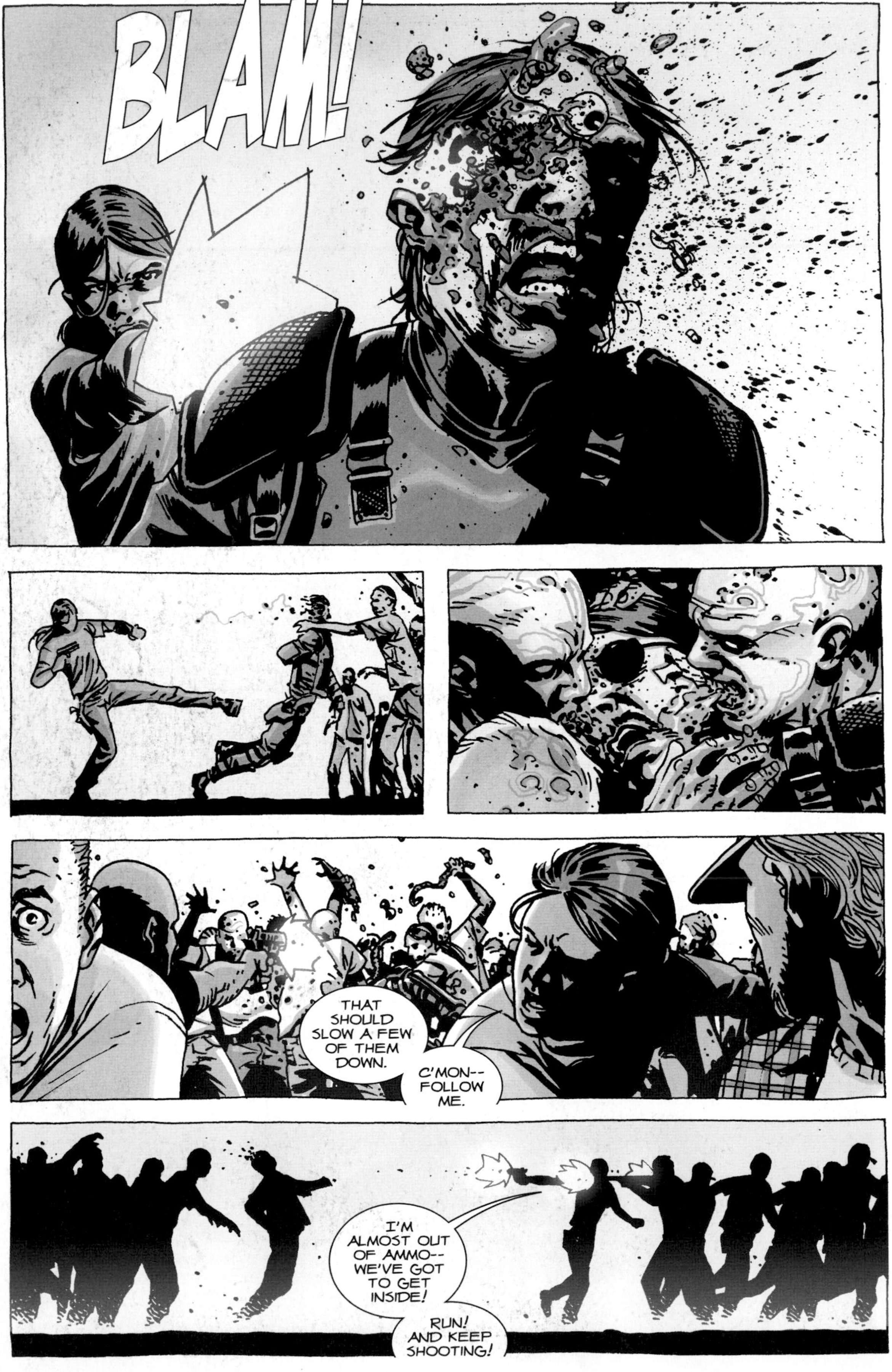
BLAM!
THAT SHOULD SLOW A FEW OF THEM DOWN.
C'MON-- FOLLOW ME.
I'M ALMOST OUT OF AMMO-- WE'VE GOT TO GET INSIDE!
RUN! AND KEEP SHOOTING!

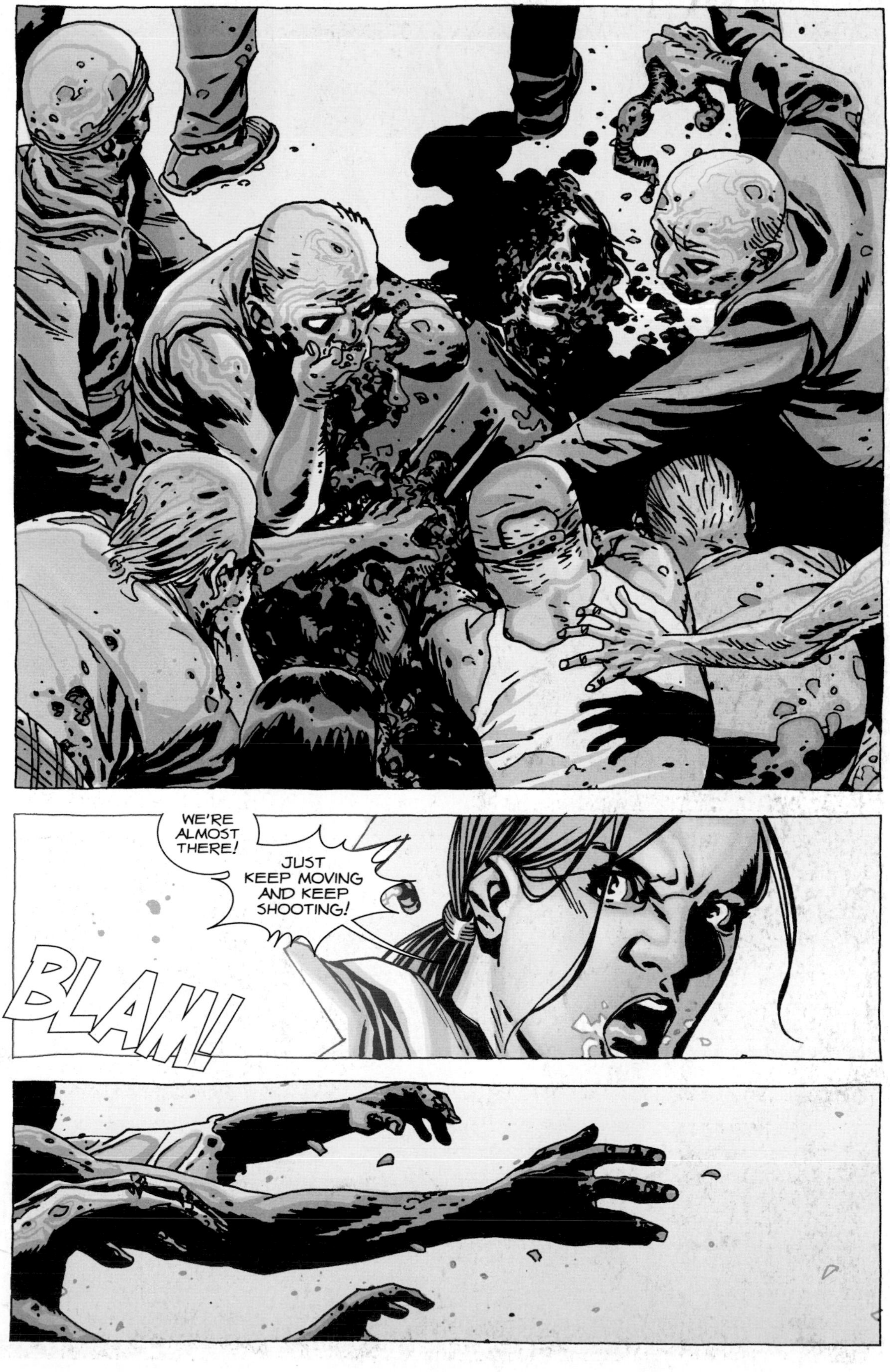
WE'RE ALMOST THERE!
JUST KEEP MOVING AND KEEP SHOOTING!
BLAM!

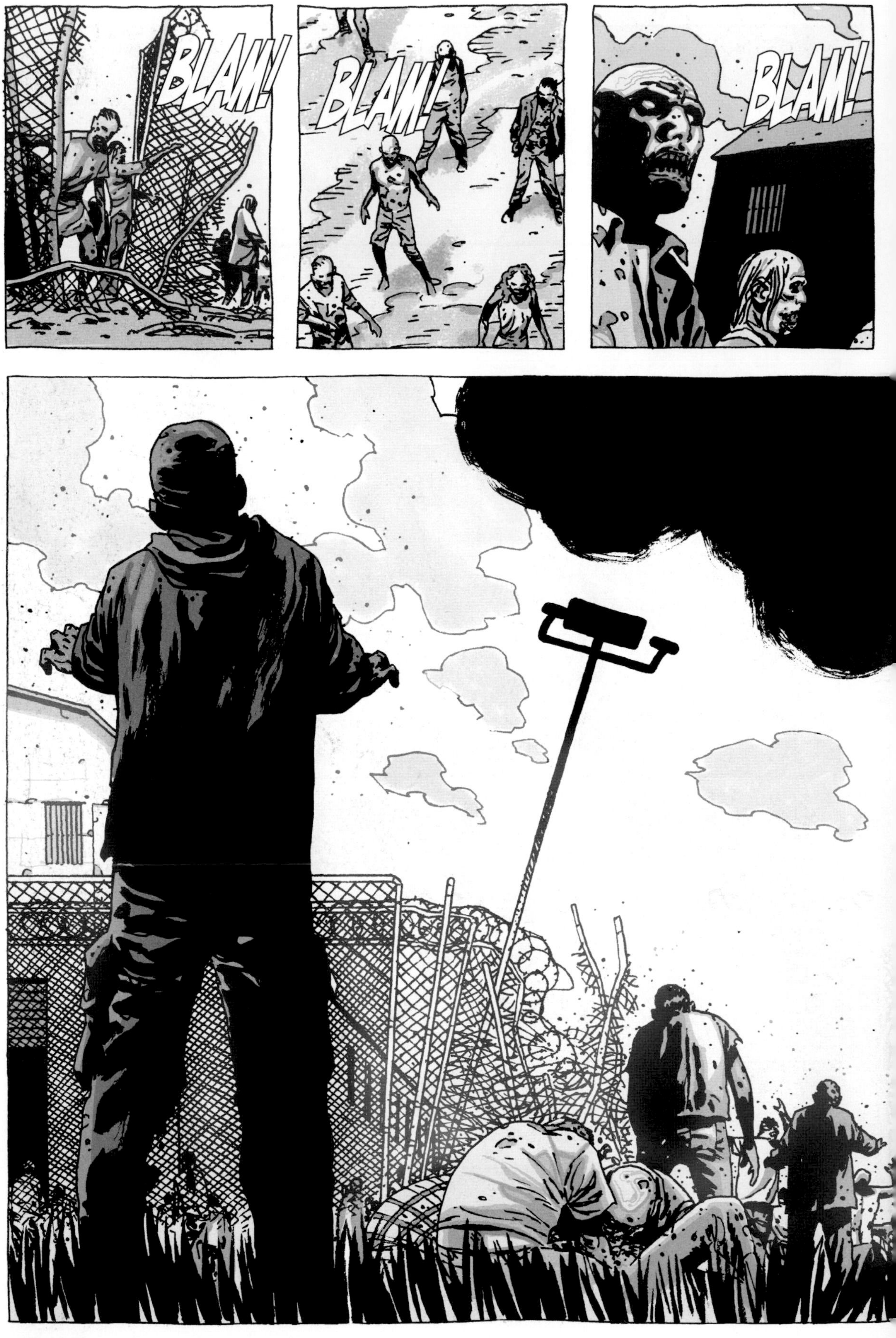
BLAM!
BLAM!
BLAM!

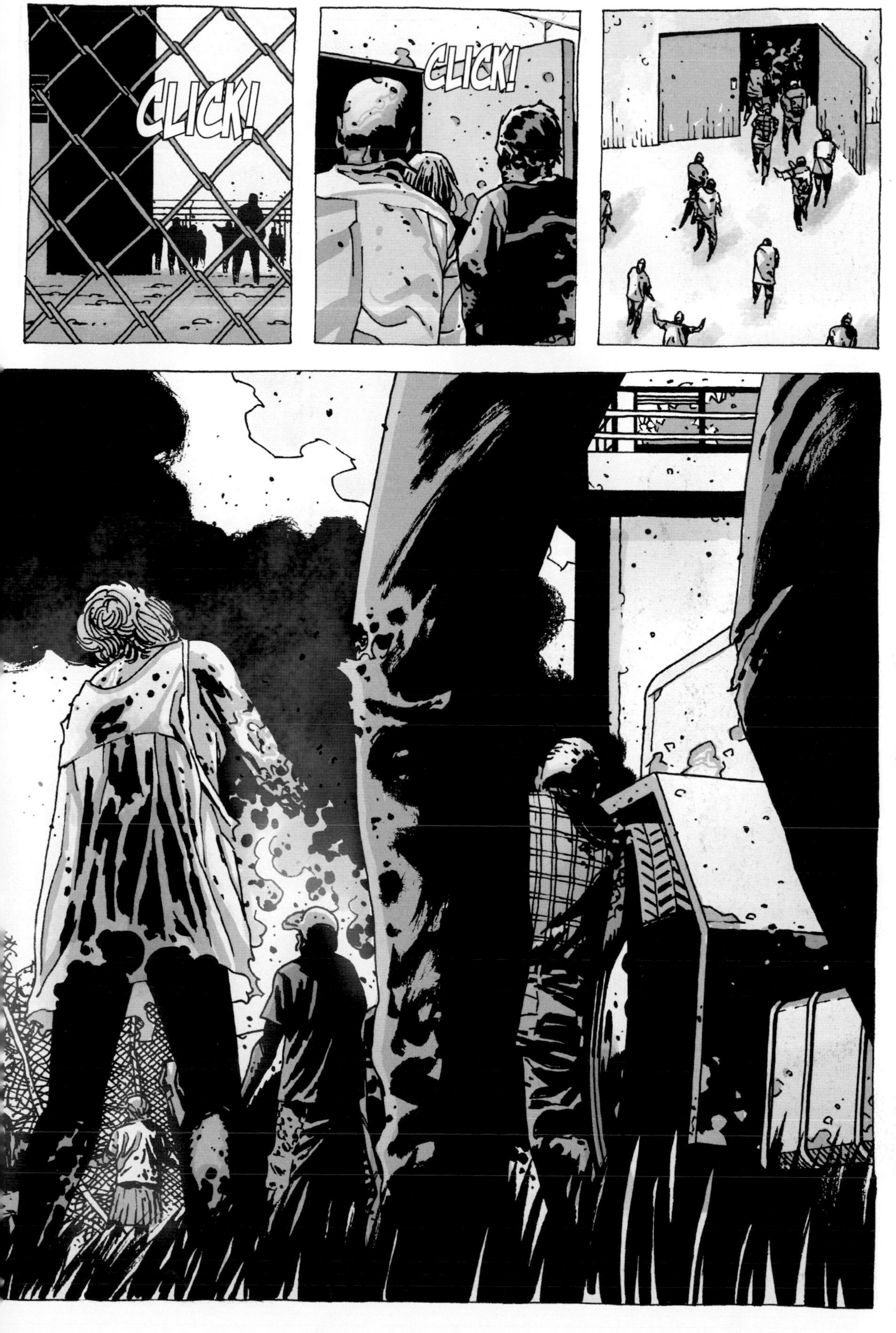
CLICK!
CLICK!

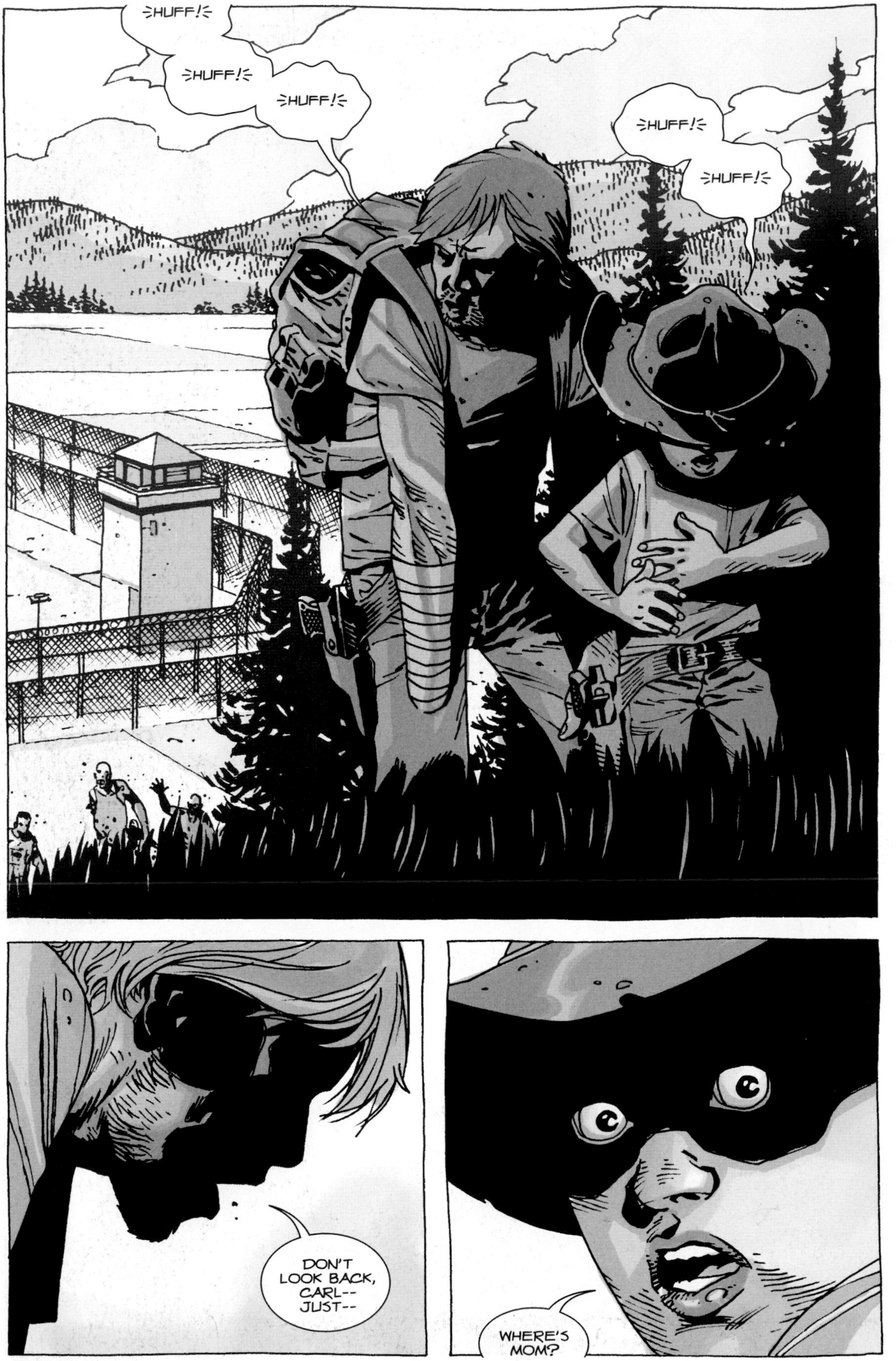

HUFF!
HUFF!
HUFF!
HUFF!
HUFF!
DON'T LOOK BACK, CARL-- JUST--
WHERE'S MOM?

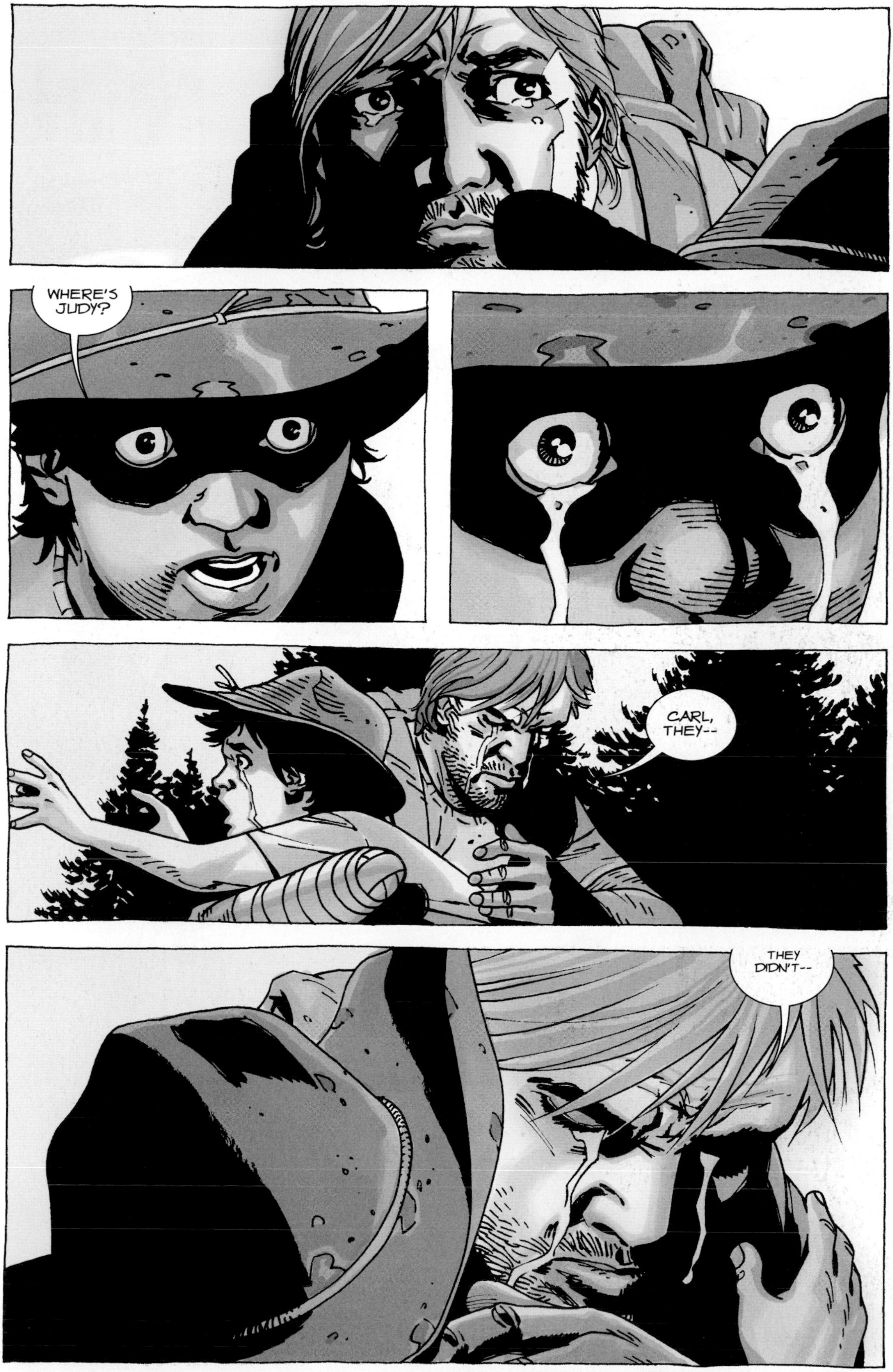
WHERE'S JUDY?
CARL, THEY--
THEY DIDN'T--

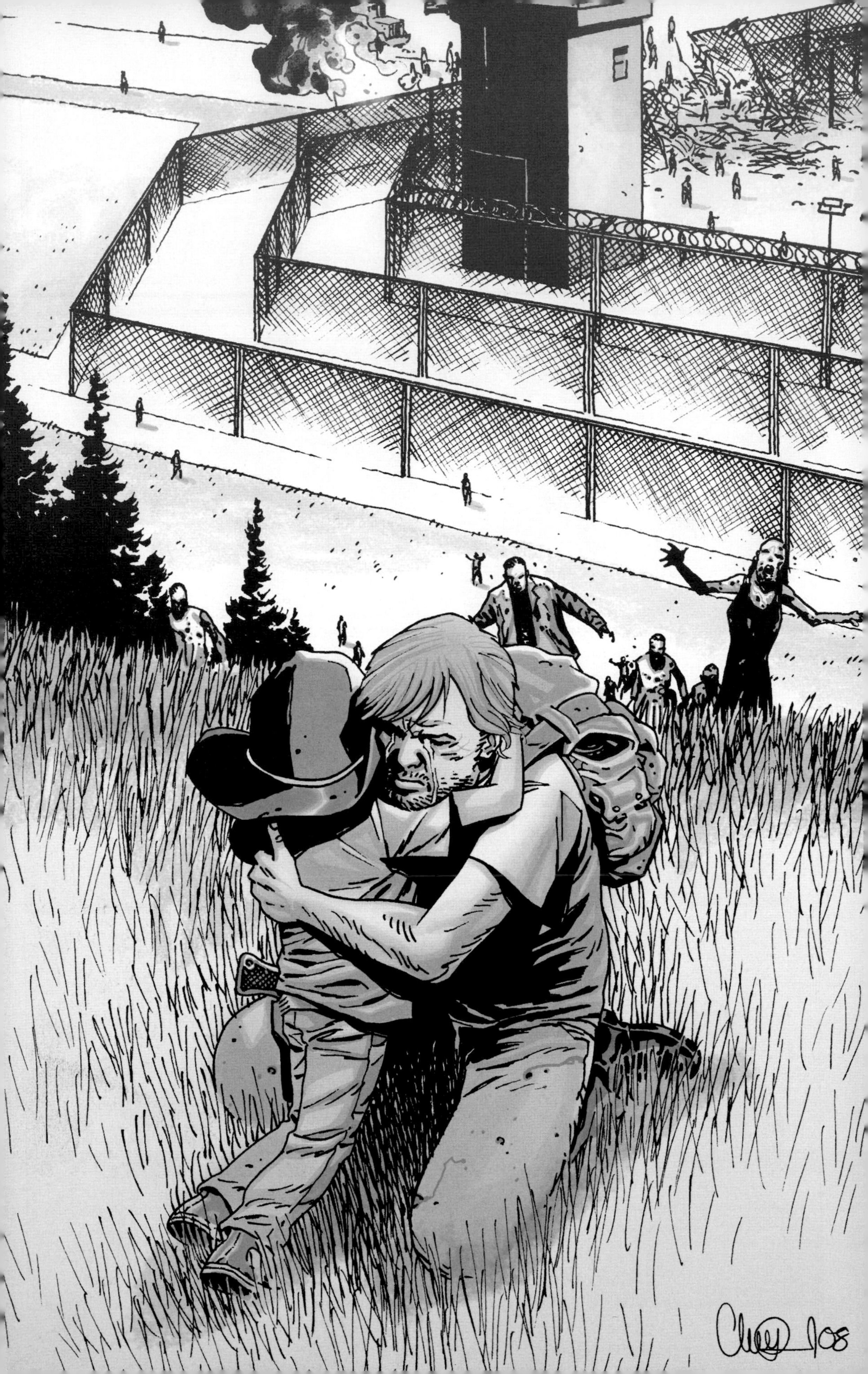

TO BE CONTINUED...

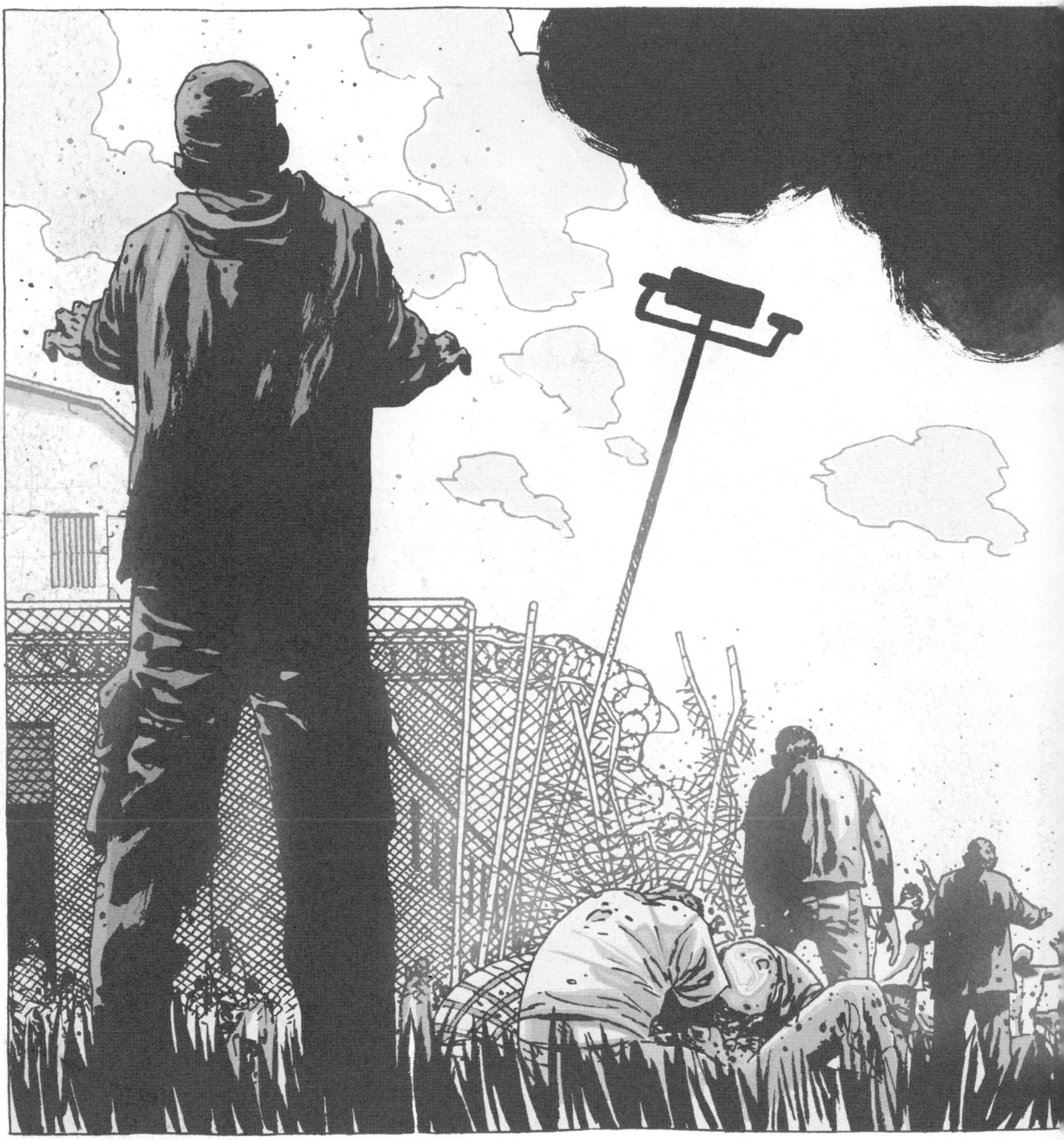

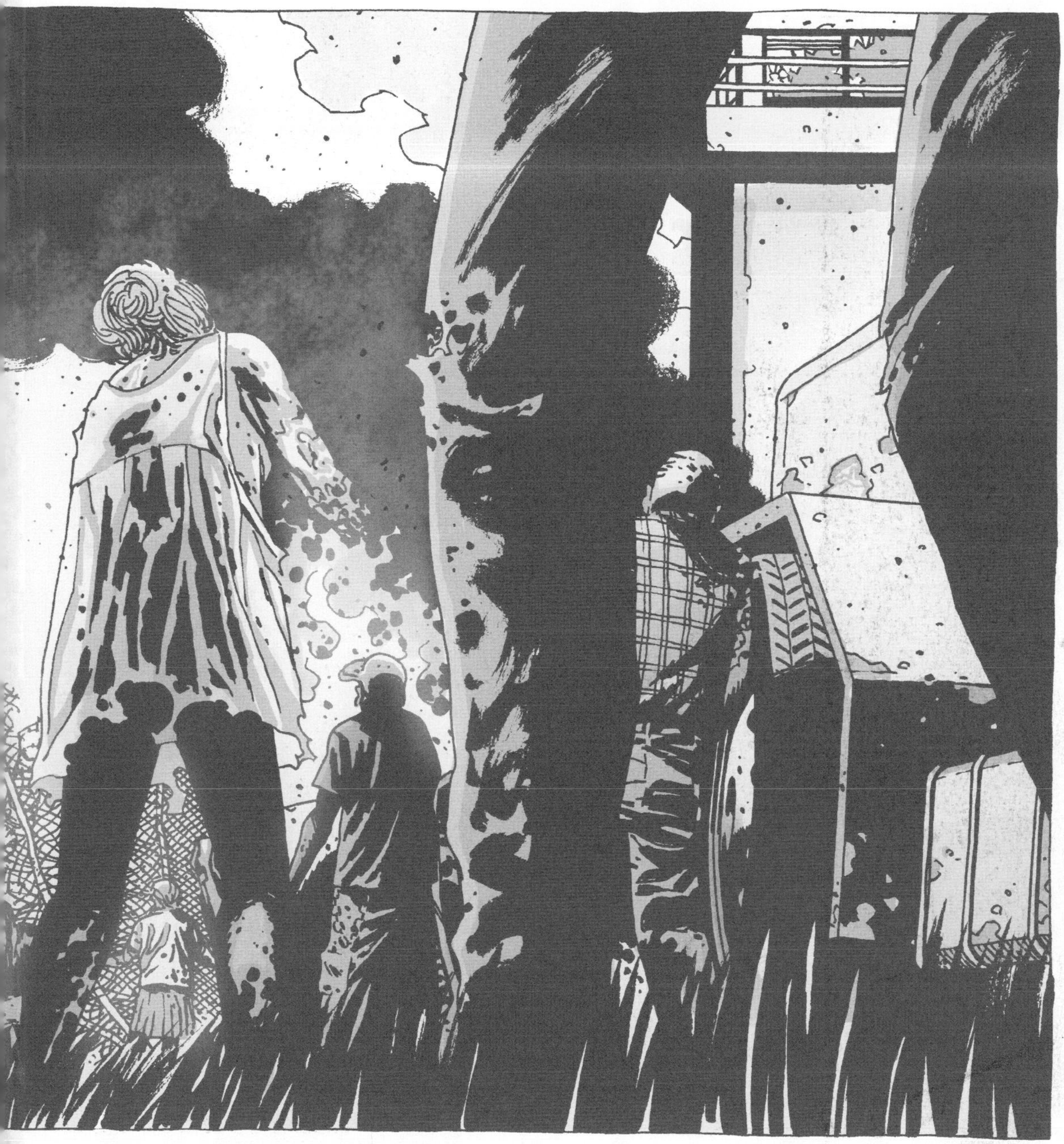

MORE GREAT BOOKS FROM ROBERT KIRKMAN & IMAGE COMICS!

BRIT
VOLUME THREE: FUBAR

THE ASTOUNDING
WOLF-MAN
VOLUME ONE

HAUNT

CAPES
PUNCHING THE CLOCK

INVINCIBLE
ULTIMATE COLLECTION
KIRKMAN
OTTLEY
RATHBURN
PLASCENCIA
VOLUME
5

THE OFFICIAL HANDBOOK OF THE
INVINCIBLE
UNIVERSE

THE ASTOUNDING WOLF-MAN

VOL. 1 TP
ISBN: 978-1-58240-862-0
$14.99

VOL. 2 TP
ISBN: 978-1-60706-007-9
$14.99

VOL. 3 TP
ISBN: 978-1-60706-111-3
$16.99

BATTLE POPE

VOL. 1: GENESIS TP
ISBN: 978-1-58240-572-8
$14.99

VOL. 2: MAYHEM TP
ISBN: 978-1-58240-529-2
$12.99

VOL. 3: PILLOW TALK TP
ISBN: 978-1-58240-677-0
$12.99

VOL. 4: WRATH OF GOD TP
ISBN: 978-1-58240-751-7
$9.99

BRIT

VOL. 1: OLD SOLDIER TP
ISBN: 978-1-58240-678-7
$14.99

VOL. 2: AWOL
ISBN: 978-1-58240-864-4
$14.99

VOL. 3: FUBAR
ISBN: 978-1-60706-061-1
$16.99

CAPES

VOL. 1: PUNCHING THE CLOCK TP
ISBN: 978-1-58240-756-2
$17.99

HAUNT

VOL. 1 TP
ISBN: 978-1-60706-154-0
$9.99

INVINCIBLE

VOL. 1: FAMILY MATTERS TP
ISBN: 978-1-58240-711-1
$12.99

VOL. 2: EIGHT IS ENOUGH TP
ISBN: 978-1-58240-347-2
$12.99

VOL. 3: PERFECT STRANGERS TP
ISBN: 978-1-58240-793-7
$12.99

VOL. 4: HEAD OF THE CLASS TP
ISBN: 978-1-58240-440-2
$14.95

VOL. 5: THE FACTS OF LIFE TP
ISBN: 978-1-58240-554-4
$14.99

VOL. 6: A DIFFERENT WORLD TP
ISBN: 978-1-58240-579-7
$14.99

VOL. 7: THREE'S COMPANY TP
ISBN: 978-1-58240-656-5
$14.99

VOL. 8: MY FAVORITE MARTIAN TP
ISBN: 978-1-58240-683-1
$14.99

VOL. 9: OUT OF THIS WORLD TP
ISBN: 978-1-58240-827-9
$14.99

VOL. 10: WHO'S THE BOSS TP
ISBN: 978-1-60706-013-0
$16.99

VOL. 11: HAPPY DAYS TP
ISBN: 978-1-60706-062-8
$16.99

VOL. 12: STILL STANDING TP
ISBN: 978-1-60706-166-3
$16.99

ULTIMATE COLLECTION, VOL. 1 HC
ISBN 978-1-58240-500-1
$34.95

ULTIMATE COLLECTION, VOL. 2 HC
ISBN: 978-1-58240-594-0
$34.99

ULTIMATE COLLECTION, VOL. 3 HC
ISBN: 978-1-58240-763-0
$34.99

ULTIMATE COLLECTION, VOL. 4 HC
ISBN: 978-1-58240-989-4
$34.99

ULTIMATE COLLECTION, VOL. 5 HC
ISBN: 978-1-60706-116-8
$34.99

THE OFFICIAL HANDBOOK OF THE INVINCIBLE UNIVERSE TP
ISBN: 978-1-58240-831-6
$12.99

THE COMPLETE INVINCIBLE LIBRARY, VOL. 1 HC
ISBN: 978-1-58240-718-0
$125.00

THE COMPLETE INVINCIBLE LIBRARY, VOL. 2 HC
ISBN: 978-1-60706-112-0
$125.00

THE WALKING DEAD

VOL. 1: DAYS GONE BYE TP
ISBN: 978-1-58240-672-5
$9.99

VOL. 2: MILES BEHIND US TP
ISBN: 978-1-58240-413-4
$14.99

VOL. 3: SAFETY BEHIND BARS TP
ISBN: 978-1-58240-487-5
$14.99

VOL. 4: THE HEART'S DESIRE TP
ISBN: 978-1-58240-530-8
$14.99

VOL. 5: THE BEST DEFENSE TP
ISBN: 978-1-58240-612-1
$14.99

VOL. 6: THIS SORROWFUL LIFE TP
ISBN: 978-1-58240-684-8
$14.99

VOL. 7: THE CALM BEFORE TP
ISBN: 978-1-58240-828-6
$14.99

VOL. 8: MADE TO SUFFER TP
ISBN: 978-1-58240-883-5
$14.99

VOL. 9: HERE WE REMAIN TP
ISBN: 978-1-60706-022-2
$14.99

VOL. 10: THE ROAD AHEAD TP
ISBN: 978-1-60706-075-8
$14.99

VOL. 11: FEAR THE HUNTERS TP
ISBN: 978-1-60706-181-6
$14.99

BOOK ONE HC
ISBN: 978-1-58240-619-0
$29.99

BOOK TWO HC
ISBN: 978-1-58240-698-5
$29.99

BOOK THREE HC
ISBN: 978-1-58240-825-5
$29.99

BOOK FOUR HC
ISBN: 978-1-60706-000-0
$29.99

BOOK FIVE HC
ISBN: 978-1-60706-171-7
$29.99

THE WALKING DEAD DELUXE HARDCOVER, VOL. 2
ISBN: 978-1-60706-029-7
$100.00

REAPER

GRAPHIC NOVEL
ISBN: 978-1-58240-354-2
$6.95

TECH JACKET

VOL. 1: THE BOY FROM EARTH TP
ISBN: 978-1-58240-771-5
$14.99

TALES OF THE REALM

HARDCOVER
ISBN: 978-1-58240-426-0
$34.95

TRADE PAPERBACK
ISBN: 978-1-58240-394-6
$14.95

BRIT
VOLUME ONE: OLD SOLDIER

REAPER

Battle
POPE
Wrath of God

THE COMPLETE
INVINCIBLE
LIBRARY: VOLUME TWO

INVINCIBLE
HAPPY DAYS

TECH JACKET
THE BOY FROM EARTH

TO FIND YOUR NEAREST COMIC BOOK STORE, CALL:
1-888-COMIC-BOOK

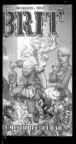

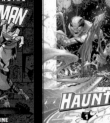

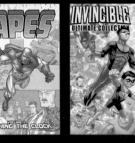

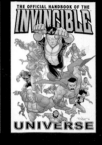

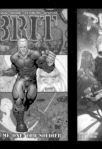

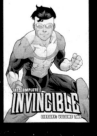

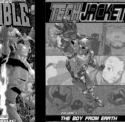

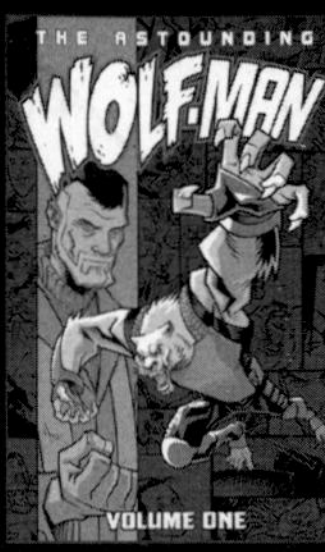

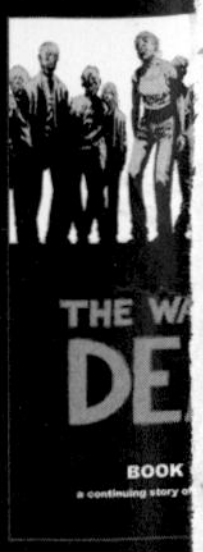

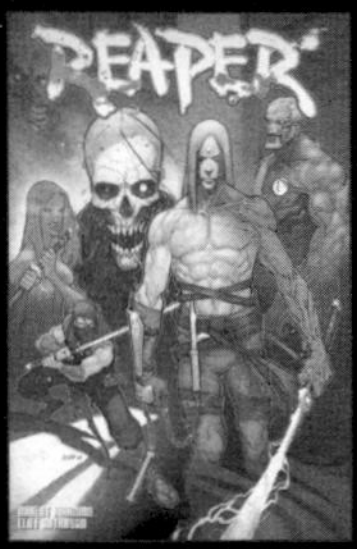

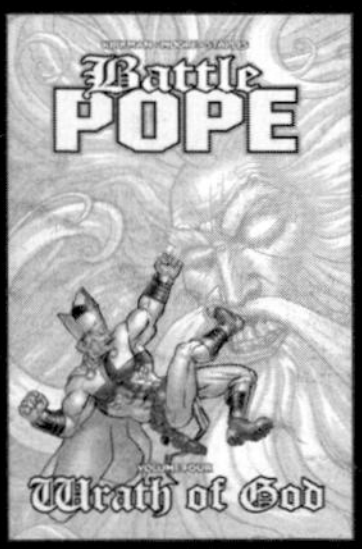

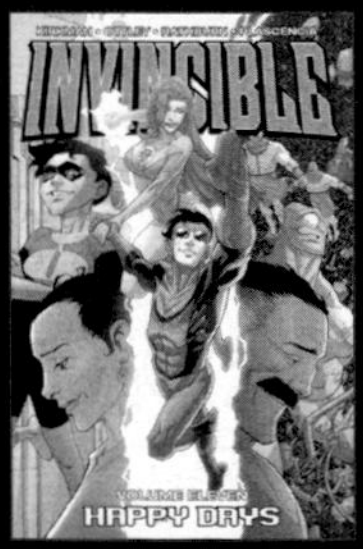

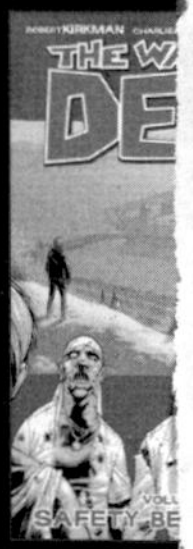